NORMAL IS DIFFERENT

LATILDA CONYERS

Published by Victorious You Press™
Charlotte NC, USA

TITLE: NORMAL IS DIFFERENT
First Printed: 2023

Cover Designer: Jadia Bellamy
Editor: Lynn Braxton

ISBN: 978-1-959719-09-0
ISBN: (Ebook) 978-1-959719-10-6
Library of Congress Control Number: 2023906659

Printed in the United States of America

For details email joan@victoriousyoupress.com
or visit us at www.victoriousyoupress.com

ACKNOWLEDGEMENTS

GLORY TO GOD

The most important source of my life is God. Father God, you always amaze me. No matter how much I think I know what I need, you always know so much more. No matter how much I expect of you, you will always give so much more. I pray that you are always at the center of everything I do. During very pivotal times when I needed to make health decisions, life-changing choices that were scary and overwhelming, you gave me direction. You sent people who knew my circumstances without me even saying a word. Most times, I would panic and cry first. I had to learn how to seek you first before calling my family and friends. At the end of the day, none of those people could do what you did and what you continue to do. Having the right resources are pointless without you. Every day I feel like I grow closer in my relationship with you. I love you God. I give you all the glory and all the praise! I commit my life to sharing you with others.

EXTENDING A WARM THANK YOU TO:

Lynn Braxton, my editor and writing coach. I thank God that he brought you into my life. A fellow survivor and a strong black woman. You are a blessing. Thank you for helping me to transform my journey into words. Thank you for encouraging me and speaking wisdom and restoration over my life. I truly feel that you are a God send. Thank you for everything!

My mother, Edna Castille- Thank you for always being there and for always encouraging me. Thank you for your strength and determination that motivates me to keep going, no matter the obstacle. You always say that the greatest gift you could ever give to us was giving us back to God. Thank you. I love you, mom.

Papa J, Jesse Castille- I've never called you my stepdad because I never felt like those words were enough. My first time practicing how to drive a car was with you. You dropped me off at my first high school dance. You showed me an example of real love. Through thick and thin, sickness and health, you have stood with my mom and with us every step of the way. So, the word stepdad just doesn't do it justice. Thanks for being my Papa J. I love you, Pop.

My father, Eugene Shanks Jr.- Daddy, I miss you. I think about you all the time. I laugh all the time just thinking of our conversations. Thank you for the long talks about everything; no subject was off-limits. Most importantly, thank you for the guidance and for always keeping God's word front and center. Rest in Peace! I love You.

My siblings: U-jhun Shanks, Sharene Shanks, and Lisa Hawkins.

My sibling in-laws-Tremayne Roberts and Amanda Shanks. Two words: Fully covered. In prayer, in conversation, in laughs, in good times, and through tough times. Whether together in the same room, on the phone, or in different states, I always feel the love of my siblings. Thank you for your teachings and for being an example of leadership. Most of all, thank you for listening and being there for me.

Family- I believe I have the biggest family in the whole wide world. My mother has twelve sisters and five brothers, and that's just the tip of the iceberg. If I don't have the biggest family on earth, then the love I receive from them certainly makes me feel like I do. Thanks to all my uncles, aunts, cousins, and extended family members and friends. Aunt Gustavia Moreaux and Uncle Joshua Moreaux-thank you for the daily text and the daily words of encouragement. I love you all.

To My Fellow Warriors: I've met so many wonderful people along this journey. So many powerhouses. Thank you for your strength and courage.

Thank You to The Physicians and Amazing Friends God Brought into My Life!

Georgia

Dr. Randy W. Cooper, Surgeon-I felt like I was your only patient, like family. From the phone calls at home after surgery to the jokes that made me laugh when all I could do was cry. Not only did you explain to me so I could understand, but because of you and your amazing team, I know how I want to be treated as a patient, and I don't accept anything less.

Augusta Oncology-Special thanks to the entire staff at the University Health Care System in Augusta, GA. I can't tell you enough how special you all made me feel. From the kind words to the laughs, it was awesome. This is the only staff I ever made cakes for. I'm not a baker, but I had fun doing it. I will never forget how much I laughed watching ya'll eat my pineapple upside down cake. Thank you for making my time with you unforgettable!

Greenbrier Fitness Evans, GA- When I parked my car, the owner of this place asked me my name. Two weeks later, when I went back, they still remembered my name and treated me like I was a part of the family. Fresh out of chemotherapy and radiation, sore and achy, this place was right where I needed to be. Thank you for being a part of my journey.

San Antonio, TX

Dr. Marisa Sandera, Oncologist- I love my oncologist. If you've ever been diagnosed with cancer, then you understand how important it is to have a good medical team in your corner. Dr. Sandera is straight-up, sharp, and will go to bat for you when needed, but she's also very kind, gentle, and understanding— and wears some badass heels.

Dr. Brian Szender, Gynecologic Oncology Surgeon- Needing surgery can be scary. Having to accept a complete hysterectomy without having any children was life changing. I am thankful that I had a surgeon who went out of his way to demonstrate the compassion behind what he does. For me, that's a God-given blessing. I'm very thankful for having you as my surgeon and as an intricate part of my treatment.

TABLE OF CONTENTS

INTRODUCTION

Am I normal? Yes. Is my normal different? Absolutely. Am I ordinary? Never, and neither are you! I believe there are special and unique qualities about each one of God's creations. For some, it may be in the form of a talent or gift that can feel so overwhelming at times, one may struggle to find the right form of expression. Yet, when others get a small glimpse of it, they are speechless and in awe of your innate ability. For others, their differences may be a physical feature that forces them to stand out from the crowd. But because of a longing to fit in, they try their best to hide what others may not understand.

In full transparency, I must often remind myself that God's creation of me is not a mistake. Just like a light that is destined to shine and cannot stay hidden, neither can the differences that shape and mold me into the person I am meant to be. So, despite every enduring challenge, my long list of shortcomings, failed relationships, and heartache, I must remember that I am made perfect in his image. And it's okay to love myself, just as I am.

As you read this book, Normal is Different, go with me on this rollercoaster ride of the ups and downs, and the highs and lows of life that the main characters experience. It's a journey that deals with the pain of acceptance, while embracing the struggle and the peace that comes from learning to love our God-given differences—especially the ones that some people may call weird, ugly, or strange.

At the end of the day, it's not what others say about you that matters most. It's believing in God's Word that says we are all "fearfully and wonderfully made" (Psalm 139:14). So, look in the mirror, hold your head up high, with shoulders back, and confirm your affirmations because what we believe and tell ourselves should be based only on God's Word not what other people say.

MY AFFIRMATIONS

I am valued for who I am, not just what I do.
I am whole and complete.
I am created in God's image.
I am loved by God.
I am fearless.
I believe in myself.
I am exactly what God created me to be.
My worth is defined by God's grace, not man's words.
Why? Because I am fearfully and wonderfully made!

One

A SEXY HYENA

"SHEESH!" Dani yelped, hitting her pinky toe on the corner of her bedroom set again. "You big, stupid idiot," she said as she hopped on one foot, punching, and kicking the oversized leg that was responsible for her throbbing toe. Her bedroom set was a bulky, cherry oak, queen bed with a massive headboard that lightly brushed against the crown molding. With rich mahogany tones and engraved leafy designs, the set came with a massive sectional dresser surrounded by a tripod of mirrors. A smaller version stood on the opposite side of the wall. After they were married, this pile of polished wood was the first thing she saw when she stepped into their newly constructed home.

"This set is fit for a king and his queen," the contractor had said.

Although clearly, it was meant for a queen to keep clean. There were twenty-six drawers in addition to a storage chest at the foot of the bed. Dani used eight drawers for her personal things, and her husband used his fair share. While she didn't mind the extra storage space, keeping the dust, fingerprints, and crap away from the surface tops and crevices of the leafy patterns was a headache. It was never clean enough. Dani felt it was just too big, boisterous, and far too much trouble since they relocated often due to their jobs. When traveling for work, they rented out their home, taking the furniture with them, and ensuring it fit in every home they owned or leased. The idea of choosing something simpler to avoid potential damages and expenses was something they didn't agree on.

Her husband worked hard, and he earned the right to have his home the way he wanted, and Dani understood his perspective. So, when he served her with divorce papers after years of cleaning and polishing, fighting with contractors over bad repairs, and after knockdown, drawn-out disagreements, she felt like she earned the right to have it, even if she loathed it. Whenever she hit her toe on the end of its bulky leg, she had to resist the urge to chop some wood and start a fire.

"One day, one day," Dani said, pointing to the bed as if it understood her and was openly laughing at her pain.

"Alright," Dani said, taking a step back and staring at her reflection in the full-length mirror. "Girl, you betta work," she smiled, sticking out her tongue, dancing, and admiring the results from the late-night workouts. "Not quite the booty I'm going for, but it's doing something back there," she said, standing on her tippy toes, admiring the view from the back. She was most impressed with her arms, appreciating the details and the length of her shoulders and biceps. "Hair and makeup, check. Sexy little black dress, check. Stilettos, check. Time to roll."

It had been nearly three years since she'd been out with another man. After her marriage was over, Dani took some time to get to know herself and figure out what she wanted for her future. And now, here she was in her forties, a published writer for a global fashion company, a homeowner, and a dog owner, going on an actual date. For the first time in her life, she felt the confidence of putting herself first, mentally, spiritually, financially, and physically. While still a work in progress, her heart and mind were finally at peace, and as much as she wanted a partner, she wasn't willing to settle.

Her friend, Becca, stopped by to hear everything about the "new" guy. "So, he's handsome and tall, and he sent you a diamond tennis bracelet, but you don't know what level of fine he's ranking in at?"

"That bracelet was delivered to the wrong address. I returned it back to the sender. I've told you over a hundred times already, Becca. I wasn't paying attention to this man's body to rank him like that."

"Well, what, pray tell, were you staring at the whole time he was cheesing and grinning all up in your face?"

"I don't know, but let's see, what does a grown woman look at when conversing with a grown man? Maybe eye-to-eye contact? You know, like is he looking at me or is he looking away from me while speaking to me. Is he paranoid? Anxious? Can he hold a decent conversation, and does it make sense? Does it interest me? Do we have anything in common? I mean, really, we're grown folks out here in these streets. There's more to people than just looks alone."

Dani had met Dr. Jacob while doing volunteer work at the senior community center. After scraping snow-filled driveways for what seemed like hours, they decided to meet for coffee, followed by a shared plate of warm miniature toast, prosciutto, and cheese. They exchanged phone numbers and made plans to meet for dinner. That gave her plenty of time to prepare, but also, too much mental space to ponder the negative.

"It feels good to meet a man who shares my interest," Dani said. "Although, to your point, I probably should have paid more attention to the whole package."

"It's okay, honey. I get it," Becca replied. "I'm not trying to beat a dead horse here, but I just need you to make sure you get a good look at him this time, okay? It's been a while since you've been out with a man, and well, I don't want you to choose a man from a lonely state of mind. You know, when we get a little bored and in our feelings, sometimes, any ole dog in a muscle shirt with a grin starts looking good. I just don't want you to wake up one day to a spotted, crusty ole snaggle-toothed hyena lying in bed next to you."

"True, but I think I would have noticed if he was snaggle toothed," Dani said, recalling a few past choices she considered that made her shudder at the thought. "Now that you mention it, I'll be sure to call you with a detailed report, maybe shoot you a text photo mid-date." Thinking about the overall experience made Dani want to cancel, as she had zero patience for dating games. But, thanks to Becca and a slew of prayers, she held out hope that at some point, it would be different.

When she first met Dr. Jacob, she wore a New Orleans Saints beanie hat complete with a jersey, long sleeve thermals underneath, sweats, and a fresh, clean face. Nothing special, just her regular at-home look, but he was still interested. While she felt an attraction to him, it wasn't enough to consider going on an actual date. After their brunch conversation about health and community work, which meant a lot to her since losing her dad and dealing with her own health issues, Dani saw something under the surface, something different.

"Hi, I'm Dani," she said to the hostess, "here for Jacob Henry."

"Right this way, Ms. Breaux," the hostess smiled, leading Dani down the hall and into a closed room overlooking a view of the city. In the middle of the room was a table set for two with wine and long stem glasses. "Dr. Henry called and said he's running a bit late. Please, have a seat," she said, pulling out Dani's chair. "My name is Samantha, and I'll be your hostess for the evening. May I pour you a glass of our finest red?"

"Wow," Dani said, taken aback by the view and the ambiance of the restaurant. "Yes, please. Thank you." This restaurant was a bit snazzier than her usual semi-healthy foodie-type-of place. The atmosphere was very elegant and posh, not quite formal, but definitely a heels and nice dress-type of environment.

Just as she was starting to relax, her stomach did a quick somersault stirring her back to reality. Realizing her error, Dani closed her eyes and rubbed her stomach as it continued to grumble. *Shoot! I should've stopped at Le Ric's for a vegan chicken wrap,* she thought, knowing she became hangry when she waited too long to eat, especially after a workout. Le Ric's is a vegan food truck that sits two blocks away from Dani's house. Concerned that the restaurant food may not be as sexy as the atmosphere, she looked through the glass window, searching for an image of a plate of food on somebody's table, something to provide a description of what was to come. "Le Ric's might be closed on the way back home, and I'm starving," Dani whispered, mimicking a fake-sounding cry as she looked at her watch.

Dani was truly addicted to the food truck. Her favorite was the chicken made with chickpeas wrapped in a buttery tasting, non-buttered, gluten-free bread. *Mmmm, I'm so hungry,* Dani said to herself again, imagining biting into that first crunchy bite topped with greens and a creamy, spicy, coleslaw-type-of sauce. *Enough! Stop sabotaging the evening. The food here may be good; just give it a chance,* she thought as she focused on her deep breathing routine, hoping the exercise would soothe her growling stomach and calm her inner alter ego, Daniesha.

After a few minutes of inhaling and exhaling, Dani opened her eyes, and that's when she saw him. Dang! He needs a theme song to match that level of fine. "You better walk, Dr. Jacob," Dani whispered and smiled, admiring the confidence of the strong black man commanding everyone's attention as he sauntered through the room. At six foot seven, Dr. Jacob had the body of a leading actor in an action film that every woman was dying to see. He moved like a man of power with his chiseled cheekbones, full lips, and pearly white smile. *Are those real?*

At the coffee shop, Dani was so intrigued by their conversation, she never noticed the depth of his physical features. As he made his way through the restaurant shaking hands and greeting the staff, her eyes wandered over the detailed fit of his grey slacks and how the casual pullover short sleeve shirt stopped perfectly at the center of his upper arms, tastefully revealing the curvature of his biceps. With a subtle look and a classic James Bond style, he had just the right amount of sex appeal to make the ladies swoon, topped with an unpredictable intrigue that could wipe out all the bad men in the room without breaking a sweat. "Hmph, come on through with the shoes then, Dr. Jacob," she mumbled, recognizing the sleek appearance of his dark brown shoes as a brand she often saw worn by the designers and rich executives at her office. "Okay, so the price tag on those shoes alone is at least several months' worth of my salary," she mumbled, while texting Becca all the details.

"Sweetie, what a vision you are," Jacob smiled, eyes squinting while biting his lower lip. Standing to greet him, they briefly touched cheeks as Dani's eyes unintentionally looked over his shoulder, catching a glimpse of the clock in the corner of the room. *It's 9:30pm. Le Ric's will close in exactly two hours,* she thought. "Knock it off, Dani," she mumbled to herself, praying the food here would soothe the hunger in her tummy. *If the food sucks, I could totally get to Le Ric's just in time if I removed my heels, jog a little bit, or just call an Uber,* she thought to herself. Knowing she was pressed for time, Dani needed to order now to see if this place was worth the gloss.

"Baby girl, I am famished," Jacob said, grabbing his incredibly toned stomach for emphasis.

"Yes, famished, so am I…"

"Why are you so beautiful?" Jacob interrupted, cutting Dani off before she could fully express her degree of hunger.

"Thank you, I…"

"You know, before you respond, I know exactly what we're having to start us off," Jacob said, cutting her off again. "You are going to love, love, love this food," he gushed, sipping on his glass of cognac. I took the liberty of placing an order with our hostess. I hope you don't mind."

Smiling, Dani realized she was not giving this evening a chance. *I mean, look at him! He is gorgeous and can carry a conversation. He has great eye contact, too, and he likes food? Jackpot!* she thought to herself. Suddenly, her shoulders relaxed, and her mouth watered as the waiter came closer with their plates. *I could forego Le Ric's for tonight and stop by early morning on my way to work. Some hot golden milk and a crispy sweet potato breakfast bowl topped with crunchy greens, candied pecans, apple chunks, and plant-based sausage. Hallelujah!* Dani did a little chair dance in her seat, excited for the evening with her date, the idea of her favorite breakfast in the morning, and the array of delicious food coming towards her now. *I think I hit the jackpot with him. I might even have a little dessert. He definitely looks like the type to eat a little something sweet after dinner and get a hard workout at the gym the next day. Yep, he's definitely a foodie. Lord, I need to calm down. I am not this greedy. I will never work out and go out on a date again without eating.*

As the waiter sat the bowls of green soup down, Jacob quickly dug in, scooping large spoonfuls into his mouth, "Mmm, mmm, mmm! Oh, that's it," he moaned, pointing to the green substance in the bowl. "Sweetie, I have been dreaming about this all day. Dig in, babe. I promise you won't be disappointed."

He was already into his fourth scoop by the time Dani picked up her spoon. Taking a small sip of the green liquid, she recognized a familiar taste and smell. "This tastes like green beans and coconut?"

"Very good Ms., Breaux, sexy and smart," Jacob replied, seemingly amused. "You know, it took me forever to figure out what was in this soup—green beans with a ton of herbs and spices, and yes, the coconut part is my favorite. Mmmm! That hit the spot," Jacob said, sitting back in his chair, rubbing his non-existent belly. "I think I ate that too fast; I'm stuffed. Maybe we finish up here and go for a walk? It's a nice night out," he smiled as he waved down the waiter for a cup of tea.

NOOOO! No, no, no, no, no! I know this fool is not serious! I got all dressed up for this? Dani's inner voice, Daniesha, hangrily burst into her thoughts as she sat still with a painted-on smile, watching her date sip his tea.

Okay, okay! Whew, breathe, Dani breathe, she thought, calming herself. *Maybe it's me. I've gone on outings with friends where we just had a snack, and that's it. Why am I triggered?*

No, bump that. This green shit stinks so bad. I can't eat this! It smells like a bowl of farts. Stop breathing and start asking questions! Daniesha said, her thoughts getting angrier by the second.

Am I tripping, or did he suggest I bring my appetite tonight? Wait, let me check my phone text because maybe it's me, Dani thought as she scrolled through her messages.

Nope, there it is. "BRING" your appetite, her inner voice Daniesha confirmed.

Who the heck is eating pureed green beans? WHO is pureeing green beans for dinner? I mean, I like a soup just like anybody else, I love pureed soups, but this is not what you mean when you say "BRING" your appetite! I'm so hungry my stomach is touching my back, Dani thought again, squirming in her seat, trying to make sense of her feelings, as her therapist advised. *It's just that I've worked all day, did my usual workout after work, even threw in a few extra deadlifts and squats so I could look good in this dress. That's why I'm moody, just a little hungry, that's all,* she thought as she exhaled through her nose, still smiling. *I'm just so sick of these daggone dating games. Why we just couldn't have a normal evening with comfort food, or is that too old school?*

"Sweetie, sweetie? Hello? Are you okay?" Jacob said, confused at Dani's expression. "You seem like you're in pain?"

She wanted to say no, that she was not okay, and was on the verge of a full-on panic attack from the natural disaster brewing in her stomach. "Of course, yes," she said, picking up the menu. "Just a long day at work," Dani replied, taking a deep breathe. *I'll just find an entrée on the menu. That's it, Dani thought,* shutting angry Daniesha down for good. Realizing she was overreacting, Dani started to smile, feeling silly, as she read through the menu.

"Gotcha, I had a pretty exhausting day myself," Jacob said. "I had this patient, right? And…"

Does this menu say all raw cuisine? If you don't carry your little thick ass up outta here, Dani thought. You have not gone grocery shopping yet. You got some stale oats, cucumbers, and nut butter at home. Get yo' behind up and get moving!

"Umm, excuse me," Dani said, stopping the waiter as he walked by. "I know this is an all-raw restaurant," she wanted to seem like she was familiar with the place, "but where are the salads?"

"Oh, yes, of course. Here they are. You can pick whichever one you like, or we can make something special for you."

"That won't be necessary. I'll have a large Mediterranean salad with extra green olives," Dani said, feeling confident in her response.

"Ssssure, um, we normally lean towards the root vegetables or the green bean or celery soups but, we can do this as well. Would you like that on ice, in a glass or bowl?"

"Sweetie, it's a raw juice and soup bar tonight—everything is raw," Jacob said with a sound of arrogance. "I thought you knew."

"Oh, okay, I must have forgotten," Dani said, waving her hand. "Water will be fine."

"My man, she'll have the collard and pineapple smoothie made with nut milk topped with cinnamon, turmeric, and ginger. I will have another green bean soup to go with pureed peas, broccoli, and garlic on top. Add a spicy tomato juice with extra lemon and cilantro."

I didn't even need to wear my grandma panties tonight, Dani thought, recalling the big black panties under her dress that were nearly touching her breast. *The way he is drinking these vegetables, his ass gon' be fastened to the toilet.*

"Oh, and tell the chef he outdid himself again," Jacob said, laughing out loud and pointing at his empty bowl as if he'd just finished an amazing meal.

Dani could hardly believe Jacob was satiated. While listening to him ramble on and on, she thought about their brunch after scraping snow at the community center. *Was this the same man who shoveled prosciutto, cheese, and crackers into his mouth by the dozen? Chasing it down with two large mugs of hot cocoa-after he drank coffee the whole morning.* Sipping on her collard greens and pineapple juice, Dani felt her stomach flip, and not in a good way. *Now you know you can't hold your farts, she thought. Leave now! Before it's too late. The vegetables are already separated from the liquid,* she thought as she stared into the warm concoction. *I need my chicken wrap right now and a bathroom! What the heck is he rambling on about,* Dani wondered.

"I'm sorry, what was that?" Dani asked, attempting to catch up with the conversation?

"I was just asking what you thought about dinner tonight. It was amazing, right? They handpick the green beans, organic, of course, and they extract out all the juices. Then, they hit it with just a squeeze of lemon juice, add some Moroccan spices and coconut, and voila. Absolute perfection."

"So, if it's not pureed, then where are the green beans?"

"Discarded, I suppose. The first time I tried to make this at home, I spent hours trying to replicate the recipe, and I just couldn't get it right. With a little practice, I think I'm coming in at a close second," Jacob smiled. "Hopefully, you'll allow me to prepare our favorite dish, just for you," Jacob said, licking his lips.

Fake ass L.L Cool J looking fool, Dani thought.

"So, anyway, Ms. Dani B, how about you? What's your favorite food? What's your thing?"

"Well, it's funny that you mention it, but there's this place called Le Ric's, it's more like a food truck, but the food is ama—"

"Ah! Did you say Le Ric's? Oh, hell yes, I love that place!"

"Oh, my gosh, yes," Dani sat up, ready to grab his hand and charge out the door.

"That name reminds me of this quaint little place back home called Arlebu," Jacob said excitedly. "They serve the best meat in the world, hands down, nothing like it."

"Oh," Dani said, somewhat relieved. "I wasn't sure if you still ate meat."

"Well, technically," Jacob smiled, "I'm more of a savor the flavor type of carnivore. They actually boil the meat, extracting all the juices and nutrients from it, and they serve it warm, cold, or however you like it."

"Sooo, basically broth," Dani said, squinting her eyes, hoping he could see she was on to the level of BS he was serving.

What type of mental madness is this man doing to himself? Have the green bean soup, but don't eat the green beans. Love the meat juice, but don't eat the meat, just the prosciutto.

Dani barely touched her seventy-five-dollar cup of green bean water. She was done with this evening. Every time she tried to speak about anything, Jacob cut her off. Every time he asked her a question, he cut her off before she could answer. Every time she fell silent and tried to focus on anything but hunger, he cut her off. And to include her back in the conversation, he complimented her eyes, her cheeks, or her smile. But before she could respond, he redirected the conversation back to himself and cut her off again. *Shoot! Becca was right. He's a dog in a muscle shirt, a sexy one, though.*

"You have the most beautiful hair, just gorgeous. You know, it's one of the first things I noticed about you the day we met," Jacob said, as he smiled, reaching across the table to grab Dani's hand.

Knowing that she wore a beanie hat the first time they met, she didn't understand how her hair attracted him the most. He had never seen her with hair, except for tonight. Dani had alopecia universalis, an autoimmune disease that causes hair loss. In her case, she couldn't grow hair on any part of her body. The wig she wore on their date tonight was simply a part of the outfit that Becca thought was a good idea, suggesting she introduce her baldness to him slowly.

"Pardon my interruption. You said that my hair was the first thing you noticed when we first met. Was it before or after I got drenched by snow?" *Hint, hint, idiot! Hellooo! Community service. Shoveling snow. A bald-headed woman in a beanie!*

"Well, call me crazy, but I actually loved brushing the snow from your hair and staring into your eyes. I mean, come on,

Dani, you're beautiful. I had to build up my nerves just to ask you out," Jacob said with a shy grin.

That ain't no dog in a muscle shirt, Dani thought. *That's giving him too much credit. That's a rabid-faced hyena in a muscle shirt!* Dani laughed while tossing her head back and whipping her hair from side to side like a possessed woman.

"Are you okay?" Jacob asked.

"Totally," she said as she stood up and grabbed her purse. "Thank you for a nice evening," was all Dani could manage to say as she struggled to get to the exit before her inner thoughts took over her mouth.

"What are you doing? Where are you going? Dani, at least tell me what's wrong."

"This, all of this," she said, circling her index finger in the air for emphasis. "This is not it, but thank you for having me," she said as she moved towards the door.

You're almost at the door, Dani thought to herself. You got this! Don't you let this fool see you cry.

"Typical," Jacob said loudly, gaining the attention of the only other couple in the room. "I'm sitting here having dinner with you, going all out for you! What's the problem? Nah, never mind, I get it. I just never pegged you to be one of those. The old 'nothing is good enough for me' type of woman. Damn sisters! All the same, all the time," Jacob mumbled under his breath, still loud enough for the couple in the corner to hear his every word.

Dani stopped in her tracks; disbelief flooded her face. *He never pegged me for one of those,* she thought. He was definitely asking for it, but she was doing all she could to keep Daniesha at bay.

"You're soooo hurt from all the abuse from every man in your life that you take it out on innocent people. Try taking some accountability for yourself, for the situations that you put yourself in. Too damn broken to notice something good right in front of your face," Jacob mumbled. "Do me a favor, get yourself some counseling. Better yet, here's my card. Call my office, I'll have my assistant recommend someone."

"You got all that from what I said? How nice of you to suggest someone," Dani said, reaching for the card while holding back angry tears.

"Least I can do. I guess I thought you were different," he said. "Turns out you're just another patient in denial."

Take his dignity and pierce his heart, but don't go to jail. "You thought I was different? What does that mean?" Before Jacob had a chance to respond, Dani purposely interrupted him. "Mind if I go first," she stated, while moving towards him, as not to disturb their audience. "Different is me standing here telling you that this evening with you has been a beautiful, yet hungering disaster."

Dani moved closer to Jacob until she stood so close, she could smell his aftershave. Staring directly at him, she realized he wasn't as handsome as he was earlier. It was something about his eyes that seemed lost, empty, and too familiar. She wanted to cut him up with words, but she sensed something was already broken there. "Thank you for inviting me to share this lovely scenery with you," she said. "The 360-degree views of the city are breathtaking. And you, Dr. Jacob, with your chiseled frame and your gorgeous smile, you sir, are an exquisite looking man," she said.

Fully aware that she could walk out now, but something inside kept urging her to finish it. *How will he learn if I run? What about all the other women? This beautiful fool actually believes I'm someone else.*

Dani knew if she didn't speak her heart in this moment, it would haunt her, and she would take it out on the next man, or worse, on herself. She turned away from Jacob and faced the door before she started to speak because if she looked him in the eyes, her words might come from a place of hunger and frustration. She needed to leave him with something peaceful and loving because she sensed that he needed it.

"When we first met, and you grabbed my hand in the cafe, my fingers brushed across the hard calluses on your hand. You immediately apologized, trying to explain the life of a hand-washing surgeon, combined with an exercise enthusiast, but all I saw was a hardworking man. When the sun set over the snow and you removed your sunglasses, you tried to explain the circles around your eyes from the overnight shifts and long days at the hospital, but all I saw was someone with a heart for others."

"That day as the group of us set out to shovel snow, we were met with some pushback from a few of our elderly favorites," Dani smiled, thinking about Mr. and Mrs. Hoffman on McGullum Street. He was a retired surgeon, and his wife, a retired financial advisor. Everyone knew Mr. Hoffman did not take kindly to just any ole body offering him a hand.

"I don't think any of us will ever forget Mr. Hoffman coming outside with his pistol hanging off the side of his belt and a rifle draped over his shoulder. Even then, you responded with a slight touch to his arm and a friendly hand on his back. As I recall, you did this to every elderly person that we met that day, offering a sense of calm and reassurance.

"Dr. Jacob, you are a man who saves lives, committed to giving your time to others. You're a heart surgeon who volunteers on his days off. I came here tonight to be a part of your 'you' time, honored that you chose me to spend this free evening with you. I thought we would kick back and chill, like at the cafe. Unfortunately, sometimes things that are so beautiful from the outside can be empty and hollow on the inside. Like your conversation tonight and this food. I want you to know that while I can see through all of this, I still feel like it would be an honor to get to know the real you."

"As lovely as that sounds this evening, whatever this was, is over," Jacob replied, clearly upset as the couple sharing the room had been giving him disgusting looks all night. He was certain it was Dani's energy rubbing off on the room. "I'm glad you were able to gather a good assessment of me. At least you got something out of the evening, right? Something to compare with the next man you judge without reason. Hopefully, you can find a way to apply whatever you learned to yourself, that way you don't disrespect the next man's time." Seemingly satisfied with his response, Jacob called for the check. "Oh, and can you please see her out? Get her a cab or something."

"You know when I met you, I was just me," Dani said. "Foolishly, tonight I thought I needed to add to myself because I wanted to *look* like what I felt. Free from wondering what anyone else, including you, would think of me when you saw me. After sitting here with you, I realize that maybe you needed to see me, just me."

"The evening is over Dani," Jacob interrupted while placing a hundred-dollar bill on the table.

"Since my beautiful hair is what drew you to me, you can keep it," she said, ripping the wig from her head and tossing it in his lap. *This* is who you met two weeks ago, wearing a New Orleans Saints hat and a jersey. No makeup, no hair, no lashes, just me! Take it all in," Dani said, as she closed her eyes, swallowed her tears, and did a full spin.

At that moment, Jacob was shocked as he now remembered Dani. "The cafe," he mumbled, suddenly recalling that exact day. *We talked for hours,* he recalled. While she wasn't the type of woman he normally dated, he thought she was cute and sexy, but in a tomboy sort of way. Looking at her now, in that dress and those heels, even without hair, she was stunning and different. Looking at his phone, he realized he had confused Dani with his date for tomorrow night, Debbie, the brunette.

"Dani, I—"

"The wig," Dani interrupted, "her name is Alicia. It's amazing that you remember *her* as this was her first time meeting you, or maybe you met Alicia on someone else." Reaching into her clutch, Dani pulled out her silk scarf, as she never left home without it, and wrapped it around her head and neck Grace Kelly style.

Standing near the door in her slinky, black dress and stiletto heels, she said, "One more thing, stop it with the lies. Drinking seventy-five-dollar cups of green water and broth! Meat juice? Really? Two weeks ago, I watched you devour two platters of meat, cheese, and crackers, not to mention the donut and sausage links you ate at the community center. Now, suddenly you only drink meat juice?"

"Dani, I can explain."

"No need. If green juice and meat broth is your thing, then do you, but do it because that's what you like. Don't do that for me or for the woman you thought was me. Because no matter how much you lie or how hard you try to hide who you really are, some people can still smell dogshit even when it's smothered with expensive cologne."

"Dani, wait," Jacob said, walking towards the door to stop her. "Can we just start over? This was a bit of a shock for me, not a bad shock. What I mean is, I know I'm not the first man to say this to you. I think you're beautiful just as you are, and I'm sorry."

At that moment, all Dani could think about was standing there naked, with no hair—bald, while Jacob was thinking she was someone else all evening. Although his eyes seemed so sincere, she could never give him a fair chance. "No, do your own inner work."

"But I…"

"No! Do your own self-work Jacob. Read some books, get some counseling, call your mama, find your daddy, and gimmie me back my wig," she said, snatching Alicia from under his arm.

Dani moved with grace, sexiness, and elegance, knowing that Jacob was watching her every move. Then, she slowly stepped into the cab.

Girl, this a camera moment right here, she thought, *if you didn't have that damn wig in your hand.* Refusing to look back, Dani simply waved the cab driver forward.

"Where to, ma'am?" the cab driver said, turning on the meter before she could slowly close the car door for full effect.

"Le Ric's food truck on 17th and Milton. Please, step on it.

Two

FIGHTING TO SURVIVE

The best part of Dani's day was always waiting when she came home. "Hey, mama's boy! Who's got your favorite doggy biscuits? Whose got your favorite doggy biscuits, huh? Yummy, yummy," she said, kneeling down, nestling her face against his furry wet nose. After years and years of wanting a dog, Jackson, her chocolate Goldendoodle, was a personal gift to herself after the divorce. "What'd you do, huh? What'd you do tonight? Mommy missed you too," Dani said as Jackson jumped onto her lap.

In terms of besties for life, Jackson was right up there with her two best friends, Becca and Cammie, and he was definitely leading the pack. They slept and ate at the same times, seemingly understanding each other's moods. When Jackson had his shots, Dani made him his favorite pumpkin snack, and when Dani felt sad, Jackson always made her smile. He even cuddled with her when she cried herself to sleep. Standing in his usual spot next to the door, Jackson smothered her face with more than the usual doggie kisses, as if he knew her date was a total bust.

After settling into her pajamas, Dani sat on the couch with Jackson's head in her lap, crying silently. Her tears were not from a place of pain but rather from a feeling of gratitude for creating personal boundaries for herself and finally finding inner peace. After her divorce, she was so alone and broken that she would have settled for someone like Dr. Jacob. But thank God, she was not that person anymore.

TOUGH TIMES

A string of events took place during the first few years of marriage: Dani lost her dad to Parkinson's disease. A year later, she found bald spots around her hairline that eventually spread. Two years later, she miscarried. The following year came with breast cancer, surgery, chemotherapy, radiation, and years of hormonal treatments. After ten years of marriage, they decided to go their separate ways. The months following the divorce were some of the hardest times of her life. Not sleeping well, unhealthy eating, overworking, exercising, and crying became her daily routine.

Often feeling like she was losing control, Dani prayed, meditated, and read her Bible. There was no one she wanted to talk to or be around. Yet, she craved the presence of a hug and not just any hug; a strong, encompassing, never-ending kind of hug, something her friends and family couldn't fill.

She recalled the hot summer day when she realized everything she planned for her life had failed. Feeling defeated, all she wanted to do was run. One lap after another, she ran while telling her frustrations to God, until her best friend Cammie intervened. "Dani, who are you speaking to? Cammie said, realizing there was no one else around. "Let's get you cleaned up, and I promise you, we can sit in the cool air and talk all day," she said as Dani stood next to her, drenched with sweat.

"Nah, I'm good, thanks."

"Dani, I'm in the middle of a very important case. You're not answering the phone, and you're not sleeping. Clearly, you're overworking yourself, and I know you're not financially okay."

"So, you stalking me again? You know that's illegal, right? Stay out of my bank accounts Cammie. I have everything I need."

"Really? Illegal? Then call a cop. I'm not just your lawyer or advisor; I'm your friend. I'm not asking you to let me help you Dani, its already done! So, here's what's gonna happen next. You're gonna get in the shower, throw on something cute, and we're going to brunch. We need food in our bodies! We have moves to make and a lot of retail therapy to get done."

"You know I hate retail therapy. I have a house I'm trying to buy, Cammie, a new job full of responsibilities that I'm not yet sure I can handle, and you wanna go shopping? What purpose is in that? How is that feeding into any of my plans or my destiny?"

"You been watching T. D. Jakes and Steven Furtick this morning, huh?"

"There you go, always judging just because you choose to live in a false sense of reality."

"No, no, I didn't mean it like that," Cammie said. I'm just saying that when you start speaking words like 'purpose, journey, or destiny,' either you've been fasting and praying, or meditating on something, that's all. Come on Dani, a little shopping during these times can lift the spirits, shift the atmosphere.

"Whatever! Maybe you're right. I just don't know what's going on with my life. I keep making moves, doing all I know how to do, only to find myself right back at square one, starting all over again. I'm exhausted! I feel like I've been fighting to live, fighting to beat cancer, to be healthy, fighting for my marriage, fighting to have babies, fighting for my career, and now I have to add a hysterectomy to the list."

Fearing that Dani would start doing more laps, Cammie stood in the middle of the running path. "Look, I don't have all the answers, but you know that Becca and I will never leave you. As for the hysterectomy, I promise to make it the ultimate recovery experience of the decade. You'll be staying at my penthouse with a full staff waiting on your every whim. Also, let's not forget that you are still standing and looking very well while doing so. Honey, in my book, that's not losing, that's living."

"I know. It's just…whew," Dani said, exhaling. "Have you ever read that story in the Bible about the woman who bled for twelve years? She believed that just touching the hem of Jesus' garment would make her whole. Can you imagine twelve years of constant pain and disappointment? Yet, she believed that just a simple touch would restore it all. I've read that story dozens of times throughout the years, but these days, it reads differently. Sometimes, I feel like the buildup of everything has been incredibly overwhelming. My mom always says that God never puts more on us than we can bear, and I get that. But I never knew that accepting the tough times would hurt so much. Yet, I'm too ashamed to admit it.

When I think about how blessed I am and how much worse things could be, I feel so selfish and ungrateful for crying and complaining about anything," said Dani. "Yet, on the other side of that, I can't tell you how many times I've told myself that if I could just get God's attention, if I could just touch him, then all of this would go away, and everything would be made whole. I don't even need it to make sense anymore. I just want the rollercoaster ride to stop."

"Dani, people get divorced. As awful as it is, I have a whole department in my firm dedicated to that very subject. Rejuvenation of your mind, body, and spirit is the best thing for you right now. In the meantime, a little retail therapy won't hurt. Trust me, it will make you feel better."

"This is not just about the divorce, Cammie. During those first five years of marriage, I felt like I lost everything. The years after that were just a waiting period to accept what had already happened. The divorce was hurtful and humiliating, but losing my fertility too? Heck, I can't even grow hair anymore. I'm not sure what type of man would want someone like that."

"Excuse me? I'm bald, too, and I don't have any problems in the man department. Maybe it's how you own it. Dani, you are one of the most beautiful bald women that I've ever seen, next to me of course. Even without a face full of makeup in a hundred degrees of heat dripping sweat, you are still sexy. However, and please hear me out, we cannot ignore the fact that as women, we have got to stop raising grown-ass husbands with man-boy perceptions on life. We have enough to deal with on a regular basis. Unnecessary stress adds up and can have an ill effect on our bodies. All women are not cut out for that ride or die life, just as some men are not the type to deal with a woman's daddy issues. Please, I beg you, let me handle him, Dani. I can get him together, so this doesn't become a pattern for him in the future. I can save him. You know I don't lose."

"Lose what? That's not gonna change anything, Cammie. You can't make somebody stay if they want to go. Besides, you know he's not a bad person."

"Dani, he left!"

"Cammie, he needed to leave! Everybody's not meant to stay throughout every journey of your life. This has nothing to do with him or anyone else. This is about me. Sometimes, I think maybe I pissed God off, or perhaps he's trying to get my attention or something. I don't know. One thing is for sure, I'm listening."

"Okay, but you don't get to beat yourself up. Just let me handle it," Cammie pleaded.

"Lately, I've been feeling this hole in my heart, and you know what? Maybe it's been there for years, maybe since I was a little girl when the first man walked out of my life. I didn't know it, but perhaps whatever remnants that pain left behind has been there all this time. I thought that working hard, moving forward, getting married, and starting a family was the answer. But it's not, not right now. Whatever it is that's bringing me right back to this space, I need to deal with it."

"I agree," Cammie said. "We all have that come to Jesus moment at some point in our lives, but I don't know if this is a 'woman in the Bible, touch the hem of his garment, help me God' type of situation," Cammie said.

"Then what type of situation is it? Is it a shopping fix? It can't be because everything will be waiting here when I get back, except I'll have less money. Or maybe it's an 'I need a career change and more money type of thing, or perhaps just a few drinks and some spa time with my girls or maybe I just need a new man right Cammie?' Girl, we're in our forties. At some point, we have to grow up and realize that we don't always have the answer, and everything we keep trying to do to numb the pain, does not produce a long-term result. How bad does it have to get before it becomes a 'help-me-God' type of situation?" Dani said.

"What do you mean?" said Cammie.

"I'm just tired of going back to the same place," said Dani. "Tired of watching the world go by while I'm still trying to figure out this part of it. I just wanna learn whatever I need to do to produce a different result. When I was diagnosed, I had never seen anyone fight something like that before. I wasn't sure how to survive cancer or how to do that in a new marriage. I didn't know how to be this new person I was evolving into while my husband was still getting used to living with his new wife. I wasn't sure how to keep being strong and keep believing in God while feeling so disappointed and let down on the inside. Some of the same friends who congratulated us, expressing all kinds of love and admiration of him, of us, are some of the same ones now sharing what they would have done differently if they were me."

"Screw them! Cammie said. "I didn't have to be with you 24/7 to know that you prayed for him, for the both of you, before you acted on your feelings. You had a courtship, a friendship, and that's why even in the midst of your hurt, you still have love in your heart. Trying to navigate loss and transformation in a new marriage without a blueprint can be difficult for anyone," said Cammie.

"Exactly. Having a God-fearing man by your side is what I've always wanted, but I have never felt so chosen as I did when I saw how God showed up in our lives during the most difficult times in my marriage," Danie recalled. "He loved on me like I was his only child. I prayed for a man to see me like that, but if I would have understood the depth of 'Seek God first, and everything will be added,' I would have focused more on my relationship with God, before man."

"Girl, most of us out here think we good with God simply because we go to church, read the Bible, tithe, and all that. We really don't know the strength of our relationship until our faith and beliefs are tested," said Cammie.

"Look at you? Talking about I'm listening to T. D. Jakes and Steven Furtick. Sounds like you been sitting on the couch right there next to me," said Dani.

"No shame in my game. I gets mine. Seriously, you got this, and we have you," Cammie said. "If you're interested, after the hysterectomy when we get you all healed up down there, I know a couple of single guys in my office."

"Do you? Hold on, let me ask Jesus," Dani said as she bowed her head. "He said no, we good.

"Okay, you got jokes, but you can't stay single forever. Plus, it's a whole other world out there. You have to properly vet these dudes before you get involved Dani, I'm serious. Fool around and fall asleep next to a gorgeous killer and forget to wake up."

"You should know," Dani said.

"You play too much," Cammie replied, turning to walk away.

"I hear you. I'm just focused on other things right now," Dani said.

"I know, and we just talked about them. We can't fix everything in one day, especially if we don't have all the answers. In the meantime, while we're waiting on Jesus, we can shop. My treat."

"Fine. I just have one more question, how do you see God? How do you envision him?"

"Dani! It's too hot out here to keep going this deep into conversation," Cammie yelled.

"Like I imagine him as this giant figure, bigger than anything ever seen. When I go to him, he picks me up and sits me on his lap. Next to him, I'm like a little tiny speck of dust, but because he's God, somehow, I fit just right. I'm like a child sitting on her father's lap and…"

"Dani, stop," Cammie said. "I'm sorry, it's too hot. I'm sweating off lashes and makeup. I get it, you're sitting on God's lap, wrapping your arms around his neck, and all the pain goes away, just like with your daddy. Am I right? Many little girls around the world have that image, Dani. It's one of the only things I remember as a child with my dad. I even have a picture of me as a kid with my arms wrapped around a man's neck, but his head is cut off from the photo. My mom said it was my dad. And to this day, it's still my favorite picture, but that nigga left too. It happens, Dani. Daddies leave their children; husband's leave their wives. And mothers? They become a superwoman left behind to raise superwomen and sometimes supermen."

Dani nodded in agreement.

"You and I? We are built for the shit we deal with," Cammie continued. "We come from a long line of superwomen who kicked ass because they had no other choice. THAT is who we are! We work hard, and we go hard for those we love. You need to accept that!" Cammie said.

"You're right, Cammie. That is who we are, and daddies do leave…but in my image, it's not ME wrapping my arms around God's neck; its him wrapping his arms around me, refusing to let ME go. When my arms are too weak and my heart is broken, he holds on tighter. No matter what I do, he always shows up for me. Nothing in the world can separate us. I may be a superwoman, but I'm human, and I get tired of fighting sometimes. I know you do too. He makes me feel like I don't have to fight, and I don't always have to be a kickass or prove myself to anyone. I can just be myself. He's always waiting for me with open arms, comforting me as I sleep, as I breathe, guiding my every move. I've sat on my dad's lap too, but the feeling is not the same."

"Okay," Cammie said, swiping away tears, forgetting about the heat. You think that's in the Bible, she said as she pulled off her lashes?"

"I don't know, but it's in my heart, and I believe that's where my focus should be."

In the weeks that followed, starting with the first page of the Bible, Dani read and meditated on one scripture, one day at a time. After reading, she journaled and talked to God out loud about everything, like he was her best friend sitting next to her on a park bench having lunch. At first, she felt crazy, like her conversation wasn't holy enough, but as she continued to talk and read scriptures, she had read dozens of times, she felt like she had reconnected with someone from her past, but yet it was new.

Raised in a small town in the south, Dani was no stranger to the church. As the youngest of three siblings, she grew up singing in the choir, acting in plays, and ushering in the church. Every night as a child, Dani recited one of her father's favorite scriptures, the twenty-third chapter of Psalms. He taught her to read this chapter in her darkest moments, like when she failed to graduate from high school, or when some guy broke her heart. One of her favorite memories was the time when she lost her job while living alone in a small town out West. Back then, Dani made decisions to benefit her feelings in the moment, failing to consider the long-term effect. When she got laid off from her job, it was like her world shattered; how would she take care of herself? Who would pay her bills? Would she have to go back home as a failure? She raced back to her apartment as fast as her overpriced, not needed, brand new muscle car could carry her and dialed her father Edwin's phone number.

"Hello?"

"Hey Daddy, it's me, Dani."

"Hey, I know who it is. What, you think your daddy don't know when his baby calling? Guh, I know that ring before I even pick up the phone," he chuckled, laughing through his teeth. "What's wrong?"

"How you know something's wrong, daddy, I ain't said nothing."

"Because I know my baby. How you like that," he chuckled again. "What's wrong? Talk to your daddy, come on."

"I lost my job today. They laid me off, and I don't know what I'm gonna do."

"It's okay, baby, that happens sometimes. They gon' call you back, or you gon' find another one. Somebody gon' call you. You know you running that business over there."

No matter how many times Dani told him she wasn't running anything, he believed that she ran the company and that God told him she would someday own the business. It didn't matter that it was a billion-dollar industry she worked for, and Dani didn't even have a college education at the time.

"Daddy, I'm not running anything. I need my job. What am I supposed to do? I never expected this. I'm not prepared. I don't have any options here."

"So, you wanna come home? You can come stay with me until you get yourself together. But what is it that you really want to do?"

"I don't know, daddy. I'm just trying to figure everything out. I'm so frustrated with everything," Dani sobbed.

"Okay, it's okay," her dad said. "Let it out and pull yourself together. Then, stop all that crying before you make yourself sick. Have you read the twenty-third chapter of Psalms? Have you read your Word today?"

Knowing she did not read her Word today, yesterday, nor did she remember the last time she really read it. Dani started to lie and say she did just to move on to something else. *Why can't he just be my dad,* she thought. *I don't want to talk about the Bible right now. I don't want him to be a minister right now. I need my earthly father to rescue me, show up for once!*

"No, I haven't read it yet," Dani replied in a short tone, ready to argue with him. As much as she loved him, she still harbored feelings of anger for him leaving when she was a child. *Maybe if you would have stayed where God put you, then I wouldn't have moved here chasing after some resemblance of you, and we wouldn't be on the phone having this conversation, Dad,* Dani thought to herself.

As if she had spoken the words out loud, Edwin's tone and line of questioning became firmer and more direct. "Look! What is the purpose of what you're doing? What are your daily tasks? What actions are you committed to doing that are speaking life and purpose into your future while helping the lives of others? We may not have made the best choices together, but me and your mama gave you a strong foundation in God, and we love you. We taught you to seek God and learn of him and his will for your life. We can pray with you, and we can pray for you, but you have to talk to God for yourself. You hear me? You have to pray, read, and seek him for yourself, and he will guide you. Didn't he say, 'he will never leave nor forsake the righteous?' But you have to trust him, baby, beyond what you can see or feel. But if you're running from anything, you need to stop. Your daddy is right here if you wanna come home and get yourself together."

"I know, Daddy."

"Tough times will happen, and when they do, the Holy Spirit will remind you of his Word, and it will guide you. That's why it's so important for you to read the Bible, so you know God's voice when he's speaking to you, and you can expect him. Okay? In the meantime, do your pushups and toughen up so you can stay looking good and fine, like your daddy."

Laughing through her tears, Dani picked up her Bible and read the Twenty-Third Psalm with her daddy, and they prayed together. Afterward, they went on talking for hours about recipes, his church, her guy friends, his lady friend, and sports. Years later, before his memory left him for good, he made sure she still knew the Twenty-Third Psalm, ready to repeat it long after he was gone when he knew she would miss him most but need God more.

"I miss you, Dad, as I'm sure you know." Yearning to talk to him, Dani picked up her Bible and read the twenty-third chapter of Psalms, and his personal favorite, the twenty-seventh chapter of Psalms. When she finished, she recalled that conversation again, when her dad told her to toughen up and do some pushups so she could stay good-looking, just like him.

"Well, Dad, you always did have great skin and a smooth baldhead! If only you could see how much we look alike now." And just like that, Dani burst into the loudest laughter as if her dad was right there with her, admiring their similarities. Sitting on the couch with Jackson, she cried tears of joy, thankful for those experiences and the woman God was allowing her to become. "Life is good," Dani whispered as she cried herself to sleep, peacefully, in the comfort of her own home.

"Hush, Jackson! Shush," Dani muttered through barely opened eyes. The intercom blared, alerting Dani that someone was at the door. "Whoever it is, get away from my door," Dani yelled into the speaker.

"It's Beccaaaaaa," her best friend cheerfully replied in her best singing voice. "I come bearing treats and love, my dear."

"Hmm, come in," Dani said, keying in the code for the entryway.

Becca Lynn Carrington and Dani had been best friends for the past ten years. Born and raised in Texas, Becca was like wonder woman. At six feet one with long silvery, golden blond wavy hair and blue eyes, she was sweet as pie, gorgeous, and bougie. With an athletic build from years of competing in every sport to satisfy her father's dreams of having a boy, Becca developed an attitude to go along with the muscle. She was known for delivering a total knockout to her share of men who came a little too close to what her mother called the cookie jar, without invitation. Throughout the years of getting to know Becca, both Dani and Cammie joked that at first sight, she was as doting and loving as a classic Nicole Kidman from the *Stepford Wives*. But in the blink of an eye, she could switch to a modern-day Charlize Theron from *Atomic Blonde*, hashing out punches and sidekicks while wearing a pencil skirt and stilettos. With a classic Texas accent that turned powerful men into puddy in her hands, she was a force to be reckoned with in the fashion industry. At the age of twenty-five, Becca earned her first million and developed her brand as a tailored online clothing designer. She then opened her first brick-and-mortar lingerie boutique at age twenty-nine. Fifteen years later, she's now a global brand for high-end lingerie, undergarments, and most recently, women's clothing and accessories.

Bam, bam, bam, the sound reverberated through the house. "Come in, and if you don't stop banging on that door!"

Knowing her best friend suffered from early morning frustration, especially when being suddenly awakened from her sleep, Becca softened her tone, anxious to hear all the juicy details from last night's date.

"Good morning, sunshine. I come bearing your favorite beverage and pastry from Le RRRRic," Becca said, rolling her tongue to give the name an accent."

"Thanks, girl," Dani replied in a softer tone, smiling at the cup of Le'Rics golden milk, her favorite morning coffee substitute.

"So? What happened? Did you guys fall in love? How long was the date? Ooooh, is he still here? Are you basking in the afterglow?" Becca laughed, gyrating her hips and wildly shaking her thick blond curls from side to side as they landed perfectly back in place? "You really should put something else on, so he doesn't see you looking like that," Becca said, sipping on her hot coffee with one perfectly manicured hand, while holding her Valentino clutch in the other.

"Becca, shut up," Dani said, feeling the ease from her golden milk starting to wear off.

"Dani, honey you can't look like last night today. I've told you time, and again, nobody wants to wake up to a grouchy ole mess. Men want to see that same sexy angel from the previous night. Come on, let's brush your teeth and get your face on. I got something special in my car. Just one look at you, and y'all gone be in the bed all day," Becca said, pulling Dani towards the guest bathroom.

"Girl ain't nobody here," Dani said, jerking her arm away from Becca. "You know I love you, but it is too early for this much talking," Dani said, feeling somewhat embarrassed thinking about her stupid date.

"Hmph, what happened," Becca said, as she smiled and tilted her head slightly to the side in her traditional, yet unpredictable to others, 'Do I need to kick somebody's ass' attitude?' Just like that, bougie Becca was sitting in the corner while her alter ego, Beccuh Lynn from Texas, took over.

"Calm down! It was the norm experience. One that I have been on too many times and not interested in doing again."

Seeing Dani relax in her chair, bougie Becca took over, "Oh, honey, I'm sure it wasn't that bad."

"No, I actually learned some things, like how some restaurants serve green water for seventy-five dollars a bowl."

"Ewww."

"Right? Though the most important thing I learned is to never allow anyone to convince me to wear a wig ever again."

"What? Oh, no! Did it slide off? Dani, I told you to use extra spray and clips to keep that thang on. Otherwise, a good breeze or a feisty bird can just swoop in and carry it away! Did it come off in the restaurant? Outside? Where did it fall off? Did he see it?"

"No, it did not fall off, at least not like that."

"You ripped it off again, didn't you?"

"I guess so," Dani replied.

"Well, he must have been a total bum. I'm so sorry, hon, but you know I think you're beautiful with or without hair. Wigs are like accessories these days. No one needs a red-bottom stiletto, but sometimes a good shoe is a total mood enhancer."

"Yeah, that's true," Dani said, still slightly feeling the sting from Jacob thinking she was a completely different woman the entire night. She was nowhere near as important as the woman he was trying to impress.

"Don't you let that pig's turd ruin your day!"

"Of course not. I'm just feeling a little tired right now," Dani said, doing her best impression of a fake yawn, hoping Becca would take the hint and leave her alone.

"Well, I have two bottles of wine in the car, and it's Friday. We should get a buzz, have some breakfast, get a little gym time, a massage, hell let's do a weekend."

"Girl! It's seven o'clock in the morning, and not all of us run our own business. I have to go to a work meeting this morning. In fact, gimme a few minutes to throw on some shoes and a hat. I'll walk down with you," Dani said, jumping up to brush her teeth, do a quick change of clothes, and grab a hat.

"Looking like you look? Honey, you know that I love you too, but you look a hot mess. Dani, you work for a global fashion company."

"So, what. It's not like I own it."

"Well, as the owner of my company, I can't have you hanging out with me looking like that. If I've told you once, I've told you time, and time again, you have to represent for the job you want, not the job you have."

"Oh, my gosh," Dani said, grabbing her head feeling a headache brewing from the conversation. "It's casual Friday."

"Then casually carry your ass back to that room and put on something that compliments this body that God done saw fit to bless you with. Put on some heels, and ditch the hat, please." Becca hated when Dani walked around looking defeated. "Now listen, I hate seeing you like this. Have a good cry, get back up, and keep it moving. I've gotta go. Call me later, and we'll meet for drinks and high-calorie carbs," Becca yelled back as she rushed out the door before Dani had a chance to reject her Friday night offer.

Dani and Becca met at a local gym in DC when Dani first started losing her hair. Mesmerized by the girl with the neatly tapered mohawk, Becca would stare at Dani, often forgetting to concentrate on her own exercises.

"Who is that woman?" Becca asked her trainer.

"I think her name is Dani. Why do you ask?"

"I don't know. It's just something about her that is so different. She's regal, but she seems so sad."

"Hmm, I don't know about sad, but I admire her work ethic. She kicks ass."

"Exactly! She kicks ass, almost like she has no other choice." Becca watched her a few times, intending to talk to her and possibly make a new friend. A few months later, Dani was lying on the workout bench completing her last set of bench presses when someone brushed past her, knocking her hat to the floor. Realizing her head was cold, Dani struggled to quickly place the heavy bar back on the rack and put the hat back on before anyone noticed the large bald spots in the middle of her head. Before she could sit up, Becca was there placing the hat back securely where it belonged.

"I think you lost something here. Excuse me if I'm being too forward, but you really don't need it. Hair is pretty overrated."

With a look of panic and embarrassment, Dani simply replied, "Thanks," and immediately left the gym. After realizing that she could use a friend who knew the real her, Dani turned her car around and went back to the gym. The two of them have been inseparable ever since.

Becca was right; Dani had finally landed a job she loved with a high-end fashion company she was proud to represent. She needed to show up looking like she owned the title. After the divorce, she hit a dead end with her job in finance. Being a writer gave her room to be herself while connecting with the community. The best part was the sample gifts and access to old clothing, shoes, and makeup which were outdated trash to them but brand new to her. And no one cared that she was bald. There wasn't some imaginary ambiguous corporate culture that she had to fit into. In fact, she felt like a badass every time she walked into the building. Dani stood out in her own little category, just like everyone else, walking in her own fashion show every day.

"Maybe it won't be so bad. I could use a real night out," Dani said to herself.

Becca loved to hang out at this semi-ritzy restaurant that turned into a live music scene after ten pm. Friday nights were a combination of 80s and 90s classics. Becca and Dani liked to feast on boiled crabs and sing along with the band to all the old-school jams, but Dani just wasn't in the mood for going out and singing.

"Jackson, are you still sleeping?" Seemingly annoyed, Jackson quickly looked over his shoulder and turned back around, cuddling deeper into his plushy lounge chair. "I hear ya, Jack. Mommy feels the exact same lazy way today."

After a long work week, Dani liked to unwind on Fridays. Her workday typically started at eight every morning, but she was usually in the office by six-thirty am. Today, she just felt out of whack and tired. Standing in the kitchen, drinking her warm beverage, she remembered that her morning had started off in an unusual way. She had not done her prayer and meditation, and judging by the way she was feeling, she needed it.

If it's one thing I've learned throughout the years is that God gifts us grace and new mercies every day, and the enemy knows that too. "Come on, Jackson. Outside you go," Dani said as she let him run about in the backyard. "I need to get a fresh word and meditation into my body before I start my day."

Three

TIME TO SHINE

While meditating, Dani's mind wandered to the morning meeting with her boss, Talia. More than just a boss, Talia was a mentor, her confidant. Coming into Sari as a new writer, Dani needed a lot of attention. Her first day in a new corporate culture was a disaster. Unaware of the popular dress climate, Dani wore brown slacks, a cream-colored sweater, and dark brown pumps. Definitely not the worst, but after seeing her environment, she quickly realized she had to do better. After making her way through the crowded lobby, moving from floor to floor of the computerized building, she finally made it to her office, where she sat, awaiting instruction. Hours later, she was confronted by Talia's assistant, and not in a good way.

"Ms. Breaux? Dani Breaux?"

"Yes, that's me. Nice to meet you," Dani said, standing to her feet and extending her hand."

"You missed the morning meeting. Why?"

"I…I wasn't aware of a morning meeting."

"Everything was emailed to you in that neat little computerized box on top of your desk. Did you check your emails?"

"I'm sorry, this is my first day," Dani said, pulling back her hand as it was clear she was not going to shake it. "I don't have access to the passwords or anything."

"Hmm, then you go to admin and check-in. No excuses. Here at Sari Unique, we will not tolerate unpreparedness or tardiness."

"I wasn't tardy. I was here. On-time. Six-thirty am sharp, and my shift starts at eight."

"But yet, here you are, clueless as to your assignment for the day because you missed the morning meeting. Every day, we have a morning meeting, and it's your job to know that."

"Got it. It won't happen again."

"Good, but again, why did you miss the morning meeting?

Did this heifer hear what I just said? This ain't it! Nope! I will go to jail messing with this thang every day. I'm about to call human resources and get my old accounting job back.

"My apologies, as I just stated, I did not get the communication. I do not have any information, as it is my first day, and I haven't even met my boss yet. So please, who was I supposed to meet this morning?"

"Me," a distant voice called out from the hallway. "Dani Breaux, nice of you to join us. I'm Talia, your boss. Now that we've officially met, follow me to my office, and we'll get started.

Oh, and this is Yuri, my assistant. That'll be all, Yuri. One other thing? In an hour, I want you to walk Dani through the norm, show her our day-to-day."

"Yes, ma'am," Yuri said.

"Oh, that won't be necessary," Dani said. "I can find my way around just fine. I'll check with admin for access to everything. Thank you."

"Ms. Breaux, Dani, don't do that. I like things to be done a certain way, outside of admin. I get *to know you, you get to know me, and we won't ever need a 'Yuri moment' to intervene. Yes?"*

Hmph, Yuri is clearly unaware that I have nothing to lose, and I will drag her tail through this office if she don't come up out my face.

As if reading Dani's mind, Yuri extended her hand to Dani, complete with a warm smile. "Nice to meet you, Ms. Breaux. Welcome to Sari Unique."

"Everybody gets a little ribbing around here when they first start, but no worries, I got you," Talia said as Dani followed her to her office.

Talia French graduated at the top of her class from one of the most prestigious law schools in the country. Her mother is a former district attorney, and her father, a retired military general. Talia and her siblings followed the family legacy with her brother as a Navy Seal, and her sister following her auntie's path as head of obstetrics.

Talia's celebration party for making partner at her firm turned into her retirement party. Using her connections, she strolled into Sari Unique and into the office of CEO Langston Sidreaux Jr.

"Mr. Sidreaux, my name is Talia French, a former partner at Beckle, Ridgeforth, and French. I am here to offer you my services as the Editor in Chief of Sari Unique Magazine."

"Please, call me Langston. It's nice meet you, but seriously, Ms. French, why on earth would I agree to something like that? I'm sure I don't have to tell you that this is a global corporation. We can't risk someone with no experience in that position. However, I would be honored to have someone of your stature on my legal team. I'm sure I can meet your salary demands."

"Mr. Sidreaux, this is a one-time offer. If you refuse to accept, then I will join your lowest competitor, and I will bury you. Before you answer, consider this small piece of advice as a gift. Every word and image this company prints, speaks to the culture and work ethic behind the brand. You have one of the oldest African American ancestries in the world, yet your creativity as CEO does not represent what you pretend to value most. You say you speak for the voice of the community, setting a platform for those you serve, but your publications lack any type of diversity, speak very little about real-world issues, and you have absolutely zero inclusion for anyone outside of your frame of reference. As the current acting CEO of Sari Unique, what you do with your time defines your legacy. You can solidify your place as the top contender in the industry to bear your name, or not. You have twenty-four hours. My card."

In less than a year, Sari Unique Magazine went from being known for its flawless pages and high fashions to creating a category of its own with a strong emphasis on community development, diversity and inclusion, career progression, in addition to high fashion.

With a newly acquired interest in his family legacy, Langston Sidreaux Jr opened an art gallery to honor his family's history of art and dance. He developed culinary institutes and performing art schools. He extended funding for improvements, programs, and land development at Historically Black Colleges and Universities (HBCUs), sponsored paid internships with a clear path for career progression, and donated millions in scholarships and grants.

Langston established different genres of magazines, catapulting Sari Unique into more than just high fashion. That was one of the things Dani loved about working for this company. Rather than attaching a mission statement to a bunch of ambiguous comments, leaving the public and employees to form their own perception, the culture at Sari demonstrated everything they printed. From ballet and art to culinary creations, body products, high fashion, homeware, and world issues—Sari was everyday life. This is why Dani felt comfortable pitching ideas to include a space for people with "normal" differences like alopecia and to brand cover pages and document stories with images that represent the many facets of beauty. While Talia supported most of Dani's ideas, this one, she said, would be Dani's calling card, as it spoke to her identity, and, perhaps, her purpose as a writer.

Feeling excited and recharged, Dani took Becca's advice and dressed for the day. Slipping on a pair of pale jeans, a cream-colored sweater with a low cut back, a pair of silver pointy toe heels with diamond stud earrings, and a bracelet, Dani left home feeling like a boss.

Since working at Sari Unique, Dani learned a thing or two from the models about her daily fashion choices and makeup, like less fuss is more, and simple pieces are classic. In her first couple of months at Sari, she enjoyed getting to know the models, seeing them enter the office in their original state of beauty before being transformed into the monthly cover issue. While the photos were spectacular, Dani thought the before was even better. As a result, she aimed for natural beauty with a soft rose lip, complete with her favorite eyelashes.

"I don't understand why women think men care about eyelashes," said Johnson, a sportswriter for Sari who often spoke too loud and too often. "You ask a perfectly fine woman out on a date, and she shows up looking like two caterpillars are glued to her face. What's wrong with just looking normal?"

"While that may be true for some, perhaps others don't have any lashes or eyebrows, possibly due to a sickness or autoimmune issue," Dani said.

"Okay, I get it, Dani, truly I do. And yes, it would freak me out if I saw a fine ass chick from behind, and she turns around with zero lashes and eyebrows on her face. I'm just saying, can women tone it down? Maybe try and fool us a little bit with some level of reality behind the fake hair and make-up? I mean, we know your real eyelashes are not touching the top of your forehead. Maybe you should do an article entitled, *'We Know They're Not Real,'*" Johnson said, as the guys rolled in laughter.

Frustrated with his comments, Dani walked away knowing people like that would never understand the process of buying "so-called realistic lashes" or trying to draw a perfectly framed eyebrow where there is none. Thinking back to her own eyelash experience, no matter how hard she tried, the glue would not bond to her hairless eyelids. Other times, the chemicals made her eyes red, swollen, and itchy.

Thanks to a small lash company, Lashes Lashes & More, run by another bald sister, Dani had finally found her dream lashes. Unable to contain her excitement, she emailed the owner:

> *Thank you! Thank you, thank you, thank you! I can say that a million times, and it still wouldn't be enough. Perhaps it takes a bald woman to understand the daily difficulties of applying lashes to a naked eyelid or attempting to draw on the perfect eyebrows which are either halfway gone or barely visible before walking out the front door. And as for a lace wig, that's a whole other story in itself. I received an email about your new line of products! I can't wait to see your wig line and eyebrow makeup. I am forever your customer, and I will send everyone I know your way.'*

Dani was so happy to find Lashes Lashes & More that she signed up for a monthly subscription, never buying store-bought lashes again.

This was the kind of story she wanted to feature in her article, entrepreneurs who turned their pain into purpose by creating products that filled a need for others based on their own differences. Thanks to Lashes Lashes & More, and a skin care routine created by a mother with autoimmune skin disease, Dani finally had the natural look that she had wanted since losing her hair—nice skin, realistic micro-bladed eyebrows, and healthy-created eyelashes that looked like they grew from her eyelids.

Even with an extra edge of confidence, at times, Dani felt weird walking down the street. She could hear people talking behind her back, "It's probably cancer. What's wrong with her? Is it contagious? I'm gonna touch her head." Dani quickly turned and said, "Touch this bald head, and you will have a noticeable difference of your own." Along with her daily positive affirmations, she had to remind herself that the world was not focused on her little bald head.

Arriving at work with just enough time to make her morning meeting, Dani announced her presence to the mass of employees. "Hot cups coming through, make way," Dani said, walking into the crowded lobby of Sari Unique. "Hey! Boy!" Danny stopped abruptly to rebalance both hands full of steaming hot tea. "Get your head out of your as-uh phone and watch where you're going!" *Shoot, there I go cussing after I just talked to Jesus this morning.*

While approaching the elevator to her department, she knew it was only a matter of time before someone would bump into her again. Playing out the scenario in her mind, she would cuss each and every person out, lose her job and then smack the hell out of that lil' boy who was still texting and walking into people. Her face would then be splayed across social media as the bald girl who eventually lost it, and people who never knew her would tell the news outlets that she finally snapped from the sequence of bad events going on in her life. She would go from being a sexy bald baddie to that baldheaded angry black woman who finally lost it over spilled tea.

With her future in jeopardy, Dani made a beeline for the stairs. "Okay, now if I could just scan my badge and open the door while carrying my briefcase, these breakfast pastries, and the two hot cups at the same time, I'd be golden," she mumbled. After scanning her badge and using her left butt cheek to prop the door open, she shoved the box of pastries under her left arm and used the strap to carry her briefcase on her left shoulder. With her butt in the air, Dani bent over to grab the cups from the floor. "Got it!" Just before she could stand up straight and declare victory, the door swung open, causing Dani to lose her balance and tilt backward, right into the grasp of none other than Langston Sidreaux Jr, the CEO of Sari Unique.

"Shhhhhaaat," she screeched!

"I got you. You're okay."

Standing up straight, Dani felt her heart racing, and it had nothing to do with her near fall. *Ain't nobody got time for his magnificence today,* Dani thought to herself as her streak of boldness slowly started to fade, leaving her feeling shy and struggling to find the right words.

"Ms. Breaux, how's your morning going so far?"

"Mr. Langston," Dani replied with a shy smile, "nice catch. I mean, not as in me and you, nice catch, just in you not letting me fall type of nice catch."

"No problem. Bit of a tea fetish this morning?"

"What makes you think it's tea or that it's all for me? Can't a girl simply share a warm beverage with a fellow co-worker?"

"Ah, who's the lucky guy?"

"Well, I don't know about luck, but I have a meeting with Talia, and our meetings are better when hot beverages and pastries are involved. Besides, this tea is amazing," Dani said, ready to advertise her secret spot.

"Yes, it is," Langston agreed. "Le'Ric's teas are nothing short of a miracle in a cup. One-of-a-kind type of fragrance and taste, might I add. The lavender vanilla is my personal favorite."

"Really," Dani said, trying not to sound too surprised? *What the hell does the prince of Sari know about a food truck,* Dani thought. *You have to walk on the cement outside to get to the food truck. I've never seen the man wear a pair of shoes for less than $30,000 dollars, and that's when he wasn't wearing one of his own million-dollar designs.*

"Does that alarm you?" Langston asked. "I would have you know that I have my own list of my favorite food trucks in this city, and Le'Ric's is in my top five."

"Really," Dani laughed.

"That's right," Langston smiled. "If I didn't know any better, I would think you were mocking me."

"Oh, no sir, not at all. It's just that, well, there are stories."

"Stories? Ah, of course. The old rumor mill," Langston smiled. "Let me have it! What do *they* say?"

"Well, rumor has it that, uh, your highness doesn't walk on pavement."

"Okay," Langston replied nonchalantly. "What do I walk on?"

"Well, rumor has it that you drive your cars into your own privately waxed garage on the basement floor of the office building. Then, you take the winding staircase up to the daily scrubbed ground floor where you occasionally visit the employee café, and then you make your way up the stairs to your penthouse suite," Dani said, feeling somewhat embarrassed to know the office gossip. "I'm not saying I believe it, but you can literally eat off the bottoms of your shoes," Dani said as she glanced down at his fresh out the box designer footwear.

"Okay," he smiled. "Maybe one day I'll sh—" *His phone suddenly blared in his pocket.* "One sec. This is Langston."

Thankful for the distraction, Dani slowed down to give him some privacy because, in reality, being cute in stilettos while nervously conversing, holding in your stomach, and climbing several flights of stairs was a hustle. Dani took this time to catch her breath and let her gut relax, allowing a stream of co-workers to go ahead of her so she could gather her thoughts. *Wait, was he about to ask me out?*

THE SIDREAUX FAMILY

Langston Dean Sidreaux Jr was the prince of Sari Unique Global Designs. With a family history dating back to the 1800s, the Sidreaux dynasty was rich in culture and talent, ranging from art to education, culinary, fashion, medicine—the list is endless. In the early days, the Sidreaux women created the designs while the men ran the business. The oldest living Sidreaux male became the owner of the empire, and his oldest son succeeded him. The title passed down from generation to generation. While Langston Sidreaux Jr is his mother and father's only son, his mother Naomi Winston remarried and has two sons of her own.

Just like their big brother, Langston, the Winston brothers are future heirs of their mother's global legacy, *Naomi's*. At five-ten with waist-length platinum hair, steel-grey eyes, and caramel skin, Naomi drips class and grace. She started her business using a kitchen mixer to create her now trade-marked body butters, handing them out as freebies at Sari Unique events. Within months, she began selling her beauty products in the lobby gift shop, which Sidreaux Sr. turned into her very own exclusive boutique.

Once sales expanded beyond the lobby, Naomi purchased her own building, which now has several locations around the world. In addition to the beauty line, her sons expanded the business to include professional makeup artists for movie and theater productions, a complete line of men's products, and recently, a line of children's organic body products. Per Becca, rumor has it the Winston brothers recently launched into the farm-to-table food business, marketing fresh products from farmers in state-of-the-art grocery stores located in select cities.

After the Sidreaux's very public divorce, Langston Sidreaux Sr. relocated from his palatial estate in Potomac to migrating between his Los Angeles and Dubai mansions. The Sidreaux triplet sisters, whom he has with his current wife Claire, run the day-to-day operations in Beijing, Dubai, and Paris.

Coincidentally, the Sidreaux sisters are the same age as Langston Jr, meaning Sidreaux Sr. was in the business of expanding more than just operations.

DANI'S CRUSH

"The only thing I can confirm without a shadow of a doubt is that Langston Dean Sidreaux Jr. is extraordinarily fine. His skin is like caramel, he has a pearly-white smile I can stare at all day and hazel green eyes you can get lost in. He's gotta be at least six-seven. And forget about a theme song; this man deserves his own album, okay! Oh, and his hair, a bald fade in the summer and a head full of curly hair complete with a full beard in the winter. He is always camera-ready without effort."

"Well, Dani Breaux, if I didn't know any better, I would think you may be having your first post-divorce crush," Becca said, excited, since Dani had never spoken about men since the divorce.

"I don't think so."

"You don't think so?"

"I don't know. He's just so smart. Did I tell you how we first met?"

"No, and as much as I wanna hear it, I have to be honest here for just a sec. You don't shit where you eat, Dani. Oh, honey, he's the first man to get your attention after all that pain and agony you felt, and that's a good thing. All I'm saying, before you act on anything, just give it some time so you can meet the real him. And then, if it's worth the stench, then I say shit on."

"Yeah, I know your right? Truthfully, as gorgeous as he is, I really don't have a desire to get to know the real him. I just wanna dream," Dani smiled, sinking into bed, and pulling the thick comforter up to her neck. Staying at Becca's place until she got on her feet turned out better than she expected. Although she resisted at first, she had to admit this place was like a hotel spa. Chef prepared meals, a guest suite with a balcony and a weekend masseuse, Dani was in her own little paradise. The best thing about it was Becca. Together they were like two peas in a pod, laughing when something was funny and crying on each other's shoulder when the weight of the world seemed unbearable.

"Well, dream away, honey," Becca said as she turned off the lights, switched on the sounds of rain and jazz, and went to her master suite on the opposite wing of the mini mansion.

Closing her eyes Dani reminisced about the first time meeting his royal highness. It was during a time when everyone was so excited for the winter months, it was like Christmas was coming early, and everyone was getting a car from Oprah. Every time Dani asked one of her co-workers, the girls would say, "Oh, yeah, the cold months are brutal," with a weird, almost giddy smile.

Dani spent weeks watching the news, waiting for something to indicate the expected snowstorm. She assumed it would be like a catastrophic icy event combined with a hurricane and a tornado wrapped into one, where the city would lockdown due to dangerous weather conditions. Too afraid to ask the whisperers at the office, out of fear of bringing more attention to the new bald girl, Dani just simply prepared her house with plenty of groceries and supplies for her and Jackson.

When the first day of winter arrived, nothing happened. The second and third weeks were just like the first, except it was much colder. Weeks later, snow covered the ground. On one particular day she remembered wearing a red blazer over casual leather pants, a fitted-white open collar t-shirt with ankle boots, and a fedora hat styled to the side. Just like any other wintry morning, Dani walked into her office, sat her Le Ric's hot tea down on her desk, and removed her hat, scarf, and coat. Grabbing the hot tea from her desk, she headed down the hall to her morning meeting, while texting Becca about their Friday night plans. Suddenly, she hit her head on something that felt like a brick wall. "Ouch!" Dani shrieked. Grabbing the top of her head, she held onto the brick beam for support.

"Uh, oh. Hey, let me see. I got you," the strange man said, gently moving Dani's hand away from the throbbing area above her right eye.

Dani bit back tears as her eyes watered from the impact.

"Hey," he said, with her face gently cupped in his hands as he dabbed her tears with his fingers. "You're okay, open your eyes."

When she opened her eyes, Dani was sure she had passed out as she was surrounded by four of the most gorgeous men she had ever seen, but the one holding her face was like a vision.

"We good here?" Langston smiled as he bent down, trying to catch Dani's gaze, still gently holding her face.

Speechless, Dani nodded her head, yes. It was him! While she had seen plenty of pictures of Langston Jr around the building, wall to ceiling portraits on almost every floor, she had never met him. As she stared into his eyes, she noticed his loose curly hair, sprinkled with grey and a full beard groomed to perfection. With a leather jacket hanging across his arm, he wore tailored jeans over snakeskin boots and a simple tan, short-sleeve shirt that fit like a glove over his shapely arms. He had the appearance of someone that was jet-lagged and had just jumped out of bed and threw something on to get to the office.

Having done this herself many times before, Dani would try her best to make it seem like a jet lagged day was just like any other workday, but most times, she failed miserably and was a walking zombie by lunch. The man from the wall pictures made the look seem easy because while his eyes were tired, everything else was simply flawless.

"Ma'am, your phone," said one of the beautiful Arabian men.

"Thank you," Dani simply replied, still amazed at their presence. Once she snapped back to her senses, she noticed everyone staring at her again. This time, it was not because she was bald, but today, she was bald while wearing leather pants in the middle of a rom-com scene with the office crush.

Damn, Becca, you and your damn leather, Dani thought to herself, feeling foolish.

"Beautiful," the stranger from the wall photos spoke in her direction.

Did he just call me beautiful?

"Your shirt, it's from our *Beautiful* collection," the stranger said with a smile that Dani couldn't look away from, no matter how embarrassed she felt.

"Yes, it…it is," Dani fumbled her words."

"Well, have a nice day, Dani."

And just like that, with the four towers of beauty trailing him, he walked away as she stood staring in their direction along with everyone else on the floor. Turning to walk away, she remembered that he knew her name. Later that morning, he sent someone to her office to replace her cup of tea with an expensive cafe brew from the lobby.

Interesting how the thought of that day still brought a slight smile to her face. She could still hear him saying, "Have a nice day, Dani."

"Dani? Hellooo, Dani, are you there?"

"This is your floor, right?" Langston looked down into her face with a concerned tone.

"Ugh, yeah. Yes, yes, it is," Dani answered, snapping back to the present, not realizing that she'd finished the flight of stairs. "Long night, working on a piece," she lied.

"I see. No worries. I'm sure it will be outstanding," Langston replied as Dani peered up at him with a surprised expression written all over her face. "What?"

There he goes smiling again. I just can't, Dani thought.

"Come on, you know you're bad. Seriously, when you can write inspirational pieces that speak to your sensuality while still representing the voice of our readers, that's badass."

"Well, somebody is feeling very gracious in words today," Dani smiled sarcastically, eyeing Langston from head to toe.

"Ha, ha, ha," Langston roared, throwing his head back in laughter. "I am always supportive of your creativity."

Dani knew that when she really put her heart into a piece, Langston always noticed by sending her an email or giving a shout-out in the morning meeting. She appreciated how he saw her passion for creativity, but she wondered if he really saw *her,* or people like her. She wondered if he cared about what it could mean for his brand to shine a light on the millions of people with alopecia.

Looking for more than just a feature for alopecia month, she wanted to consider the possibilities of high-end fashion, treating those with differences the same, just like all the other features they printed throughout the year.

"Thank you, and hopefully, the boss lady will agree," Dani said as she smiled and headed to her office.

"Hey Dani, there's something I wanted to uh, ta…"

"Langston, there you are. What are you doing down here? I have those blueprints from Rob. I think you might be interested in this."

"Right, uh-we'll talk," Langston said, nodding his head towards Dani as he walked away with his assistant.

Wait, what just happened? What could he possibly have to talk to me about? Hmmm, maybe he's ready to leave his gorgeous model girlfriend and confess his love for me, Dani fantasized to herself. *Girl, please! She is a model, with hair flowing down her back and legs so long they reach to the ceiling. He ain't leaving all of that for your cute, bald head self.* "Get it together, girl. You have a meeting," Dani sighed.

They met on the first Friday of every month to discuss new topics as the monthly column, 'Something to Think About' was Dani's section. While the monthly issue was filled with interesting articles and designs to mesmerize the readers, Dani believed that her stories were the voice of the community. The Sidreaux brand was 100% undisputed beauty and class, but it was also built on creativity and individuality.

"Good morning, boss ladyyyyyy," Dani sang in her best soprano voice as she walked into the conference room.

"Dani, I uh, completely forgot our meeting this morning, Talia blew her nose while speaking through a cascade of tears.

"Talia, what's wrong?" Dani asked, concerned as she had never seen Talia like this before. Known for her classic Type A personality, crying was not something one expected.

"Dani, please, come in. I would like to introduce you to Kevin Delane, one of our chairmen of the board, and you know Sidnae Kaye from marketing."

Assuming these people were responsible for bringing Talia to tears, Dani moved away from Sidnae, just in case Daniesha tried to make an appearance.

"Dani Breaux," Sidnae said, stepping forward to shake Dani's hand. "No need for introductions as I am a huge fan of this one's work. It is nice to finally meet you. I was just telling Talia…"

"Nope! I got this," Talia said, sitting on the edge of her desk.

"Of course."

Okay, hell no! Are they about to fire me? Dani thought. *Damn, just as I was starting to get adapted to things.*

"As you know, I am fully dedicated to the needs of this company and how we represent our community and our readers. But today is bittersweet. I'm resigning from my title because I have just been promoted to vice president of the organization," Talia said, smiling through a constant flow of tears. Ms. Kaye will temporarily take over until they find a suitable replacement for my position."

"Wow, congratulations," Dani replied, unsure of whether she should be happy for Talia, knowing that she earned that promotion or be sad because there was only one Talia at this company who really cared about Dani's future with Sari and respected her creativity. Realizing the inevitable, Dani wanted to scream for Talia not to leave, but when she opened her mouth to speak, she burst into tears, knowing that every creative idea she discussed with Talia would be intercepted by Sidnae.

A former international model and Princeton graduate, Sidnae Kaye found her second career in marketing, generating millions from ad sales and sponsors. Sidnae was the woman everyone wanted, and the girl many young girls and women wanted to become. With dark brown hair and cat-like eyes, in her middle age, she had a body many of Sari's twenty-year-old models envied.

Typically, Dani would be more than happy to have Sidnae as her new boss. The problem was the rumors that recently started to circulate about her and her former spouse, Gavin Kensley, better known as the Robin Roberts of the organization. As the face of Sari Unique, he covered all media footage, appearances, and interviews. Sidnae and Galvin Kensley met during a cross-segment interview for a well-known television personality. Immediately drawn to her, he put in a word to Sari, and she was hired the following day. Within a year, they were married and pregnant with twins fourteen months later.

Rumor has it that six months ago, Gavin walked into their sprawling estate and announced to Sidnae that marriage just wasn't for him. Other than full custody of the kids, she could have all things acquired during the marriage, including their home and beach property in New York. A week later, Gavin & Sidnae Kensley released a statement:

> *It is with sadness that we have decided to end our marriage. While we love each other very much, we have grown apart. Our focus now is on being the best parents to our boys. We would appreciate privacy at this time. Thank you.*

Two weeks later, Sidnae came back to work better than ever, refreshed, vibrant, and glowing. In her first month back, she managed three separate campaigns, bringing in new sponsors and increasing revenue for the digital platform. Sidnae was also a hands-on mom, attending after-school games, leaving the office before dinner time, serving on school functions, and the occasional monthly slumber party. A regular wonder woman, she was the "it girl" around the office.

It wasn't long before people started to realize a pattern of events, vandalized cars in the parking garage, damaging leaked stories to media outlets, home break-ins, food poisoning, company rumors. It all seemed to fall back on Gavin Kensley, who was forced to take a brief hiatus away from the company. Sari was doing better than ever with Sidnae running lead on Gavin's responsibilities as well as her own.

Dani cried harder just thinking about the possibility of Sidnae disregarding every one of her ideas.

"Dani, it's okay. Here, come, come, come," Sidnae said, walking toward her with open arms.

"Good morning. Sorry, I'm late. Dani, what is it?" Langston said, grabbing her forearm while cutting Sidnae off.

Looking into his face, Dani noticed the concern in his eyes; his expression seemed so real. "Nothing," she said, removing her arm from his grasp. "I'm just happy…for Talia. I'm going to miss her, is all. It was a little unexpected," Dani said, wiping her eyes while ensuring her eyelashes were still intact.

"No, ma'am," Talia replied. "Do not expect me to get soft on you just because I'm moving to another floor. We still need you, and you still have a story to cover that I intend to see through to completion."

"Of course," Dani said, relieved that Talia was still supporting her project.

"Good, because we need kick-ass material to spearhead our anniversary issue. Something unique and fresh," Talia said, pacing across the floor. "Dani, You're up! The stories of women with Alopecia, kicking ass in the newest fashions."

"I figured we can do cross-over marketing," Dani interjected, branching into our other magazine genres, like homeware, theatre, art, and hopefully movie production. I just think it would be awesome for the world to see a more frequent presence of reality, and what normal is as it relates to millions of people throughout the world."

"Mmmm, I like it," Sidnae replied, "but I see bald women on commercials sometimes and shaved models on runways. It's certainly not a new concept."

"That's because it's not a *concept!* It's a reality! Take our most recent magazine cover, for example," Dani said, grabbing the most recent Sari magazine from the table and holding it in the air for all to see. "She's gorgeous! The designs are fresh and unique, it's good. But we also see this more frequent in commercials and runways. It's not a new concept. I'm certainly not saying do away with models. I love models; their work ethic alone is some of the most committed I've ever seen. I'm just saying that we pride ourselves on being inclusive, but are we really including the differences in people as a part of the norm?"

"That's excellent, Dani! Sari preaches a foundation of diversity and inclusion, and I think it would be sexy to introduce a fresh take, really show it off," Talia confirmed. "Sidnae, we need marketing to go crazy on this one, pulling out all the stops. Dani, the commentary must be as powerful as the photos, with every article more powerful than the last. I don't have to tell you guys that every two years, the company comes out with a killer campaign, shocking the industry while celebrating Sari's anniversary. I think this is our best one yet," Talia said, smiling at Dani.

"Yes! I already have models on hand with stories for days," Dani agreed, trying carefully to contain her excitement.

"Then, it's settled. Dani, get me a formal presentation in my office by the end of the week with everything we just discussed written out," Sidnae said.

"Done."

"And, Dani, I love the idea, but I need to feel like I can see inside your head. We have to sell it," Sidnae said, holding her index finger in the air to solidify her point.

"Of course," Dani said. "The more involved, the more exposure we get, and the more revenue we generate, right?"

"That's my girl," Sidnae laughed, putting her arm around Dani's shoulder. I think this partnership will work out just fine."

Four

THE AFTERGLOW

Bursting with excitement on the walk home after work, Dani could hardly believe her prayers were coming true right before her eyes. She thought of her mom praying with her, asking God to allow her gifts to make room for her, to provide for her life. Dani thought about the people she would help by sharing their stories. Opportunities were coming her way, and she was finally getting a seat at the table doing something she loved. The rest of the workday was like a blur, as all she could think about was celebrating with Becca.

Picking up the pace on the walk home, Dani intensified her stride to prepare her body for an evening of carbohydrate delight, spicy falafels, garlic aioli fries, along with cosmos and martinis. Cosmopolitan had become her go-to drink ever since she and Becca binge-watched everything *Sex and the City*. After three drinks, Dani was done. But tonight, she thought about having one extra, just to put the cherry on top.

Smiling to herself, Dani imagined being interviewed by media correspondents for Sari: *So, Dani, great issue. Was it difficult to share this part of your life?*

"Thanks, it's truly an honor to be here with—."

A blaring car horn snapped Dani out of her fantasy.

"Dani, it's me, Langston!"

Dani noticed Langston waiving through the passenger window of his fall/winter Rolls Royce SUV.

"Mr. Langston? What are you doing?" Dani said, moving closer to the curb. *Oh, my gosh, I can smell him all the way over here. He smells so good.*

"Please call me Langston. Where are you off to? Jump in."

"Ugh, I'm okay. I need the walk, tryna' get my steps in." *Girl, you betta' not get in that truck,* Dani thought. After having her favorite broccoli salad for lunch, she was a fart machine, and she could feel the pressure building again. *You smell like broccoli farts and spicy tuna. Don't you even think about getting in that truck! Nope, I will not allow my first experience in this beautiful ride, WITH THIS MAN, to be compromised by holding in gas. And what if he has the heater on? I know he has heated seats in there. Oh, my gosh, I can smell myself,* she thought.

"Nonsense, get in here," Langston smiled, leaning over to open the passenger door from the driver's seat.

Think, Dani, think! "Oh, wait, a smoothie shop that sells coffee," Dani mumbled as she thought of random ideas. "Let me just grab a drink. I'll be right back," she said, pointing to the smoothie shop down the sidewalk.

Hit with the smell of coffee, fresh vegetables, and fruit as soon as she walked through the front door, she suddenly knew exactly what to do. "I'd like a blended coffee with celery and uh.... whatever other kind of strong, pungent green vegetables you have, please."

"Yep, I got broccoli and kale. You want this with ice?" the guy asked, completely unbothered by the concoction he was about to make?

"No, nice and warm, room temperature," Dani replied. As Dani walked back towards the Rolls Royce, she took a small sip from what smelled like a hot porta-potty in the middle of a construction site sitting in the hot sun. Suddenly, releasing the last bit of gas she was holding, Dani breathed a sigh of relief as her stomach flattened from the pressure. Feeling embarrassed, she purposely dropped the warm concoction partially on the street and onto her jeans to disguise the smell.

"Dani, are you okay? Hold on, give me a second. I got you," Langston said, jumping out of the SUV to assist.

What? Boy, if you don't get your ass back in that truck! Girl, you ate a plate of broccoli salad. Stop acting like your farts don't linger. Do something! The thoughts in her head screamed.

"Langston, stop! You don't want to get this smell on your shoes, please. I would feel awful if this green sludge got into your vehicle. I mean, it's good for you, but the smell is horrible."

This man is a billionaire. He could care less about that truck, Dani thought. "It would just kill me if I ruined your shoes, she said instantly. You know how the rumor mill can be. You have several months of my salary on your feet. I would never be okay with not being able to replace them."

It was true, Langston didn't care about what he was driving or his shoes, but he knew it would bother her if she couldn't cover the damage.

"No worries, it's just stuff," he said, pulling a towel from the trunk and tossing it to Dani. While wiping bits of the thick concoction from her jeans and shirt, Langston grabbed a second towel and placed it over the leather passenger seat. Motioning for her to remove her heels and place them in the towel.

Dani paused, still trying to think of a way out of the situation. *You know you just had your feet done, right?*

"Oh, thanks, but no. It's a little nasty on the sidewalk for bare feet, and it's cold." At least she wasn't lying, she thought. Her pedicure was still spa fresh. It would be a waste of money to place her freshly scrubbed feet on the nasty street. "Mr. Langston. I mean Langston, really, it's okay. You have my number. Whatever it is, just call me, and we can talk later."

As he shut the back of the Rolls Royce SUV, Dani thanked him for being there for her, again, while apologizing for the awful smell. "I'm so clumsy," she said, still wiping at her jeans, thankful the gassy smell was replaced with coffee-soaked greens.

Suddenly, with one arm, Langston swept her off her feet. She squealed in surprise as he carried her to the passenger side of the car, gently placing her on the towel-covered warm leather seat and removed her heels.

As she sat back in the SUV, she felt the warm-heated seats under her butt and the fresh leather smell mixed with a patchouli scent.

"Now," Langston said, climbing back into the driver's seat, "Where are we off to? Sniffing the air with a puzzled look on his face, he said, "It smells like coffee and grass in here. What on earth were you drinking?"

Dani chuckled, breathing a sigh of relief while laughing hysterically on the inside. She couldn't wait to tell Becca every detail.

Once they arrived in front of her house, Dani opened the door and tried to quickly get inside, but Langston was tagging along right behind her. Jackson came barreling to the door, wagging his tail.

"Hey buddy, what's your name," Langston said, grabbing the friendly dog's ears and nuzzling his nose as he barked and wagged his tail.

"Langston, this is Jackson. Jackson, this is Langston, the Prince of Sari, gracing our humble abode with his presence," Dani laughed while pretending to bow in his honor.

"You know, I'm starting to really think you believe that."

Jackson was always excited when she came home, but she didn't understand why he was taking to Langston so quickly. It's not like she had ever introduced him to any of her male friends before. "Okay, Jackson, let's not wear out our company," Dani said, walking down the hall and opening the door for Jackson to go outside.

"Nice place," Langston said as he took a few more steps forward, stopping short of the deck.

"Coming from you, I guess I consider that a huge compliment, I think."

"Coming from me? Okay, I get it. Yes, I was born into wealth. I've never had to work for my needs, my wants, or desires. While I have my differences, it doesn't mean that I don't respect and admire those that build their wealth from scratch, in spite of adversity."

"Okay. I can appreciate you for respecting what you don't understand," Dani replied.

"Ditto," Langston said with a gentle smile.

"And while you certainly do seem sincere, you are still the prince of Sari.

"And that, I am. So, let's hear it," Langston said, standing tall with his hands cupped in front of him. "What else do *'they'* say?"

"Well, rumor has it that you live in these rolling estates in some part of Virginia, but you have mini-mansions all over the world."

"All over the world?"

"Yes, and you have chickens and alpacas."

Langston threw his head back as his laughter bellowed throughout the house. "Alpacas? Well, I believe that one can live well and still admire the beauty of another," he replied, staring back at her.

Dani got the strange feeling he meant something else. *Girl, please, his girlfriend makes you look like a bald-headed chihuahua,* she thought.

"I hate to cut this short, but I have to change. I'm meeting my friend Becca for drinks." Knowing he would decline, she extended the invitation, "You are welcome to join us if you like."

"I would love to, but I have a prior engagement myself. I actually need to speak with you about your project."

"Wait. I know I've never done anything like this before, but Mr. Langston, I can do this. I already have everything written out."

"I trust you. In fact, for the next three issues, I want you to take creative control over the project, the photos, the commentary, everything. Sidnae will cover the overall spread of the issue. She'll get with the ad sponsors to ensure they're on track with their designs. Talia will oversee from a distance, but you, you will have creative control."

"What? No, that's Talia and Sidnae's domain. I'm just a writer. They will never go for that. I'm not so sure I want them to. I'm not qualified for th—"

"Talia is my VP now," Langston said in a curt and straightforward tone. "I need someone on the ground," he said, softening his voice, "someone who is familiar."

"Sir, uh, Mr. Langston, I appreciate that but…"

"Dani, this is not a request," he said as the stare she thought she saw earlier now looked more like a glare.

"You and I both know that if I mess this up, or if I make the slightest mistake, I'm done," Dani said, with tears already welling in her eyes. *Don't you let this gorgeous fool see you cry,* she thought, quickly swallowing her tears. "On the anniversary issue? This will be career suicide for me."

"Then don't mess up," Langston nonchalantly replied.

"So much for respecting what you don't understand," said Dani.

"Dani, you are a bald woman," Langston said, smiling as he stared at Dani.

"Why the hell are you telling me what I already know?" *Okay, mortgage payments, bills, health insurance, Jackson. You better simmer down,* Dani thought to herself. Dani knew that her response came with a little too much attitude, but she didn't care. She was tired of selfish men crossing boundaries she had never given them permission to cross. How dare he think anything she holds close to her is about him.

Langston's smile grew across his face as he shook his head at Dani.

"Respectfully, let me tell you something, Langston," Dani said, saying his name like it was any other word.

As if he saw what was coming, Langston held his hands in the air in front of him, surrendering his once stoic position. "I just meant that you are beautiful, strong, and I need you. I need for you to put words to what I see, what everyone sees, when we look at you in this cover series, in your own words."

"What's so special about this for you?" Dani asked.

"It could be a huge push for Sari Unique and you, as an up-and-coming writer. You know I stand by you and everything you've done so far. I need you on this, and I promise I'll make it worth your time."

As she pondered his last statement in silence, Langston continued, "Because as charming as your winter cottage may be, perhaps we can find something more on a regular basis."

"Cottage? This is not a cottage," Dani quickly replied before catching herself."

"Pardon me," Langston said with his head slightly tilted to the side.

She knew that look. It was his "who the hell you think you talking to kinda look," and he couldn't even do that right, looking like the cover of somebody's Ralph Lauren magazine. It's amazing he thinks that look actually scares anybody.

"I'll have you know that the owner who sold me this house was intending to use it as his home when working from his DC office," Dani replied, feeling vindicated.

"Is the owner here now, in the area?"

"As a matter of fact, he is," she replied, suddenly understanding what he meant since it was, in fact, wintertime.

"As great as this conversation has been, I need to change and head out." She had been around too many men like Langston, who always felt better about themselves by making her feel small. She didn't have the energy to deal with another one, even if he was her boss.

"Hey, Dani, I know this is scary for you. I just need you to trust me. I won't let you fail; I promise."

Something about him made her want to believe that. *Hmph, he would never let his company fail,* she thought. For some reason, she also felt like he would never let her fail.

"May I drop you off at your destination? Personal driver, perhaps?"

"No, I could actually use the walk. On second thought, I change my mind. Give me ten minutes! Oh, and one more thing, can I drive the Rolls Royce?" Dani asked, peeking from around the corner of the wall.

Smiling from ear to ear, Langston replied, "No."

"Fair enough," she shrugged as she hurried to her room to get dressed.

Sitting next to Langston made her feel like royalty. She closed her eyes and allowed her thought to take over her mind. *Is this how his girlfriend feels riding next to him? Nah. That woman is gorgeous. He probably feels like royalty standing anywhere near her. Whatever, I look good, too! If I had hair down to my ass, he would feel the same way standing next to me. Whewwww! Shut your negative self-up, Dani, and just enjoy this moment. For the next ten minutes, I just want to feel like I belong with a man that makes me smile like Langston and loves me with the heart of God. Nothing wrong with dreaming,* she thought.

Dani paid special attention to what she wore for her evening with Becca. She wanted to savor the moment riding next to Langston, not as an employee, but as an equal, even if he didn't know it. She wore a pair of dark, fitted jeans that elongated her legs and tightened around the ankle, revealing a perfect pair of black stiletto Louboutin's— they were Becca's but hers for tonight. She wore long, silver earrings that grazed her shoulders and a fuchsia off-the-shoulder peplum blouse adorned with asymmetrical ruffles on top with a huge bow hugging her curves around the middle, stopping just above the top of her jeans.

"Nice," was all Langston said when Dani walked to the truck.

As they pulled up to the front of the bar, Dani saw Becca stepping out of her Ferrari SF90 Stradale, a gift from her "so-called" male best friend, Javi, who both Cammie and Dani knew was more than just a friend.

As they came to a complete stop, Langston got out of the car and opened Dani's door. Reaching his hand to grab hers, she stepped out of the car, and for the first time in her life as a bald woman, she felt comfortable in the company of a man, not trying to fit into anyone's world of what she should look like, or who she should be.

Dani's ex opened doors for her in the same way, but she felt like she was in some type of motion picture, always trying to maintain the perfect role. It was weird wearing wigs everywhere they went. He had never asked her to cover her head. But she always felt like she needed to, just to fit in and be the woman he would proudly have on his arm.

"Thank you," Dani said. She couldn't help but smile, meeting Langston's gaze as he was grinning from ear-to-ear like he was proud of her or something.

"So," Langston said, grabbing Dani's double-breasted, black wool coat and placing it around her shoulders, "I hope you have a great night," he said while looking down into her eyes. "If you need anything, with uh, the cover issues, don't hesitate to call."

"Will do," Dani replied, feeling somewhat anxious from all the eyes on her, especially Becca's, knowing that by now, she was probably burning a hole through the back of her head.

"Langston, thank you for the ride, and if you have any other ideas on how to ruin my life, let me know how I can make that possible for you," Dani said, half-way joking.

"Will do," he mouthed back.

"Will do, what?" Becca said. "I'm sorry, I read lips. My great Aunt Tandy taught me how one summer when I was in Georgia. "What a lovely man," she said, stepping forward to shake Langston's hand.

"Wait, aren't you…"

"Becca, this is Mr. Langston, my boss," Dani interrupted.

"Charmed," said Becca.

"Ladies, enjoy your evening," Langston said as he nodded towards the doorman.

While walking into the restaurant, Dani could feel Becca's eyes on her, warning her to steer clear of the fashion industry prince and not to forget that he has a girlfriend, and no one ever sees him with another woman outside of his main squeeze. AND more importantly, not to shit where you eat.

Dani was fully prepared to lay it all out, her possible promotion for work and Talia's title change. She decided to start with the fart story first.

"So, work today was crazy, but the broccoli casserole you made, no ma'am."

"He likes you," Becca intervened "It's different, I can tell."

"What? Mr. Langston? The prince of Sari?"

"I know what we call him," Becca said, "but I can feel it, honey. I can just feel it."

"Bec, he's my boss. I am a mere chihuahua in his world. Have you seen the legs on his leading lady? Even if I did see him in that way, someone like that could never be into someone like me."

"Stop! I don't care who she is," Becca confirmed in her best "I know what the hell I'm talking about" kind of way. I don't care what he is or what he has, he doesn't have you, and he knows that's what he's missing. I'm so happy and excited for you, she said, tearing up. Drinks! Bartender, we need drinks. Lobster and mac over here, and bring the best bottles this way, please," Becca said, waving down the waiter.

"No, you are clearly and emotionally PMSing. I'm treating tonight," Dani said. "Sir, we'll have the red, and we'll start with the house salads. No tab tonight."

"Afraid I can't do that, ma'am. Mr. Sidreaux took care of the tab. Everything is yours for the evening. Be right back with those lobsters and bottles."

"Shut up, Becca," Dani said, interrupting her 'know-it-all' response.

"Oh, I can't wait to be your maid of honor."

WHAT'S FOR YOU IS FOR YOU

Dani had a newly constructed three-bedroom, three-and-a-half-bathroom house she purchased from the owner almost two years after her divorce. Bill Cartwright of Cartwright Construction International had several condos in the area, but this particular house he intended for his primary residence when working from the DC office. Within a year after landing the job with Sari Unique, Dani decided it was time to stop living in Becca's spare room and find a place of her own. With Becca by her side, they spent months wandering the streets of Maryland and DC-into Georgetown, window shopping and fantasizing. While every home they saw fit perfectly with Dani's taste, they were more affordable for Becca's wallet.

"Becca, I'm exhausted. It's been a long day. I love this area, but I am perfectly satisfied with an apartment for now. Let's just pick an apartment building, make a deposit, and complete an application at one of these places."

"Absolutely not! We still have one more house to look at and were almost there. Plus, my agent says this is the one for sure."

"You said that five houses ago too."

"Dani, this is a process that takes time. You think I stepped in and bought a house within five minutes of searching? No, trust me, this is a task. You'll know your space when you see it, like it was destined for you."

"Becca, I get it, but these are all million-dollar homes. The taxes alone will send me to the poor house."

"You've been using that saying that for years, and I've never seen you in one," Becca replied. "Honey, my mama always used to say nothing will stand in the way of what God has for you. You just have to believe it."

"Okay, okay, the last house, let's finish this Becca, please. My feet are killing me."

"Oooh, you smell that? Smells like boiled crab. You know how much I love me some crab," Becca said, looking around trying to find the location of the smell."

"Yeah, I smell it too. I think it's coming from that food truck. It must be good. The line is wrapped around the corner," said Dani.

"Yeah, we can check it out on the way home. We can spend the rest of the day sitting out on the deck, cracking crabs, and sipping wine. Who knows, we may be eating on your deck by the end of the day Ms. Dani. Okay, here it is!" Becca yelled with excitement. "Well, honey, it's just gorgeous! It's all fenced in with the perfect little walkup away from the street, just as you requested."

It was true. Each house along the winding road was fenced in with its own walkup. The whole neighborhood was like a mirage in the middle of a desert. Only in this case, the desert was high-end shops and restaurants with some of the best-looking food trucks Dani had ever seen. "Beccaaaaaa! I can't afford this type of stuff."

"Come, come, come, come. Let's just see, let's finish the day strong." Becca ran towards the stairs, her voice trailing off as she met the realtor at the door and disappeared on the other side. "Dani, get your behind in here, you gotta see this!"

As Dani trudged down the cobblestone pathway and up the stairs leading to the huge oak double doors, she noticed floor to ceiling dark shield or glass on the side of the house. Whatever it was, she couldn't see through it. "Yep, that's gonna add another million or two. She thinks everybody's rich like her," Dani mumbled." *Okay, just take a look. Walk through and get on with it,* she thought.

Inside was a small foyer and a coat closet that opened up to a large office on the right. "Whoa! This room is definitely going on my vision board," Dani said, snapping a picture with her phone. The room interior was covered in dark woods, with a crystal chandelier and a leather couch in the corner that looked as if was designed to resemble bubble wrap. A large, cherry-oak desk with a matching chair fit for a king sat in the center of the room surrounded by bookshelves and modern art.

"This room was definitely built by a man," Dani said. Next to the office was a half bath with custom-designed fixtures. The initials BC were carved in the heavy marble sink that took up half the wall. *Who needs a sink this big? I wish we had something like this as kids when we had to wash up and couldn't get in the bathtub. I could put my whole body in here,* she thought, laughing to herself.

Just like the others, this house had basic beige walls, vaulted ceilings, hardwood floors, and soft cream-colored beams with splashes of chocolate brown.

"And this is the sitting room with heated floors, complete with a custom-built fireplace," the realtor said. "All of our remodeled homes in this area under Cartwright Construction have these two features."

"And the pool table?" Becca asked.

"Uh, no. As I previously advised, this home is not for sale. It is a model of the Cartwright Homes Premier," the realtor confirmed.

Premier? If we can't afford the regular, how the hell we gon' get premier? Dani thought? Perhaps it was because she loved to cook and considered herself a real foodie, Dani was mesmerized by what appeared to be a smaller version of a state-of-the-art kitchen. The cabinetry was all made of glass with wine racks built into the custom-designed island. Everything was top of the line, from the stovetop gas range, smart fridge, double ovens, mixers, and more appliances than she could ever imagine.

Once they officially signed in, the realtor led them through the spacious sitting area, to the outside deck and then to the upstairs floor. Unsure if it was the heated hardwood hugging her bare feet or the floor-to-ceiling spacious windows in the back of the house, but Dani was starting to feel something was familiar about this space. I mean, it wasn't as grand as the homes she'd seen throughout the day, not even as grand as Becca or Cammie's home, but there was something about it that made her feel protective of it. Although it was small, with the vaulted ceilings and everything built into a wall or shelf, it was grand to her, and that's all that mattered.

"Dani, Dani," Becca whispered from the upstairs bathroom. "Hey, I'm gonna go sit on this smart toilet and see what happens. If I'm gone more than five minutes, then honey, that's one heck of a toilet, and I'm ordering one before I leave here today."

"You so nasty. Enjoy yourself and make sure you wash your hands," Dani said, leaving Becca to the toilet device.

"Am I dreaming, or is everything in the kitchen and bathrooms marble stone or something? I can only imagine the cost of this place."

"You are absolutely correct," the realtor said. "The marble is all customized. Construction is in its final stages, and we only have one other home that is similar to this one. As we previously discussed…"

"I know, I know. This one is not for sale," Dani confirmed, repeating the realtor's mantra.

After playing with the kitchen appliances, they walked around the spacious back yard, what appeared to be a second upstairs living room with a built-in fireplace and a large plush throw rug that Dani desperately wanted to take on the way out. She could just buy this rug and use it as her bed in whatever apartment she would eventually lease.

As they went from guest room to guest room and again to the hallway bathroom, that feeling started to come back again. Suddenly, she was reminded of the home she shared with her ex-husband. It was a three-story modern home with wall-to-ceiling windows. The second floor was her favorite spot, as the back of the kitchen was all windows facing a heavily wooded area. No one could see through the other side, so she would sit on the windowsill in her pajamas in the early morning hours, watching the deer run through the snow-covered grounds.

She would read her Bible, meditate, talk to God, dream, and just marvel at the blessings in her life. She missed that part of herself, that feeling of just being, without the constant reminders that she was no longer that person anymore. What would her peers from the ritzy diners and high-end social gatherings think of her now without her knee-length cocktail dresses or cute little hairstyles and updos? Would they still think she was a beautiful host and an amazing cook, or would they just feel empathy for her previous illness, baldness, and infertility?

Suddenly, Dani no longer wanted to tour this house or any other house outside of her financial means. She did not want to be reminded of what she could not afford while she was trying to celebrate her new job. Becca was generous with providing her a place to stay, but she was ready for her own space, and this home was not it.

"Ladies, brace yourselves. This is the spot I was telling you about. It makes everything worth it," the realtor gushed as she swung open the double doors leading to the master bedroom.

It was a very beautiful master suite, but it was just like all the others Dani had seen that day. The floors were a different type of dark wood but still warm to the touch. The room had two sets of double doors, with the first one leading to the master bathroom. A large claw foot tub and a step-in shower was surrounded by shower heads on each wall. Mirrors, and marble fixtures covered the entire space. The toilet was enclosed in a room off to the side with a panel for seat warming features and other settings Dani had no idea existed for a toilet. It was what was behind the second set of double doors that brought her to tears.

When the realtor swung open the wooden doors, it was like someone had taken the view from the second floor of the house she had shared with her ex-husband and planted it there. It resembled her room with a view—but on steroids.

"How could that be? I was just thinking about that," Dani mumbled to herself. It was an enclosed terrace. As they walked onto the outside living space, Dani could feel the buzz of the jacuzzi under her feet. The opened closet door on the right housed a hot sauna, and the area on the left was complete with a mini kitchen and a bar. While she was taken aback by the spa-like features, it was the floor-to-ceiling windows complete with a windowsill and cushions that made her burst into tears.

"Honey, it's okay, you don't have to get a house with a view," Becca said, rubbing Dani's shoulder.

"Uh…well, she's in luck. The only home we have left does not quite have this same view, and remember, this one is not for sale," the realtor said.

While the realtor continued to break down the features of the outside space, Becca stared at her best friend, remembering the many times they shared coffee and conversation sitting on the windowsill of Dani's house. As if reading her mind, Becca replied, "You are just as beautiful now as you were then. Thankfully, he recognized that he was not the man for you because he's an insecure asshole."

"Becca!"

"He is! And while I am thankful for him doing the right thing, I still wanna beat his chicken-shit ass at the same time. Dani, this is just the confirmation you need. You are beautiful, and what's for you is for you! No one will ever take this away from you again. Your experiences with that asshole-I'm sorry, Dani, but I have my own opinion here. Those years with him have helped you to recognize your worth. You're no longer that shy little girl from the South. You're a kick-ass, confident woman who's not afraid to stand up for herself and fight for what's yours."

Dani thought back to the day she packed her things and left her home. She didn't want to leave, but she didn't have the means to support her environment. She was still healing from her diagnosis and was doing her best to maintain a steady nine-to-five job.

"Everything okay in here?" a strong booming male voice bellowed from behind?

"Ah, Mr. Cartwright, this is Dani Breaux and Becca Carrington, hopefully our newest homeowner," the realtor gestured with an opened hand towards Dani.

"Once again, sir, the beauty of Cartwright Homes can be a lot to take in," the realtor said.

"It's beautiful, truly breathe taking," Dani said, taking in the view once more.

"Yeah, well, it's not for sale," Mr. Cartwright replied nonchalantly.

"Of course, it's not," Dani said. "No one should ever willingly depart from a view this peaceful. It just warms your soul," she said, staring into the sky as the sun washed over her face.

When Dani turned to face Mr. Cartwright, his facial expression and hardened demeanor softened as he glanced at her tear-streaked face. It wasn't just her tears, he'd had his share of tears in his life, but it was something in her eyes that understood what it felt like to have that kind of peace in your soul. The kind that no one could ever give or take away. As the realtor continued her spill to Dani and Becca, Mr. Cartwright wondered how a woman so young could understand the vision behind the custom-designed views he built, mostly for himself.

Bill Cartwright had lived all over the world in houses of every size. His entire life was spent building things with his bare hands since he could stand on his own two feet. No one had taught him anything. Either you were born with it in your blood, or you weren't. That was the motto for Cartwright Construction that was passed on from his daddy and from his great grandfather to his grandfather. But after his wife died, Bill Cartwright Jr buried himself in his work, expanding the family business to a global empire.

Outside of his work, he spent most of his time alone. He had a series of dead-end relationships. He refused to pretend to feel something for someone just to avoid being alone. So, he built his own space in every city where he spent the most time, just to have that special place that made him feel love. Sometimes it was a house; other times, it was a camping site overlooking the mountains where he would set up a tent outside and watch the sunrise and set for days. Many women saw his freshly shaved head and ocean blue eyes and fell in love at first sight. With his Paul Bunyon-like height and broad, muscular shoulders, he was what some called easy on the eyes. While intimidating to any stranger who met him, to his friends, he had the biggest heart anyone had ever known.

"Thank you for sharing your space with me," Dani said with a slight smile.

"So, as I said, construction will be complete in our next available home within the month," the realtor said. "Are you making an offer? Before you answer, please understand, we cannot hold it, and this home will sell fast."

"As beautiful as this place is," Dani said, "at this time, I have to de…"

"Yes, she wants to make an offer," Becca interrupted, writing her numbers on a slip of paper, and handing it to the realtor.

"Seriously, not even close," the realtor replied. "Did you read the price sheet?"

"Okay, well, this is my final offer," Becca replied, writing another number on the slip of paper, only to be met with another hard no from the realtor.

"Listen," Becca said, wrapping her right arm around Dani's shoulder, "my sister, here writes for the number one fashion company in the world."

"Becca, no, stop, it's okay," Dani said, feeling embarrassed.

"Yes, it *is* okay," the realtor replied. As much as I have enjoyed your presence today, along with your emotional outburst, I have serious clients that are more worthy of my time. Mr. Cartwright, my apologies, sir. I had no idea they were simply trolling."

"What did this heifer just say? Yeah, uh, Mr. Cartwright, Bill, is it? My name is Becca Lynn Carrington of Becca's Fashions, uh Lingerie Designs, and up and coming Becca's Babies? Or maybe your more familiar with the Carrington family dynasty out of Texas." Dani knew that when Becca started speaking her resume, she was about to go from zero to sixty. "I want to buy the place that looks just like this-all cash, right now, for the price written on this here paper! And that, little Ms. Shit, is my final offer," Becca said, tossing the paper towards the realtor's face.

"This is not a negotiation, Ms. Carrington," the realtor replied, using her fingers to emphasize the word "Carrington" while looking to Bill Cartwright for backup.

"Becca, no," Dani pleaded, fully aware that she was wasting her time. It took a lot to piss Becca off, but once she was full-on, there was no going back.

"Now, Angela, that's your name? You think because I'm here in a pair of shorts and a t-shirt that you can talk down to me and treat me and my sister like trash or trolls just strolling by? Oh, you poor soul," Becca whispered. "What have they done to you? How many did you have to screw to be his hand puppet?"

"Ah, *excuse* me!" Angela shouted, grabbing her make-believe pearls.

"Sooo many of us women know what it's like to work endlessly for these robotic corporations with these hard-ass men in charge, Becca calmly continued. They expect us to be cutthroat and sexy. Do the shit they won't do, or can't do, because they don't have the balls to, or in Bill's case, they're too damn rich to give a shit. So, they keep a cute little mouthpiece like you around, one with many talents might I add. But that's alright, honey, no need to be ashamed of it. The trick is, you gotta know when to use those extra skills, especially in this crazy old world we live in, right?"

"Becca, please, your roots are showing," Dani mumbled.

"Because if you don't know how or when to use them their talents," Becca continued as she drew closer to Angela and looked her dead in the eyes, "well, the crazies in the world just might gut you up like a pig, straight line it from the snout to the tail," she said pointing her finger from Angela's mouth to her lower parts.

"Becca!" Dani, exclaimed. "Enough!"

"Honey, at the end day a sliced pig is a sliced pig, it all roasts up the same. Nobody won't know the difference, because nobody won't give a damn," Becca said with a crazy twisted chuckle. "It's just another pig gone out to that big, beautiful pasture in the sky."

"Now, Bill, I won't deal with your side piece okay," Becca said. "Honey, this is between you and me or not at all."

"Bill, darling, sorry to interrupt. I'm ready now, love. You were right, dear. This place is beautiful," said a gorgeous blonde woman standing in the doorway.

"Ladies, it has been an eventful pleasure," Mr. Cartwright said with a slight smile and nod of the head, stopping to whisper a few words to Angela.

"Ms. Carrington, I'm so sorry. I had no idea; please accept my apology," Angela said through tearful eyes. "I can have the paperwork sent to your office within the hour."

"That won't be necessary, but thank you," Dani said, feeling embarrassed for Angela. As they walked back onto the street in silence, Dani whispered to Becca in a somber tone, "I have to do this for myself, but thank you for being that kind of friend."

"Dani, I can do it; let me do it. It's a write-off for me. You know I don't have any biological sisters or brothers. You and Cammie are all I have. What good is money if you can't do little things like this for the ones you love? It's not like it's a mansion or something. I'm just gonna drop the check off in your account, and I will never come back for it. Oh, heck Dani, if this is a problem, then I can only imagine what you gonna do when I die, and you see my will."

Dani never responded, and they walked in silence for the next two blocks until they spotted an ice cream store and stopped in for cones. Giggling like two schoolgirls, they people-watched for the next hour and stopped for boiled crabs on the way home. For the rest of the evening, they ate crabs and sipped wine on the deck, laughing at each other's antics, never mentioning Angela or the Cartwright house again.

Two weeks later, Dani woke up to a delivery at Becca's house. Looking puzzled, she slowly opened the envelope and read, "Dear Ms. Breaux, I accept your offer on one condition. You must purchase the very unit you saw. And before you seek me out to find out why I am selling you my personal unit, just know that someday you will find someone you can share that loving feeling with, and you will realize that it's too big, too far, and too wide to keep to yourself. I pray that this place brings you peace. God bless you. Enjoy."

Five

GET YOURSELF TOGETHER

After dinner with Becca and plenty of Langston conversation, Dani sat at home, on the terrace talking to God, analyzing her new work assignment. Every time she tried to focus on ideas, her mind drifted to Langston. *I need you,* his words played back through her mind over and over again. "Tsk, I need to focus on what's most important, which is work. My God, he is nice looking though, but in an unpredictable type of way. I can never tell what he's thinking; his expressions are blank. I'm just saying, God, he's easy on the eyes, that's all. I know it's the words and actions that flow from the heart, over all the other stuff. Thank you for always reminding me of that. I know my husband-to-be is still out there, somewhere."

Before getting married, Dani had expectations for the type of man she wanted—tall, handsome, accomplished, down to earth, someone she could grow with, a God-fearing family man. Years later, after everything she endured, the last thing she cared about was another list.

Just like Becca says, "After the newness fades, the lusty eyes are opened, and you experience what really lives and breeds in the heart."

"My gosh, preach!" Dani laughed out loud, just thinking about how Becca had a way with words. "Oops, sorry, Jackson," realizing she scared him out of his sleep. As many times as she read the Ten Commandments as a child, she was a whole grown adult before she realized the depth of "loving God with all your heart, mind, and soul," and "loving your neighbor like yourself."

For years, Dani thought that as long as God was in her heart, and as long as she loved her neighbor and treated them how she wanted to be treated, she was honoring her relationship with God. Somewhere along the line, she'd forgotten about her response to things and people and the nasty words and thoughts that flowed from her mouth like a fountain. "Are those feelings and words living in my heart?" she thought.

Dani recalled the counseling session after her divorce, sobbing to her therapist, Dr. Sheila? "Am I harboring a level of pain that someone has the power to provoke? I love my neighbor, but I don't love myself the same. I allow people to mistreat me time and time again, and I do whatever is necessary to stop them from leaving. Maybe subconsciously, I wish I could have done that with my dad. But in reality, I knew I couldn't. How can I truly love anyone if I don't recognize and embrace real love for myself? How do I love this new version of me? I look and feel so different, like an alien. I can't stand to look in the mirror. I don't think it started with the hair loss. I think that insecurity was already there. I said some of the most horrible things. I spent years defending myself against someone else's perception of me and my family because I knew in my heart it wasn't true. Why didn't I just leave?'"

"Perhaps you were hurt, and you spoke from a place of hurt," Dr. Sheila said. "We are human, and we make mistakes. What's important is that you recognize the changes that you want to make, and you understand why it's important to do so."

Two years later, Dani was well on the journey of accepting herself and living her life. So far, her faith and relationship with God were increasing her perception of real love and she was learning how to respond to the hurdles and barriers along the way.

"I should have called Cammie. She would get a kick out of this whole creative concept stuff for the new Sari campaign. Wait, I think I have an idea," Dani said to Jackson, who was completely knocked out in the corner of the room. For the next two hours, everything poured from her mind to her laptop. She wrote until she could no longer keep her eyes open.

AND THEN CAME CAMMIE

Cammie was Dani's baldie sister who lived in New York, or Boston, or D.C. No one really knew what place Cammie called home, but Dani always reminisced about the day they met. Two months after her second miscarriage, Dani visited several reproductive specialists, eagerly trying to better her chances at carrying a baby full-term. Every one of them said she was healthy, and despite having a few fibroids, nothing was preventing pregnancy or stopping her from carrying. She didn't understand the healthy diagnosis. Dani was so enamored with her condition that she took additional studies in school to focus more on health and wellness and self-care.

Dani's hair fell out from what they said was stress-related or hypothyroidism. Research insisted that many women in her condition had healthy, full-term pregnancies while living a long quality of life. Her last medical referral recommended Dr. Marie Lawfton, a reproductive gynecologist in New York who also practiced functional medicine. After doing her due diligence of research, Dani discovered that Dr. Lawfton was very popular with an elite list of celebrity clients and high-end professionals.

"Why would she want to see little ole me? Goodness knows I am nowhere near her typical clientele," Dani whispered to her friend, Justice, as they exited the elevator to the receptionist desk.

"Because you are a patient just like everyone else, and money is money, and so is insurance, as long as she takes it," Justice said.

"True that. Thank you for coming with me."

"No, thank you for trusting me to be here with you. We got this," Justice said, wrapping her arm around Dani's shoulder.

The first time Dani met Dr. Marie Lawfton was on a video conference. She insisted on Dani completing a full workup at one of the satellite locations in D.C. and discussing the results. Dani was glad to meet with her doctor via telehealth, considering she had never been to New York and could barely understand D.C traffic, let alone New York. After their first two virtual healthcare visits, Dani felt like she was on track to becoming a healthier version of herself. Dr. Lawfton was heavy into functional medicine, so she did a lot of blood tests while the nutritionist on staff eliminated certain foods like full-fat dairy or gluten and carefully reintroduced some of them along with more vegetables, supplements, and daily sleep patterns.

On her own, Dani had tried many different approaches, including Paleo, Keto, and Vegan. While they all had their benefits, she still wasn't sure which one was best. During her first conversation with Dr. Lawfton, she quickly learned that her situation was not black and white, and what works for one may not be the same for all. Through her classes, she also learned that health and wellness was not just nutrition and exercise specific, nor was it the absence of illness. It involved several dimensions, and she would not stop until she learned how to successfully establish herself in each one. Dani noticed the differences in her body. The aches and tiredness she felt every day began to slightly improve, and her skin was flawless.

With everything going exactly as planned, she never expected the mammogram she took in D.C to find anything, but it did. So here she was, two months after the lumpectomy, waiting in the lobby to see Dr. Marie Lawfton face-to-face.

"Dani, Dr. Lawfton will see you now."

Dani stood up to follow the nurse. Justice quickly rose from her chair to accompany her friend.

"I'm sorry, Ma'am, but the doctor will only see the patient."

"Oh, that's fine," Justice said, "I'll be right here, Dani."

"Thank you," the receptionist said. "I'll be back to show you to the waiting room, and you can help yourself to a complimentary breakfast."

"Complimentary? I'll be waiting right here," Justice said. "Don't worry, girl. I'll stash a lil' something for you in my purse for later," Justice laughed as the nurse whisked Dani away and onto the elevator.

With her heart pounding in her chest, Dani had no idea what to expect. Dr. Lawfton seemed lovely and down to earth, but was she prepared to hear this woman tell her whether or not she could harvest her eggs? Just the idea of more doctors poking at her body made Dani feel emotionally exhausted, and she still had chemo and radiation to complete.

"Here we go, right this way," the nurse said as she led Dani down the carpeted hallway of what now suddenly looked like a corporate office.

Upon entering, the scent of fresh-brewed coffee and cinnamon filled the air. "Gluten-free pastries," Dani mumbled the words from the sign next to the mini buffet.

"What would you like for breakfast," the nurse asked?"

"Breakfast?"

"Yes, ma'am. It's the most important meal of the day, and it's 8:00 am. Based on your chart, your first meal of the day is in thirty minutes. Should we start with your regular smoothie?"

Dani had a breakfast smoothie a few times a week that consisted of steamed greens, fruit, homemade nut milk, hemp or soaked nuts, vitamin powder, and herbs.

"Um, okay."

"Great! And then we'll fix you a plate of breakfast while you wait. Make yourself comfortable. The doctor will be with you shortly."

Dani quickly noticed the large reclining chairs and the chaise lounges next to the windows with a great view. Her eyes scanned the hardwood floors, the fluffy throw pillows, and the huge desk nestled in the corner, covered in family photos. It was like she had just stepped into a home magazine for design and décor, complete with lavender smelling oils and sage.

"If 'Ms.-Stress-Begone' was this room, I think I just met her today. Dang," Dani mumbled to herself, surveying the lavish comfort space/office that instantly made her body relax.

"Well, I'd be happy to get you an autograph," said a familiar voice from the doorway.

Dani turned to see Dr. Lawfton smiling as she approached her.

"Dani! How are you dear? I tell you, I am just loving this new gadget on my wrist! I am getting my steps in today. No more guesswork for me. Still beautiful as always, I see," Dr. Lawfton said, her bubbling personality filling the gaps in the comfort room, removing any leftover remnants of anxiety in Dani's mind.

"Thank you, so are you," Dani said, admiring Dr. Lawfton's casual green summer dress and loafers. Instead of her usual high ponytail, dark spectacles, and white coat, she looked like a model in a summer ad for Gap magazine with her long wavy hair hanging over her shoulders.

Shortly after Dr. Lawfton entered the room, someone knocked softly on the door.

"Yes, come in," chimed Dr. Lawfton.

"Yes, ma'am. I have Ms. Dani's morning smoothie here and a few things for you to nibble on."

"Very good," Dr. Lawfton replied. "You have to keep your schedule even when you're not at home, yes?"

"Absolutely," Dani replied, "although I don't have much of an appetite." Within the hour, the doctor gave Dani the news she had come to hear, egg harvesting was certainly in her future, but she could not carry them at this time due to the circumstances surrounding her illness, but there were other options.

Before Dani could respond, someone knocked on the door again. "Yes, come in." *Oh please, I am not hungry. I just wanna go home now and figure out what to do with this new information,* Dani thought to herself, assuming the receptionist was coming in with more food.

"Dr. Lawfton? Well, you are looking quite spiffy today," the voice from behind the wall said. "Oh, you have a patient. Pardon me, they told me to come right in," the woman whispered.

"It's fine, dear. Dani, I want you to meet my daughter, Cammie-Liana."

"Call me, Cammie, please," said the strange voice from the corner."

When Dani looked up, her mouth dropped open in shock. This lady had no hair at all, and here she was standing here, bald like it was just another day. No hats, no scarves, just the most perfect woman she'd ever seen.

"You're so beautiful," Dani said, clutching her chest.

"Oh, thank you," the stranger grinned shyly. "Perhaps, I would say the same to you, but I really can't see you behind that hat. Is it meant to cover your face too?"

"Sorry, no, it's just a hat," Dani said as she removed it, revealing her own bald head.

"See there, and you are gorgeous. Just look at those eyes," Cammie said, but her smile quickly faded as she noticed Dani's face was wet from crying. Cammie quickly realized that she was standing in the home office. Her mother rarely came into this office unless she was meeting a new high-end client, or she needed to comfort a patient after delivering some sort of shocking news. Since her mother's roster was always full, Cammie knew it was the latter.

"Yes, this is my one and only daughter, Cammie-Liana, or as we sometimes call her, Cammie."

"Wow! You're beautiful," Dani said again through bright, wet eyes and a tear-stained face.

"So are you, just don't put that hat back on. Actually, girl how old is that hat, and why do you still have it?"

"Cammie-Liana! I will be with you shortly. Please wait in the adjoining room."

"Will do. I just have to say this. No disrespect. I get it with the whole bald thing, but baby, this is a gift that you have to own, or at least wear a hat with some personality to it."

As Dr. Lawfton sat on the side of her desk watching her daughter tear up just from noticing Dani's pain, she realized her plan worked better than expected. Cammie didn't have any real female friends, partly because she was too brutally honest, and that honesty always broke the friendship. Dr. Lawfton also thought it was the type of women she chose to befriend as well. All from a certain type of elite class. None of them yet understood the trauma of hair loss for women or the complexities of life. Knowing that Cammie could bring a sense of energy and empowerment to Dani, she purposely asked her daughter to meet her for breakfast during Dani's appointment. What she didn't expect was for Dani to bring a sense of real compassion and understanding to Cammie, something she could not always do as her mother.

"Bummer, I think I may have double booked myself. I am so sorry, Dani. My daughter and I were supposed to do an early morning brunch."

"Oh, it's okay. I think we're done here, right? I was just leaving," Dani said as she stood up to leave, trying to decide if she should put the hat back on or not.

"Of course, if you would like to stay and join us, that would be great," Dr. Lawfton said, fully expecting Cammie to intervene with a quick no, demanding the time with her mother all to herself. Instead, she stood silently waiting for Dani's response.

"Um, I have a girlfriend in the waiting room that drove up with me."

"Yes, of course, you do," Cammie snapped. "Nice meeting you, Dani, and please spare us the pain of ever seeing you again in that hat thing. Ever heard of a scarf? Geesh."

"Can she join us too? If it's too much, I understand," Dani said.

"Not at all," Dr. Lawfton replied. "I will send for her now. Shall we go to the adjoining room? I'm always starving since I started this new workout," she said, grabbing Dani's hand and leading her to a separate room in her office, complete with a cute little dining table next to a sprawling view below. The table was full of sliced mangoes, pineapple and blueberries, crab cakes and grilled salmon, hot croissants, raw greens with cucumber, sliced tomato, and jalapeno olives, fresh-squeezed juice, and coffee.

As Cammie eyed the table full of her favorite foods, she was sure that her mother had planned this little memory lapse. Knowing that Dr. Marie Lawfton doesn't do anything by coincidence, she thought to herself, *there must be something intriguing about this woman. Time will tell, I suppose.*

Throughout the years, Cammie and Dani became thick as thieves, and the introduction of Becca made them the Three Musketeers. Cammie was the only one in Dani's close circle who understood the daily chronicles of bald women; finding eyebrow pencils that didn't melt from a shimmer of sweat, the summer heat, lace front wigs that didn't look like the plastic was melted to your forehead, eyelashes that safely attached to bald eyelids, makeup that would blend the face, bald head, and neck, and last but not least, clothes that would complement her style. She was definitely a work in progress.

After completing the creative writing for the designs, Dani sat, impatiently as her best friend poured over her work, reading cover to cover. "Well?" Dani asked anxiously, waiting for Becca to finish reading the final page of the write-up for the next three Sari issues.

"I LOVE IT! I absolutely LOVE IT! Dani. This is so big. I'm so proud of you!"

"Do you really love it? I'm so nervous just thinking about it. So, Cammie, Anna K, and Stephanie are my models for the presentation. I'm so nervous, but I can't wait to knock them out of their seats," Dani said, imagining the look on Talia's face and, in the back of her mind, Langston's as well.

"Oh honey, you did it! I knew you could do this! And rest assured, we all know that Ms. Cammie-Liana herself will ensure the sisters from the Professional Bald Women's Network are serving full fabulosity for this meeting."

"Okay? She already has everybody booked for the spa as soon as their flight lands."

"Dani, mark my words, when Langston sees this, honey, they gon' have to make way for the new boss lady coming through. Sales are gonna hit the roof! My advice to you, do not take the first offer they throw at you. In most cases, they can always go higher. Wait until the others come in before choosing the best one."

"Of course," Dani said. She had no idea what she would do if she ever found herself in a position to choose from multiple lucrative offers. Those kinds of things never happened to her. She was just fortunate enough to be considered for the opportunity. *I never thought of including that in my dream or even asking God for it, she thought. Did you hear that, God? I think I might wanna include that, so long as you give me the wisdom to know what to choose and how to make a difference. What a feeling!*

For the next few weeks, Dani worked day and night, ensuring the penthouse suite was fit for a runway, submitting new samples from designers to Sidnae, and proofreading write-ups with Talia. After checking the girls into the hotel, Dani assisted with the models' outfits for media coverage: a casual white blouse, fitted trousers, jewelry, and stilettos—all courtesy of the new Sari fashion line. Dani ran through her entire presentation with Sidnae and Talia, and just as Becca said, they went crazy over it. Thanks to Sidnae, several high-end sponsors confirmed their RSVP. Dani was confident and ready for the formal presentation.

After a long night, she was finally home. Nothing else to do now but get some rest before the big day. "Hey, Jackson, hey, bookie boo. Did you enjoy your dog sitter? Mommy is back now. It's just you and me together again." Dani had to get a doggie sitter because of the extended work hours. While she always had a profound respect for her fellow employees, her level of admiration for the entire process of completing a Sari campaign was now magnified times ten. To show her appreciation, she had breakfast and dinner sent in on long workdays, as they were in the office from early morning 'til late night. She even got Langston to spring for a massage therapist on Fridays.

"This is it; this is really it," she mumbled through a yawn while stepping into the hot shower, thankful to Sidnae for pushing the presentation back two hours. Exhausted, Dani mentally checked off her list of to-dos once again. With everything in place and nothing left to do but sleep, Dani climbed into bed, confident that by this time tomorrow, her future would be heading in a different direction.

The next morning, she was fresh, rested, and sore from a gruesome workout, just how she liked it. But no matter how peaceful she felt, she couldn't seem to shake that feeling of nervousness sitting in the pit of her stomach. So, she kept repeating to herself over and over again, "God didn't give me a spirit of fear."

Walking into the office, she felt strong, brave, and ready. The lobby was busy with the normal morning buzz of employees scampering for coffee, breakfast, and trying to make it to their offices, but Dani still felt like something was off.

"It's just your nerves, that's all. Relax," she mumbled to herself. Taking one final walk through the office, she reviewed her checklist, ensuring everything was in place, starting with the food. Two weeks before, she spoke with George, the chef for Le'Ric's food truck, he agreed to cater the presentation. Instead of vegan chicken and lemon meringue, he introduced an array of different appetizers with a creole flair.

"George, everything looks amazing!" -

"Dani, hey, where you been? It's nice to see you, beautiful as always. I got your favorite drink right here. I've been keeping it warm," he said handing, Dani a steaming cup of golden milk.

"Awe, thank you, but I gotta run. I'll see you in a bit," she said, blowing air kisses while racing out the door. Still unable to shake her nerves, Dani took a moment to do some deep breathing, inhaling, and exhaling. She followed her daily routine to a point, just as her therapist suggested. Prayer and meditation, followed by strength training, combined with a love-hate relationship on the assault bike, and a good relaxation in the sauna.

She felt powerful this morning, dressed in a cream pantsuit, with a pair of closed-toe heels, princess cut diamond studs, a pendant necklace, and silver rings, all courtesy of Sari's Silver to Diamonds collection.

In her office, Dani found a large basket of cheese and wine on her desk with a note, *Good Luck*. She figured it was Becca and was thankful as the thought of her best friend rooting for her was encouraging. Before heading to the penthouse office on the top floor, Dani took one last look at herself; makeup on point, speech in hand, and the models are waiting on cue. She sighed and took a deep breath, "Okay, God be with me."

The penthouse floor was like a different building altogether, with a total of three areas. Each executive had their own private wing. It was a cream-colored museum filled with statues and black and white prints of the Sidreaux family ancestry. The open area outside the elevators housed a massive private lobby with fully armed security.

"Ms. Breaux, right this way, please," Yuri said as she led Dani to the conference room around the corner from the main lobby. The penthouse floor had showers, a full gym, and a chef's kitchen that was closed off to prevent smells from drifting into the atmosphere. This floor was an experience, a complete escape from the reality of the rest of the building.

"May I get you anything, ma'am?

"No, thanks, Yuri, but my models will be walking up soon. Please make sure they are directed to the conference room without issue."

"Of course, and best of luck to you," Yuri said before walking back towards her office.

Taking one last deep breath, Dani opened the door. "Good morning."

"Dani! Pleased that you could join us. Come, come, have a seat," Sidnae jumped up, pushing her seat towards Dani.

"Sidreaux Sr., ladies and gents, I would like you to meet my muse, the fabulous Ms. Dani Breaux. As you can see, she clearly represents Sari Unique's new bald and beautiful collection, brilliantly wearing our Sari's winter white, Bravo Dani."

"Thank you, Sidnae," Dani replied, her excitement for the moment increasing by the second. "So, shall we get started?"

"Get started? Dear heart," Sidreaux Sr. replied, looking from Talia to Langston, "we've been listening to Sidnae drone on for hours. I would like to think we are wrapping things up here. I have a flight at noon,'" he said.

"And yet, you still love me," Sidnae laughed in unison with the rest of the room. "We are indeed officially wrapping up. Yuri, send in the ladies one last time with the final designs for the issues."

The ladies! What ladies? My ladies, Dani thought?

"That won't be necessary," Sidreaux Sr. barked, standing to his feet. "I've seen enough. Now listen, I don't know if the world is ready to embrace women and femininity in this way. I certainly don't know if we should be using the different categories across the entirety of our brand to speak to something so…abnormal," he said, resting his gaze on Dani. "For some, it may seem a bit out of the ordinary, even for a global fashion company. We're certainly not in the medical profession to be deciding what's normal for people. What exactly are we saying by opening this door, and are we ready to address the differences of millions of people around the world?"

"Ready or not, we are here, sir," Dani quickly interjected. "What is normal? It's different for every person. As bald women, our look, everything we wear, everything we do may appear unusual to the common eye, simply because we are bald. Many of us are unable to grow lashes, eyebrows, or any hair at all. It is a misconception that all bald women are either sick, hurt, or suffering in silence from an undisclosed death sentence. With all due respect, sir, it is our bold attitude and how we own and represent our unique differences that intensify the presence of your brand, or any brand, with all due respect sir," she said, making note of the silence in the room.

"Hmph, Dani, is it? Very well said. A little late to the table, but good, nonetheless. To finish my first thought, I was sold from the very beginning. I just want to make sure we are ready for the naysayers, and there will be many. What's say you, are we all in agreement?"

Everyone in the room agreed in unison.

"Son, it appears as though the great women who run this company have saved your ass, yet again. Great job, Sidnae. Lucrative as well if I may add. Didn't I tell you giving her full creative control would make an excellent decision? And you wanted to use some inexperienced person to run lead on this! Sidnae, I am very grateful that you called me to talk some sense into my son."

"Anything for the company," Sidnae said, avoiding eye contact with Dani and Langston.

"Thank you, father," Langston said. "Sidnae, prepare our international partners in Paris with the last-minute changes. We need a strong introduction for the fashion show in a few weeks."

"Done," Sidnae replied.

Sitting in her seat with a perfectly painted-on smile, Dani felt like she was having an out-of-body experience. Her legs were like jelly, and as bad as she wanted to walk out the door, her body felt limp and motionless.

"Are you okay, ma'am? Would you like a drink of water?"

Dani looked up to see Langston's mother, Naomi, staring at her from across the room with a blank expression. The voices surrounding her were like a blur of tones, and she was unable to make out any real words.

"Ma'am, have a drink of water," the server said, handing Dani a glass.

"Of course, thank you," Dani said. Realizing that she was sweating, she closed her eyes, drinking the contents in one gulp.

"The food was amazing! Where did you find the chef? What a wonderful and delightful man. Sidreaux, we must fly him in," Claire gestured towards her husband.

"As much as I would love to take the credit for that," Sidnae replied, "it was all courtesy of Dani Breaux. The food and the decor were all her idea."

"Well, that explains a lot," Sidreaux Sr. said, smiling in Dani's direction. "That's why you came in at the tail end of the meeting, ensuring everything was up to par with the wait staff. I like that in a worker, young lady! I can't tell you how many things I've missed trying to get every detail just right. There are no simple jobs; every job is equal! Hard work! That, I can appreciate." Buttoning his jacket and taking the hand of his wife, Sidreaux Sr. royally left the room with everyone clearing a path as his son Langston Jr. led the way.

As the room cleared, Dani sat fastened to her seat with the same painted smile across her face, still unable to leave the barely empty room. When she attempted to stand, her adrenaline immediately rushed inside her, eager to respond with anger. So, she sat back down in silence, waiting and praying for the opportunity to leave the building. Once home, she would gather her thoughts before speaking to anyone, just as her therapist, Dr. Sheila, suggested. In the meantime, she sat, praying for tears to fall, something to release the urge she felt inside.

Meanwhile, Langston's mother, Naomi, was still sitting across the room staring at her while talking to someone Dani didn't recognize. As the sounds from the hallway began to quiet down to a faint whisper, Dani stood to leave the room, taking note of the numbness of her legs and sore muscles. After two steps, Dani felt a muscle pain coursing through her right thigh. Somehow, she knew that on this day of all days, the leg cramp was going to linger, unlike other sporadic times when they came and went. Every so often, she experienced a painful cramp, a Charlie horse is what she called them growing up, that required lots of jumping, yelling, and swearing to find relief. Tears formed in the corners of her eyes as she silently released the pain now coursing through her calf muscle.

"Dani, there you are," Cammie said, walking towards her. "We've been looking for you everywhere. The ladies are downstairs in the lobby. We tried coming upstairs, but security stopped us. Hold up, what's going on?"

"Excuse us, ladies, just trying to reach the elevator," said a familiar voice from behind.

"Oh, I am loving your hair, sis," Cammie said, pressing the elevator button and complimenting the other three shaved heads walking their way. "Yes, honey," Cammie snapped her fingers, waving her hands in approval.

"Thank you," said the familiar voice with the longest legs of the bunch. It's a bit of a shocker for me, but uh, it is what it is," she said with a half-smile.

"Agreed! I'm just looking forward to finding something to put on my head until my hair grows back," said one of the other freshly shaved women.

"No offense, ladies, but when you had hair down to your ass this morning, but you're going home with a bald head in the evening, it's a lot to take in," the familiar voice replied again, running her hands over her bald head.

"Oh, girl, listen, no offense this way," Cammie replied. "One day my hair was thick as thighs, and the next day, it was gone."

As they continued to talk, Dani suddenly recognized the freshly shaved female figure. "Run, honey, run," the woman said, peeking around the corner as Cammie held the elevator with her foot.

"Thanks, babe. Ladies, I sincerely appreciate your uh… appreciate your kindness," Langston Jr said, slowing to speak once he saw Dani standing in the corner of the elevator.

Too focused on her silence to even acknowledge him, Dani stared straight ahead, anxiously awaiting the first floor. *That's right, Jr; stare at me, get a long, hard look,* she thought. *You think you can steal from me? God help me,* Dani prayed as her breathing quickened, and her heart raced with anger. Anxious to respond to her present environment, her thought took over her mind.

Breathe, Dani, breath. Don't allow yourself to be provoked! Don't choose to respond in that place. You are not that person anymore, she imagined Dr. Sheila whispering into her thoughts.

He ain't nothing but a gutter punk getting by off the very tits that are feeding him, from his mama to Talia, to Sidnae, and now to me, said her alter ego Daniesha, itching to make an appearance. *You had to go hire your own models, even shaved their heads because real bald women just didn't make the cut! Now it's all coming together—Sidnae telling me the meeting was pushed back two hours, but that was just to keep me away while using all of my ideas. God, I need to know if there is a way I can repent later because I'm dragging that snitch on sight. I need to release! Breathe, Dani. How you gon' drag somebody when your conscious won't even let you cuss right now. It's okay to be upset, but don't let it control you. You've come too far to lose everything; pull it together. God help me, I'm so angry, hurt. I feel used and tossed aside. I don't have any good words to say, Dani prayed as she bit her tongue, tasting her own blood, finding some sense of relief in the pain.*

Once off the elevator, they were greeted by Sidnae and Talia as Dani made a beeline for the revolving door.

"Dani," Sidnae said, grabbing her hand as Dani forcefully pulled back. We need to have a final pow-wow, just a few minutes." Sidnae smiled towards Cammie, fully aware of Dani's sudden reaction, but pretending like she didn't notice. "You've met Ebony, right, pointing towards Langston's girlfriend, the new face of our concept? Would you look at the bald head on her? Isn't she stunning? Now, Dani, we want to give her a story that shakes our audience to the core. We want to emphasize the realness of her struggle with hiding this hideous, yet gorgeous secret. But we don't want to make it look like your kind of bald because, of course, her hair will grow back, right? She can't be bald forever. We want it to be more realistic. We can use the stories, your stories, and cater them towards the models. Also, we need to get a few different ones that intertwine them, like forming their relationship and their sisterhood. I know you have more stuff in that arsenal of yours. If people can relate to someone like her being bald, think of how many people we can reach—Sponsors, designers, sales, money, money, money. She's a supermodel, for crying out loud!"

As Sidnae continued to talk, all Dani heard was *you're not good enough. Your ideas are good, but you're not good enough to speak in this environment. Only the beautiful and normal can speak and be heard.* While Dani listened to the sounds from Sidnae and the words in her head, she fixed her eyes on Talia, who watched her with a stern, yet embarrassed look on her face.

"Dani, a word please," Talia said, interrupting as Sidnae droned on in unfinished sentences.

"Mmmm, I'm happy to let you two talk. I just want to be sure we have the same eye-to-eye thought process with this, Dani. Get it to me no later than twenty-four hours from now, okay?"

"I did, didn't you get it?" Dani asked calmly, head cocked to the side.

"What do you mean? You already emailed it?" Sidnae laughed out loud while two-stepping a little dance to the music in the lobby. "See Talia, I told you, Dani, are I are good. Great minds think alike, same page here, girl," Sidnae said, pointing eye-to-eye with her two fingers between the two of them. What email address did you send it to? I don't see it?"

"I mean, if we're here," Dani said, stepping into Sidnae's personal space, "we certainly don't need an email, right? We clearly have an unspoken word between us. You probably know exactly what I'm thinking right now."

And just like that, the real Sidnae surfaced, "I don't owe you shit! So, I'm only gonna say this once, we've all sacrificed things in our careers for the greater good. This is not about you or me. It's about the message, the communicator, the audience, and the money. I mean, come on, Dani, you know this. You have a master's in communications, for crying out loud! As much as we want to focus on some kind of personal moral compass, or whatever that shit is," Sidnae laughed, "this is a business. Do not embarrass me, you don't wanna do that," she whispered.

"I couldn't agree more," Dani replied softly. "I simply meant that great minds think alike. As a matter of fact, that's one of the things I like about you, Sidnae. You seem to know how to read your audience and respond accordingly, effectively. I give you my word that I will do the same," Dani said, staring into Sidnae's eyes, feeling grateful that she wore her stilettos because this heifer was tall.

"That's my girl," Sidnae said. "No, my guh! Is that how your people say it, my guh?" Sidnae laughed as she walked toward the crowd.

"She's right, you know," Talia said. "Sidnae is a whole lot of moving parts, yet sometimes you have to sift through the mess to get to the good stuff. But she's right about one thing, business is business."

Looking at Talia, Dani was finally ready to cry as words could not describe the hurt she felt from her mentor.

"Listen to me, Dani. No one can tell your story like you can. It's unforgettable moments like these that can help to lend a little more definition, a little more foundation. Take notes. Allow yourself to be fully present in this. Take the time to really feel what this moment means to you, not to the people you were trying to impress in that room, and not to the idea of whether you succeeded or failed to do so. If you can do that, and you will,

I fully believe that you will respond to Sidnae accordingly. Because at the end of the day, Dani, it's just business."

"Good night, Ms. Talia," Dani said as she walked away, refusing to allow the words boss lady to ever leave her mouth again.

Noticing that Dani called her by her name, Talia mumbled to herself, "It's okay, Dani, you gon' get that heifer one way or another."

Back at home, Langston was dying to shake the morning off. Feeling disgusted with his father and Sidnae, he poured himself a drink. "Austin? Hey, Langston Jr. here. What you got for me, chief?

"Still working on it, but I can definitely see the concern here. The origins are so unusual, different from your family lineage. With your permission, boss, I'd like to bring in an old connection of mine to do some real deep diving on this one. Something about this causes me concern."

"Concern? Something I should be worried about?"

"Ah, I'm not too sure, but as soon as I get some information, I'll get back to you."

"Of course, you know where to find me. And hey, Austin, who is this connect?"

"No worries at all. He's a very prestigious cat, very professional and respected, if you know what I mean. I guarantee you that. You know I don't do errors, boss."

"Of course, you don't. We'll talk soon," Langston said, ending the call, slightly anxious over Austin's admission of concern. A jack of all trades, the old man was never wrong about anything, including his suspicions. If he didn't have an answer to a problem, he always had an expert waiting in the wings to find it. So, when Langston discovered several old art prints underneath his great grandfather's paintings, he decided to do some research, and he couldn't think of a better person to call. "The last thing I need is more drama right now," Langston mumbled to himself, thinking of the hurt expression on Dani's face as he poured himself another drink.

Sitting in his study, Langston smiled to himself, staring at a picture of his father and his grandfather entertaining guests at the holiday gala on the family plantation, now known as the family estate. "Look at his cream-colored ass, looking like a damn clown," Langston mumbled to himself about his father. If it wasn't for his mother's full nose, lips, and tanned skin, no one would know that Sidreaux Sr. had a black son as he often went with whatever race was conveniently popular for him at the time, and it was never black.

His father's mother and her lineage were the footprint of the family's artistic side. Known as the backbone of the family, she taught her daughters ballet, which she learned from her half-Italian mother during a time when black ballet dancers were not accepted. His grandmother may have liked his mother, Naomi, as she was just the complete opposite of his father.

Naomi was excited to represent the heritage of her African American/ Spanish mother over her white father, whom she never knew. She always went above and beyond to make sure Langston Jr always remembered who he was and where he came from, often sharing with him stories of how she met his father and how they struggled to restore the Sidreaux family business and the millions his grandfather had lost gambling and doing dirty deals.

"This is why I will always spoil my mama and give her the world," Langston said, staring at his mother's photo above the fireplace. He couldn't wait to gift his mother the cylinder paintings Ebony uncovered a few months before in the fancy storage unit at the estate. The tall cylinders were filled with the ingredients marked on the labels, showing the exact amount in each figure.

Sitting back in his chair, Langston recalled the day Ebony pulled the hidden paintings from the back of the frame. "A-Shea, Z-Oil, H-Coconut. What does it mean? Feel the texture of this painting. It's still soft after all these years. What do you think it means," Ebony asked, mesmerized by the large dusty print?

"Hmph, I'm not sure. It looks like some sort of recipe," Langston said. It says butter in the far corner."

"Maybe it's your mom's signature butter? Maybe someone painted it for her," Ebony said.

"It's possible, but knowing my mother, she's too vain. She would never hide something like this. On the other hand, if it is her recipe, then this is amazing," Langston said, putting it with the others to have professionally restored for the art gala.

"No! Langston, you can't feature that. It's her signature recipe."

"You're right; I wasn't thinking. But why would they store away so much of who they are? I just don't understand."

"Well, honey, really, where would they put this stuff? This art is amazing, but it's kinda more fitting for a museum than a house."

"Maybe so, but I think this would make the perfect anniversary gift," Langston smiled."

"The perfect son strikes again," Ebony said, playfully pinching his muscular arm. "Your mom will love this painting. I can see it now, hanging as the centerpiece in her trophy room," Ebony laughed.

"Vanity is her favorite sin," he said.

"Careful, you wouldn't want to make the Winston boys jealous of their big brother."

"Please, her sons are the least of my concern," Langston said, picturing the anniversary soiree and his mother's Oscar-winning performance surrounded by her fans, family, and friends as she rips the wrapping paper away from the painting. "Hmph, Oscar-winning performance indeed," Langston mumbled as he poured himself another drink, hoping to forget the look on Dani's face as she stood in the back of the elevator staring into nothing.

Six

FEELING THE PEAKS AND VALLEYS

Once her skinny stilettos hit the sidewalk, Dani's shoulders began to sink, and her temper started to rise. She wanted to walk faster, jog, even run, but her legs were too sore, and her heels were too high. "Ugh! Why? Just why! What the hell for! What lady, what? What you looking at? You ain't never seen somebody talking out loud before?" Dani yelled.

"Screw you, you freak," the strange lady replied.

"No, screw you! Screw all of ya'll." Dani said. Kicking off her heels, she walked across the street barefoot to the athletic store on the corner. Instantly regretting her decision, she danced from foot to foot, trying to protect her feet from the cold, dirty pavement. For some people, a little retail therapy calmed the nerves. Maybe a pair of expensive heels, makeup, or jewelry was enough, but Dani's weakness was workout clothes.

After browsing the store, Dani quickly picked out an outfit and waited in line.

"Aww, when did you get diagnosed?" She heard someone from behind ask.

What? Lady, if you don't get the hell away from me, Dani thought to herself, intentionally ignoring the woman hovering from behind. *Today is not the day. How do people not know that it's rude to assume something based on appearance? Nothing wrong with a regular hello. Why is she breathing on the back of my neck? I wonder if men who choose to be bald get approached like this.*

"Hellooo, Ms? Uhhh, ma'am," the stranger said louder and with more attitude?

If this woman touches me right now! *Don't let her touch my shoulder! Don't let her touch my shoulder! Don't let her touch me! God give me the words. Why is this line moving so slow?*

"Excuse me," the stranger said, standing next to Dani where she could see her face. "Hey, so when did you get your diagnosis? Is it cancer? I freaking hate it! Like, I hate it so much. Like nobody can tell you have it or anything, 'cause you look like a freaking rockstar. But I have a shit ton of experience with it, so I can always tell when somebody did, or does, or whatever. Like my grandma had it, and then my little sister. Can you believe that my little, baby sister had that shit? She lost all her hair too, but it came back after chemo. Are you still going through chemo? Like, don't trip; your hair will totally come back."

"No," Dani replied.

"Oh, well, you look really good like that."

"Thank you. God bless you and your family," Dani said.

Pretty freaking cool if you ask me. Do you work around here?"

"Excuse me." Stepping away from the checkout line, Dani went into the dressing room. Ten minutes later, she emerged in a long-sleeve wicker shirt and tights, complete with sneakers and a hat. She stuffed her work clothes into a backpack from the shelf, grabbed a new pair of wireless headphones, and went back to the checkout line.

"Did you happen to see the woman who was talking to me a few minutes ago?" Dani asked the cashier.

"Yep, she's right over there," the cashier said, pointing to the children's shoes.

"Keep the change for her," Dani said, giving the cashier a little extra.

For the next hour and a half, Dani ran, jogged, walked, and cried up and down busy streets and staircases. She thought about Sidnae's words. *Maybe Sidnae's right, you know. Maybe this is just how it goes. I mean, CEOs get all the credit, too, and some of them don't know shit about what it takes to do the actual job that produces the numbers.* But what the heck was Sidreaux Sr. thanking Langston for? This fool didn't do nothing but lie. Ole lying, shiftless negro. "Yes, suh, boss daddy, whatever you say, boss daddy," Dani said in a deep voice, pretending to talk like Langston Jr.

"Who the hell are you talking to lady? You need to watch where you're going," a stranger yelled in Dani's direction.

Not realizing that she was now speaking her thoughts out loud, Dani continued ranting and running all the way home.

As her body slowed down to barely a jog, Dani continued talking to God. "What if there was more? What if there's always been more? Am I stagnant, too afraid to take a risk? What risk should I take? What should I do next?"

Being a writer wasn't her first job. For over ten years, Dani worked in the corporate industry, struggling to make ends meet while trying to make a name for herself. Dani had many successful projects and ideas, but she was never a part of any financial windfall or promotion that came with it. Just a bunch of plaques and awards.

"I don't know God. I just figured at some point, my time would come too, you know. Just keep working, keep pushing, keep grinding, go back to school. But even after going back and finishing at the top of my class, I still feel like I belong behind the scenes, like the imaginary seat at the table everyone talks about just isn't meant for me. Every time I try to convince myself otherwise, I'm reminded of my place, just like today."

She remembered telling Becca that those spots at the table are reserved for people who did everything right, from graduating high school, getting into the right college, marrying the love of their lives, and having kids. Not for someone like her who was anything but traditional. "Such an ignorant way to look at life," Dani said, while the negative thoughts in her mind tried to convince her different

After finishing her master's, Dani assumed everything would be so much better with a formal education and experience under her belt. She applied for one job after another in her department, hoping they would utilize her skills and offer more financial stability. Every time a rejection email came without explanation or a request to interview, she felt like a huge disappointment to herself.

"Maybe things didn't go my way in that industry because I really hated it, but that's not the case anymore. I love being a writer. How can I use what I love to help others, to bring people closer? I just don't know where I fit in anymore. I want to feel like I'm contributing something of importance, not some outdated robot, just existing but failing to live the life you called me to live. You saved my life, and that has to mean something. God help me! I'm just not sure what I'm supposed to do with my career or anything for that matter. How do I honor you? Some people would say that I'm blessed to have the job I have, and I should be settled with that. Something inside of me says that's not enough. Getting the dream job was just the beginning."

By the time Dani got home, she was all cried out. So, she fed and walked Jackson, turned on some music, grabbed her microphone and the biggest bottle of Red she could find, and hit the stage.

WHEN MUSIC TOUCHES THE SOUL

Dani loved music and was drawn to different styles and genres, depending on her mood. Growing up as a teenager in a Christian home, her family was deeply rooted in Gospel music. While she loved singing and listening to nostalgic hymns, her life was forever changed the day her brother brought home music by Commissioned and Fred Hammond. After that, she and her siblings went on to discover The Winans, Bebe and CeCe, Take 6, Kirk Franklin, Yolanda Adams, and so many others. The beats of the songs were mesmerizing, but as she progressed through the intricacies of dating, moving away from home, and growing up, the words from those songs gave her peace and comfort.

While Gospel music was her first love, Dani learned different types of soulful R&B from her aunts. Summertime weekends at her auntie's house involved everything from cleaning, cooking, talking, unwinding, dancing, laughing, and just rejuvenation. Sometimes, she even got her hair done after they were finished. She developed a love-hate relationship with the sporadic early morning summer cleaning rituals, as they often began with turning off the air conditioning before scrubbing the house, as if the heat produced a better effect.

As frustrating and sweaty as her memories were from the time before, she would do it again and again and again just to relive the excitement of everything that followed. It wasn't the familiar smell of coffee, grits, eggs, sausage, and cinnamon rolls filling the air that kept Dani coming back. It was the music lessons and the free-flowing conversations. It was Frankie Beverly and Maze, Al Jarreau, Earth, Wind & Fire, Chaka Khan, Sheila E, Babyface, the list goes on and on. She danced, laughed, and talked about everything under the sun with her aunt, respectfully. By the time they finished scrubbing the house from front to back, doing yard work, and cooking Sunday dinner on Saturday night, they were exhausted.

After a shower, they would throw on some house clothes and were laid out on the couch before sundown, watching episodes of Seinfeld and Mad About You. As an adult, Dani adapted that routine into her weekend schedule. After the divorce, she promised herself that any new guy in her life would have to share her love of music, and she would do the same for his interests.

"Dani, honey, I'm here," Becca said. "Answer your phone, I'm walking up the steps now."

Jackson stood by the door and began to bark incessantly.

"Who is it?" Dani said, attempting to quiet Jackson by rubbing his back. But Jackson continued to bark. Glancing at the camera, Dani didn't see anyone, so she turned up the volume, blasting Fantasia, singing the words into her microphone. Jackson continued to bark as Dani sang louder.

"Cammie, is that you?" Becca said as she noticed her walking up the sidewalk.

"It sure is, Ms. Becca, boo."

"Hey, girl, it's so good to see you! Oh my gosh, you look amazing," Becca said as they held hands admiring each other.

"I know. I'm like a fine wine, baby girl. I just keep getting better with time. Talking about me, look at you and all that booty, looking like the front page of Vogue. You got curves and booty for days," Cammie said as Becca did a full spin, showing off her fit and toned body.

"I know you didn't get that big ole booty just eating green grass, so dish it! Where's the food I'm starving?"

"Honey, you know me, I got the bottles," Becca said, holding up two large bags.

"Bottles are good, but I need sustenance. I need curvy people food."

"Oh, that does sound good. We can stroll on over to the food trucks down the road, best non-chicken you ever tasted, I kid you not, but first, we gotta get our girl."

"Have you knocked on the door," Cammie said, banging on the door and pressing the call button.

"It's no use. She can't hear us over the music."

"Shh, shhh," Cammie said, walking to the side of the house. "It's Jill Scott."

"Are you sure? Which song?" Becca asked.

"Nope, but it's definitely something soothing, something soulful."

"Oh, thank goodness for that," Becca said, still not convinced that Dani was in a good place. "That girl's music is a whole mood all by itself," Becca said, sitting next to Cammie on the porch swing.

"Shhidd, it's a daily soundtrack," Cammie laughed.

"Just as long as it's not like that one time when she took a bubble bath every day for weeks, listening to the same song over and over again," Becca recalled.

"Oh, right after the divorce? Oh yeah, she was a mess, devastated and depressed, but at least she smelled good," Cammie said.

"My gosh, it was just a tornado of events coming at her, one after the other. I wasn't sure how she was gonna get through it, but she did. No thanks to you, Ms. Cammie, recommending she sit in a damn bubble bath every day. Why would you tell her to do that? She had earphones plugged in her ears and a bottle of wine by the tub. I sat by the bathroom door for hours, day after day, just to make sure she was still breathing," Becca said.

"She may have been depressed, but she smelled good. We both know a depressed Dani will work out until she passes out, again and again. Not only does that shit stank, but it's not healthy, especially in her condition. She was clean, and she was eating. I think I did a damn good job. The music was taking care of the rest," said Cammie.

"Yeah, but that one song, over and over again? I was on the verge of losing it."

"Becca, that was on you." Then, doing her best impression of Becca's Texas accent, Cammie said, "Take your headphones off, Dani, let's hear what ya listening to, hon."

"Well, I didn't think it would be the same song, on repeat," Becca said. "I've never heard anyone do that before, till this day."

"Well, I can totally understand 'the same song on repeat' concept, depending on the situation," said Cammie.

"Well, I ain't there yet," Becca said. "Remember when I asked you to help me and let me have your Commissioned and Fred Hammond CD's so I could try to understand the words, and you refused?"

"Yes! Remember when I told you that we are in the days of purchase online?"

"Well, I sure did purchase everything. When I got to work one day, I told Jess to just let it play in the office instead of whatever music was playing in the store. Girl, I made them put on the Gospel station in the lingerie store. They thought I was losing my damn mind. You should've heard Jess, 'Lingerie and Gospel? Becca Lynn Carrington, what are you thinking?'"

"Hmph. So, what you saying, Becca Lynn? You got yourself a gospel card now because you got a little taste? What you know about Kirk Franklin, John P. Kee, and Yolanda Adams?" Cammie asked with her head cocked to the side, waiting for Becca to respond with her infamous 'Honey, who?' "You think you finally got yourself a seat at the church barbeque, huh?" Cammie teased.

"The church barbeque? Honey, please. What you know about them Winans, all of 'em, The Walls, Jonathan McReynolds, and Tye Tribbett?" Becca said. "Oh, and I think you meant the Saturday cookout. I been bringing your grandma's recipe for the potato salad and baked beans going on three years now. Everybody knows I'm hanging with the middle-age aunties and uncles, listening to Frankie Beverly and Maze, sprinkled with a lil' Earth Wind and Fire, playing dominoes, and two-stepping in the background. Talking about a church barbeque, honey please. I got a front row seat at the afternoon church service, the day *after* the *family reunion* barbeque," Becca emphasized, "where church starts at 1:00 and ends around 5:00.

"Awww shoot, well, come through then, Becca Boo!" Cammie said as they both laughed out loud.

"Heck, I thought you knew," Becca laughed, high-fiving Cammie. "I may not have understood it all back then, but I'm learning."

"Exactly," Cammie said. "Sometimes that one song says everything, and it's all you need, all day, every day."

"You say that like you know," Becca said as their eyes met, sharing a look they both understood. "Oh, move, move, move! Song change, song change, go, go, go!" Becca and Cammie raced, with one buzzing the intercom and the other calling Dani's cell and knocking on the windows. Finally, the door buzzed open.

As they walked into Dani's house, Jackson was nestled in the corner unbothered, chewing on his toys, and Dani was in full duet-mode with Jill Scott singing "Hate on Me Hater," complete in her workout tights, sports bra, and fluffy socks.

Looking over her shoulder, Dani knew the girls would show up because she was sad. However, after releasing her aggression through exercise and conversation, she was fine, and she knew exactly what she needed to do. She didn't know how she would do it, but she would respond, and as Sidnae and Talia said, it would be *just business*.

Looking down at the huge gift bag Becca had in tow, Cammie grabbed it and quickly gave it to Dani.

"We bought you this," she said, before Becca could intervene. Knowing that a hardcore workout was calming to Dani during tough times, Becca had picked up some boxing gear, but by the looks of it, and the smell, Dani had already decompressed.

Dani dropped the mic and opened the huge box to find designer boxing gloves, hand wraps, knee wraps, and compression socks.

"I already did that," she stated, shoving the box at Cammie and resuming her position with the microphone.

After lighting candles and incense, Becca and Cammie stood staring at Dani hopping from place to place, performing as the backup dancer, lead vocalist, and backup singer, creating lyrics that were not in the actual songs. As friends, they did the only thing that two best friends could do. Becca reached in her purse and grabbed her hairbrush, while Cammie grabbed a big wooden spoon from the kitchen, and they sang as loud as they could, but their laughter was short-lived as Dani did a song change.

Both Becca and Cammie stared at each other, silently praying for a different song, hoping this would not be a repeat of the bubble bath days.

"This song right here speaks to where we all are in this world right now," Dani said, slurring her words, courtesy of the glass of wine on the table that was still half empty. Dani was not much of a wine drinker, so a few sips was enough. "We all have something in our flesh that craves carnal pleasures like money, acceptance, and vanity. We hide that shit, deep down so nobody can see it, see us in it, see it," Dani said, stumbling through words. "We hide inside our titles, relationships, and success. That's why we feel like shit when we fail because we ain't dealing with the real. We think we can just put a blanket of success over everything, and it's gon' be good. Then we just keep needing more money, more success, and more fake love just to sustain,"

Dani moaned as she grabbed the wall, trying to control her balance.

"Whoa, be careful," Cammie chimed in.

"Stay in corporate, Dani, writers don't make money," she said, mocking her former friends. I gave them punks my ideas too. "Teamwork, teamwork makes the dream work," Dani chanted. "And every year they put five more cents in my coffee cup, took my ideas, and denied every promotion. Here's employee of the month, though," she said, pointing to herself, "for six months straight! Bunch of worthless plaques and shit that you can't spend. For years, I've sat back and made excuses for it—getting more degrees, doing more internships, broke as hell, 'But it's business, Dani, it's just business. There are no job titles, just jobs that are all important," she said in a high-pitch tone, mocking Sidreaux Sr. "Well, let's switch for a day then, how 'bout that?"

"Hey! Lil Girl! What in all the earth are you talking about?" Cammie asked. "How is this song related to all of that? This is uh, uh Michael Bublé singing about Mrs. Jones! What does this have to do with your job?"

"What you mean, how does it relate? Er-body has a Jones, Cammie! Maybe not in the physical sense of a relationship with a man or a woman…but, wait… you did Cammie, yours was a relationship. Remember that old man you messed around with back in the day? Dang, that joker was old too, and not in a sexy, rich Mr. Big and Carrie Bradshaw from Sex and the City type of way either," Dani said, recalling characters from her favorite television show.

"Oh, you mean that old fart that owned the law firm with the Porsche that used to let her drive his Rolls Royce, no, the Aston Martin," Becca recalled. "Oh my gosh, remember that time we drove down to Hilton Head in his Bentley to my uncle's retirement party?"

"Yep, that's the weekend we spent on the water on the yacht. That was awesome," Dani said.

"Yes, I do remember him," Becca laughed. "We used to call him *'ashy ashtray, looking for a bae!'* Dani and Becca yelled in unison, as they doubled over in laughter.

"Yep, he was always cutting our skin with them dry, crackly hands, never took the lotion we offered, but he always had hand sanitizer," Dani laughed.

"Now Cammie, I was still getting to know you back then, and I always wondered, did you and ole ashtray ever, you know?" Becca asked.

Looking from Becca to Dani in frustration, Cammie warned, "Ya'll don't wanna play pull the skeletons out the closet with me. Not tuhday! Especially when I'm starving as I haven't eaten since your lil' sideshow hustle this morning, Dani. What was that? Hmm? And gimme that damn microphone here," Cammie said, snatching it from Dani's hand. "Narrating these amazing classics with your nonsense. Start that song over, and let mama teach you how it's done."

After Cammie finished, they took turns singing Jill Scott and Fantasia, each one taking the lead, adding background moves and off-key vocals. They followed up with a few Commissioned classics for Becca as she was so thankful that Dani and everybody else was fine. But Cammie knew she was just showing off, singing the lead, proving that she knew the words, and she earned her ticket to the family reunion barbeque. And because Cammie wanted to remind them of the powerful sisterhood they shared, they sang India Arie, Erykah Badu, Lauren Hill, Ledisi, and Tina Turner.

Once Dani's buzz wore down, Cammie sprayed her with Lysol, forcing Dani to take a shower. Feeling drained and empty after their karaoke dance performance, they walked down the block to Le Ric's Food truck for take-out. Laying outside on the deck, they talked and acted out their favorite parts in movies until they fell asleep under the stars.

The next morning, Dani found herself alone with her thoughts. "Jackson," she called out between the throbbing beats in her head. She found Jackson sleeping peacefully in his bed, his food and water bowl half empty. "Awww, them aunties took care of that baby," Dani said, gently kissing Jackson's head.

With nothing to do, she jumped in the shower and tried to think of a plan, something she could do to solidify this project as her baby. "What difference does it make at this point? If I do anything else other than being Sidnae's wingman, people will assume I'm just being jealous or kissing up to the new boss. I need to find a way to gently bend the rules, but where, with who, and how?" So many questions, but the most important question that pondered her entire being and took priority over everything else she was thinking was, "Why is there blood flowing into my shower drain?"

A few hours later while waiting for her gynecologist, Dani's mind raced trying to find the reason why she was spotting from there. After being diagnosed with hormonal breast cancer years ago, the combination of chemo drugs and hormone therapy made her pre-menopausal. She didn't understand why she was bleeding, and despite taking the medication, why was the pain getting worse by the minute?

"Excuse me, how much longer?" Dani asked the receptionist. Dani called her primary doctor, who told her to call her oncologist, who told her to call her gynecologist, who had advised her to come in before she had to leave for an emergency labor and delivery. So, now she was in the hands of the assistants.

"Ms. Breaux, it'll be just a few more minutes," the receptionist said, leaving Dani anxious and in pain.

While waiting, her mind raced over the past years to the many times she'd heard a nurse say, *"Just a few more minutes."* While waiting for the results from the second mammogram and again for the biopsy, she heard that line, and several times later, while waiting for tests, thyroid biopsies, and vaginal ultrasounds. Every week for several months, she was in and out of the doctor's office. She lost count of how many times she sat waiting in cold, patient rooms hanging on to what little faith she had left.

Dani recalled the nagging burning sensation she felt in her left breast and the time spent trying to convince the doctor that it was more than just nerves from trying to get pregnant or a reaction from the thyroid medication. Something didn't feel right, and no one was listening.

TOUGH TIMES

Dani was just finishing a boxing class when she got the call about a second mammogram. At her age, mammograms were not a part of preventive care. After having her share of disappointments in the last few years, Dani was confident there was no way she could have breast cancer. No one in her family had breast cancer, so she was sure it must be something else, but she needed to know for sure before they continued with fertility options.

Sitting in the waiting room with a bald head and seeing how some of the patients were looking at her, Dani knew some of them were assuming she already had cancer. Dani longed to call her Dad, but he was gone. She didn't wanna call her husband as she didn't want to hear the disappointment in his voice or face the thoughts in her head. *Again? Something else is wrong with you again? Girl, you are adding too much lemon to the lemonade.*

After everything that happened already, surely God would not allow this too. As she sat, waiting for the breast cancer doctor to perform her biopsy, Dani repeated her daily scripture reading from that morning, "Whatever you ask for in Jesus' name, so it shall be," and in between she prayed, "Please God, help me."

"Well, this is breast cancer," the surgeon said. "From the looks of it, it looks like we caught it early, but we'll know more once the test results come back."

Unable to understand why she wasn't a total wreck after hearing the 'big-C' word, Dani felt at peace. It wasn't until she got home to the empty house that a flood of emotions took over, and she realized the magnitude of what was to come.

"Okay, I need to pray," Dani said as she got on her knees, but nothing came out. No thoughts, no silent prayers, just tears. The more she tried to calm herself and just pray, the harder the tears fell. It got to the point where she couldn't keep her mouth closed because she was wailing so hard. So many thoughts were coming and going, some in anger, some in fear. She fell to her knees and put her head on the floor. The weeping sounds were so loud, and her heart was pounding too fast to stay in that position. So, she sat on the floor with her legs straight out in front of her like a child having a temper tantrum and just cried. The sounds of her wailing grew louder and louder until they were full-on screams!

"What is happening? What is happening to me? How am I supposed to tell him this? What is it that you want from me?" Then Dani quickly stood to her feet and paced the floor, suddenly too angry to sit. "I'm staying in faith. I'm doing everything I know how to do! I volunteer, I go to church, I serve consistently. I BELIEVE IN YOU GOD! I keep my house in prayer. I don't understand this. Why? Why are you not choosing me anymore? First you take my babies, now this! It's too much, too fast! I can't…God! I'm so scared," she cried, falling back to her knees."

"I've brought nothing but pain to my husband, to my new marriage. Every day he looks at me, I feel like half of a woman. I can't give him babies, and I don't feel like the wife he married. What am I supposed to do with all of this? Why are you allowing these things to happen to me now—with him? I prayed, I fasted, I waited for a husband to come into my life, and now I keep breaking his heart. I don't wanna die, God. You said whatever I ask for in your name…, that's what you said! When I was bleeding and pregnant…no, no, no!"

Dani stood to her feet again, angry and pacing the floor. "I told myself to let go of the spotting and give my baby to God. I couldn't control or fix what was happening, but I knew that you could. I didn't think I would lose my baby," she cried. "What have I done? Whatever it is, whatever it isn't, whatever I'm not, and whatever I need to be, God, please help me," she cried, falling to her knees again. "Please forgive me, forgive us. If it's anything in me, in us, that is not of you, please forgive us. Please help us! Show us where we need to be."

After hours of crying, praying, and self-pity, Dani realized that she could not fight this battle with fear alone. Regardless of the anger and hurt she felt in her mind and in her flesh, she needed God. She didn't care if she felt that God had given up on her, because in her heart, she could still feel him, and she knew he was there. She could feel the Holy Spirit comforting her as the scriptures she'd read over the years flowed through her mind, responding to every fear and every pain she felt, just like her parents said they would. She just had to believe God was still God, and he didn't need a blueprint of someone else's storm for guidance. He would meet her in the midst of where she was, even if the last few years left her doubting her self-worth.

Pray, cry, talk, pray, cry talk. Every day, she sat in the corner on the floor talking to God, reading her Bible, yearning to feel something other than rage and fear. Three times a day, mostly when she was alone, she went back to the corner. Pray, cry, talk after her husband had left for work and before starting her day. Pray, cry, talk again before lunch, and once more before bed.

The corner in the room became her secret place, complete with throw pillows, a vision board against the wall, and a painting of a sunset with the words beautiful in bold words. She was careful not to share her space with anyone else as she didn't want their fears and opinions to interfere with her time with God. Dani had no idea what she was doing, but her time in the corner reminded her that no matter what she saw in the mirror or how much pain she felt, God made her beautiful in his image, and the promises of his word overwhelmed her with a sense of strength and security.

It became a regular relationship for Dani to make time for God and put him first in her life—before the gym, before checking her phone, and before work. It was her relationship with God that helped her when doctors told her she may never birth a child, and years later, when her marriage ended, and her heart was broken again.

What she didn't always realize was that while she was going through her own mental hell, so was her husband. So many days, she wanted to take his stress and heartache away. She just wanted to disappear, go somewhere else and heal, let him be with someone who didn't have any health issues, someone who wasn't bald, who could have a house full of babies. He didn't deserve to go through this.

No matter how hard she wished or tried, she could not be the same woman he married, and it hurt her deeply. She felt like she was battling with herself to be who she was versus the woman she was becoming. Letting go of her old self was another loss she grieved, but it was God who helped her accept who she was becoming. Every day, she felt him teaching her how to love herself.

An hour later, Dani experienced her first pelvic exam and vaginal ultrasound while on a full-blown period. The nurses tried to convince her that they were accustomed to almost every situation involving women and reproduction, but Dani still felt embarrassed and in pain.

After her appointment, she hurried home, swallowed some pain pills, turned on some Maxwell music, and sipped chicken and vegetable bone broth she'd picked up at a local restaurant around the corner. That's what she loved about her neighborhood; they always had an ample supply of whatever she needed, and she always felt at home.

Seven

A TASTE OF HOME

Two days later, Dani was still out of the office. She was considering making it a solid week, unsure of what was happening with her body. For the last two days, she practically lived in the bathroom, from the shower to the toilet, in fear of what may happen with too much space in between.

The buzzing of the front door caught Dani's attention.

"Delivery for Dani Breaux."

On the front porch, Dani noticed a man dressed in a white jacket, like a chef's coat, "Can I help you?"

"I have some cooked meals for Dani Breaux."

"You have the wrong address. I didn't order anything."

"Are you Dani Breaux? I'm just doing my job, ma'am, and I have a delivery for this address."

"Okay, leave it there, thank you."

"Ma'am, I don't think that's a good idea. Have you been outside your house today?"

"What? I don't think that's any of your business," Dani said, grabbing her phone to call the police while reaching for her protection, just in case."

"My apologies, ma'am, you have a lot of flo-…"

"Sir, please, just leave it there along with your card. Thank you."

"As you wish," he replied, sticking his card in the side door.

After finishing her broth and ensuring the coast was clear, Dani took Jackson outside in the backyard to throw the frisbee around. From there, they secretly crossed the neighbor's walkway to the open trail, hoping the movement would ease her mind and stomach.

"So that's what they're doing," Dani said, talking to Jackson like he understood. I guess Sidnae and Talia think they can smooth things over with some ready-made food that's probably been sitting in the freezer storage at Sari for months. Even as she said it, she knew Langston didn't get down like that, often recalling his disdain for frozen foods, preservatives, and eating two-day-old leftovers. When the chefs on the executive floor cooked too much, they brought the food down to the regular folks, and it was amazing, she recalled, salivating over the thought of the lobster bisque.

"Hmph, maybe the meals won't be so bad," Dani said. "Whatever! Come on, Jackson, let's take our walk. Thinking they can just send some food, and everything will be alright, whatever. That mess gon' be there when we get back."

After their walk, Jackson ran around the backyard chasing birds while Dani lay in the hammock, her body relaxing and the pain slowly subsiding as she drifted to sleep. While in and out of consciousness, she could hear her neighbors having a full discussion.

"I'm not sure what this is all about. This looks messy and it's very overwhelming. Where is Dani? I'll call her."

Unable to rest for the past two days, Dani was exhausted. The sound of the birds chirping, the warmth of the sun, and the chilly breeze gently swaying the hammock, lulled Dani into a peaceful, relaxing sleep. Suddenly, Dani was jarred awake by the ringing of her phone. Feeling half-drunk, she tried to compose herself, "Hello! Yes, I know, she said, clearing her throat. I'm here in the backyard. Yes, someone dropped off a delivery. I'm coming to get it now, thank you." Geesh, the nerve of these neighbors and the HOA committee to harass me about some flowers and boxes on my porch. "Jackson! Come on. Let's get these groceries before I have to tell somebody off today, Dani fussed. Yes, you're coming in the house while I get this stuff. I don't need you running up behind me while I have my hands full. You know how this neighborhood likes to talk. The next word on the street will be that I neglected my dog, and you were hit by a car," Dani mumbled on to herself. Come on, boy, we'll come back out when I'm done. It might be something out there for you."

Swinging open the front door, Dani could hardly believe her eyes. Draped across her porch sat twelve crystal vases, each filled with two-dozen tulips, her favorite flower, with a different color rose in the center. The delivery driver left his card in the door along with a note:

Greetings, Ms. Dani Breaux,

Someone is thinking of you. Please enjoy, from our heart to yours.

The flowers requested are already prepped; nothing additional is needed. If you have any questions on how to care for them, please call the flower shop at the number listed below. Thank you.

On the side of the door were two extra-large boxes. After several trips to the porch, Dani had a vase of flowers in various areas around the house: on the upstairs terrace, the deck below, the porch in the backyard by the hammock, the windowsill in the bathroom next to the garden tub, and on the island kitchen counter. Besides water, open air, and sun, Dani was clueless about how to care for so many flowers, so she left tulip arrangements on the doorstep of each of her neighbors, careful not to leave her name to draw attention to herself.

On top of one of the boxes was a card: *Read me and open this box immediately.* Eager to see a name, Dani ripped open the envelope:

Dani,

I'm not sure how I got here to the point of writing letters and sending flowers, but here I am. Trust me, the flowers were not a part of this at first. I was out for a run recently when I saw them. These particular flowers stand out more than any I've ever seen. The colors are so bold and rich. They are flawlessly stunning. I couldn't look away. They remind me of you. When you walk into a room, it changes the atmosphere. People stop and stare, not because of the obvious, but I think it's because of how well you represent what I'm sure you think are your flaws and imperfections. You see, a rare flower doesn't know that it's a rare flower. It's just effortlessly beautiful, like a work of art. I am in total awe of that kind of beauty.

This is where my attempt at writing gets a little more mushy than I'd like, but here goes: You inspire me, overwhelm me, actually. It's not very often that I feel this way about anything or anyone, but when I do, I express it. I like to create things, particularly through cooking, making music, and my favorite—making desserts. Typically, I keep my outlets of expression to myself. It's my own personal joy okay, don't judge me.

I know this sounds weird, but I'm an only child, and I've been this way my whole life. Since this is a first for me, I've decided to do something different and share it. After all, it's not like you know who I am. (Side note: If you're not freaked out yet, keep reading.)

Sometimes when I think of you, I want to reach out to you, see your smile, and hear your laugh. It's refreshing, and it makes me feel good and energized. So, it came to me. I have a go-to cake recipe that has been with me since I was eight years old. Throughout graduations, breakups, sadness, and happiness, I add to it and take away from it. Out of all the things that I've done for others, this creation is all mine, my own little occasional transformation piece. (Side note: my mushiness gets worse, keep reading). So, I was thinking, what could I add to it that reminds me of you? Buttercream icing, of course. Now, this is far beyond the typical frosting as this icing sits on top of the most exquisite cake in the world. Lol! I kid you not. You have never tasted anything like this cake. What's funny is that I hate buttercream icing. I hate all forms of icing, but for some reason, I can't seem to get enough of it on this cake. Either I'm just that good of a baker, or perhaps it's more than just the icing on the cake.

One thing is for certain, I suck at writing, so I'm keeping my day job. And because I've eaten so much cake, I'm definitely hitting the gym a little bit more. Hopefully, the words of this letter, along with the images of eating rich, decadent cake, make you smile. If not, I included some other things.

I wanted to get to know you, and I didn't want my limitations to cause me to miss out on all the unique and authentic things there are to learn about you. I wondered, 'How do you really get to know someone? How do you show them that you're interested beyond leaving just the typical hundreds of flowers on their doorstep?' I honestly don't know, but hopefully, this attempt is getting me…just that much closer. Here's to enjoying my process of getting to know you. Cheers!

Sincerely…XOXO.

"XOXO? This is definitely not from Sidnae or Talia," Dani said, flipping the nameless card back and forth. Unable to casually carry the boxes inside, Dani squatted and lifted one box at a time. "No wonder the delivery guy wanted to bring everything in, sheesh."

Dani immediately called the flower shop and the food service guy and left a tip, thanking him again for his service. Slicing through the packing tape, she could feel the cool air escaping from the box. Lifting one warm container after another from the box, she carried them into the kitchen, removing the lids slowly. The air instantly filled with the aroma of spicy seasons, roux, and okra.

"Are you kidding me right now? Somebody actually sent me some food, and it's still warm?" Grabbing a spoon, Dani stirred the dark liquid, revealing andouille sausage, chicken, and shrimp gumbo. Placing the lid back on top, she inspected the second large container, which contained seafood gumbo with some blue crabs. The third large container was a vegetable and beef soup that looked and smelled just like her daddy's.

Stepping away from the kitchen, Dani wasn't sure what to do with this strange delivery. "How would anyone know about my daddy's soup, she wondered out loud? Should I toss it, donate it, taste it? Mama always said, 'Be careful eating unknown gumbo and potato salad. Baby, gumbo is a mixture of different things that brings peace and joy to the soul, but everybody's definition of peace and joy ain't the same.'"

Following the instructions on the containers for cooling, Dani stored the savory foods in the freezer and dialed the phone number on the card.

"Hello. My name is Dani Breaux."

"Ms. Dani, good morning. This is Jean (Jon). How is everything?"

"Great! Uhh…why did you make me gumbo?"

"Well, now, I can't tell ya that, but if you got questions 'bout the food, you reached the right one here. How is everything?"

"Chef Jean? of where, Dureaux's?" Dani laughed?

"That's me."

"You're Chef Jean of Dureaux's? Seriously? No, you're not. Who is this?"

"Ms. Dani, one second, mon cher," he said, placing her on hold.

"What the heck? He called me 'mon cher,'" Dani said. "That means 'my dear,' in French," she smiled. "I mean, it sounds like him," she said, looking up a video clip on her cell phone of Chef Jean cooking live on television. "I don't know anybody that knows a famous chef."

Slowly realizing that she was talking to a real-life celebrity, Dani sat down on the edge of the couch and watched the video clip she'd seen several times. Born in Louisiana, Chef Jean Broussard was a world-renown chef. He spent half of his childhood with his father in Chicago and the other half with his mother in the South, splitting summers with his mother's parents in France and his father's parents in Italy. She recalled eating at one of his restaurants in Vegas and was floored by the shrimp and grits. It was nothing like she'd ever tasted. The bread he made was even more different. She watched all his shows. He was her favorite chef.

"Ms. Dani, thank you for your patience, baby. It was a pleasure to do this for you. Your friend is a very good person. He's always good to me and my family. Anyone who is special to him will always be special to me, always. Please, please call me for anything. Whatever you need. Enjoy!"

"Oh, Chef Jean, wait! Would you like me to taste anything? On television, you wait until the celebrity guest tastes the food before ending the show. I mean, of course, I'm not a celebrity, but I'd be willing to taste it for you."

"Oh yes, yes, yes… no. I believe the food is just as good as you remember. Enjoy," he said, disconnecting before Dani could respond.

"Jackson! Do you know who I was just talking to?" Gazing up from his empty snack bowl, Jackson ran towards the kitchen like he was going for the food. Suddenly, remembering the gumbo, Dani raced behind Jackson, grabbed a spoon, and popped open the container from the freezer. She dipped her spoon in and took a little taste, and then another, and another.

"MMMM!!! It can't be this good! This is home," Dani said as she recalled sitting at the kitchen table chopping seasonings while her aunt made a roux from scratch. She was the only who could make okra in a gumbo that made Dani crave it every time. Suddenly remembering the other box, Dani grabbed a knife and anxiously sliced through the tape. Inside was a large cream box wrapped in a silky, gold ribbon which fell apart with the slightest touch. Once opened, a bright light flashed from the corner of the box, revealing another envelope.

Please Read Before Opening.

Did I do my research, or did I do my research? I shouldn't brag; you may not even like it. Of course, I don't know how anyone could not like Chef Jean's cooking, but this is my first time doing something like this, and I am excited and hope that you will love it! Everything here is a part of you. The love for where you come from, your favorite foods, your scent, and a piece of your culture. How do I know this? Because I think, for the first time in my life, I listened. Perhaps we'll share these things together someday. In the meantime, I hope that you enjoy this as much as I loved putting it together.

"Research? Somebody researched me? Smell, I don't smell like gumbo. Do I?" The white box had four individually covered compartments. Removing the top from the first compartment, Dani stopped in disbelief. "Shut the front door! These are homemade pecan candies!" Inhaling the familiar scent, Dani quickly removed the wrapping and bit into the sugary confection, sinking back into the floor as the candy melted in her mouth. "Oh, ma ga," she said with a mouth full. "Just as I remember. Sorry, Jackson, too sweet for you."

After counting over a dozen pieces of individually wrapped candies in the box, Dani sent a text to Becca and Cammie to protect her from eating every single one. 'Ladies, *I have goodies for you.*' Pecan candy simply required a skill set one had to have. While the process seemed easy, you had to know when to do certain things based on intuition and skill. She had a cousin or two who could make a recipe that would make you slap yourself silly. Still licking her fingers, she opened the next compartment to find warm mini tea cakes and lemon pound cakes.

Like a child on Christmas morning, Dani sat on the floor, dancing and humming to her own beat while nibbling on the sweet confections of her childhood. "Awww, I'm sorry, Jacks, but this is just for mommy," she said as Jackson continued to inch his way closer to the sugary treats. "Don't look at me like that. I am always getting you surprises and spoiling you rotten. It's my turn. Go on, Jackson," Dani teased. "Let's just hope it's not from a psycho."

The cream-colored case was still too heavy to lift from the cardboard box. Inside, underneath several layers of wrapping tissue, sat a bulky white treasure chest with a key attached to the side. Carefully inserting the key, a bright light illuminated the box, revealing the entire Naomi Winston beauty collection. *'Smell,'* she remembered from the letter.

On her first day shopping for her new home with Becca, Dani remembered picking up a heavy jar of whipped body butter priced at $350 dollars for a small size. Becca insisted she treat herself, so she bought a fifty-dollar sample size that was carefully measured into what looked like a clear glass contact lens case. On self-care days, she would touch the tip of her pinky finger into the silky cream and dab a little on each side of her neck and wrists, always careful not to use too much. Dani loved how the scent of fresh honey and coconut would linger throughout the house for days.

"How would this person know about her favorite unaffordable body cream?" Here she sat with five of the largest jars she'd ever seen of it and in various scents. In addition, there were bath salts, oils, bubble baths, soaps, and an entire line of facial products with a card attached to the top of the treasure chest:

'Dani, The facial products are especially for your skin type. Please call me with any questions, Monique.'

"How could she know my skin type? I've never had a facial there." Anxious to store the beauty products on her vanity, Dani tried removing the large cream chest from the box, but it was still too heavy near the center. Shaking it, she heard a swishing sound coming from underneath. She lifted it to find three bottles of expensive red wine. "This person knows me a little too well."

After removing everything from the boxes, including all the extra discoveries from the little hidden compartments, Dani had finally put everything away. As she sat down on the barstool munching on the semi-warm hog cracklings she found in the box, along with three different types of smoked boudin and mini sweet potato pies, Dani sat crossing out names of men who she thought could be capable of doing something like this. It definitely wasn't her ex-husband as he would never spend that much on flowers.

"No man I've ever dated would do something like that. Speaking of dating, I've only gone out on one real date, and that was with…aww, heck, nah!" Thinking back to her date with Dr. Jacob, she recalled telling him to leave her alone, declining his request to start over.

"Dang it," she said, feeling disappointed at the thought of him being her mystery man. Although she had to admit, she was impressed. "It doesn't matter," Dani said, feeling like that kind of normalcy was reserved for women that looked like Becca or the models at Sari.

"Nope, Jackson," she said, gently rubbing his head, "Real men, the ones that I like, don't see me in that way anymore. I gave Dr. Jacob nothing but good intentions, and I had to damn near cuss him out for him just to see me. He can send all the flowers and food in the world. Heck, he could ship a whole damn chef in a box."

"No way I'm ever getting into another relationship right now. I'm a writer. That's my focus." Jackson suddenly picked up his head from the floor and stared at her like he was calling her bluff?

"What? Why you looking at me like that? Some men choose their careers over women all the time. Trust me, they will sacrifice a ten, twenty-year relationship for a moment of weakness and insecurity. Nope, no more relationships, at least until I'm where I need to be."

Looking down at the hog cracklings, Dani realized why she gave them up many years ago. "You will never love me like I love you," she said to the bag, sealing it and placing it with the stack of goodies for Becca and Cammie.

As she dozed off to sleep, her stomach cramps finally subsided, and her body relaxed. After a few minutes, she was suddenly jarred awake by the sound of her phone. Dani quickly sat up as she noticed the caller ID, Dr. Steward, Gynecologist.

Eight

WE ALL HAVE TO SIT IN STINKY STUFF SOMETIMES

"I can't believe she just sat there and gave away the very idea that was supposed to put her on the map, didn't even fight for it, just like that," Gina said, snapping her fingers. "We flew all the way here for this nonsense. All I'm saying is that hopefully, she learns from this experience. She needs to fight for herself, cover her own ass."

"Exactly! I said the same thing," said Anna K. "Dani has had a sequence of things happen to her, crazy life-changing things. She needs to start being more mindful of her environment and protect herself."

"Agreed," Stephanie said, "and be more mindful of who she trusts. Ain't no way I would have let my employer make a fool of me. I would have got their asses all the way together!"

"Yes, indeed. When you're right, you're right," Cammie said. "So, how are you feeling, Gina?"

"I'm good, girl. I just need to get my butt back to New York. My head chef is killing it right now. We are booked solid for months. Ordinarily, I'd be happy with that, but ever since that food critic wrote that article, he's been getting other offers left and right. I can't afford to lose him right now. I'd have to go back into the kitchen, and I have too many ventures going on right now to do that."

"I hear ya, but you know when it's worth fighting for, right? You got your father's inheritance, more than enough to last you a lifetime. Pay the chef his worth," Cammie said as the ladies looked at her suspiciously. "I'm just saying, whatever it takes, right?"

"Right," Gina agreed with a crooked smile.

"You got this," Cammie said, touching Gina's shoulder for support. "Right before we flew down, you were having a tough time too. You okay now?"

"A tough time? Cammie, I was having a nightmare," Gina said, filling in the other ladies at the table. "I couldn't fit a single thing in my closet. My stomach swelled up like a hot air balloon. To make matters worse, I had investors waiting on me at the restaurant. And Anna K, before you say anything, please know that I have been sticking to my workout routine and nutrition plan, just as we discussed."

"I haven't said a word," Anna K replied.

"Maybe it was the stress of everything, I don't know. I think I'm finally realizing how my hormones can wreak havoc on every aspect of my life, not just my bald head. With the expansion of the restaurant and the online business, ya'll know I ain't got time for these hormonal intrusions. I made an appointment with my endocrinologist immediately," Gina said.

"Good for you," Cammie said. "I must say, I was a little concerned when I walked in on you eating an entire fudge cake all by yourself."

"I was not eating the entire cake by myself. You had some too! Besides, I'm a world-class chef, it's my job to taste my food."

"Agreed, but I had about four bites of cake, and it was delicious. When I went back to your place the next day to get a second slice, the fork and chocolate-covered platter were still sitting on the countertop in the same spot. So, I took a slice of the lemon cake that someone had already started on. Are you going to tell the hormone doctor that maybe the dinner cakes are keeping you from fitting into your pencil skirts?"

"Sure," Gina said with a smirky expression. "She is a doctor, and overeating is hormonal too. Not saying that I was overeating, but if I did, then it's still hormonal!"

"Agreed," Cammie said. "Listen, sometimes my hormones have me craving too much of a good thing too. I swore off beef and pork as a trigger point for my hormones long ago, but don't tempt me with a platter of rib tips from Chicago."

"Okay? After a long day at the office, sometimes I feel like a large pepperoni pizza from our old hangout. That's all the comfort I need," Stephanie said.

"Right? And don't forget about the chicken wings. Just one whiff and my vegan diet is done," Anna K said. "I think it's safe to say we get it," Cammie said. "We all have slip-ups more often than not Gina. And here I was thinking that it was Tim's pregnant mistress that tipped you off the healthy wagon. Didn't you find out about it that day? That may have something to do with the hormonal dinner cake behavior," Cammie said.

"Ooof," the ladies moaned, stirring in their seats as they all knew about Tim's extramarital affairs. Everyone who lived in the area knew, considering he was a prominent figure in the community.

"No worries and no need for embarrassment, sis," Cammie said. "We support you, right Stephanie?"

"Of course, we do," Stephanie said, reaching across the table to grab Gina's hand. "You know we're here for you. It's okay."

"We all have busy schedules, but as sisters, we make time for each other," Cammie said. "That includes making time to discuss the stinky stuff. Speaking of busy, Ms. Stephanie, have I told you how proud I am of you? Thee baddest real estate mogul to ever grace the East coast!"

"Well, what can I say, what can I say?" Stephanie said, popping her collar and smiling through her pearly whites.

"Girl, every time I see an investment opportunity, you already have your name on it," Cammie said. "I remember when we first met, you were a receptionist at your husband's law firm, working your way through college, building your empire. Needless to say, we are all happy for you and your founding success. From one sista to another, you are doing your thing."

"Thank you, Cammie girl," Stephanie said, dropping Gina's hand to toast her wine glass with the ladies.

"Thank God for prenups," Cammie said. "When Parker left you for that happy meal, you barely had enough money to cover the rent on the apartment he was leasing you. Without that settlement we won, you and all your degrees would have been starting from scratch. We all know you would have still made it to where you are today, but you definitely would have had to take the back roads. I took your case free of charge, remember that? Fresh out of school, everyone said I was out of my lane. Parker was too big to fail, too powerful to beat. We hired that private investigator and brought his ass down to size real quick. I got you half of everything and then some."

"Touché Cammie, point taken," Stephanie said, taking a long swig from her wine glass, as silence lingered in the air.

"Anna K, not to change the subject, but, girl, every time I see you, that body is banging better than before, Cammie said. As it should be when you are training all of the Hollywood elite and the athletes too. Hell, we tight, and I can't get an appointment with you till the end of next year."

"Nonsense, I always make time for my sisters," Anna K said. "And don't start with me today, Cammie. Whatever it is you teaching this morning, you can pass me by. I didn't take no handouts from anybody, and I'm not hiding any children born out of wedlock. I put in every ounce of sweat equity on my business and my figure, as you can see."

"You are absolutely right, Anna K, but it still doesn't hurt being engaged for the last seven years to a plastic surgeon, Cammie said.

"So, are you saying that a woman with two children can't have a body like this without going under the knife? Come on,

Cammie, you don't have to be a world-class trainer to know that's bull," Anna K said.

"That's not what I'm saying at all. We all know you handle your business. Even if a person does get a little tuck here and there, if it makes them happy, then good for them! All I'm saying is with the work you put in, girl, you earned your bragging rights."

"And Lawd knows she uses them," Gina muttered under her breath. "Don't look at me like that Anna! You're always bragging about your all-natural beauty over-forty stuff. You a whole lot to take in sometimes, sis."

"Wow, you women always seem to have a problem when other beautiful women do their own self-work," said Anna K. "I'm not gonna apologize for pulling my own self up from the hood straps and becoming my own boss. That's why I am who I am, and why I do what I do. I will never be a woman who doesn't practice what she preaches."

"Ladies, ladies, ladies! This is a friendly conversation, airing out the stinky stuff, calm down," Cammie said. "It's clearly obvious that every woman at this table gets her gym time in, so chill," Cammie said to the three ladies as they all shook their head in agreement. "It's just that I have yet to see a new nose and a full set of double boobies fresh off the weight room floor," she continued, looking to Anna K for a response.

"Might I add, your ass has always been flatter than your abs," Stephanie said. "No shade, but I was with you during labor and delivery and during the last few months of your last pregnancy.

You were on bed rest. Your ass went from pancake to a full peach the day after your maternity leave," said Stephanie.

"Nevertheless," Gina intervened, "do what makes you feel good, right ladies?"

"Exactly, and none of us should have to lie about who we are or down each other just to be friends," Stephanie said. At the end of the day, we all know how much your fiancé loves a nice body and a nice ass. And It don't matter who the ass is attached to either," Stephanie said.

As silence filled the table again, Anna K threw down her napkin and jumped up from her seat, "Ladies, it's been nice, but I have a plane to catch."

"Girl, sit yo' ass down," Cammie politely replied with a smile. "Now you all know me well enough, don't make me say it again."

Anna K glanced across the table at Stephanie and Gina as they looked away. She slowly slinked back into her seat, casually draining the leftover remnants of wine from her glass.

"That's always been a problem with our sisterhood. In the same breath that we use to lift a woman up, we can't even exhale without tearing that same woman down," Cammie said. "We call it support, keeping us accountable for the work we need to do on ourselves. If it's so good, then why do we wait until one of us is down to have that supportive conversation? If it's so good, then why ya'll so mad right now?"

"Correct me if I'm wrong, Cammie, but isn't that friendship? Still, being able to support each other while speaking the truth?

To be honest, I will never be another woman's *yes* woman," Gina said.

"Understood, and yet you are fine with being a *yes* woman to your man," Cammie said. When I walked in on you at your lowest point, I should have told you then that that your glutinous behavior may be symptoms of something bigger. Perhaps a philandering husband, but then, could that be just another symptom? Perhaps I should have given you legal counsel, again, and then I should have talked to you about doing your self-work, instead of letting this half-ass-man control your actions and how you feel about yourself, again. What is the second or third child with the mistress?"

"Well, maybe not so much truth at that time Cammie," Stephanie intervened, noticing the tears gathering in Gina's eyes.

"You're right Gina. As much as I can appreciate that level of straightforward communication from the people I love, it's not for everybody," Cammie said. "So instead of responding my way, I called a dress shop and had the perfect dress sent to you, and I had my driver take you to your meeting. While you were there, I tossed everything that could be baked, fried, or cooked into the trash. Although that was obviously a mistake, I filled your house with the best meal prep service in town, right? I'm just saying, there's a time and place for certain conversations. We don't kick each other while we're down. This is the reason many of our sisters in the Professional Bald Women's Network suffer alone in silence, hiding abusive relationships, with cheating narcissistic spouses, thinking they can fix it on their own. Too afraid of the judgment they will face from us, so they dwell, comfortably squatting in shit that, in some cases, is not even their own," Cammie said.

"I understand that we help each other, and kudos to you for looking out for Gina, but you didn't really help her," Stephanie said. "It sounds like you just enabled her and gave her a clean spot to keep shitting in."

"Exactly, Stephanie, just as I did for you," said Cammie. "If you choose to dwell in your shit, that's your choice. As your sister, I will help you clean it up, and I will try my best to be a shoulder for you so we can discuss why you are comfortably squatting in shit in the first place, at the appropriate time. I will also be there with you during those times when you need to peacefully sit with some shit until you get to the other side of what's for you," said Cammie.

"That's why you treated me to a spa weekend," Gina cried. "You guys know how much I love a spa, but this place was glorious. I talked about things I haven't thought about since I was a child."

"Hopefully, you called that lawn care service I was raving about," Cammie said, keeping their conversation about Gina seeking therapy confidential until, or if, she decided to tell them herself.

"I did," Gina smiled, now fully understanding Cammie's frustration with them. "Just because things, jobs, or relationships don't work out like we intend, that doesn't eliminate all the work we've done and all the effort we've put into building our legacy," said Gina.

"*That* is what we should hold onto," Cammie said, "especially in the midst of a shitty situation. Instead, we always start questioning ourselves when things don't go well. While some of that is healthy and we learn from it, there is a time and place for us to have those discussions with each other, to even get revenge if we choose, or maybe that's just me," said Cammie."

"My mother used to say that some things we face in life are not about us," Gina said. "I didn't meet my husband that way, I didn't knowingly marry a cheater, but I settled for one. Stephanie, I'm happy and sad to say that I'm also a part of the 'prenup' sisterhood. Cammie's firm is representing me in my divorce," Gina said as the tears spilled over.

"Oh, Gina, we got you girl," Stephanie said as they all held hands around the breakfast table.

"The accepted affairs, the overeating, it was all just a symptom of something else," Gina said.

"As sisters, we should be there for each other, only discussing that 'something else' at an appropriate time, when the other person can receive it," Stephanie said.

"I agree," said Gina. "I don't know how I would have responded if Cammie would have started talking about my stinky shit while I was trying to zip my olive-green skirt."

"The Prada green skirt? You can't fit it," Stephanie said?

"Today. I can't fit it today, but there's hope for the future. Right, Anna K?"

"What if they can't receive it?" asked Anna K, withdrawing her hand from Cammie's. "What if you try to have a conversation with one of us, about the stinky stuff at an appropriate time, and we still can't receive it?"

"Anna K, we're all sisters and we love each other. So were gonna continue to support one another, pray, and wait," Stephanie said. "Exactly, and when that person is ready for that conversation, then we'll have it," said Cammie, grabbing her hand. "We will support each other, doing whatever we can, disinfecting the shit out of the 'something else,' that's bothering us so it doesn't show up in another form, or in some type of illness," Gina said.

"I think I'm ready to join the 'prenup' club too, but I guess I don't fit in because I don't have one," Anna K cried. "We haven't been engaged for seven years, more like one year. We've been married for six. I'm sorry, I was just too embarrassed to tell anyone.

"You don't need a prenup. You got a Cammie," Gina said.

"Prenup ain't got shit on that," Stephanie said as all the ladies laughed except for Cammie.

"Anna K, I am here. Whenever you're ready, I got you," Cammie said.

"Me too," Stephanie joined in.

"None of us are one hundred percent self-made," said Gina. "We've all been through…stinky stuff, but we've all received a helping hand from someone at some point in our lives. I'd like to pick up where we left off before we were led into a much-needed self-check by our gorgeous sister Ms. Cammie. The truth is, I've never met a more compassionate person than Dani. She looks out for us like real sisters."

"Yes, indeed. She's always finding the bright side of a true asshole," Cammie said. "No pun intended."

"I can agree with that. That's one of the things we all love about her," Stephanie said.

"Okay, I am so glad that we all can agree," Cammie said. "You guys know that Dani and I go way back. So, if you can't support her when she's down, then you have to find yourselves another Cammie for your group."

"We didn't mean any harm by it," Gina said. "In all truth, it just looked like she was going to snap after that mess at Sari Unique. I want what she wants for herself so bad, and we all know that she's put in the work, three times over. Sometimes, I just get carried away with the whole judging situation, like I project onto her my stuff, and that's not cool."

"Agreed, but she needs our support, not judgment or projection, because no matter how much work we put into something, sometimes it takes nothing short of a miracle to get an idea off the ground," Cammie said. "At least some strong supportive ass sisters in your corner can help."

"Maybe we can put our heads together and think of something," Stephanie said.

"Yes," Gina said, "so she can see that she doesn't need to get a seat at anybody's table, not when she can make her own." "Now you're talking, sitting over there in that sweater dress looking snatched, Cammie said, as the ladies laughed in agreement and Gina stood up and struck a pose, showing off her physique. "Girl she ain't seen a morsel of food since you walked in on her eating that cake," said Anna K. "Exactly, look at how full her plate is now, girl gimme that biscuit," said Stephanie, swiping it from her plate. Cammie smiled as the ladies went back and forth.

CAMMIE LAWFTON

Knowing she had the power to cut people with words, Cammie picked up the breakfast tab for her friends at the ritzy restaurant downtown. While her communication was a work in progress, Cammie believed that harsh words were sometimes necessary to establish a real breakthrough when done at a proper time, of course. Her character assassination through words made her one of the most sought-after attorneys in her field.

Cammie was born and raised in the Bronx to a mixed black, Italian mother named Maria Lawfton, and a white father, Richard Lawfton. Her daddy was a prominent attorney who dabbled in politics and spent most of her formative years in DC, with his new family and kids. She didn't remember being around him as a child, and she had never seen a picture of him until much later in life.

One summer, while Cammie was in DC touring Georgetown University with her mother, she saw an attractive, seemingly wealthy white man talking to her mother. Judging by the limited-edition Bentley parked on the curve, this guy had to be somebody important. Smiling to herself, secretly hoping her mother would step away from the operating room and give this one a chance, she took a few steps toward them, trying to get close enough to read their lips.

Cammie's mother, Maria, always said she had no time for men. After opening her own medical practice for obstetrics, she spent most of her time with pregnant women delivering babies. Maria worked hard, which set the foundation for Cammie and her older brother, Bennie, to become successful in their fields. They never spoke of their father. While they never needed anything, Cammie always wondered what it would be like to have a father of her own. Her mother tried to ease the pain, gifting her with dresses, toys, and a pet rabbit, but when Cammie became angry, someone completely different took over.

It all started downhill when Cammie was twelve years old. Her brother, Bennie, fifteen at the time, often picked her up from ballet class two to three times a week on his way home from football practice. The nanny usually did it, but as Cammie got older, Bennie stepped in more and more, picking her up from ballet class, cheer practice, and school.

"Look at my son, enjoying the time with his little sister. Who needs a little brother when they have each other?" Maria always bragged to everyone who saw them together.

It was true, Cammie and Bennie were attached at the hip, never far from each other, but not for the reasons their mother assumed. They had sibling secrets, and both were committed to keeping them until that fateful day after ballet class when everything unraveled. As usual, Bennie arrived to collect Cammie on his way home from football practice, but today something felt different. On his way into the building, he passed a police officer and an EMT exiting the building. In his mind, he already knew it was Cammie. As he approached the door to the room, his heart raced in his chest.

"Bennie? Come with me," said Lauren, the ballet teacher.

"Where's my sister?"

"I called your mother several times and left messages."

"Where's my sister?" Bennie yelled frantically.

"There's been a terrible accident with one of the other girls. Our sweet little Stacy, she stepped out to use the office to call her Mum and apparently slipped and fell off the second-floor railing."

"What?"

"How the hell could you let something like that happen? Where is my sister?"

"Cammie-Liana is fine. She was in the bathroom at the time. Bennie, she is the one who found our dear Stacy lying in a pool of blood. She was rushed to the hospital in critical condition. Cammie was devastated, of course, screaming and crying, but she is much calmer now.

"Bennie," Cammie said as she ran to her brother and fell in his arms sobbing.

"Please, take her home and have your mother call me if she needs anything, anything at all."

Lifting Cammie into his arms, Bennie walked toward the door and was greeted by their mother Maria.

"Bennie, what's happening? What's going on? Cammie-Liana, what is it? Here, give her to me," she cried, reaching for Cammie.

"Mother! Mother, no, she's fine. Just let me get her home.

"Bennie, give her to me. Cammie, mommy's here, honey."

"Mother, stop! Please go and talk to Mrs. Lauren. You have to be the parent right now and talk to your daughter's dance instructor," Bennie said, glaring at his mother through dark, slanted eyes. "I'll take Cammie home."

Shocked into silence as she had never heard Bennie speak to her or anyone in that manner, Dr. Maria Lawfton gathered herself and walked into the building to speak with Mrs. Lauren.

After getting home and finishing her bubble bath, Cammie hurriedly slipped on her pajamas. Sniffing the familiar smell of fresh-baked chocolate chip cookies in the air, she raced downstairs, unprepared for what would take place once she got to the kitchen. As Bennie was taking the cookies from the oven, he was dropping them, one by one, into a sink filled with bleach and water.

"Stop it! Those are mine!"

"Make me," Bennie replied.

Reaching into the drawer and grabbing a knife, Cammie lunged at Benton. He quickly placed the pan on the counter and put Cammie in a headlock. With her arm trapped behind her head, Bennie removed the knife from her hand. Pushing her up against the wall, still in a locked position, he questioned her about the accident at ballet class.

"What happened? You think you're the only one that's crazy in this family? Tell me, or I'll break your arm, and you know I will!"

"Okay, okay! I did it! I pushed her. One day she saw me adjusting my wig in the bathroom, and she called me bald. She's been threatening to tell everyone at school that I wear a wig. She said I was the reason why Daddy left because he was too ashamed to have a daughter that looked like a boy. I begged her over and over again to take it back and to swear she wouldn't say anything, but she promised she would tell everyone in school. So, when I saw her leaning against the rail smoking, I snuck up behind her and pushed her over. She didn't see me, so it's okay. Bennie, no one saw me."

"How could you do that?" Maria said from the doorway, dropping her purse and her belongings to the floor as her body went limp against the wall. Cammie-Liana how could do that! Do you have any idea what you've done? While I was speaking to Mrs. Lauren, they received a call that Stacey had died. The cops believed her fall was either accidental or suicide. They were called out to Stacey's home several times this year, as she ran away often. Just last year she tried to kill herself after her parents' divorce." The room grew quiet, and no one said a word for a long time.

For the rest of the evening, they talked about the sudden disappearance of the rabbit, the newspaper boy who refused to come back, the slumber party that ended with a call to the fire department, and why Bennie's last girlfriend threatened him with a restraining order.

Bennie noticed Cammie's rage right after he found the bloody rabbit in the backyard. Experiencing bouts of anger himself, football and drawing had become an outlet for him, combined with therapy from his school counselor.

"Why didn't you tell me, Bennie?"

"Cammie, get upstairs now," Bennie said.

"I just wanna talk to mom," Cammie replied. Bennie looked sternly in Cammie's direction. Knowing what her brother was capable of, she quickly jumped to her feet and flew up the stairs faster than her legs could move. Once she was out of sight, the darkness of his gaze quickly turned toward his mother.

"Did you really want to know, Dr. Lawfton? You are a doctor, a mother, and an adult. I was eleven years old when I noticed my little sister had the same fits of rage as me and our father. Tucking him away does not erase the mark he left behind, mother."

"I understand you know more about your father than Cammie, but Bennie, are you aware of how serious this is? Cammie is a real danger to others as well as herself."

"Unlike some, she has a conscience, mother. She strikes only when someone is hurting her deeply and won't stop. Debate classes and self-defense training is her outlet, but of course, you want her to take ballet and cheer class."

"Bennie, she's a child. She needs structure. She needs to enjoy life, not some self-defense stuff that she will only use to hurt someone else."

"No, mother. Your dreams of a perfect little girl who attends a perfect school, as a perfect little ballet dancer, are over. Stacey is dead, and your daughter cares more about the cookies I dropped down the kitchen sink. Innocence and purity of heart are not what we have here. Cammie is perfect! She is a beautiful, bald little girl who is sensitive but hard— tough but passionate. She is slow to anger and quick to listen. If you don't nurture who she is instead of who you want her to be, then one day she will kill you in your sleep. Oh, I think the next batch of cookies are done," Bennie said, turning off the alarm on the kitchen stove. "Cammie-Liana, dessert is ready. But first, we'll have cheesy, gooey burgers," Bennie yelled from the kitchen as Cammie ran down the stairs, cheering with excitement.

The next day, Maria enrolled Cammie in karate classes, which led to boxing classes and sparring matches. She also joined the debate team and became the fiercest competitor in the state. After a few years, Cammie's hair grew back enough to keep it cut in a cute lil pixie hairdo. This pattern seemed to work well for Cammie until her mother began stressing her more about going to medical school. Her hair started to shed again during her senior year in high school. It seemed the more she stressed about her studies, the more her hair shed. After getting accepted into one of the best schools in the country that would surely prime her for medical school, Cammie gave a speech that her mother still talks about to this day.

"Thank you, everyone, for all the support you've given me over the years. I am happy to say that I have also been accepted to Georgetown University in DC. I have set aside a lucrative amount of money to fund additional expenses, outside of my scholarship funds for the next four years of my education. Before you speak, mother, I love you, but I cannot be a doctor because I am a lawyer." Cammie had no idea that her father was a prominent attorney with his own law firm in DC. It was true; her family always knew that she was her father's twin, in more ways than one, and no amount of medical school would change that.

Now, standing outside of Georgetown University, staring at her mother and the handsome, rich man, she couldn't help but feel drawn to his presence. He was physically fit and flawlessly tanned. He had a head full of dark brown hair with a perfect hairline, just like Bennie. Maria smiled a familiar smile when he touched her arm, not like the glares she gave the cute guys who came on to her at grocery stores or the gym.

As Cammie approached them, her heart started to race once she got a closer look at the stranger's face. When he smiled, she noticed he had the same small little gap between his perfect white teeth just like hers and the same ocean blue eyes as Bennie.

"Daddy?" she said as silent uncontrollable tears flooded her face.

Cammie's mother and father looked at each other as a smile of relief came over Cammie's face. But that smile was short-lived, and neither one noticed Cammie's expression disappear behind a dark, evil smirk. Before they knew it, Cammie had punched him in the face and broke his nose.

"Dammit, Cammie-Liana! I'm sorry, Richard. It's those damn boxing classes," Maria said as she grabbed some tissues from her purse and popped his nose back into place.

"It's okay," Cammie's father smiled, holding his nose to catch the trickles of blood while extending his hand out to keep his security detail away. "I love the aggression. We just have to teach her how to use it."

For the next eight years, Cammie and her brother, Bennie, grew close with their father and his other children. Having been divorced from his second wife for many years, they believed something was going on between their father and mother but neither cared to admit it. Cammie was a mixture of the gentle side of her mother with a double dose of ass-kicking from her father.

Last year, Cammie successfully defended a high-profile political figure. After a flawless victory, outside on the court steps, Cammie addressed the press, "People, please vote in your local elections, or else you will always have shitty representation like this man, good day." Her ability to defend and dislike you at the same time was something she was well known for, in addition to being a baldie badass.

Cammie removed her wig for good after suffering overwhelming humiliation her first time before a judge. In the process of taking hormonal treatments, hoping to grow her hair back, she suffered from waves of hot flashes, at least three at a time, back-to-back. While in court defending her client, she called for a recess which the judge denied. With no further option as the wig continued to slide around her head, she decided to remove it. The courtroom went silent, and everyone stared at her. "Hormone injections," she said. The judge recessed for the rest of the evening. The next day and every day going forward, Cammie rocked her baldhead proudly, refusing to sweat behind another hot flash or hormone treatment ever again.

TEST RESULTS OR BEING TESTED

"So, everything looks good?"

"Everything looks good," advised Dr. Smith. "Your endometrial biopsy came back fine. I spoke to your oncologist, and she's going to change the hormonal drugs you've been taking as your body becomes adapted to them after a certain amount of time. You looked surprised. Perhaps, we should do another biopsy," Dr. Smith laughed.

"That's not funny," Dani said, remembering when Dr. Smith suggested they schedule the endometrial biopsy. Dani hated the idea of doctors taking a piece of anything from that place, but even more so, she hated having to think about what it would feel like and anxiously waiting for the day to get it done. So, she stepped into the ladies' room, said a silent prayer, and convinced the doctor to do it now, holding her breath the entire time until it was over.

"So, call me if you have any other symptoms or issues, but everything looks good. Are we still good for the hysterectomy early summer?"

Dani nodded, acknowledging she had made the final decision that sealed her status as a single woman, Dani confidently replied, "Yes, yes, we are still good."

Leaving the doctor's office, Dani felt relieved. After breast cancer, little things would spring up like a quickened heartbeat, pain in her muscles, or irregular heavy menstrual bleeding, making her feel like something was happening to her body again.

"You have to stop running to the doctor every single time your body does something unfamiliar," Cammie said. "You're human, baby girl. Just live your life."

While she later found most of her issues were nothing to overreact about, Dani was always concerned when something new came about. The truth was perhaps she was overreacting by checking on every out-of-the ordinary glitch, but she would learn to adjust and manage. In the meantime, Dani didn't see any reason to stress or beat herself up about an unfamiliar pain when she could just go to the doctor. "That's what my health insurance is for, the doctor. I pay a heck of a lot for it, so I'm using it," Dani replied.

Feeling better, Dani decided to stop by the office on the way home. Hoping to avoid running into Sidnae, she took the elevator, walked, then ran to her office and quickly shut the door. "Ah, home sweet home." As frustrating as it was with the whole Sidnae thing, it felt good to be back in the office, in her creative zone. "Emails done and calls returned."

"Dani? Is that you? Hey, I thought you weren't feeling well?"

"What's up, Sidnae? I'm just checking in, and I'm fine."

"Hmmm, I don't know, you don't look it, but that's all about to change. Have you read my emails?"

Heck no, and I'm not, Dani thought to herself. "Not yet. What's up?"

"You, me, and Paris. Your flight leaves Monday, first class. I booked you a luxury five-star suite for the next few months. Give it to me!" Sidnae said, holding her hand up for a high five, but quickly realized Dani wasn't reciprocating. "You're in shock, right?"

"Paris? for how many months? I can't do that at the last minute. I have responsibilities here."

"Nope. Sari is your number one priority. It's all expenses paid, Dani, don't worry, I got it. I need you on point for this campaign, so go home. Next week, we'll be so busy, you will barely have time for sleep."

"Okay, why do you need me in Paris? You have the pieces I wrote. What more do you need?"

"You. I need you, Dani! It's something about your writing and how it fits the imagery, like a glove. Hell, it makes me wanna go out and buy whatever you're writing about, and I probably already own it."

As much as Dani hated to admit it, in this moment, it was true. When Dani had hair, she thought it was everything. A great hairstyle hid her PMS bloat, occasional acne, and up-all-night tired eyes. Put a nice pair of heels with a kick-ass haircut, and it didn't matter what you had on. But losing her hair gave her something like a sixth sense, so to speak. It made her feel naked. With nothing to hide the imperfections, Dani focused on how a pair of heels elongated her legs and the lengthened her thighs or how the glare from a simple pair of diamond stud earrings sparkled against the melanin of her skin. That's what made her pieces real because she wrote from her heart.

"We haven't decided on the designers yet, and I need you to add that something special, that thing you do. I mean, who better to get the perspective of a bald woman than a bald woman, right?"

"So, you want me to use my experiences to write how a fake, bald woman feels wearing these designs from the perspective of a real bald woman?"

"Isn't that why we hired you?"

"Nooo, not that I'm aware of, no."

"I get it, the whole integrity and honesty thing, I get it, but this is what we need now. Dani, I'd, like to share something personal with you," Sidnae said as she sat on the edge of Dani's desk, popping open a fresh jar of homemade glazed pecans. "My mama used to tell me all the time, mmm, my gosh, these are so good. Sorry, no, she said that God blesses everybody with a gift, you know like singers sing, and actors act. Believe it or not, I used to always wonder about my gift and why everybody always sees just the outside of me. You know the body, legs, and hair. Goodness knows I've never seen a gym a day in my life, and I eat like a pig," she chuckled.

Is that the glazed nuts my mama brought from home when she traveled all the way here from Louisiana, Dani wondered?

"I finally realized that our gift is our destiny. It's our calling card to change the whole damn world."

"I'm sorry, Sidnae, I'm not following."

"Listen, I have a gift I didn't ask for, and so do you. While sometimes our gifts can be a pain, we don't get to choose what they are, but we can use them to our advantage. My advice is let's just get this coin, touch a few hearts in the process, and keep the personal feelings at home. K?"

Dani stared at Sidnae, trying her best to take in what she had just said.

"Oops, that's me," Sidnae said, grabbing her cell phone. "Hello! Oh, hey. Gimme one sec. Dani, I gotta skedaddle. I'll see you in Paris on Wednesday. I'll be going back and forth, you know. I have to juggle with the kids and all. Oh, no, you don't know, that's right. Ugh, I'd be a wreck if I couldn't have kids, but again, it's a gift you didn't choose, right? Heck, it's destiny, girl. Okay, okay, okay, I gotta take this call. Catch you in Paris, baby," Sidnae said, closing the door behind her and taking Dani's glazed pecans.

Sitting at her desk, Dani desperately tried to block out the sound of Sidnae's voice down the hall. Her laugh, her conversation, her words, everything about her was insulting and arrogant. "I will never resort to violence, but a good old fashion ass whipping ain't never hurt nobody." *Who gon' pay your mortgage? Who gon' hire the angry black woman who lost her temper at work?* she thought to herself. *Inhale, exhale. Inhale, exhale. "Whewww!* "Nope, the breathing is not working today, and she ate my mama's gift to me, too. Sometimes you have to stand up for yourself, even if it means what it means," Dani said as she quickly walked from behind her desk and swung open her office door.

"Talia? What are you doing here? And why are you out of breath?"

"Dani, I'm so glad I caught you. We need to talk! I have news. Yuri is right behind me, bringing us some tea."

"I was just about to step out," Dani said, inching closer to the hallway.

"This won't take long, I promise. Shut the door, please."

Nine

JUST SHUT UP AND PRAY

The incessant buzzing of the doorbell and Jackson's barking woke Dani from a deep sleep. "Quiet, boy!" Dani said, attempting to calm Jackson down, but to no avail. "Jackson, please, it's one in the morning! Nobody knocks on my door at one in the morning. Jacks, shush and go lay down, now!" Jackson refused and continued to bark at the door. Someone was buzzing, and he was fixated, standing guard by the door. Dani grabbed her phone, and it instantly started buzzing. "WHAT?" she shrieked into the phone, sounding very irritated.

"Girl, get yo ass down here, and open this door!"

"Cammie? You know what time it is, right? Buzzing folk's doors this late at night," Dani mumbled.

When Dani opened the front door, she was shocked by Cammie's appearance. Cammie was always beautiful, but tonight she was glowing. Her slinky red dress and red bottom heels were popping against her caramel skin, but Dani was far too frustrated from lack of sleep to compliment her best friend.

"Well, good morning to you too, ole grouchy one. I have pastries," Cammie said, strolling past Dani and into the kitchen.

Washing and drying her hands, she pulled a baking dish from the shelf and gently placed six vegan donuts into the oven. She then proceeded to make coffee using her own coffee grounds. "Oh, I almost forgot, I have your lil weird orange milk from that food truck around the corner," she said, pouring the contents of the cup into a small pot to keep it warm. They even threw in your very own container of non-dairy whip cream to top it off."

As Cammie moved around the kitchen, Jackson and Dani quietly watched her go from coffee pot to stove, humming to herself like it was her kitchen, and they were visiting. "Cammie, what is hap-wait, Le'Rics? It's two in the morning, and Le'Rics is not open. Where did you get that orange drink? Please tell me what you're doing here," Dani said, half asleep.

"See? You look so tired. That's why you need to make some changes. Start by drinking some real coffee and not this walnut water you be playing around with."

"Almond milk," Dani replied, "and they make it fresh every day. What changes?'

"Whatever, and it's twenty minutes to six in MY morning, so I'm not sure why you still stuck on two a.m.," Cammie replied.

Dani looked at the kitchen clock and it was after five a.m. She looked at her phone and realized she had confused the last missed call at one am with the time. Cammie then went over to Jackson's bowl and filled it with his favorite morning breakfast and water, kicked off the baddest multi-colored stiletto heels Dani had ever seen, grabbed the pastries from the oven, and put two coffee cups on the counter.

"You're drinking coffee this morning," she said as she turned the stove off. "I need your mind fresh and ready for this conversation."

"Conversation? I'm just gonna visit the ladies' room while you busy yourself in my kitchen. Oh, and I don't care what time it is in *your* morning. If it's before daybreak, it's still too early to be talking," Dani said.

"Well, good morning, sis, from my morning to yours. I'm gonna take Jackson out real quick," Cammie said, shuffling her feet into a pair of Dani's flip flops and racing out the front door.

Once back inside, Jackson lay lounging in the corner as Dani sat on the deck, wondering what was so important that Cammie was there so early. As she waited for Cammie to finish changing her clothes and join her for whatever this was, Dani felt a ping of excitement in the pit of her stomach. Anytime Cammie appeared with an unexpected conversation, Dani was always left speechless, with her mouth hanging open. Dani thought about the time Cammie sent Becca and her a text message to meet her at The Four Seasons. *Once we got there, this heifer told us she had a full hysterectomy,* Dani recalled. *And a few months before that, she had her breast enhanced. Oh goodness, that time she showed up on my doorstep at 3:00 a.m., deciding now was the time to take over her father's law practice, which she successfully accomplished.* "What has she done now?" Dani mumbled to herself. "Why am I sitting here tired and lazy on this rainy morning? I could be lounging in bed. Why is Jackson in the corner passed out, and why, *why* is Cammie still in the bathroom?" Dani exclaimed loud enough for Cammie to hear.

"Cammie!" Dani yelled, just as the doorbell chimed. "What? Is this a family reunion? It's open, Bec," said Dani. "I think I may have some coffee this morning. These women are on my last nerve," Dani fussed. "It's like they don't understand people need sleep. Everybody is not a daggone CEO!"

Dani rolled her eyes when the doorbell chimed again. "It's open, Bec! Hold on," Dani said, barely opening the door, and then realizing it wasn't Becca.

"Hi, I have a delivery for Dani Breaux."

"This early? You can just sit it outside. I'll get it."

"I'm sorry, I wouldn't be able to do that. I can slide my credentials under the door if you like."

Oh snap! It's Mr. XOXO, Dani thought, glancing at herself in the hall mirror as if her secret admirer was watching her from the doorway. "Just a second," Dani said, bracing herself for another surprise when she suddenly felt the door open wide as she was hurriedly pushed to the side by Cammie, who stood at least six feet, just a bit taller than Dani.

"How can I help you?" Cammie asked the stranger in a stern yet calm tone.

"Of course. I have a breakfast delivery for Ms. Breaux."

"Breakfast for Ms. Breaux? Perfect, come on in."

"Cammie? You don't just let strangers in like that," Dani mumbled. "It appears that I have a secret admirer, and he could be crazy."

"Hmph, secret gifts. I like it. I thought the vanity area in your bathroom was looking a little expensive."

"This is courtesy of Chef D, yours truly. Where can I set up?"

"You can just leave it out there," Dani replied, uneasy about letting someone she didn't know named Chef D into her home.

"Nope, you can just follow me right this way," Cammie said, leading him to the deck.

While they were outside, Dani quickly grabbed the phone and listened to her voice mail. There were five from Sidnae, all regarding the trip to Paris. Realizing that it wasn't a good idea to pair Dani and Sidnae alone together, Talia insisted Dani work on the project from home while remotely communicating with Sidnae. To sweeten the deal, she threw in a promotion and a raise.

"Dani, congratulations! Talia emailed me the changes to the schedule. I'm not gonna say I told you so, but, oh what the hell. I TOLD you this project would pay off in a big way! You have to trust me on these things. Anyway, listen, email me the bios so the girls can rehearse their parts. We don't need them drawing a blank face on media day. Also, I need daily detailed writeups regarding every image I send. The words should stand alone. They must express the humility of a bald woman, her boldness, and the way she owns her image. Oh, and try to see if you can get some additional stories from those bald ladies that came to the event, something juicy we can tie in."

"Ugh," Dani screeched, pressing delete on all five of Sidnae's messages. "Every time I hear her voice, I just wanna punch her in the face." The next several messages were from the ladies in the Bald Professional Women's Network congratulating her and offering to share their stories. As Dani listened, she thought about how to tell them that Sari only wanted to use their stories for their own benefit.

"Ms. Breaux, thank you for allowing me into your home," Chef D said, handing Dani a letter from Mr. XOXO. "I hope you enjoy it. If you need anything else, please, don't hesitate," he said, handing Dani his card and walking towards the door.

"Hey, Chef D, are you gonna tell me who sent you? I mean, I did invite you into my home. This secret admirer may be crazy for all I know," said Dani.

"I'm sorry, Ms. Breaux, I am sworn to secrecy. If it's any consolation, I know this gentleman personally, and while I have never known him to do things like this, he could never be a danger to you. Also, if you don't mind my saying so, I can see why he would go through all this trouble. My uh, my mother had cancer. It was very difficult for her to go through that alone. Years later, both my sisters had the same sickness at the same time. The fact that you and Ms. Cammie have each other to lean on right now is a blessing."

"Come again, D? I'm a bit lost on what led you to that conclusion," Cammie said.

Usually, Dani was a voice of support for the occasional random stranger who was bold enough to assume Cammie's bald head was cancer-related or that it was the reason behind her baldness, as well. After the humiliation she felt at Sari, she didn't feel like coming to anyone's rescue. Curious to hear his response,

Dani stared, waiting for him to speak while frustratingly preparing to stand up to Cammie in his defense.

"I…I was just commenting on your bravery. No offense," he said, holding up his hands in surrender.

"Chef D? Is that you? Looks like I'm just in time," Becca said, confused as to why he was standing in her friend's doorway?

"Pleasure to meet you, ma'am. Good day ladies," he said, eager to shut the door.

"Hey Chef, I'm sorry to hear about your family," Dani said. "Thank you for coming."

"My pleasure, Ms. Breaux," he replied.

"Next time, try reading a book before jumping to conclusions Chef D," Cammie said. "A science book, a medical journal, whatever floats your boat. It's all fundamental," she said, slamming the door behind him.

"Becca, welcome. I brought pastries, but clearly, Chef D had other things in mind," Cammie said, ushering Becca to the spread on the deck.

Dani was surprised by the display of food. Fresh cut mangoes—her favorite fruit, shrimp and grits, corn fritters, cinnamon rolls, and coffee. "This is so sweet," Dani said, sneaking off to a corner to read the letter.

Good morning, Princess,

Last week I had the most amazing shrimp, grits, and stuffed corn fritters cakes. The only thing missing from my perfect evening was you. As a foodie, I wanted to share my experience. I am a hundred percent sure Chef D did not disappoint. Please enjoy.

Oh, and one other thing, the thought of you keeps a constant smile on my face.

Sincerely, XOXO.

"I really needed this kind of feeling today," Dani said as the early sun showered her face, soothing her mood.

"Well, I don't know what's going on, but I'm damn sure about to eat," said Becca.

"So, now that we are settled in with no further distractions, we need to talk," said Cammie.

"Sorry to interrupt, but honey, this red dress is divine," Becca said.

"Oh, this old thing," Cammie smiled as they went back and forth about the style and cut of the dress.

With so many questions and no answers floating around in her mind, Dani was beyond frustrated. *Why is Becca here? Why were they both here? Why did Mr. XOXO send a chef so early in the morning? What made him think I would want a strange man in MY house before six a.m.?* Dani took a big bite of the warm cinnamon roll, followed by a sip of hot coffee. "Mmmm, this is good," she said, scooting down in her chair, intentionally ignoring her friends.

Cammie and Becca soon joined in, and the sounds of chewing food and slurping on hot coffee filled the atmosphere.

"So, all I know is both of us are going to be your maid of honor," Dani said, smacking on a crunchy corn fritter.

"You are so nosey, and this conversation is not about me," Cammie said.

"Oh my gosh! Would you look at the size of that thing? Oh, honey, he did good! He did reeeally good," Becca said.

"Suri, play Sunday Morning," Dani said as she and Becca danced around the deck, singing into their utensils, pretending they were microphones. One summer, five of their mutual acquaintances were married, and this song played at every one of their weddings. Just as Dani was about to go into the bridge, Cammie turned the music off.

"Enough! While I live for your joy, this is not that conversation. However, I'm just gonna say this one time so we can move on. Good enough?" she asked, looking to Dani and Becca for agreement. "I said, good enough?"

"Good enough," they replied in unison.

"You already know who he is, and yes, he proposed while we were in Italy. We flew back early because, as you know, the NBA season is starting soon. So, that's that," Cammie said as she sipped her coffee and hummed Sunday Morning to herself.

Becca and Dani looked at each other, waiting for the other to ask the follow-up question.

"No," Cammie said abruptly. "I haven't responded yet. Don't look surprised. You know how I feel about marriage, and not even his fine ass will change that. First, you tie the knot, and it's marital bliss, everybody's in love. Then, suddenly out of nowhere, you end up in front of Judge Judy, fighting over assets and money. No, ma'am, that's not for me," Cammie said, shaking her head.

"Oh, honey," Becca said with a somber expression, "you do know Judge Judy won't be handling your divorce, right?"

"Yes, and *that* Becca is one of the reasons why I said no, AND the fact that his mother hates me. But that's a story for another time."

"Yes, Cammie, we know about your fascination with courtroom drama's and how they inspire you to do your job while telling your clients to go straight to hell," Dani said.

"Only if they truly need to, Dani," Cammie replied. "The real hard truth is what people need to hear sometimes rather than some 'yes, ma'am, no ma'am," and 'whatever you need' type of nonsense. That's why folks are so spoiled because businesses are too busy competing for 'likes' instead of just being real," Cammie said. "I'm sorry that you couldn't pay your bill on time, Mr. Customer. I know that must be difficult," Cammie said, pretending to speak to an imaginary customer. "Hell, nah! How about, 'Hey, Mr. Customer, I'm sorry that you didn't even have the *respect* to call and advise my organization that took a chance on your trifling ass that you were going to be late paying on the car, the house, or the credit cards provided to you. Oh, what was that Mr. Customer? You said I owe you a break for never being late? Didn't I just give you a break last month, Mr. Customer? No sir! I don't owe you nothing! Pay the bill, Ricky boy, or I'm coming to collect my shit!'" Cammie said. "How's that? We need to be honest with folks in this country ladies. That's all I'm saying."

As much as Dani wanted to argue that Cammie's commitment issues were not about business, judges, or anyone else, Dani understood her fear. "It's not like Harris is a replica of E.J.," Dani said, referring to an old flame from Cammie's past.

"Hmph. Same height, both good looking," Becca replied. "They have a few similarities."

"I'm not sure why we're comparing men. E.J. was just a season, and Harris brushes his teeth daily," Cammie said.

"Of course, he does, honey, and I'm sure his breath smells minty fresh," Becca said as they laughed, recalling the stinky mouth story Cammie shared with them.

For months, all they heard was E.J this and E.J that. They knew Cammie was head over heels crazy about her newfound attraction for the wealthy investment banker—until one Saturday evening, Cammie showed up at Becca's drunk and in tears. Once they covered all the formalities, Cammie shared with them one of the most embarrassing moments of her life. On occasion, when Cammie flew into L.A, she often picked up E.J from the office gym, so she was used to the smell of sweaty armpits and protein shakes. He had a great body, so she didn't mind sacrificing her nostrils for a few hours.

"We decided to meet up at a sports bar, which was great. It gave us both time to shower and change into something a little more comfortable. Except when E.J got there, he still had on the clothes he wore during the layover at the airport, which was the same clothes he wore the day before when he pulled an all-nighter at the office. After we ate, he jumped into my car, and we rode back to his house. The smell, it was different this time.

During the ride, I assumed he bought a to-go box of wings or something. My car was filled with the stench of butt, just smelling like hot tar and toilet sewage. Anyway, we got into a small disagreement. When he tried to make up and kiss me on my cheek, I got a whiff of his breath. Now, I've smelled stinky breath before, but this was something that was abnormal. And he was comfortable with it. I don't understand, he has the most beautiful teeth money could buy. Anyway, I told him he needed a shower or at least some mouthwash. Long story short, he said if he is fine with me being bald, then I should be fine with him not brushing his teeth every single day."

"So, you have to be okay with smelling some stank breath because you're bald? You should be ever so grateful," Dani said.

"What happened next?" Becca asked.

"Let's just say he won't have to worry about brushing his teeth for a while."

Thinking back to that conversation and what she now knows about Cammie's temper, Dani suddenly understood what Cammie meant by that statement.

"E.J? He also shaved his head bald in solidarity for you," Becca said. "Dani, remember when he showed up at the Christmas party in all that black leather looking like an R&B rock star?"

"Yes, I remember, but I don't think that was E.J. he was already bald," Dani said.

"Yes, yes, yes, you're right," said Becca. "It was Andrew, whose hairline was already touching the back of his neck way before he met Cammie. He tried to pull that solidarity nonsense, knowing doggone well if it wasn't for Cammie being bald and bold, his hair would still be looking like the parting of the Red Sea," Becca laughed.

"Are ya'll done reminiscing? Again, this conversation is not about me," Cammie said, pulling out her phone. "Dani, I need you to confirm your airline ticket for Spain. I have a glorious week planned with some of the ladies from our Professional Bald Women's Network. Before you think you can say no, please hear me out," Cammie said. "You must learn to celebrate your successes in life. The world will give you enough crap to deal with. Why not celebrate the victories? I know I'm not the most holy person around, but even I can see that God has blessed you with so much. Just a few years ago, this crazy evil thing tried to take you away from us. It attacked your body, your family, and your life. It saw something in you, and it tried to destroy you…but God. While I see you attempting to go after your purpose, I'm afraid your fears are causing you not to experience your full potential and creativity. Baby girl, you were built to create, to tell your story. All of us have come through so much, and I will not let either of you miss out on what you are destined to do," Cammie said. "Before you speak, please know that I understand the responsibilities of work. You can bring your laptop, and you can get two hours a day to handle your business."

"Alright, well, this is very CEO-ish of you and very unexpected, considering I have an employer to report to daily. I may need some time to think it over," Dani said.

"On to the next order of business," Cammie said as she confirmed Dani's flight. "You can just pay me back," she said.

"What about Becca?" Dani said.

"Oh honey, my seat is already booked," Becca replied.

Cammie reached into her bag and pulled out a bottle of Macallan 30 and three shot glasses. "Now, I know ya'll don't drink this, but this next topic is a bit of a conversation that will only last up to eight minutes, ten at the most, 'cause I'm running late for an appointment. After I'm done, you each get two minutes to respond, and then we drink to the moment and leave it. Sit in it, go on with our day and let it marinate for a future date," Cammie said. "Both of you ladies are some of the baddest women I know. Nope, sorry, I don't have enough time to butter ya'll up for this part. I have to get right to the point. I want you guys in New York. Dani, I don't need to go over the opportunities you would have in New York; I just covered that. Becca, I know your business is here in D.C, and it's also overseas. Expand it to New York, where the love of your entire life lives, breathes, and waits on you twenty-four hours a day using planes, trains, and automobiles, literally. You are fortunate to have a soul mate. Some people spend a lifetime looking for that, and you're hiding him. It's been years! Stop wasting time."

"What man are you referring to Cammie? Sounds like you're in my business, and you have no idea what you're talking about," said Becca. "Girl, stop! We're in our forties. No one has time for hide-and-go seek boyfriends," said Cammie.

"Becca, it's true. We both know you're in love with Javi. There's nothing wrong with that. He's a wonderful man. He made some mistakes, but nobody's perfect," said Dani.

"Look," Becca interrupted, 'I love you both, but D.C is my home. This has nothing to do with Javi. My business is here."

"Let me stop you right there," Cammie said. "I love you too, but you are comfortably stagnant. I see what you're working with, and I hear your dreams, but I don't see any movement. Am I wrong?"

They both knew she was right. Dani was at a stand-still, unsure of her future but afraid to take a risk. While Becca's business was steady, she yearned to take it a step further, and New York had always been her primary focus since she was a little girl. She also wanted to see Javi more than just a few times a month. She just wasn't sure she was capable of committing to that extreme. Besides, she knew deep down inside that Javi wasn't going anywhere. They just had some kinks to work out.

"We can go over all the details and concerns when we reconvene back here exactly two weeks from today." Cammie stood up and finished her drink in one gulp. "My town car is downstairs. Ladies, none of this talk on our girls' trip, please. Oh, and before I forget, when we get back, we need to discuss what the heck Chef D was doing here in the first place and why Dani got all that damn creole food in her freezer. Oh, and Becca, your greedy self barely touched that pastry. You must've "Javi-ed" yourself a good night last night, huh? HA! I crack myself up," Cammie laughed. "I love ya'll, but please do not contact me with insecure conversations about what you think you can't do. Just shut up and pray. Deuces."

After Cammie left, Becca and Dani sat in silence for over a minute before they burst into laughter. "She think she running everything," Dani said.

"It's our fault. We raised her this way," Becca laughed. Once the noise died down, they sat together quietly on the deck, sipping McCallan 30, refusing to discuss the conversation as promised.

While Becca was deep in a trance, Dani thought about her life in DC. *I finally have my own home, a nice retirement account, and I've made a life for myself here, independence. I don't know what's gonna happen at Sari, but at least I have a job with a possible future. I think. Or maybe not? Shoot, who the heck am I fooling. I'm never gonna accomplish my goals with this company. Maybe Cammie's right. Maybe I am stagnant, afraid to stay, and too afraid to go,* she thought. Trying her best to shield her thoughts and remain positive, Dani gave Becca a half-smile.

Becca was too deep in thought to notice Dani's supportive gesture. She had become a designer because she wanted to create different things outside of the traditional concept. She prided herself on giving other designers that no one wanted to work with a fair chance. She had a platform bigger than life but spent much of her time hiring people to find models that fit society's expectations of what a woman or man should look like. *My gosh, Dani is so beautiful, and she's just as gorgeous on the inside, so different from what the world expects. I've been a horrible friend to this woman,* Becca thought. *Back when I first started, I would have given my right arm to have someone like Dani wear my work. Goodness knows this woman has the power to light up a room, let alone the world; she just doesn't know it. I don't know why I love New York so much, and with Javi being there too? Everything just fits. Maybe Cammie's right.*

After Becca went home and the bottle of Macallan 30 had reached its halfway mark, Dani lay on the deck, dozing in and out of consciousness. Like everything else in her life, when Dani faced a decision, she prayed. This time was no different. After she prayed, she couldn't help but imagine what it would be like, what it would feel like to live in New York. She could hardly contain her excitement as she talked out loud to God like he was relaxing on the recliner chair next to hers.

Ten

SHOW US HOW YOU LIVE IT

"That's it! Snapping out of her Macallan 30 buzz, she raced from the deck to the storage closet, emptying boxes until she found her video camera. "It's been a minute since I used this thing. Okay, Jackson, look at mommy? That's perfect. Okay, go, go, get the ball, get the ball." Always ready, Jackson sprang into action, grabbed the ball, and moved it around with his nose. "Perfect! I think we're ready," Dani said, feeling confident after setting up the video camera on the tripod. Before pressing play, she quickly washed up, and just as she was about to put on full lashes and makeup, she stopped. "Real Dani, not made-up Dani. Just be yourself," she repeated over and over in the bathroom mirror. Settling for clear lip gloss, a small amount of eyeliner over her naked eyes, face moisturizer, and a pair of tiny diamond stud earrings, Dani felt camera ready. Barefoot in a pair of black jeans and a V-neck t-shirt, she pressed record. "God give me the words."

What's up, world! My name is Dani. I'm forty-three years old, and I write for one of the biggest fashion companies in the world. Since becoming a professional writer, I've had the opportunity to represent the heart and soul of many different communities, giving people a voice and a platform to speak their truth. Today, I decided to represent my community of people living with alopecia. Alopecia is an autoimmune disease that can be caused by a number of different things. Doctors don't really have an underlying factor or cure. But this is not about a lesson on alopecia. This is about embracing our uniqueness and acknowledging that our differences are what makes us normal. We are surrounded by people who are unable to grow any type of body hair, including eyebrows, and eyelashes. They feel compelled to cover themselves, because they're afraid of being bullied or falling short of society's expectation of what looks and feels normal.

"This makes me question some of the brands, including my employer, who caters to what is considered normalcy instead of reality. I've met many children and women, myself included, who are bullied and talked about for something that is not within their control, feeling forced to hide behind wigs and products just to fit in. While a wig may feel good and somewhat normal for many of us, once removed, we are right back where we started. Now many of you out there have already accepted the reality of who you are, and I commend you on your authenticity. However, some of us are still struggling every day.

So, what can we do to change it, to help? First and foremost, we have to love ourselves just as we are, because we are all gorgeous! Have you seen yourself today? You are beautiful! Own it! I encourage you to take a good look at yourself and appreciate that one thing about you that you admire the most. Maybe it's your smile, your eyes, your shoulders, your mind, your bald head.

Whatever it is, celebrate that feeling of gratitude and who you are destined to become. We have to love ourselves first, right? Second, let's challenge big industry with the same message. What can they do to reshape the stereotype of what's considered normal? And let's be clear, we're not looking to celebrate a person's differences for a day or a month. Why? Because it's our daily lives. It's also some of your children's daily lives in a world where social media is front and center every second of every day. How many times have you checked your thread today? If you're watching this video, then you may wanna add this to your count.

We see all types of messages. I don't know about you ladies, but when I see bald women breaking glass ceilings as professionals, and when I see them featured in movies, ads, commercials, and billboards, I feel overwhelmingly proud to be a bald woman. Shout out to the bald sisters who represented in Black Panther, by the way, one of my favorite films. I just wish we could see representations of us more often.

What if there were just as many fashion ads, movies, and superhero roles for all kinds of people, regardless of their differences? And before anyone says it's already out there, of course, it is, but maybe I'm greedy. I want to see it so much that it becomes the norm. I don't know about you, but sometimes when my friend and I walk down the street, it's only one of us that gets asked about cancer or treatment options. How many people stopped to pray over you this week, praying that your hair comes back so you can look normal? Or the hard stares, my gosh, the stares. What about the ones that just walk up and rub your bald head like it's a statue? While it can be embarrassing for many of us, it can also be a teachable moment to help others understand that we exist, and we are not some alien being. We are not all sick and trying to pray our hair back into existence. For some of us, this is how we were born. Despite what you think you see, we are healthy and beautiful, just as God intended.

Now, for those of us who like to wear makeup and can appreciate a beat face every now and then, how many name brand waterproof eyeliners and brow pencils, powders, and pomades have you had to throw away because they sweated off your hairless face before you even left the house or because the 'all natural' ingredients littered your skin with bumps and rashes, Dani said raising her hand. If I'm the only one with my hand in the air, then so be it. This is my video! Make your own, no shade. We have to make room for other people's experiences, right?

Okay, back to me. I was doing research on a beauty piece a while back, and a very popular on-screen male co-worker, that shall remain nameless, thanked me for my work. Then, he began adding his own comments. He suggested that women are too lazy when it comes to getting the right kinds of makeup and products for their skin, advising that the beauty industry has a product fit for everyone. He said, and I quote, 'It's ridiculous for a grown woman to wear the wrong brand of makeup or have a pimply, blemished face. There is no sufficient reason for this type of error. I refuse to deal with a woman who cannot properly care for her own skin.'

With all due respect to his point of view, for many of us, the error is not due to a lack of effort. Let me show you something,

Dani said as she popped open a makeup box. Here we have thousands of dollars spent on facial products, makeup, soaps, oils, and some are dermatologists recommended. While I tested a few of these for marketing purposes, most of the items you see here were purchased with my money for my own personal use. Unfortunately, they didn't work for me, but that's okay. This is not a one size fits all type of situation, and it certainly doesn't mean that I or any other adult who has done the same thing is lazy. For many of us, our concern is not just about oily, dry, or combination skin. I'll tell you this, after losing my hair, I felt like I had to become a professional artist just to draw a set of even eyebrows on my face every day. Then, most times they came off before I could leave the house. That was all before I finally had my eyebrows micro bladed.

Don't even get me started on my gym look or trying to master a lace front wig for work. Hats off to the folks out there that can make a daily look appear like you woke up that way. Much respect to you. Especially when you are starting with a completely bald platform every day. I had no idea what I was doing. My eyebrows didn't come off just because the products in this box didn't work. It's because they just didn't work for me, regardless of the expense or the labels. Maybe it was the hot flashes throughout the day from the hormonal treatments, who knows, but it wasn't working for me. It took me some time to find myself, and later on, to find the products that actually did.

Now, this is just an example about my daily drama, but what's your story? How many missed job opportunities and relationships have you had because people refused to acknowledge what they didn't understand, or perhaps you were too afraid to challenge their perspective with your own personal experience? Studies show that there are millions of bald women out there. My question is, 'Where are you?' How are you doing with all of this? How do you make it all come together and work for you? What's your daily like? If you're having trouble, what can I do to help? We can challenge perspectives, we can ask questions, we can make our own lanes, but first, we have to show up. We have to come out of the shadows.

So, I challenge you brand companies, designers, and fashion moguls. And I'm not talking about just using someone else's story to fit your own narrative so you can sell more products and defeat your competitor. If you wanna do that, fine, do you. I'm talking about working and collaborating with real people and really living by the mission statement and values that you set forth. Acknowledging the successful and talented people who have exceeded expectations in their field despite their daily personal challenges. Use them for your billboards, ads, and movies so that our children can see more than a once-in-a-lifetime opportunity. If Becca, with the long hair, can be a supermodel, actress, lawyer, doctor, performer, writer, journalist, show-stopping stunner, so can Megan with the bald head. All day, every day.

Maybe someone will step up, or maybe not. Maybe you guys will watch this, or maybe you won't. But one thing is for sure, I will never stop writing your stories, speaking your truths, and empowering our community. Who knows, I may see you in your city, or maybe even on your job to do a feature on you. Until then, my beautiful bald people, grab your camera and introduce yourself. Tell us who you are, share your experience. Show us how you live it!

"That's a wrap, Jackson! Oh my gosh, that felt so good! Okay, don't think about it! Don't think about it! If I think about it too much, I won't share it. Just share it, Dani, share it. Here goes nothing, she said," and posted to her social media.

Silencing her phone, Dani took advantage of the sun and walked to the park, where she was greeted by the neighborhood children. Knowing how much they loved playing with Jackson, she gave them some space to run around the park and wear each other out. After working up a good sweat, Dani and Jackson walked the downtown area stopping for fruit and cucumber cups before making their way back home.

Dani made a mental note to start shopping her resume around New York, knowing Sari would never support her social media message or stop using her life as their own. "New York? Where would I even start?" Tempted to glance at her phone to check for messages, Dani busied herself with making dinner, feeding and bathing Jackson, and taking a shower.

"Enough! Just do the obvious thing and check your ph—." Before Dani could finish speaking, her cell phone blared. "That has to be Talia," she said aloud. "Shit, I done lost my damn job on my day off. This is Dani. Hello?"

"You know, dear, if you're going to question the masses, it may be a good idea to prepare a proper response."

"Who is this?" Dani asked.

"Pardon me? Surely my ex-husband's minions have taught you better. Honestly, you're a writer, dear. Show some respect."

"Naomi? I mean, Mrs. Winston?"

"That's better. So, why me? Why would your little public tantrum interest me? I mean sure, my heart goes out to all the little boys and girls who are different, but why should I use my company and my products to create a lane just for you? I'm making more money by simply ignoring this issue, just like everyone else."

"Okay, I get it."

"You get it? Very well. Then, we're done here. Goodbye, Dani."

"Wait! Please!" Dani called out. "Let me explain. Your lotion? It's like cashmere and silk wrapped around your body. This product is unrelenting, it saturates my skin to the very core. You also created your masterpiece in the kitchen using real ingredients that by themselves seem simple enough. But together—together, they are life-changing."

"I'm listening," said Naomi.

"The first couple of years after the breast cancer treatments and surgeries, my bones ached, and my skin was painfully sensitive. When the seasons changed, I felt it in the tips of my fingers and toes and my surgical scars. Sometimes it affects my normal exercise routine, even writing. Doctors say it gets better with time, but they don't tell you how much time because they don't know. In the winter months, when fabrics brush up against my skin, it feels like bristles. I've tried hundreds of lotions, body butters, dermatologists-tested prescriptions, but nothing lasts, nothing works."

"My first experience with your product, was a fifty-dollar tablespoon sample of your Signature Body Butter. Just a slight dab of cream on the wrist and I immediately felt the tingly sensation coursing through my fingertips as I rubbed and massaged. Like the sleeve of a thick cashmere sweater, my arm felt warm and relaxed while the rest of my skin was still brittle and cold. In a situation like that, one would assume any relief is better than nothing. But most times, the coverups are worse than the underlying issue itself, often leaving patches of blotchy welts and itchy rash."

"The Signature Body Butter is nothing short of amazing. The fragrance engulfs your senses while the cream nourishes your skin from the inside out. However, as much as I love the quality of this cream, it's not affordable for the everyday woman that you boast about. That woman that you pride yourself after who created this product in her kitchen."

"It's called scaling dear," Naomi said. "It's business. I meet the demand of the consumer, my audience. If you want the best, you have to be willing to pay the cost. You won't find my products in some grocery store chain or some mall outlet."

"You sold them for fifty dollars a jar back then, but five hundred now? I understand the scaling perspective, but when you created it, it wasn't just about making money; you had money. It meant something else to you back then. What was it?"

"Enough! I've heard enough. I'm in, but I have one condition—You. I want your voice, your face, your writing, everything with this deal," Naomi declared. "If we join together on this little project of yours, we will push the competition right into the palm of our hands, making ourselves quite the stack of money, while giving you people your little lane."

"Yeah, but money is not the primary concern," said Dani.

"Rubbish. Money is always the central focus. I assure you I can top anything my ex-husband is paying you."

What? No, this can't be real. She can't be for real, Dani wondered, as her thoughts smothered Naomi's voice. *Pray. I need to pray. Can she see my face? She can't see my face; she can't see me. I need to get on my knees,* Dani thought as she knelt down. *"God, guide my steps, be a light into my path, in Jesus' name, in Jesus' name. Is this the right thing for me? Am I making the right choice, Lord? My hands are so sweaty. I'm gonna have to postpone the trip to Spain. Cammie will understand. No, she won't.* Reaching for the Macallan 30, then, quickly deciding against it, Dani took silent deep breaths.

"Dani? Are you there?" Naomi called out. "Did you hear me? You say that you want to celebrate your differences but yet you want to be seen as normal. What's more important to you, dear? Do you want to be different, or do you want to be normal?"

"Yes, I'm here, sorry. Different or normal? I'm already both. They're one and the same."

"So bald women like yourself want to be included, but they also secretly want their own category, like plus-sized women, same but different. Tell me, what are the sensitivities besides the eyeliners, skin, and the lashes fiasco?"

"Of course, I—"

"Hey, hey, hey!" Cammie said, bursting through Dani's door, completely out of breath. "Naomi, we should talk about this a little more in detail, face to face. With Dani employed and currently under contract at Sari, we wouldn't want a conflict of interest. I'm sure you understand that. Anything she agrees to with you right now will be null and void, and she could be sued or terminated. None of us want that, right? Of course, we don't," Cammie declared before either had a chance to reply. "While the copyrighted video Dani shared has some great ideas, we should discuss your offer from a business perspective first Naomi, don't you agree?" Cammie asked.

"Copyrighted video?"

"Oh, yes, ma'am," Cammie smiled, aware of Naomi's shady tactics.

Dani was so excited about New York and the social media video, that she forgot to lock the door when she came home from her walk and never noticed Cammie entering her home. Five minutes after sharing the video with The Professional Bald Women's Network, Stephanie immediately sent it to Cammie to help protect Dani.

"Cammie-Liana Lawfton, my, my, my what a pleasure. My assistant will be in touch."

"My assistant will be at your office with a few details of our own," said Cammie. "Looking forward to hearing from you soon."

"Very well then."

"Oh, and ladies, I prefer to keep business separate. Mrs. Winston, Dani will not be attending our meeting, and there will be no further private conversations until all parties have reached agreeable terms," Cammie stated.

"Hmph," Naomi grunted and disconnected the call.

Eleven

TRUST AND BELIEVE

After nearly a week of sleepless nights, Becca had made her choice. She knew that if she didn't act on it quickly, she would have a change of heart. "Ma'am, can I get you anything else? Another glass of wine, maybe?" The flight attendant asked.

"No, I'm fine, thanks," Becca replied. After spending the night with Javi, she was tired and mentally drained. Dropping him off at the airport this morning was harder than usual. Especially since she was boarding the next flight to the same destination and staying in a hotel thirty minutes from his house. Several times throughout the night she just wanted to blurt out, "Javi, I'm expanding my business to New York," and then cry on his shoulder until her fears of failure went away. Becca knew that lingerie shops like hers came a dime a dozen in New York. But the chance to reinvent in a new territory and use more of the creative edge that drove her passion years ago was an idea too good to pass up.

Once she checked into The Four Seasons, Becca threw on her sneakers and jeans, found the nearest food truck, and gobbled down two hotdogs before she could finish chewing. She then had her driver take her to various areas, hoping that something would catch her attention. A place she could envision her company growing.

"Rebecca? Hey, thank goodness you answered my call. Melanie here, I have terrific news. Remember the first property we discussed? The one that you fell in love with that was under contract. Well, the contract fell through, but we have to act fast!"

"You're kidding? That's amazing," said Becca.

"I can hardly believe it myself. The head contractor is headed this way now. How fast can you get here?"

"I'm on my way," Becca said, excitedly giving the driver the address. "Wait, please pull over. Quick, please!"

"Yes, ma'am."

Once the car stopped, Becca opened the door and vomited her lunch, the wine from the plane, and everything else that was bubbling in her stomach. "I can't believe this is happening. My God is real! He is so real!" Becca exhaled.

"Everything okay, ma'am? There's some ginger ale in the drawer back there," the driver said.

"Oh, bless you," Becca said, downing the small bottle of ginger ale in one gulp and popping open another."

"No problem. First time in New York?"

"No, not at all. New York always feels like home. I've been coming here since I was a kid with my dad. He used to force me to tag along with him on these long boring business trips, telling me to focus and learn something. I used to cry and complain the whole time. I hated it. Until one weekend, I had an idea, ran it by them, and they loved it. Every business trip after that was like a trip to Disneyland for a twelve-year-old girl. I went from being a tomboy in overalls with a ponytail to a little entrepreneur with her own pajama line. Once my dad noticed my muddy sneakers turned into leather pumps, my business trips to New York with him turned into NFL games, hotdogs, and lonely nights in a hotel room by myself. He made me promise never to move here, said the city would swallow me up whole and take everything away from me that I love, eventually killing me. I've always wanted to open my business here, but I was never confident enough. I've never shared that with anyone," Becca said, wiping teardrops from her cheeks.

"When Cammie, my best friend, mentioned moving to New York, I went home that night, called my agent, and told her about my dream location. I prayed and promised God that if that location was available, I would go all in, no doubts. The next morning my agent called and said it was under contract for someone else. I decided to fly to New York anyway and look at other locations, just to see if anything grabbed my attention in the same way. My agent just called and said the pending contract fell through, and now the property is available. I'm sorry, I don't know why I'm telling you all this," Becca cried.

"It's quite alright. It seems like New York is meant to be then," the driver said.

"Yeah, I guess we'll see just how much," Becca mumbled, feeling slightly relieved and anxious all at once. To own anything in this area of New York would cost her nearly everything in her savings account. Since running her own business at an early age, Becca kept an "expansion only" savings account, ensuring she would never have to depend on the family trust fund to follow her dreams. Partnering with some of the biggest beauty brands in the industry made expanding her business overseas a reality. In fact, the money she made from that partnership alone would replenish her "expansion only" savings in no time. Her main concern was failing in New York as her father's words kept replaying in her head, over and over again. As the driver pulled up to the curb, she could feel her heart pounding in her chest.

"Becca, you made it," Melanie said, swinging open the car door.

One look at the multi-floored building, and it was love at first sight. While the realtor talked, Becca busied her mind connecting the dots from the move, staff, ideas, to decor.

"So, what do you think? Maybe take a few days? How long are you in New York? I can hold off new offers for at least a week."

"No need, I'll take it."

"Fantastic! Should I call your attorney, James?"

"Yes, please. I don't mean to be short Melanie, but I think I've seen enough."

"Of course. Have a nice trip back to D.C, and we'll be in touch."

Anxious to leave the building, Becca stepped outside and exhaled, taking in long, deep breaths. The anxiety in her stomach was slowly replaced with excitement. She felt at peace, like a new woman. "This little girl from Texas is facing her fears," she cried through deep breaths as she paced up and down the sidewalk.

Becca wanted to call Javi, go to his house, and tell him how she felt, but she had to stay focused on business first. Once Javi found out she was officially moving to New York, he would want all of her time, and she would want all of his in return. As much as she loved him, she wanted to maintain her own independence. Plus, Javi would eventually want kids, and that was something Becca could never give him, according to her doctors. When she told Javi the devastating news, he simply said, "Eh, we'll just adopt. What kinda man would I be if I left the woman of my dreams simply because God made her perfect, apart from everyone else in this world?"

As she climbed into the backseat of the car, Becca pulled on her sweater and fell asleep. When the driver dropped her back at the hotel, she went up to her room, took a long hot shower, ordered a large burger, fries, and a chocolate shake, and slept like a baby.

"Welcome home," Becca whispered to herself the next morning as her flight took off the next morning for Spain. She couldn't wait to have some much-needed time alone by herself before the rest of the ladies arrived.

"Dani, Dani, Dani," Cammie said, flopping down on the couch, thankful that she'd shown up just in time to stop her best friend from making a deal with that evil creature, Naomi.

"I know what you're thinking," Dani said, "I screwed up, and I'm probably gonna get fired. I didn't think the girls would share it across social media, and I certainly didn't think it would get this much attention. I don't know, I had a gut feeling, and I ran with it. Sometimes you have to stand up for yourself and take a risk. I guess New York is not looking so bad after all. Hopefully, my unemployed ass can find a job really quick. In the meantime, you think you might have room for a girl and a dog?"

Cammie raised her hands in the air and began clapping as loud as she could. "That's my muthafreakin friend! It's about TIME!" Cammie yelled. "I knew you had it in you. Sis. I just...ughhhh," Cammie growled through clinched teeth and balled fist. "Hello, Dani, my name is Cammie. I'm so glad to finally meet you. I've been waiting for your boss ass to show up for the past several years!"

"Whatever," Dani shyly said, secretly feeling the adrenaline rush from taking a risk for the first time in her life. "Now I need to work on strategy. Cammie, I really need your guidance, but don't you have to meet with Naomi?"

"Girl, please, I got that covered."

"Good, because I have an idea. Remember when we went to Texas and met up with that organization of bald women?"

"For the music festival? Yeah, I remember. Some of our baldie sisters from the organization in Georgia was there too. What's your point?"

"So, there's probably a network of bald women in almost every state, maybe even across the country. What if they all made videos discussing their own stories? Maybe we can edit them down to one statement, one team, one sisterhood. We can record our own video in Spain since the ladies within our network will be there and finish the final edit before we get back to the states. Then, we can release it ahead of the Sari campaign."

"We can finish it just in time for Naomi's anniversary celebration," Cammie replied with a sly grin.

"My thoughts exactly, I think," Dani said, unsure of Cammie's twisted expression.

"You see, *this* that shit I'm talking about!" Cammie smirked, with a look of satisfaction across her face as she stared at Dani. "Between you and Becca? It's about to go down," Cammie said.

"What about Becca?" Dani said, "Have you heard from her?"

"Never mind that. You just keep the thought process flowing. Feel free to pour every idea from that beautiful brain of yours without worry because I got you, and Jackson. Now, I have a slight detour to make before I catch my flight. I emailed you your itinerary. Remember, no more discussions about New York when we get to Spain."

"For sure," Dani said. While she was excited to have Cammie on board, she couldn't help but feel like her best friend was up to something.

The next morning, Dani left Jackson with the neighbor and took an Uber to the airport. She had a couple of phone calls to make before her flight departed. She prepared herself for that one conversation that would seal her master plan.

"Time to leave a message for the royal liar herself," Dani said. "If I know her like I think I do, she always has to have the last word. I just have to make my message good enough to poke the bear and provoke an interesting response. 'Hey, Sidney, this is

Dani. Just checking to see if you received my emails on the write-ups I sent. Let me know if you need anything else. Also, I'm sure you're already aware, but my friends sent you at least a dozen more stories for you to use for the models. I guess you were right, they were willing to sacrifice their personal journeys about hair loss and illness to save my job. Hopefully, this is enough, and it will secure my position at Sari, so you can stop reminding me that my career is in your hands. Also, while this really sucks, it's also an honor to have friends that would sacrifice intimate pieces of themselves just because they love me. I'm sure you wouldn't understand that being the blackmailing, lonely, old washed -up, hag that you are. It's unfortunate that you lack even the smallest amount of integrity. You'll probably never know what true friendship feels like. But, as you previously stated in my office, perhaps that's your gift, your destiny. Anyway, talk to you soon.'" *And so, we wait,* Dani thought to herself as she turned off her cellphone and sat back in her seat on the plane, clutching her Bible to her chest.

"Dangit! I hate flying," she said, popping a Benadryl. For the first time in her life, she felt a freedom that she couldn't really explain. But if she had to put it into words, it felt like driving a fully restored1968 Dodge Challenger on the open freeway—without gas. "Driving on grace," Dani mumbled. Reclining back in her first-class accommodations, Dani closed her eyes and slept like a baby.

MEANWHILE, BACK AT THE FORT

"I'm sorry, Langston, but this is my honest opinion," Talia said. "This story, this video has tripled in views across social media, and numbers are still climbing. A simple google search will reveal exactly where Dani works. People will question the authenticity of the new Sari campaign. I recommend that we pull back from Paris for now and let Dani have free reign. Let her finish what she started. Looking at the numbers, if we stand behind her, this will work out very well for Sari in the end."

"I agree," Langston replied. "Let's see where she's going with it."

"I disagree," said Sidreaux Sr. "She's fired, and the campaign continues. We'll hold off on telling her until after she completes this fiasco. Whatever business this generates, it belongs to us since she's still under contract."

"Firing her in this way will ruin any future opportunities for her," Langston said. "Come on, Dad, you know how unforgiving this industry can be, especially for newcomers. She's been through so much already."

Sidreaux Sr. remained silent, staring at Langston with the old 'Sidreaux' blank expression.

Langston knew not to press his father any further on the issue. Just as he was known for his charming, good looks, he was also known for his incredible mean streak. "As you wish, father," Langston whispered.

"I knew you would see it my way, son. Talia," Sidreaux Sr. said as he nodded his head goodbye and left the teleconference.

Feeling defeated, Talia and Langston hated what was coming and secretly hoped Dani was prepared for the hell storm headed her way.

Since he was a child, Langston Jr. was always meeting new family members—uncles and cousins he'd never known. Then one day they would disappear, never to be heard from again. It seemed that every time someone disagreed with his father or made too many mistakes, they suddenly went missing. At one point, he thought his dad was some type of undercover gangster, convinced that his extended family's mysterious disappearance was his father's doing. What he couldn't figure out, though, was why. It's not like his dad was selling drugs; it was fashion. Several years later he would discover the truth, and it was just as bad, solidifying his perception of his father from that day forward.

After college graduation, Langston had a bad argument with his Sidreaux Sr. Instead of flying him and his friends to Italy as promised, security whisked him away to an unknown island overseas. While slightly disappointed over being separated from his friends for the summer, Langston had no complaints. He was living in a mansion on an island surrounded by crystal blue water and beautiful women. In that moment, he remembered thinking that his father was completely delusional about discipline. Langston eagerly accepted his father's idea of punishment. He looked forward to relaxing on the beach and meeting some new friends before heading back to the states to complete his master's degree. Only Sidreaux Sr. had other plans. Langston quickly learned that he no longer had a position with the company, his bank accounts were frozen, and his check for school tuition had bounced. Sidreaux Sr had shut him out, allotting only a small allowance for his basic, daily necessities. From sunup to sundown, Langston Jr. was flown to every Sari location across the globe, where he worked, learning the ins and outs of every function.

Along the way, he ran into quite a few of his long-lost uncles who were now working in factory lines, and mailrooms. Surprisingly, he recognized Sidreaux Sr's only brother, his blood relative, Uncle Andrew. For years Andrew Sidreaux lived on the family estate with his brother, working day and night as they struggled to resuscitate the business from bankruptcy and loan sharks. Once the company started to exceed quarterly projections, Sidreaux Sr announced that his only brother had run off, and was nowhere to be found. When Langston saw Andrew in the factory, he ran up to him with excitement, "Uncle Andrew, it's me, Langston Jr."

His uncle looked at him as if he had never known him and continued working. Later on, Langston found out that his dad had Uncle Andrew's millions tied up in a trust that only his oldest son, Triston, could access. The two brothers had a disagreement. Sidreaux Sr demanded that Andrew's only son give up his dreams of being a basketball star and join the company ranks, insisting that he have a quality education just so he could work under Langston Jr. If Uncle Andrew agreed, then the company would continue to provide him with a lucrative salary that would take care of his wife and children. If he disagreed, then he would be disowned. At first, Uncle Andrew resisted, refusing to allow his brother to control every aspect of his life and ruin his son's future. Andrew Sidreaux left the family business, found his own job, and took care of his family. But that all fell apart when their youngest daughter became very ill, and they couldn't afford the medical expenses. Andrew went back to working for Sidreaux Sr. until he suddenly passed away.

When Triston turned thirty, he claimed the family trust and disowned his father for failing to stand up for him. He chose to honor Sidreaux Sr., keeping all of his father's hard-earned money to himself. He now lives abroad as a millionaire, running a small piece of the Sidreaux family business while taking care of his mother, his new wife, and their children.

Uncle Andrew had lost everything. Whenever someone disagreed with Sidreaux Sr, he set out to make their life miserable, and Langston didn't want that for Dani.

"Austin," Langston here. "We need to meet soon."

Twelve

LOYALTY TO ROYALTY

One by one, the ladies arrived in Spain, each flawless in a black cocktail dress and diamond accessories. Cammie's itinerary was a detailed agenda on how to dress, look, and feel without giving any clues about planned activities. The ladies slept on the plane and freshened up after landing as the agenda advised there would be no time to lag. When Dani arrived at the airport, Becca was the first person she saw, a true vision in a lacey black dress, a plunging neckline, and red bottom stilettos.

"No, no, no, no," Dani said, rushing into the bathroom before Becca made eye contact. She needed to freshen her makeup, put on her heels, and make a grand entrance. Normally, she would have summoned Becca to meet her in the bathroom, but she hadn't seen or spoken to any of the ladies since the social media video.

"You got this, Dani," Dani said to herself. "Those are your sisters out there; they love and support you. Even if they don't, so what! It's not about them. It's about the message, period!" As she walked down the corridor to meet the ladies, Dani was instantly taken aback by the sea of gorgeous bald women filling the small area in the corner of the room. No longer nervous or anxious, Dani threw up her arm in triumph and began a 'whoop-whoop' chant.

"Ladiessss! Can we show up and show out or what? We make bald look so good!" Dani said, exciting the ladies and bystanders as they walked by.

"Woohooooooo," the ladies replied as bystanders clapped and cheered them on.

"I have never been more proud to be bald a woman than I am in this moment," Dani said. Looking over her shoulder, she cued the photographer and videographer, "Let's make history, guys." *This is going to be epic,* Dani thought.

"Well, it's about time you got here, ladybug," said Becca. "I thought I was gonna have to race to D.C. and drag your butt on the plane!"

"Becca, you made it," smiled Dani.

"I'm so proud of you," Becca said as they embraced. "Thank you for inviting me to share this experience with you all."

"Bec, you're our sister. We wouldn't have it any other way," Dani stated, as she noticed the sadness in Becca's eyes. "What's going on with you? Something's not right. You know I know when something's up. Spill it."

"What do you mean?" Becca said, looking puzzled. "I'm fine. Honey, don't I look fine?"

"You look beautiful, you always look beautiful, but those piercing blue eyes never lie," said Dani. "What's going on?"

"Honestly, Dani, really, I am the happiest I have been in years," Becca said.

"As you should be," Cammie chimed in from the back, wearing a long sleeve, fitted-black velvet dress, exposing full cleavage and long legs.

"Dang," Dani and Becca replied in unison.

Cammie did a full spin while doing her best Beyonce walk, modeling her curvaceous, fit frame across the room.

"My queens, I'd like to welcome you to what will be the most memorable experience of your lives. My name is Miguel. I am the Head Concierge and will be assisting you for the next week."

"Week? I thought it was two weeks," Dani whispered to Becca.

"It was. The second week is just for the three of us. To be determined. Check your email," Becca whispered.

"Whatever you need, whatever you want, I will ensure that you have it," Miguel said. "As we speak, your things are being loaded into the cars and taken to your villas to be properly arranged before your arrival. You will find your accommodations are just as requested, including your very own private concierge and drivers to escort you wherever your heart desires." Miguel announced. "Shall we go?"

One by one, the fifteen ladies separated into a fleet of Mercedes cars, stopping to pose for a group photo before arriving at their first destination.

"Okay, ladies, may I have your attention, please?" Cammie said as they stepped out of the cars. "Sisters, the title of this trip is Royalty," Cammie said, rolling the 'R' off her tongue. "Collectively, we have worked so hard to become the women we are today. This is not just by title or profession. We have reinvented the very foundation of how we see ourselves as women. For many of us, life showed up in the middle of our most vulnerable years, like childhood and puberty, threatening to rob us of the femininity that we had barely come to know or understand. For others, life showed up at graduation, in our college years, and at the brink of fresh, new relationships and life transformations."

"Many of us felt forced to trade in our softness for a much thicker skin, foregoing our bashful vulnerability for a more ruthless, kick-ass type of boldness and bravery!" Cammie said. "But every now and then, even that strong, brave spirit gets humbled. Sometimes it just by a simple glance in the mirror before bedtime. Other times, it's over the loss of another failed relationship, or the humiliation from being passed over for another promotion because we just weren't a good fit. Oh, and my personal favorite that I used to get when I first started my law career, 'This case is going to be very strenuous Cammie-Liana, which may not be good for someone in your condition.'" Cammie said, mocking her former superiors, as the ladies laughed. "Like many of you, I knew then that I had to open my own practice so I could rightfully tell people like that to get the f…, you get my point," Cammie said as the women replied with 'amen' and 'speak sista, speak.'"

"This trip is a reminder that we were chosen to wear this royal crown," Cammie said. "At times, it may get a lil heavy, causing us to lean a little bit too far to the left or right, but don't you worry, I got you," Cammie assured the ladies. "As a network of Professional Bald Women, we got each other, yes? Can I get a whoop whoop for sisterhood?"

"Whoop, whoop," the ladies screamed.

"On this day," Cammie continued, "we solidify our pact that we will never let a sister suffer in silence! We will lift each other up, and we will stand in the gap for one another! Why? Because that's what a muther-luvin sista does!" Cammie yelled.

"Whoop, whoop! Hell yes, you better speak it, honey," the ladies shouted.

"Queens, line up and take your seats. Your royal throne awaits," Cammie said, as she motioned for the women to step forward.

As the ladies walked into the room, each one escorted by muscular gentlemen dressed in white dashiki's, *'oohs'* and *'ahhhs'* and screeches of surprise filled the air. The gentleman carefully removed the shoes of each lady as they walked barefoot on rose petals and baby-soft plush carpet to their reserved seating. The inside of the building was covered in a white tent with ceilings as high as the sky. Long-stemmed white roses were embedded into the fabric of the walls. Crystal chandeliers shaped like raindrops danced from above. In the center of the room, a high table filled the space with fifteen throne-like chairs intricately placed.

"Sisters," Cammie said loudly, struggling to speak over their excitement, "I would like to introduce you to the fabulous world-renown Chef De'Leon. You may have heard of him, but none of you has had the privilege of attending one of his exclusive soirees. Tonight, he has selected this location and created this event, especially for you."

Right before their eyes stood the most gorgeous man any of them had ever seen.

"Ladies, I am Chef De'Leon. It is my honor to serve you throughout the night. Whatever you need, whatever you want, please come to me. I promise each of you will leave here fully satisfied, needing and wanting nothing more."

"I'm first," Stephanie said, standing straight up from her royal throne.

"No, ma'am, I'm the oldest. I wanna go first," Dr. Foster said.

"Yes, and after her, I'm next," the ladies chimed in as they all laughed, forcing Chef De'Leon to smile at their anticipation. As they sat on their thrones enjoying the live music, the gentlemen in dashikis massaged their feet while they sipped their drinks and nibbled on appetizers.

"Mmmm, the steak just melts in your mouth," Dani said.

"You need to try the lobster tails with the sauce," said Anna K, licking her fingers in between bites.

"Everything is so succulent," Becca said, devouring a taste of everything in sight.

Glancing to her left, Dani met Cammie's glaze, both realizing they were thinking the same thing but choosing to ignore it and table the discussion for another day.

Cammie held up her wine glass, "A toast to my sisters for love, life, health, and happiness."

"Cheers," the ladies replied in unison.

For the rest of the evening, they feasted on paella, seafood, rabbit, pork, potatoes, breads, vegetables, cheeses, and spreads. Cammie finally advised the staff the ladies were completely stuffed. The men took the ladies' hands and danced well into the night, with the photographers capturing every moment. Exhausted and yearning for their accommodations, the ladies were escorted to the resort, where they sleepily climbed out of the cars and into their beds. Later the next day, they would marvel at the extravagance of the accommodations. The reserved villas were surrounded by water that was as clear as diamonds and stretched as far as the eyes could see.

Exhausted from a long day, Dani passed out as soon as her head hit the pillow. She could have slept well into the next evening if it wasn't for the loud noises outside her door. "What?" Dani said as she sat straight up in bed, initially confused by her surroundings at first. "Go away," she said, making an instant decision to sleep in.

"Dani, rise and shine. Let's go! We got plans!" Cammie said, rallying the troops like a drill sergeant. "You can sleep in at home, she yelled through the closed door. We ain't got time for that here. It is NOT on the itinerary!" Cammie said.

"Oh, my gosh! I thought I was on vacation," Dani yelled."

"GET UP! We got shit to do. Let's go! Let's go," Cammie said, banging on what sounded like pots clashing against each other.

"Okay, I'm coming," Dani yelled, slowly crawling from the bed to the shower. Thirty minutes later, Dani stood admiring her slightly bloated belly in the fitted tracksuit she purchased a week ago, thankful she opted for a matching wind coat and hat to use at her discretion. After a meal like that, exercise was what she needed, but she promised Cammie she would forego her normal routine for the precious pre-planned itinerary.

"Ugh, a perfect vacation would be no itinerary, more sleep, and less talk," Dani mumbled as she put on her hat and made her way to the dining area.

The next few days were filled with shopping, sightseeing, massages, slumber parties, pool parties, photoshoots, and exclusive chef dinner parties. Everywhere they went, they were treated like royalty.

At night, Dani worked with the photographer and videographer editing the footage, which included the videos coming in from various bald and beautiful social media platforms across the globe. Unknown to Cammie, Dani included quick sessions in the gym, as exercising kept her creative juices flowing. "Thirty more minutes, guys, and I'll meet you there," Dani said to the photography crew, putting her phone back on silent so she wouldn't be disturbed during her gym time.

"Excuse me, are you still using this machine?" a gentleman's voice drifted through the air.

"No, I'm good. Thanks," Dani responded.

"You're welcome. You from here?"

"Am I from here? No, I'm visiting. Have a nice evening," Dani said, suddenly anxious to get back to work.

"My name is Aaron. What's yours?"

"Um…. Dani, my name is Dani."

"Alright, well, Dani, I'm Aaron from New York, and it's nice to meet you."

Dani refused to look at him. *I'm just not in the mood to be judged by another man,* she thought as she tugged her sweat filled beanie hat down further to prevent revealing her bald head and any type of eye contact.

"So, where you from, Dani?"

"I'm from D.C.," she said, racking the weights back on the shelf.

"D.C in the house. Okay, I just wanted to compliment you on your routine. You was over there slanging and racking like a pro."

"Thank you. I appreciate that. Aaron? It was nice to meet you, but I really do have to go," Dani said, blushing her way towards the door.

"I go to D.C quite a bit, several times a month, actually. Maybe we could meet for coffee sometime? I would say have dinner with me tonight, but I don't want you to think I make it a habit of picking up beautiful women at fancy resorts."

Beautiful? Whatever, Dani thought. "Well, I appreciate your honesty, but I have dinner plans," she said.

"Of course, you do. Can you gimme a second though, just a second, maybe two minutes? Please don't leave," Aaron said as he raced out the double doors and down the hall.

This is sweet, Dani blushed, *or crazy. This man could be a psycho, and I'm standing here waiting to get chopped up,* Dani thought, suddenly rushing through the doors to get back to her room.

"Dani, hold up!" Aaron said, jogging to catch up to her. "I know you have to go, but here's my card. I wrote my cell on the back. Maybe I can show you my foodie spots in D.C. sometime. I like to eat…feed the muscles, you know."

"Is that right?" Peering down at his card, Dani said, "Okay, Aaron Saltern." Then, she slowly raised her eyes and looked up at him for the first time. *Shhhhnits, I knew he was gon be fine,* she thought. "We'll see. Maybe I'll text you my number."

"You do that. In the meantime, I gotta get back in the gym. I plan on doing some real damage at dinner tonight. Let me know if you get hungry later, maybe a late-night snack or breakfast. I mean food, not something freaky or anything like that."

"Will do," Dani laughed as she stepped outside into the cool breeze.

With the editing done for the night, Dani prepared herself for their last chef's dinner. She had a little more pep in her step as she slipped into a backless baby blue dress with a thigh high split. With Toni Braxton playing in the background, Dani was definitely feeling herself, giddy from her newfound risk-taking boldness and all the attention she was getting lately. While flattered, she still chose to focus on her work and her time with the ladies.

"My sista, my sis-tuh, you are wearing this blue dress," Stephanie said.

"Yasss, Baby! Ms. Dani has been serving body all week," Dr. Foster said.

"Thank you! I feel like I fit right in with my beautiful sisters. Although I'm still tryna get my arms diesel like Dr. Foster over here," she said as the ladies laughed, admiring Dr. Foster's strong biceps.

"You mean these lil ole things," Dr. Foster said, playfully posing for the cameraman.

"Yes, we are all showstoppers indeed," Cammie said to applause as she entered the room wearing a baby blue wraparound mini dress and silver open toe stilettoes. "Okay, ladies, they are ready for us. Please direct your attention to Miguel and follow the escorts."

"Where's Bec?" Dani asked

"In her room with a headache," Cammie said.

"Hmph."

"Yeah, I know, and I agree, but we'll talk about it when we get back to D.C."

"Oooh, girls, don't look now, but it's a stream of fine men coming our way," Lisa said.

When Dani looked up, she locked eyes with Aaron and five other equally attractive men. *Oh my gosh, he is gorgeous. Someone like that is interested in me?* Trying to think of something to say as Aaron and his friends walked towards her, all she could muster was a quick, "Hey." To her surprise, he walked right past her as if they'd never even met. Once they were seated at the dinner table, Dani noticed him and his friends climbing into the back of a limo. *Don't you dare beat yourself up,* she thought. *You are Dani Breaux, and he should be so lucky. He gave YOU his number, not the other way around. If he can't see you without a gym hat on your head, then he is simply not it. You have no time for small minds.*

"You okay, Dani? You look like you seen a ghost," Gina said.

"I'm good! Better than ever," Dani smiled, amused with her newfound self-esteem. Once she got back to the villa, Dani decided to slip into the hot jacuzzi just outside her bedroom. Assuming Aaron saw her when they made eye contact, she removed his card from the nightstand and used it to light the candles around the water. Singing along with Toni Braxton, she slid her tight muscles into the foaming steam. "Now, this is a vacation."

On their last evening, Dani surprised the ladies with the presidential suite she reserved for the night. While everything was planned to perfection, the staff had gone beyond her expectations. When she arrived at the suite, all the furniture from the room was replaced with dozens of full-length body pillows, cashmere throws, and luxury mattresses, like a bougie all-white slumber party. Fluffy area rugs covered the hardwood floors with throw pillows casually strewn across the room. As a parting gift, the hotel purchased white pajama sets and thick, plush robes, which they wore that night.

"Welcome to our last night of Royalty," said Cammie. "Once everyone slips into their pajamas, we'll start our evening."

"Good," Lisa said, "because my whole body is so relaxed from that massage, I ain't fit for going nowhere else tonight. Look at my skin? I'm glowing."

"Me, too," Gina said. "The skin on my head is blending with my face and neck, no makeup involved. I didn't know scrub and moisturizer could do that on its own."

"I am beyond fascinated with their skincare," said Anna K, "but my fiancé is going to kill me when he sees these receipts."

"Girl, please! You're looking at a ghost right now. I bought the whole damn line. I'm already gone," Lisa said as the women fell out laughing.

"Ladies, we shouldn't have to wear makeup to achieve a natural glow," said Meredith. "Every week I visit my barber or a tanning salon to keep my glow on point. On days when I can't get to my barber, then I simply use my clippers and my facial steamer. *Her* skin," pointing to herself, "is always perfect," Meredith smiled while striking a vogue pose. "That's my lil secret to y'all. You're welcome," she proudly said.

"So, Meredith, you're not completely bald," said Dr. Foster?

"Really Doc? I'm sitting in front of you with a bald head," Meredith replied. "Do you really want me to answer that question?"

"No, my apologies. What I meant to ask was, do you have alopecia?"

"What? Girl, yes, she has alopecia. The invitation for the whole damn trip is about royalty for women with alopecia," Lisa said.

"I'm aware of that, Lisa," Dr. Foster said. "I'm simply asking for clarification. Meredith mentioned clippers. Most of us here can't grow any hair to shave, and the ones that do shave, do so because of the bald spots throughout their head. We all know how hard it is to blend our bald spots with the few areas that still grow hair, but Meredith's shave looks really even."

"Ah, girl, that ain't nothing but spray," Lisa said. "Don't get caught outside on a rainy day is all I can say."

"It's hair dye," Meredith said, aggressively gulping down the rest of her drink and quickly pouring another.

"Hair dye? How is that possible? How does it stay on your skin?" The ladies began asking all at once.

"Meredith, when were you diagnosed with alopecia?" Dr. Foster asked again.

"No disrespect, *Doc,* but don't you think you're a little out of line asking me these questions? I mean, we all know you're a doctor and all, but hair loss is not your field," Meredith replied.

"Well, it is *my* field," Dr. Joy yelled from across the room, "And no, you do not have alopecia, as I have told you several times. I thought you said you made that clear to the group years ago?"

"Dr. Joy, you have never been my doctor either," Meredith said. "Clearly your diagnosis of me is based on your opinion."

"Hey, ladies, everything good?" Dani asked, carrying out snacks from the kitchen?

"Meredith, do you have alopecia?" Dr. Foster asked again.

"I have an autoimmune disease of my thyroid. I'm allergic to almost everything but deathly allergic to coconut. My hair gets dry and brittle, so I keep it shaved," Meredith said.

"There, that's that, Doc," Lisa said. "Ya'll leave her alone. I have hypothyroidism as well. Don't you have that too, Dani? It can lead to hair loss and brittle hair."

"It can, but some of us have been knowing Meredith since high school. This girl dyes her hair like she changes her underwear," Dr. Foster replied.

"Ladies…please," Becca said, looking from Dr. Foster to Meredith.

"Okay, fine, so I'm bald by choice. So, what," Meredith said. "I shaved my head after a violent relationship. I grew up in an abusive home and watched my father beat my mother like it was a hobby. When I got married, it was like watching my mom all over again, except this time it was me getting my head bashed in. I always thought my mother was the most beautiful woman in the world with long silky hair, and I looked just like her too. My beautiful, thick head of hair was a gift and a curse. So now, I look like me, and I'm happy with that," Meredith touted, holding back tears.

"So, you DON'T have alopecia," Dr. Foster confirmed.

"Dr. Foster, please," Becca said.

"I'm sorry about your experience. My heart goes out to all women who have suffered abuse at the hands of another. I grew up with domestic violence too, which led to me becoming a doctor. I watched my sister and her unborn child bleed out on the floor from being kicked dozens of times by her boyfriend. I was a child, and there was nothing I could do. It traumatized me for years. Once I became an adult, I went and got some help, and now I devote my time to saving lives," said Dr. Foster. "With all due respect Meredith, that's not what this organization is about. You can let your hair grow back if you feel like it. You don't ever have to think about going without your natural eyebrows or eyelashes or worry about how the world sees you. Or better yet, how you really view yourself in the absence of what is considered normal. So, why are you really here?" asked Dr. Foster as she scowled at Meredith. "On second thought, forget I asked. Ladies, thank you all for an amazing week, but I am very tired," she sighed. "I would really rather go back to my villa and relax."

"Yeah, me too. But with all due respect, Ms. Meredith, I understand exactly why you're here. I just don't necessarily agree with it," Lisa said, while shuffling her feet into her fluffy slippers and grabbing her overnight bag.

"Meredith, you've known everyone in this room for many years. None of us has to use clippers anymore," said Gina.

"When you give us advise on how you maintain your glow and visit your barber, what audience are you speaking to?" Gina asked.

"I'm not sure," Meredith replied. "Who cares? It was just small talk. I thought this trip, this organization, this whole social media video was about celebrating our differences. I didn't know we had to segregate ourselves to be a part of this group. I bet the media won't like that very much!" Meredith snapped.

"Check the banner, boo," said Gina. "What's the first word you see?"

"Oh, so because my baldness is not like yours, I'm not welcome here? What about people who have suffered something, and their baldness is an outlet of expression? Are you telling me that women who have been raped, molested, beaten, and choose to be bald are not welcome in your little group? Is that right, Dani?" Meredith said, looking toward the camera guy.

"Alright, enough! I don't know what ya'll talking about, but it's time to play these games and get this party started," Cammie intervened, pouring shots for everyone in the room. "Dr. Foster, where you going, sis? I know you not tryna waste my money like that," Cammie stated, frowning, and glaring until Dr. Foster and Lisa joined the rest of the ladies. "Alicia is going to be our game host for the evening. Ya'll better woot woot and let's do this!" Cammie yelled.

"*Woohoooo,*" the ladies yelped and cheered.

"This is our last night of Royalty, and before we settle down into what Dani has planned, I think we should have a few shots, relax, and play a game. Pay attention as I explain the rules," Cammie continued. "I am not a tape recorder. I made a deck of cards with movie names and scenes from the best movies ever, and I'm sure we've all seen them. Two people from your team have to act out the scene from the movie, while your teammates try to guess the name. You get one chance. No yelling out the answer because if one of you gets it wrong, then you miss your chance, and your whole team has to take a shot while the other team can steal it. If the other team misses it, then your whole team has to take two shots."

"Woohoo," the ladies whooped in excitement.

"Let's go, let's gooo," Cammie said as she joined her team.

"Okay, first up is Meredith and Cammie," said Alicia.

"Oh, I don't know how to act," Meredith whined. "Ya'll will never figure out what I'm trying to do."

"It's okay. You have to discuss the scene with me. I'm your partner. I can show you the video of the movie scene on the phone to jog your memory," Cammie said.

"I get it, but I can't act. I refuse to look stupid in front of this bunch of ladies," Meredith replied in disgust, "especially after tonight."

"Meredith, we're on the same team," said Cammie. "Don't worry, just follow my lead."

"Okay, okay, whatever. Let's do this," Meredith said as she stood next to Cammie watching the muted scene from the movie on Cammie's phone. As the 90s classics played in the background, the ladies danced on their pillow cushions, waiting the sixty seconds for Meredith and Cammie to yell action.

"Hey, let's do a dance contest instead. Same rules apply, and for extra points, we guess the song that was popular when the dance came out," Alicia said.

"See, now you talking," Lisa said. "Y'all know I like to get down."

While the ladies were occupied, Dani decided to complete the setup, pulling the suitcase full of products from the closet. As much as she tried to focus on setting the perfect scene for the presentation and the camera crew, she couldn't help but dance too. Scanning the room once again, Dani noticed the look on Cammie's face. She was standing with her back away from the camera and the other ladies, whispering something into Meredith's ear. *Now, why is she making a nasty face?* Dani wondered as Alicia passed out pre-game shots.

"Drink up, Dani," Alicia said.

"What is it? I can't drink hard liquor; you guys know that," Dani said.

"Try it. Boss lady just ordered this from downstairs. I think you'll like it. It's kinda sweet."

"Umm, it tastes like a coconut snow cone with a twist," Dani said, sipping on the frozen concoction. "What is it?"

"Not sure," Alicia yelled over the music. "I think it's coconut rum or something."

"Nice, but a little too sweet for me. Cammie, I'm opening the expensive wine," Dani said, looking in Cammie's direction, expecting a loud 'hell nah.' Instead, she saw that nasty face again, but this time with a more sinister grin. The look jogged Dani's memory as she hadn't seen that expression in years. Remembering several years back on Bennie's birthday cruise when Cammie's future sister-in-law suddenly fell into the water from the moving ship. Several guys, including Cammie's brother, Bennie, quickly jumped in to save her, but her body was limp and lifeless as they pulled her into the small rescue boat.

That next morning at the hospital, everyone was scared, assuming the worst. Cammie sat next to Bennie, stoic, with her arms wrapped around his for support. When the doctors came out, Dani jumped from her seat and stood over Cammie, placing a hand on her shoulder.

"Ms. Lawfton, I'm Dr. Pierce. Brittney took in quite a bit of water, but your quick actions may have saved her life. However, she has suffered a severe concussion and a deep gash. She must have hit her head on the railing when she fell. She also has a broken collar bone, several bruises, and cuts. She won't remember much of anything, but she'll be alright."

"Oh, thank God," one of the groomsmen said, crying into his hands. As Dani reached over to pat Cammie's brother on the shoulder, she noticed a half-smile on Cammie's face. It was later discovered that the fiancé was sleeping with the best man. *Why am I thinking of that right now?*

Once everyone had their shot glasses in hand, Cammie yelled to the crowd, "Ladies raise your glasses and let the shenanigans begin." As the ladies raised their glasses, toasting to good times, Cammie's face relaxed, and her lips curled into a half-smile as she faced Meredith.

"Hey, Cammie, I'm gonna open the wine," Dani yelled in her direction, but Cammie's attention remained focused on Meredith. "Cammie! Cammie!" Dani tried her best to yell over the music, "May I open the wine now? I'll take that as a no," Dani said, taking another sip of the coconut concoction. "Too much coconut. Coconut! Oh, my gosh! Meredith's allergic!"

"Turn up the music," Cammie yelled to Alicia, almost like she heard Dani coming to Meredith's rescue.

"It has coconut," Dani yelled, slamming into Meredith, intentionally causing her to drop the shot glass onto the floor.

"Girl, what are you doing? Move out the way, Dani," the ladies yelled.

Ignoring them, Dani went into a full centipede dance, maneuvering across the floor, making her way over to Becca.

The ladies all yelled, "Centipede!"

Even with all the laughs and cheers surrounding her, Cammie's face was still frozen in time, staring at Meredith.

After dancing every move she could think of, Dani finally lost her turn since no one could guess what dance she was doing. Finally convinced that none of the women realized the drama that was unfolding, she left the room to look for Cammie. She found both Cammie and Becca in the master bathroom.

Cammie appeared to be in a world of her own, staring intensely in the mirror as she washed off her makeup. She looked up and glared when she noticed Dani evading her quiet space.

"Dani, if I've told you once, I've told you a thousand times, you can't win in life always seeing the good in everything and everybody," Cammie calmly said. "You have to be mindful of your enemy always lurking in the distance," she said as she threw away a piece of dental floss.

"What do you do when your enemies are silently plotting behind your back, and you can't see it?" Dani asked.

"Never been in that situation before. I always see it," Cammie laughed, "like a sixth sense. I guess that's just my blessing," she said nonchalantly.

"Well, I think that's a good question," Becca said. "What do you do, Dani, when you can't always see the danger ahead?"

"Trust in God," said Dani. "He's never let me down before."

"Enough!" Cammie yelled, slamming her hand on the countertop. Grabbing the electric toothbrush from her kit, holding it in front of her face, she scowled, "Don't you dare bring that self-righteous, holier than thou mess up in here. I trust in my god, which is why I heard what that demon said. Threatening to tell lies to the media. At *my* event? After all the work you've done with your campaign, all the work I've done? That's the difference between you and me, Dani. You scared to get your hands dirty, so you wait for your angel of mercy to show up and save the day. I *am* the angel of mercy. Don't LOOK…AT…ME…and act like you didn't hear what she said!"

"I heard what she said, including the part about being allergic to coconut. I'm sure everyone in the room heard what she said. Did you hear her, Becca?" Dani asked.

"I did. She was being a bit of an ass. But, so what!" Becca said. "Honey, who gives a shit?"

"I do!" Cammie said. "I always have to be the one to show up and save the day because you heifers are too nice and too sweet. So, yes, that's what my god told me, Dani," Cammie said as she gargled with mouthwash and spit. "It's just coconut," she sneered. "Ya'll act like she was gonna die or something. Besides, Becca always has EpiPens. Right, Bec?"

"I do, but I didn't bring them to Spain."

"So, God told you to feed that woman coconut, knowing that she is deathly allergic, with a room full of cameras watching?" Dani asked. "I guess your god has an EpiPen waiting in the wings, too, since Becca didn't bring hers."

"Yep, that's right," Cammie said while nonchalantly applying face moisturizer. "You have your relationship with God, and I have mine. Don't judge what you don't understand. You guys should really try this moisturizer. It's amazing!" Cammie said. "We can probably use this in the video."

"Cammie, sorry to change the subject," Becca said, "but my mama used to always quote a scripture from the Bible, 'My sheep know my voice.' Everything that talks to us ain't of God, even if it's somehow protecting you at the moment. Honey, we have to pray for discernment. We can't listen to all the voices in our head," Becca said.

"And you can't keep doing dangerous things thinking they won't catch up to you," said Dani. "One day, you will get caught and we won't be there to stop it. Even if something happens and I lose everything, God will restore it all, in a greater way," Dani said.

"So that's what you counting on, Dani? Losing everything again and waiting? Hallelujah, sis. I'm just gon call you Job then, from the Bible. In the meantime, I'm just supposed to be like you, fearfully waiting for that restoration day to happen while I'm barely surviving?" Cammie retorted. "Nah, I can think of better ways to spend my time."

"When you met me, I wore an old peeled-up baseball hat with the plastic showing, trying my best to hide my bald head,"

Dani said. "I was so ashamed to show all of this, all of me. No, my hair hasn't come back yet. Sometimes I think it's my Achilles heel. It keeps me invested in my relationship with God, humbled, maybe. I don't know. But I believe God gave me something better, and it's so much greater than hair. He gave me you and Becca and a whole life that I could never have imagined living before. I'm not sitting in fear of what I've lost. I'm living in awe that he thinks enough of me to be everything I could ever want or need. I'm not concerned about every man that has ever left, or situations that didn't work out, or things I can't control. God is the blueprint, the infinite realness of love and life. After everything I've lost, Cammie, I don't want for nothing."

Bursting into tears, Becca reached for a napkin, "Oh, my goodness, I love ya'll so much. Praise the Lord," Becca sobbed.

"That hat was a monstrosity," Cammie said. "Why wouldn't you just buy another one? You could have gone to the discount rack."

"Becca, if you don't get your overly emotional self together and stop crying on me," Dani said, pushing Becca's wet face off her shoulder.

"Girl, Becca is not overly emotional; she's pregnant. Probably about three months," Cammie said."

"Hey! What ya'll doing in here?" Dr. Foster said as she entered the bathroom, half-drunk, or maybe a little high off the chocolate-covered mini brownies. "It's time to get some grub and get this party started right."

"They can't possibly be hungry with all them snacks," Dani said.

"Yeah, those snacks have a little something special in them, so they might be a little hungry. Alicia, get some room service up here, burgers, whatever," Cammie yelled as Alicia came through the door.

"Will do," Alicia said as she headed to the kitchen.

"Ooooh, burgers! Ya'll we bout to get some burgers and fries," Lisa said. "Heyyyyy," Lisa sang as the ladies made up a dance for burgers and fries.

"Everything okay," Meredith asked from the bathroom door, staring at Cammie like she'd seen a ghost.

"Of course, we are," Cammie said. "Just doing a little pre-cleanse. We'll be back up shortly. Oh, and Meredith, just wanna say you are always welcome in our sisterhood. That's never gonna change. With that said, I need you to understand something. I will drag you to your grave if you ever threaten to come for the women in this bathroom again. I promise, when I'm done with you, no one will ever find your body," Cammie said, with a blank expression and a half-smile like she was anxiously hoping Meredith would try her again.

"*Set It Off!*" Becca yelled, looking from Cammie to Dani. "This scene, it's from that movie, *Set It Off,* right?"

"Exactly! That was excellent, Cammie, right, Meredith? She really missed her calling," Dani laughed.

"Of course," Meredith smiled as her hands trembled, struggling to hold on to her wine glass. "*Set It Off,*" she shook her head and laughed as her body relaxed and her face softened.

"I'm trying my best to show love and meet people where they are in life," Cammie said as silent tears rolled down her smiling face. "Just let me love you," she said as she hugged Meredith.

"Now, that's the movie *Mommie Dearest,*" Becca said. "Dani, have you seen that movie? I watched that with my mother when I was just a lil one," Becca said. "Scared the bejeezus out of me."

"Burgers or steak? I think I might want both," Dani said, grabbing Cammie's hand.

"Meredith, what about you and Cammie, what would you ladies like?" Becca asked, "And please stop it with the movie scenes Cammie. Honey, you're scaring Meredith," Becca said, motioning for Meredith to follow her to the kitchen.

"It's the brownies," Dani whispered to Meredith as she walked by. "I hope you didn't eat any."

"Oh, my gosh, thank God. I wasn't sure what was happening. Are they spiked?" Meredith asked.

"Yep, look at everybody," Becca said, pointing to the ladies munching on chips, chocolate, and pickles, as the three of them made their way into the kitchen area to join the rest of the group.

"Meredith, you can help me finish setting up," Dani said. "I wanted to get your expertise on something. Take a look at these products and tell me what you think," Dani said as she put her arm around Meredith's shoulders and walked back into the party room to join the others.

Once the ladies settled down with their burgers and fries, they watched the final video, which included bald women and children from various organizations around the world sharing their least favorite beauty product along with their journey of perseverance.

"I get the challenge," Gina said. "I think we can all give a lil individual testimony on achieving success, despite the odds. The bigger question I have is how are you going to get major brands to care that their products don't work for everyone?" Gina asked. "Isn't that just the norm?"

"Good question," Dani said. Just as Dani was preparing to share samples of the facial products and body butters she was gifted from her mystery box, Cammie unzipped a large suitcase full of Naomi's signature body butter and various sample's from her product line. She also had samples from other brands who responded to Dani's video over the course of the last two weeks and had express shipped their products to the hotel.

"Don't ask," Cammie said to Dani. "Seriously, don't ask."

"Okay! Ladies, so there's enough samples for each one of us to try them out and give our honest opinion," Dani said.

"Ooh, girl, I love you more and more," Lisa said. "Can we keep what we like?"

"Yes, the samples are yours to keep, right, Cammie?"

"Of course, and please be very thorough. We need honesty," said Cammie.

As the women read the labels and sampled the products, they noticed the ones with the 'all-natural labels' either felt sticky, too thin, or too oily against their sensitive skin. All the ladies loved Naomi's Signature Butter, but at over five hundred dollars a jar, the average woman would never be able to afford it. The lotions made with essential oils from an independent brand were also a favorite among the room. Most of the facial products failed due to the ingredient list, as the ladies preferred less in their daily routines due to easily clogged pores and skin irritation. After their analysis, they posed for their final group shots and enjoyed their last night while the camera crew went to work doing the final video edits.

As soon as her flight landed back in D.C, Dani went to work making phone calls and talking to various independent brands. Most of them were excited about possible exposure, but they wanted assistance with funding, which was not something that she could afford. Her original video had been shared over a million times across social media, but now the buzz was drawing down, and it was time to make the next move.

"Dangit, I'm fresh out of ideas. Jackson let's go for a walk. Some fresh air may be just what we need." Always eager to get outside, Jackson was waiting by the door before Dani finished her sentence. With the sun beating down on her face, the smell of restaurant food and just a few blocks away—the scent of leather in high-end department stores, Dani couldn't help but smile. "I love it here. Why am I running off to New York? God help me. I'm not sure about anything except those shoes in that window," Dani said, mesmerized as she made a beeline for the ritzy store.

"Whoa, ma'am! Do you have a disability?"

"What? What did you just say to me? So, because I'm bald, you think I have a disability?"

"No. I'm asking because you're trying to bring a dog into my store who clearly would rather do anything but come up in here."

Unfortunately, the guy with the long, bone-straight hair tied back in the neatest ponytail was right. For some reason, Jackson hated shopping for anything other than toys and food.

"For the record, I love your video, and I adore your bald head," the strange ponytailed gentlemen said.

"Thanks. I guess I'll have to come back another time to look at those shoes, right over there on that little pedestal, those burgundy ones, in a size eight and a half," said Dani.

"Yeah, I think the red would be so much better," ponytail smiled.

Is he flirting with me?

"Tell you what, come back in about an hour, and I'll keep him company while you get a little retail therapy."

"No, that's okay. I'll just come back another time," Dani said.

"You should," said ponytail.

"I will," Dani replied.

"You should."

Okay, walk away, walk away. "Oh, one more thing," Dani said, embarrassingly turning back around to find him watching her walk away. "How did you see my video? I mean, I know it's shared everywhere now, but how did you get it?"

"From one of my contracts who sells out of my store. She has a nice little setup right over there," he said, pointing to the table in the back. "Body lotions, candles, you should check it out."

"Does she have a card?"

"Sure. I'll do you one even better. One sec," ponytail said as he ran to the back and came out with a candle and jar of lotion tucked into a leather tote.

"Nice bag," Dani said, inhaling the fragrance through the bag.

"I don't know, but they fly off the shelf as soon as she stocks up," the pony-tailed guy said.

"Okay. Thanks, I'll be sure to give my honest review," Dani said. "How much do I owe you?"

"A trip back for the shoes."

Speechless, Dani flashed a smile and walked away, trying her best not to look back.

After her walk, Dani made a quick salad, answered all twelve of Sidnae's emails with a simple yes, no, and maybe that one, and took a hot shower. Sitting down at her computer, Dani thought about ponytail. "The bag!" Jumping to her feet Dani ran to the kitchen to grab the leather tote. "Dang, I can smell it through the bag." Nothing prepared Dani for the creamy oil that moved with ease across her skin. Her body glowed, basking in the essence of the essential oil and the warmth of the ingredients. "If I didn't know any better, I would think that this stuff is making my shoulder feel somewhat better." Glancing at the tag dangling from the candle, Dani read, *'Bells & Me. Owner Catera Bell.'*

While dialing the number on the tag, Dani noticed a card at the bottom of the bag that made her smile grow even wider, *'Michael R. Chase, Owner-Please come back for the shoes.'*

"Hello? Catera Bell? My name is Dani Breaux. Do you have a minute?"

Thirteen

CHANGING OLD HABITS

"She's late! I hate late. Did you receive a communication? A text? I haven't received any messages from her, and I have things to do…or maybe not," Cammie said.

"Calm down, Cammie. She'll be here," Dani said. "I mean, it's Friday evening, downtown D.C traffic. Give her some time, and yes, you absolutely have things to do. You have soon to be in-laws to meet, and they will love you. What's not to love?"

"I don't know, Dani. I think his mother has it out for me."

"Nah, she doesn't. He's her only son. Just be yourself, and everything will work out fine."

"You're right, and I need to start by being on time. Hmmm, hold on, hold on, look over there. I might need a little popcorn for this show," Cammie said, sliding her shades down her nose to improve the view. Stepping out of a shimmery, black 1967 Chevrolet Camaro was Michael R. Chase. As he walked, his thick, lustrous hair moved with the wind, flawlessly settling back into the perfect position. His clothing complimented his tall, lanky, muscular frame as he wore tailored grey trousers, a black cashmere sweater, and chocolate loafers without socks.

"My guy is working the hair, the beard, and the body," Cammie said.

"Oh, that's ponytail!" said Dani, unable to stop smiling.

"That's ponytail? Girl, let me see his card again," Cammie said as she snatched the card from Dani's hand. "Thank you, ma'am! I'll be keeping this," Cammie said, sliding it into her purse.

"Sam? Drop Dani off at her house, please."

"No, I'm here to meet Catera Bells, that's it. Ain't nobody looking at ponytail," Dani said, still blushing towards the store.

"Hmph, look at your face. Go home, Dani. Try on the dresses my stylist sent you for Naomi's anniversary gala. Choose one, just one, and Alicia will come by and pick up the others. Make sure you have your speech ready."

"What speech? It's Naomi's party."

"We have some interesting events planned, and you need to be on you're A-game."

"Exactly! That's why I'm here, on my A-game, meeting Catera Bells," said Dani.

"Which you've already done," Cammie replied. "I'm looking forward to seeing how great she is for myself. Dani, because of you, the bases are loaded, and we're about to score. But it's my turn to bat. We agreed that my firm is representing you. Let me handle my business."

"Fine. I'm still not sure why I need a lawyer for this, but cool. May I have my card back, please?" Dani asked as Cammie stepped out of the town car.

"You mean your ponytail man card? No! We at the playoffs. No nookie, no potential plans for nookie, and no nookie candidates. Stay focused. This card will be in safekeeping."

"Fine, what about dinner, Cammie? I was looking forward to some girl talk?"

"Awww, I'm sorry, sis, duty calls. Plus, you know I know when you're lying. You were looking forward to eating high-calorie food. Sam, stop at the spot and treat yourself and the family too. I'll be done here in an hour or so, tops," Cammie said as she stepped out of the car and walked into the store.

Later, sitting alone at the dining room table, Dani stared at the large foil container of hot jumbo lump crab cakes, grilled salmon, sauteed green beans, and buttery mashed potatoes, one of her favorite cheat meals. After a few bites, Dani decided to store it in the fridge and head to her office to pick up a few things.

Yesterday, Sidnae emailed the prints of the latest cover photos. In one of them, Ebony was wrapped like a burrito in a black sheet, standing against a white background, posing for a selfie. She had one eyebrow removed, and the other plucked really thin with her head shaved completely bald. Ebony sat on the floor with her legs tucked under her butt, eyes closed, and her head lifted toward the ceiling. The photo was stunning, but it was the story behind the photo that made Dani feel like she was stabbed in the back. During a lunch outing with Talia, Dani recalled sharing those very words with her boss after she spent over twenty minutes asking Dani what it was like to suddenly have no eyebrows or lashes. Dani's response was now staring her in the face, under Ebony's picture.

Facial hair was never something I paid attention to outside of my eyebrows, eyelashes, and the occasional upper lip. Losing my hair was a progression that happened over time. I remember waking up one morning to little hairs all over my pillow. I prayed that it was just more facial hair or even nose hair and not the last bit of my eyelashes. As soon as the house was empty, I wrapped the bedsheet around me and ran to the bathroom mirror. I never knew how much my eyebrows and eyelashes framed my face until they were completely gone. I was too overwhelmed to cry, so I sat on my bathroom floor, grabbed my phone, took a selfie of the new me, and sent it to my best friend, who shaved her one brow in response.

"Wow, and here you are now, looking like you were born to be bald. I love your story," Talia replied when Dani shared with her those very words.

Clearly, you must have really loved it, Talia, Dani thought to herself.

"Dani, can you hear me? Are you still there?" Sidnae yelled through the speakerphone.

"Yes, I'm still here," Dani said, forgetting Sidnae had placed her on hold for another call.

"Well? Are you surprised? Listen, I told Talia, I said we have to pay homage to Dani in all of this. Without her life and stories, this whole campaign wouldn't be happening. Have you seen my new email this morning? We released the new products."

"I know about the products," Dani said, cutting her off.

"Great! So, then you saw the special edition issue of Sari Magazine, with the models sitting together? You know, testing the authenticity of the ingredients against their hairless skin, like you and your friends filmed on your little girls' trip to Spain? Yeah, that would have been a great follow-up video for your social media tell-all. Too bad we released our images first. You don't wanna be a copycat. There's no integrity in that," Sidnae said, recalling the voice mail left questioning her character.

"Well, aren't you resourceful," Dani said, fully aware that Cammie leaked the footage to keep Sidnae occupied. "All that time in this industry and you finally get the opportunity to run lead on something, and all you can do is steal from someone like me," Dani said. "I don't even have half your expertise. You should write an article on how it feels to reach that level of failure at your age. Except you can't because you're not actually a writer, but I am."

"Ouch! Careful, Dani. I know you've been under the weather lately, but I've warned you before not to cross me," Sidnae sharply said. "I just wanted to let you know the press is all over the article, and they loved it! It's real, it's raw, and emotional."

"It's real because I lived it! But I didn't write that piece, nor did I give you permission to use it to promote Ebony's photo shoot. You can't just sign my name on something without my permission! Isn't that illegal?" Dani asked.

"Relax Dani. You're starting to sound like a bad after-school special titled, 'Isn't that Illegal?'" Sidnae said, sarcastically, then laughing and mocking Dani. "Do you have any idea how many people took from me in this industry, used me like I was nothing? So, yeah, whenever I see something good, I take it back! And when someone crosses me or threatens my reputation, I simply destroy them. It's as simple as that. Just ask my ex-husband," Sidnae laughed.

"And you're okay accepting the reward for someone else's work?" Dani asked.

"Like a leading lady on Oscar night," Sidnae said. "There's so much I can teach you Dani, but let's not get too emotional with the whole stealing thing. Afterall, you shared your story and you never said Talia couldn't use it."

"Exactly! I shared it with her as a conversation over lunch, not an interview," Dani said.

"As a matter of fact," Sidnae continued, "you approached her with the idea to give your story a platform. Again, you should be thanking me instead of questioning my integrity. At this point in your career, I'm all you have Dani. A lot of your kind are competing for jobs like this, and well big industries like Sari can only *give* so many spots away. The rest of us have to earn it. Somebody has to have the qualifications to keep the company running," Sidnae said. "Anyway, I have to check on my kids. I'll email you the—" was all Dani heard as she immediately clicked off before Sidnae could finish.

Feeling anxious and frustrated, Dani decided to take a long walk, hoping to clear her head. After pacing up and down the wintry streets for over an hour, she found herself standing in front of Sari Unique. Dani pushed through the rotating glass doors and made a beeline straight to her office, exhaling as she shut the door behind her. Everything was just as she'd left it. Her co-workers shuffled around from meetings to coffee breaks to phone calls. Sitting behind her desk, Dani realized that for the first time since working at Sari Unique, she had officially become what she despised, a spineless puppet using her talents to promote someone else's dirty agenda. "Damn, I thought those days were over. It's like leaving one bad relationship and falling ass-backward into another," Dani mumbled to herself. She sat in her office staring at the wall, trying to think of a reason to stay at Sari besides paying her mortgage.

"Wait a minute, Sidnae said they confirmed the final products for the campaign. Normally they stash a supply before they hit stores," Dani said. Unable to quiet her curiosity, Dani found herself scanning her badge into what they called the dungeon. Carefully looking over her shoulder, she waited until security made their rounds for the hour. If she got caught, they would assume she was stealing and immediately terminate her employment. The dungeon, as they called it, was known as the room of old products, out-of-season clothes, shoes, makeup, bags, and jewelry. Employees dreaded the dungeon assignments. As rumor has it, they would be down there for hours cleaning, scrubbing, scanning, and organizing.

The truth was not many had ever really experienced a dungeon assignment because if they had, they would know that the dungeon was just a fake name for fabulousness. The basement warehouse was like a dream come true, pristine, and clean. Security took extra measures to ensure no one had access to the dungeon except the creative director, Adrian, who had a gold star on his badge giving him and his sworn-in minions unlimited access.

MY FAIRY GODMOTHER

Just being in the dungeon made Dani misty-eyed for her old friend, Adrian Fablis. "Ugh," Dani said, wiping her hands on her jeans from the dusty shelves. It was clear no one had been maintaining the dungeon in Adrian's absence. She thought about how much she missed him and their lunch time gossip sessions, sharing details from his date nights while sipping wine and trying on shoes. Nothing was the same at Sari without her buddy Adrian, who started out as somewhat of a nemesis. The first day Dani met Adrian, he looked her up and down, removed her hat, and simply said, "No, and don't ever do that again," as he sashayed away in his Fuchsia colored harem pants and white, off-the-shoulder top. The next day he stopped in his tracks, backed up, and said to her in front of everyone in the morning meeting, "No," garnering a chuckle from those in attendance.

Feeling bullied and humiliated, Dani cried on bathroom breaks, coffee breaks, after work, and before work. She was a walking teardrop, full of hormonal treatments, fresh from divorce and breast cancer.

Walking through the park after work, Dani yelled into the speakerphone to Becca, "Who the hell does this guy think he is? The nerve of him to tell me to stop being bald and put on a wig. I will not conform to this societal bullshit!"

"That's right, honey! You stand your ground. Don't you let them treat you like a puppet."

Dani felt embarrassed, but she refused to cover up. Every day she continued showing up bald. When she was really angry from dealing with the divorce, she'd intentionally go to work with a naked face and no lashes, praying that Adrian would say something and give her a reason to snap. One day, he finally answered her prayers.

"Hold the elevator," Dani said to one of the employees as she attempted to step in before the door closed.

"Thank you," Adrian said to the guy holding the door. Stepping in front of Dani, Adrian almost tripped her as he pushed everyone aside to enter the elevator first. Clearly, he was having a bad day as he yelled into his phone at one of his minions.

No longer feeling brave, Dani put her head down, anxiously waiting to get to the first floor. *I just wanna come to work and go home just like everyone else,* she thought.

"Hey! Ms. Girl, I have warned you time and time again," Adrian said, while the elevator audience smirked and chuckled out loud.

Refusing to spend another evening crying behind the actions of some heartless man, Dani replied, "Screw you! This is who I am," she said, taking a step forward. "You know what? Just because you yell and make a fool out of yourself doesn't mean that you're right. And these people who you *think* are your friends, are not laughing with you; they're laughing at you! Too chickenshit to stand up for themselves out of fear that you'll bully them next. So yeah, go screw yourself! And if you ever touch me or anything I'm wearing without my permission again, you will draw back a nub."

"Sometimes change is relevant, Ms. Queen," Adrian calmly replied just as Dani stormed off the elevator.

"Yeah?" Dani said, walking back, refusing to let him have the final word. "And some things on people cannot be changed! So, mind your own damn business," Dani snapped back before the elevator doors closed. That night she caught a taxi home and cried herself to sleep again. Embarrassed to go back to work that Friday, she wore her faithful hat, thankful the weekend was about to start.

"Honey, I don't know what you're so afraid of. You stood up for yourself," Becca said the next morning over breakfast.

"Yeah, hopefully, by Monday, everyone will forget about my little elevator tantrum yesterday. I'm just gonna keep my head down today and do my work," Dani said.

"Exactly," said Becca. "It's Friday, people are excited for the weekend. By Monday, it won't even be a thought."

As soon as Talia saw Dani, she assigned her to the dungeon for cleaning and reorganizing. Dani embraced her so-called punishment as she would be hidden from the stares of her co-workers and the painful reminders of the previous day. Once in the dungeon, Dani quickly realized she had been set up when she looked up and saw Adrian sitting patiently on a stool, waiting for her.

"Nope," Dani said, swiftly turning around and heading back towards the door.

"Stop! Sit," Adrian said, standing to give her his seat. "Sometimes, less is more, and less is enough. May I?" he said, asking Dani's permission to touch her? After removing her hoop earrings and long, beaded necklace, he replaced them with diamond-studded hearts and a barely-there silver charm necklace. He grabbed his makeup bag and added a little color to her cheeks and lips.

Looking at herself in the mirror, with just a few tweaks, Dani saw a difference. The diamonds lit up her eyes and brightened her smile. Adrian had her slip on a white undershirt with a push-up bra, dark jeans, and a pair of red-bottom stilettos. He added a fitted blazer and a darkened lip for finishing touches.

Dani looked at herself in the mirror, her eyes watered, ashamed to admit that she hadn't felt this beautiful in years without the addition of wigs, eyelashes, or hats. This was just her, nothing extra.

As if Adrian knew what Dani was thinking, he simply repeated the words from the elevator, "Sometimes, change is relevant, and don't you cry that makeup off," he added.

For the rest of the day, they talked, laughed, had lunch, and enjoyed each other's company. She even helped Adrian pack four large suitcases of clothes and three duffel bags filled with shoes, bags, jewelry, and makeup for the Los Angeles photoshoot he was leaving for first that evening.

"You gon be alright, Ms. Girl?" Adrian asked. "It's a hard game out here in this industry, but anytime you need me, just call," he said, handing her his card. "However, as much as I'm starting to like you, we cannot be best friends. I have a reputation to uphold around here. But no worries, I'll pop in, and we'll get a drink or two every now and then." A few months after the LA photoshoot, London came calling, and just like that, Adrian was gone.

It had been nearly a year since Dani last saw him. After her first make-over with Adrian, in the dungeon, Dani came home to five large boxes waiting by the door. Once inside, she discovered it was the four large suitcases she'd helped Adrian pack for the photoshoot along with the three duffel bags. "Oh no, there must be some mistake," Dani said, calling Adrian several times with no answer. She then called Talia and got no answer.

Inside one of the boxes, she found a card: *Sweetie, less is more, but we must always have more options. Regardless, always remember that you are enough! Enjoy, my little bald queen.* The tops, dresses, pants, and shoes from the suitcases filled her little closet. Adrian had even added lingerie for her to sleep in. Dani had never owned so many expensive brand items all at once. Maybe a pair of shoes or a dress here and there, but never a closet full.

Reminiscing about the memories of her dear friend made her sad. "This place is not the same without you, Adrian," she pouted, surveying the cold, dark dungeon. "What I wouldn't give to hear your voice right now in the midst of all this drama," Dani said. Realizing time was of the essence, she pushed her memories aside and focused on the task at hand. She opened the new deliveries and stuffed a sample of each one into her gym bag. She noticed a few jars of the Signature Body butter from Naomi's shop. "Why is that here?" she mumbled. She also saw a few new pieces that she wanted to take for herself but put back as she instantly felt guilty for attempting to steal. It took her over a month to even consider wearing any of the items Adrian had given her, thinking she had done something wrong. Talia had to end up showing her the receipt, which confirmed that the items Adrian gave her were covered under his expense, and he could use his money for whatever he wanted.

After wrapping up in the dungeon, Dani took the elevator back to her office, which was now locked. "Ugh, security!" She raced to the lobby, immediately finding Larry, head of security, coming her way. "Thank goodness," she mumbled. Dani had come to really like Larry. He was her go-to person when she forgot her badge and her office keys at home, or when she was just having a hard day. He always gave her a wink and a smile. She often brought the security guys pastries and hot coffee from Le Ric's just to show her gratitude.

"Larry, hey, I'm locked out of my office. I need some help, please," Dani smiled.

"Ms. Breaux, may I see your badge?"

"Absolutely, thanks, Larry."

Directly behind her, one of the security guys reached for her bag. Not expecting it, Dani let go of her bag, but then reached to grab it back after realizing she had let it go.

"Hey, what are you do—"

"Ms. Dani," Larry said calmly, sticking her badge in his pocket, "let's talk."

Dani realized that she was being escorted from the building. Before the other guys went through her gym bag, Larry grabbed it, and held it under his arm. The other security guy seemed to be in agreement not to search her bag.

"Ms. Dani," Larry said sadly, "we have orders," he said, looking down at her.

"Is this about the dungeon?" Dani asked. "I have a gold star on my badge. I didn't take any clothing, just samples for the shoot." Suddenly recalling the body butters, she said, "Oh, and maybe just a—"

"Stop!" Larry cut her off before she implicated herself in anything else. "We received orders last week, Ms. Breaux. I thought you knew."

"Last week?" Dani asked, puzzled. "I just spoke to Sidnae this morning." As Dani looked around, she saw three security guys standing around her, barely able to look in her direction.

"Ms. Dani, I took the liberty of packing your things," said Jim, another security guard. "I know how much they mean to you."

"Thanks." Dani remembered when Jim told her that his fifteen-year-old daughter, Kelsey, had been diagnosed with cancer. While the surgery went well and they removed it all, she had to have chemo and lost all of her hair. She was depressed and ashamed to go to school. Dani spent quite a few evenings talking to her, baking cookies, and sharing Adrian's makeup tips. Sometimes she would even pop up at the high school to take her to lunch. Just a month ago, Dani, Cammie, and Becca picked her up in Becca's drop-top convertible to celebrate her making straight A's. They took pics throughout the day and Dani had them framed for her office.

"You're a part of my family, Dani," Jim said, choking back tears. "And you always will be," he said, staring at the ground. "Kelsey showed me that video you made. That thing was kick-ass," he said.

"Hell, yeah," said Ray, another security officer, as they all laughed in unison.

When Larry looked up, the guys returned to their professional stature. "Ms. Dani, you are now free to go," Larry smiled, handing her the full gym bag and the box of things from her office.

Dani walked out the double doors of Sari for the last time. When she looked up, Larry winked and gave her one last smile. While she didn't live that far from work, that day, the walk home seemed extremely long and depressing. She had a feeling this was coming, but never expected it to happen so soon.

When Dani got home, she found herself sulking, unsure of what to do about job security since her career at Sari was officially over. "Looks like it's just you and me now, Jackson," Dani said, as she watched him play in the backyard.

Later that day, Talia called and explained that the company decided it was best to part ways due to a conflict of interest. For years, Dani has been saving almost every dime of her paychecks outside of her bills, transferring monies to interest earned accounts, and ensuring her stocks were still lucrative. Financially, she was doing okay. Talia offered her a very nice severance package that would last her for quite some time with budgeting. In addition, Talia had a connection who offered her a two-year government contract that she could parlay into a more permanent position. Without thinking twice, Dani happily accepted. While she had only been unemployed for the last four hours, the feeling was just too much to bear.

The rest of the day felt different, like a bad dream. Still in a daze, Dani took Jackson for an evening walk to the neighborhood store and picked up groceries for the week. She had money in her bank account, and a new government job that insisted she work from home. She was following her dreams to do something different, yet she felt a sadness that she just couldn't shake. Moving in a steady trance, Dani nearly walked past her house until she spotted Becca and Cammie sitting on the porch.

"Hey, what are you guys doing here?" Dani said. "Who cares, just come in," she said. "I've have had quite a day! Get in here, and grab a glass," Dani said as she pulled the expensive wine from the shelf, courtesy of the gift box.

Once inside, Cammie aimed straight for the kitchen. Grabbing the set of miniature shot glasses she'd left the last time she was there, she brought them to the bar counter and sat a glass in front of Becca and Dani. Before Dani could ask what was going on, Cammie went back into the kitchen in search of snacks. She went from cabinet to pantry, unable to find anything salty or sweet enough to count as a bad snack.

"Dammit! Where are the simple carbs? Dani, you have got to do better," Cammie said, breathing a sigh of relief after finding the stash of goodies from the mystery gift box. "Girl, I know you don't have no cracklins up in here," Cammie said with excitement as she scarfed down the crunchy seasoned snacks. "Mmm, everybody, grab a chip, and pick up your glass," she said, filling them with a shot of Crown Royal and squeezing lemon juice on top. "Now, on the count of three, let's toast."

"Wait," Dani said as she looked at Becca who was not raising her shot glass.

"I took a few tests, and they were all negative," Becca said.

"Good catch, Dani," Cammie said. "Now, let's try this again, on the count of three, everybody toast. Cammie cleared her throat as she swallowed the strong, brown liquid. "One more, straight up," she said, pouring another round.

The ladies all grabbed their throats, reeling from the burning sensation of the brown alcohol tingling in their chest.

"Dani," Cammie said, "Joshua got married last weekend, and his wife is six months pregnant with, twins. I'm sorry sis. There's no easy way to say that shit."

Becca filled their three shot glasses again and took her time licking a chip she had placed against her tongue to soak up the salt before drinking again.

"Well," Dani said, "I guess one can't stay single forever." She grabbed her glass and held it up, waiting for the ladies to join in. "To my ex, congratulations, and may you have the family of your dreams that you've always wanted."

"Salud," Becca yelled.

AND, Cammie interjected, "May you experience one hundred percent! DOUBLE FOLD! The entirety of the legacy that babies, toddlers, children, teenagers, and young adults bring to their parents."

"Come on and preach!" Becca yelled.

Cammie continued, "AND, may your children be a spitting reflection of you in every… single… way."

"Salud," Becca said.

"In a good way, with showers of blessings," Dani interjected before they drank.

"Uh, in the way I said, I can handle my own toast," Cammie grumbled.

"So, how are you feeling with all this, doll?" Becca said, reaching for Dani's hand. "I know this is a lot. Did you know anything about it? Did he call you?"

"I saw the missed calls. I made a mental note to call him back, but with all the work stuff, I simply got sidetracked. I'm good, though. At some point, we all have to move on with our lives. Contrary to popular belief, we do not hate one another and really do want what's best," said Dani.

"So, you good with all this?" Cammie asked, feeling like Dani was holding back.

"Yep, I got bigger fish to fry. I got fired today."

"Oh, no," Becca said, wrapping her arms around Dani's shoulder and pulling her in for a cheek-to-cheek hug.

"Good," Cammie said while throwing back her last shot. "They did what you didn't have the heart to do. They let go. Isn't that grace or mercy?" Cammie asked, gulping down another shot.

"Sari Unique," Becca said, pondering the name in a drunken buzz.

"More like uniquely sorry," Cammie said as they burst into laughter.

"Sounds like you guys have had a little too much to drink," said Dani.

"Bull!" Becca replied, "It'll take a whole lot more than that to fill this tank," she said, whipping her hair side to side, attempting to do a dance she saw on television.

"Girl, you better stop. You gonna mess around and get a crook in your neck," Cammie said.

"A what? A thief gonna get in my neck? Whatever! I need some food," Becca said, half stumbling into the kitchen.

"Oh, I got something! Wait, wait," Dani said as she jumped up and ran to the freezer, anxious to showcase the smoked boudin from the mystery box.

"What's that? What you got?" Cammie asked as she followed close behind, both her and Becca looking over Dani's shoulder.

"Oh, heck, nah! I'm not eating nobody's pig colon," Becca said. "I'm ordering a pizza."

"No, ma'am! Don't you cuss our Louisiana people like that," Cammie said. "Dani and I know what boudin is! But we're eating it because it's good," she commented while breaking off a piece and stuffing it into her mouth. "On second thought, you're right, order the pizza. You won't like this," Cammie said as she wrapped up a frozen link to take home.

"Oh, no, you don't," Becca said as she marched back into the kitchen and grabbed the link from Cammie's hand.

Pushing them both to the side, Dani grabbed a smoking hot link of boudin from the oven and set it on a plate. She opened the cabinet above the stove, and with a long pair of tongs, pulled at the family-size bag of Doritos until it fell on the floor. She picked it up and put a handful of chips on her plate next to the hot boudin. She then grabbed a cold, strawberry Fanta from the bottom of the refrigerator, tucked away in the back.

After Becca and Cammie stopped playing, they watched as Dani took a bite, pulling back the skin as the smell of the seasoned link filled the air. They quickly let go of each other and followed Dani's lead. After eating boudin, Doritos, and pecan candy, they packed up all the leftover food from the mystery box. Cammie called her connection to deliver it to a homeless shelter. With their bellies still full, they lay on the living room floor talking about Becca's so-called secret relationship with Javi, Cammie's NBA lover/undercover fiancée, and Dani's secret admirer.

"I think it's Larry, the security guy at Sari Unique. That man is so fine, and he got the hots for you, boo," Cammie said.

"Nope," Becca said. "It's Langston Jr. I could see it in his eyes when he dropped you off at the restaurant that night. That's your baby daddy," Becca laughed, obviously buzzing from the alcohol, as they knew Dani could not have children. "Oh, Dani, I'm sorry. I didn't mean that."

"It's okay," Dani said as she closed her eyes and laid back down.

"I'm so sorry," Becca cried. "I can't imagine how you feel. Your ex-husband getting married and having the babies you always wanted, and then having to lose your ovaries to a damn hysterectomy, and not being able to have babies ever!"

"Becca, did you really take the pregnancy test?" Cammie asked.

"Pregnancy test? What for?" Becca said, blowing her nose. "Y'all know I can't get pregnant. I paid a whole team of doctors to tell me that. I don't need no dang pregnancy test to confirm nothing. Besides, it's the hormone pills they started me on last month that has me missing my period."

As they went back and forth, Dani closed her eyes for what felt like a second. She just wanted to be alone with her thoughts just for a minute.

"Dani, you okay?" Cammie asked.

"Yep. Just thinking," Dani sighed. "I was so focused on trying to get pregnant again more than anything else. I was willing to put my body through whatever surgery it took to make it happen."

"But why? That's not what you wanted; you were terrified. So many babies out there needed a home. I never understood why you made your body the only option," said Cammie.

"Because it wasn't just about me or my wants, Cammie. But you're right! I was terrified. I just couldn't live with myself unless I did everything in my power to have children. I was so terrified of those surgeries," Dani laughed. "I was praying to God every time I walked into a doctor's office and saw a needle. I asked him to protect me through whatever procedure or surgery was ahead. And if it wasn't for me, then to remove it from my path and give me peace. One surgeon told me that as much as he was thankful that my obstetrician recommended him, he did not believe invasive surgery was the answer, and he refused. Another doctor advised the same, but I still kept going, from doctor to doctor," Dani said. "You should have seen their faces," Dani laughed. "They would walk into the patient room and see this exhausted bald woman with bags under her eyes, less than six months from the previous miscarriage. As they read through my medical chart, I swear, I could literally hear their hearts hit the floor. Still, nothing they said was gonna make me stop trying. That is until the week before another scheduled surgery, when breast cancer showed up. At that point, I finally took a breath," Dani laughed again, as Becca and Cammie listened, shedding silent tears.

In the stillness of the room and the crackling fireplace, the soft sounds of Sade filled the air, easing their hearts as each of them thought of their own struggles with men, their careers, and having children. Dani closed her eyes, and by the time she opened them, her house was dark, and she was covered with blankets. Becca and Cammie lay beside her, and Jackson came running, seemingly knowing this was not their daily routine. Dani struggled to stand up and walk to the kitchen sink. She drank three cups of water, and then poured some into Jackson's bowl. She cleaned the kitchen, brushed her teeth, and lay down on the floor, quickly falling back to sleep. When she woke up the second time, Becca and Cammie were gone. They put everything in its place, just as it was before, like they were never there. On the table, she saw a Le'Ric's cup of golden milk and a breakfast bag with a note leaning against it:

"Dani, take the time you need and then call me. We have work to do. See you at my place tomorrow. P.S. We got you. Love, Cam & Bec.

As Dani climbed into the shower to get ready for the day, she thought about her next writing assignment. She had already received an email from a local magazine requesting her to write a piece. As she smiled to herself, she couldn't help thinking about new beginnings and the opportunities coming her way. Doors were closing and opening at the same time, and she wasn't sure how to feel about it.

Dani recalled a time long ago when she stopped pursuing her dreams, and hustling became her reality. At the age of twenty, after barely being married a year, Dani was already divorcing her first husband. She knew at that point it was important for her to hustle because she refused to stay in an unhealthy relationship just to get by.

Several years later, when she met Joshua, she was trying to make a name for herself in the corporate industry. When Joshua asked about her dreams, she said, "Dreams? I write pieces here and there as a hobby. I used to have this fascination with physicians when I was a kid. I wanted to be just like them and save the world, but then life happened. The hustle is real," Dani said.

"So are dreams. Never stop dreaming," Joshua said. He reminded her of the importance of never giving up on herself even if someone you love gives up on you.

As she smiled to herself, thinking of that moment, her heart broke with sadness for the babies she lost, the husband who gave up, and the possibility of childbirth that would never be her reality. And just like that, Dani broke down. She sat against the wall of the shower, sobbing, and praying for the water to wash away the pain.

"God, sometimes acceptance hurts." She recalled hearing the baby's heartbeat at the doctor's appointments, and the moment she felt blood trickling down her leg while she was standing in line at the grocery store. "God, I gave him back to you," Dani cried. "My miracle baby. I know women lose babies all the time, but the cancer has taken away my ability to even try again. Maybe it's part of the process of whatever you have for me. It's just that sometimes accepting it hurts so much," she cried, sobbing on the shower floor until the hot water ran cold.

When Cammie first realized Dani was struggling with her loss, she pressed Dani to get counseling, and she did. In the beginning, she could barely watch a baby commercial without breaking down, and she never celebrated baby showers or even showed up for acquaintances who had given birth. While she was happy for them, it was too hard to be present. After some time, Dani realized that after all her body had gone through, she did not want to birth a child. The chemotherapy, radiation, and five years of monthly shots made her physically and mentally exhausted. She prayed to God for guidance and scheduled the final part of the process to remove her uterus, as her doctors had recommended five years before.

Dani believed that her restoration would be greater than anything she'd lost. Once the water in the shower turned cold, Dani dried off, sipped her golden milk, and ate the soft, oatmeal blueberry muffin. She took her allergy meds and climbed into bed. As if he understood, Jackson jumped up on the bed and snuggled against Dani, and they drifted off to sleep.

"Kevin? Cammie here. I got it! Yes, it's a wrap, my friend," Cammie said as she threw her head back with excitement. "Dammit, I love what I do! Get here as soon as you can. Okay, I'll see you soon," she said as she happily plopped her cellphone down on the couch.

Cammie had a hard time trusting anyone, and while Kevin, her assistant, had proven himself to be trustworthy, this particular deal was not something that could risk any errors. Immediately after Kevin left, she decided to call her right-hand man, well, technically her father's right-hand man.

"Uncle Johnny, it's done. Kevin's on the way with the documents."

"You really need to take some time off, kid. Uncle Johnny's got it, alright?"

"Of course. I just wanted to tell you I love you."

"Awww, don't make an old man cry, right back at ya kid, he said in his old Italian accent. Call your father when you get a chance. I just seen him; he misses you."

"Will do. Thanks, Uncle Johnny." Cammie looked forward to taking some time away and letting the business run for itself. And with the venture she was working on, she and her sisters would be set for life. Most importantly, her father could finally retire. "Pretty soon, I'm gonna have time to be a real girlfriend to my man, or maybe even a wife, who knows," Cammie said to herself. "All I know is that history is about to be made."

Cammie never wanted to have kids, and she was happy that her rumored fiancé, Harris, understood that. She didn't mind adopting a child, but she would never birth her own baby, and she had a hysterectomy to confirm it. When she finally broke down and told Harris the news, she assumed he would break up with her at some point. Instead, he convinced her that he was fine with it, and they would use other options to have children. Struggling with endometriosis and fibroids had taken a toll on her health, and Cammie grew tired of fighting it. The constant battle of losing weight and being bald stressed her self-esteem and led to depression. Once she decided to give up the wigs for good, she focused on living the life she wanted to live, even if it meant removing her uterus. She worked hard to maintain her health and wellness, often appearing selfish to others.

Last summer at a Professional Bald Women's Network event, one of the pregnant ladies jokingly asked Cammie when she was going to sacrifice her figure and join the ranks of motherhood. Cammie simply replied without explanation, "Sacrifice my figure for children? Never!"

Unbeknownst to the ladies in the group, Cammie had shared her concerns about pregnancy with Becca and Dani years ago. She feared that if her stomach grew, she would look like Uncle Festus from the Adams Family. She chuckled as she remembered the time she dressed as Uncle Festus for Halloween. Only she didn't need the fake stomach; her real one worked just fine. It was the worst Halloween ever as everyone kept telling her how much she looked just like him. All Cammie could think about was that it was true. She never wanted to go back to that place, not even to have kids. She knew it was selfish, but no one understood the level of depression that followed. The kids made fun of her so much as a kid, she swallowed a bottle of pills. She wasn't going back to that place for anybody. She was thankful for the painful periods and the diagnosis that followed, giving her a reason to follow through with her decision on motherhood.

Later that night as Cammie relaxed in her hotel suite, she assumed Dani was not going to show up once the clock hit eleven pm, so she headed upstairs to bed. Just then, someone knocked on the hotel room door. "Who is it?" she said, swinging the door open.

"I think you're supposed to wait for an answer before opening the door," Dani said as she walked into the penthouse suite with her backpack thrown over her shoulder.

"Dani, nice of you to show up. You know where to find the guest bedroom. Goodnight," Cammie said, heading back towards her room.

"What? So, you don't wanna work?" Dani asked.

"You're aware that no one messes with my sleep time, right?" Cammie said. Still excited about the venture that lay ahead, she decided to forego her sleep schedule and fill Dani in. "I'm making coffee, and you're drinking it," Cammie said, making a detour towards the kitchen. "Nobody has golden milk for you over here. Spoiled ass," Cammie joked, secretly excited over the idea of working with her best friend. "I guess I can call downstairs and have them get some nut milk, she relented."

"I'm fine with coffee, but you can get me some fries with garlic aioli and ketchup," Dani said."

"You can't just have ketchup with the fries? You gotta have garlic aioli," she joked. "But it does sound good though," Cammie said as she dialed room service, adding her favorite truffle sauce to the request.

For the next few hours they worked, plotted, and planned their next course of action. As Dani's head bobbed back and forth in and out of sleep, Cammie stared at her best friend with a newfound confidence. Without a shadow of doubt, she knew that Dani would carry out their plan perfectly. She wished she could tell Dani all the details, but she knew that Dani would not approve. If she felt like she was hurting anyone, she would pull out and ruin everything. Cammie just couldn't take that chance. Maybe it was selfish, but she had too much to lose to give it a second thought. Satisfied with herself, she turned off the lights and went to bed, anxious for the upcoming events.

Fourteen

THE LEGACY

"Hey boss, it's Austin. I'm outside."

"Come on up. Security is expecting you."

For months Langston Jr. waited on the results about the art prints he found in the shed at the family estate. Knowing his old man, Langston had already figured it out. The proof was just going to confirm what he already suspected; that his father had stolen his mother's designs. When his mother found out about it, he used some of the money he made restoring Sari to fund her business. The story the two of them concocted of Naomi selling so many products from the lobby that she opened her own business was a complete fabrication. Langston checked the real books, not the ones his father used for taxes, and there was no record of revenue. In addition, there was no real record of his mother's business until two years after it was opened. "That's the only weird part I can't seem to figure out," Langston mumbled as he poured a drink for Austin and one for himself. Langston smiled, envisioning his mother's reaction to the fully restored painting of her stolen masterpiece. All he needed to do now was secure this last piece of evidence to officially remove his father from the company. Thanks to Austin and his connection, he was able to secure records and signed statements of illegal practices from previous workers whom Sidreaux Sr. had abused, blackmailed, and mistreated for over a decade.

"Boss?"

"Austin," Langston smiled as he hugged his old buddy. Austin was more like an uncle, closer to him than his own father. "Look at you, man! I'm so proud of you," Austin smiled as he took the drink from Langston and sat on the barstool.

"It's really good to see you, son."

"Same here. It's been too long," said Langston. Austin was the only long-time family friend who never mentioned Sidreaux Sr. Everyone else always marveled that Langston Jr. was an exact replica of his father during his younger years. Like a parental guardian, Austin attended all of Langston Jr's football games and school events. He even helped him with his science projects and talked to him about his first crush.

Unknown to Austin, Langston was eavesdropping the day his father tried to blackmail him. Sidreaux Sr. used the same tactics on Austin as he did with the other crooked employees of the estate, or as his mother called them, goons. Most of them caved at the idea of being blacklisted, banished from the country, and unable to support their wives and children. Austin was different. He was quiet, observant, nonchalant, and strong-willed. Born in the South and raised by a single mother, as a young man, he did what he had to do to make ends meet. That's why it shocked Langston to see Austin go toe to toe with his father, respectfully declining his offer and resigning his position as a family goon.

The next time Langston saw Austin was at his mother's funeral several years later. Langston overheard the butlers at his father's estate mention to Austin about her passing as they were still friends. Langston admired him like a son to a father. After the funeral, he promised himself that he would never lose contact with Austin again.

"I know you don't like to mince words too much, boss, but I think you might wanna take a seat for this one," Austin said.

"Very well," Langston said as he sat in a nearby chair. "I thought you were bringing the uh…contact with you?"

"Oh, I just spoke to his secretary on the phone; he'll be along shortly. I told security he was coming in right behind me."

"Perfect. Before we get started, I received the return envelope from you, for services rendered. I figured you might do that, so I had your pay placed into an account in your name."

"I appreciate that, boss. But that's too much money for just a couple of leads here and there. Besides, like I told you, I enjoy the freelance work that I do."

"Austin, I am not my father. You are like family to me, one of the best parts of my childhood. I take care of my own, no strings attached."

"I appreciate that," Austin said, visually ready to move on from the conversation.

"Should we wait for your contact," Langston asked?

"Nah, I'd say you and I should get a head start. You were right to be concerned about the prints. The origins, technique, everything about them is completely different from the other paintings by your ancestors. Nothing in your family history like it."

"Okay, so what are you saying?"

"Well, Isaac said they reminded him of his hometown."

"Isaac? Isaac is from West Africa. Well, that can't be it," Langston chuckled. "I think I know exactly what happened, and this is all starting to make sense to me."

"I'm not so sure you do, boss. Turns out Isaac's right. Once we got a professional to determine the origin of the paintings, we ran the signature. We couldn't find anything, but my connection was able to put all the missing pieces together."

"Put all the pieces together? You're speaking in code. Tell me what this connection was able to find." Langston said.

Austin, standing to his feet when he heard the doorbell ring, said, "That's probably him right there."

"I got it," Langston said, placing his drink on the edge of the bar and swiftly walking towards the door.

"Langston, good to see you again. Oh, you probably don't remember me, do you? We never officially met. Austin? Is that you, or have I just met my future husband?"

"Well, my eyes must be deceiving me, Cammie-Liana Lawfton is that you?" Austin said, squinting his eyes to get a better look. Girl, if you don't get over here and put your arms around this old cowboy's neck!" Austin laughed with joy as he and Cammie embraced. "You are the spitting image of your father! Oh, my goodness. This is such a wonderful surprise!" Austin said, embracing her again.

"Yes, it is," Cammie said, dabbing away tears. "My daddy wanted me to give you this," she said, handing Austin a cooler.

"No, he didn't," Austin said in disbelief, opening the cooler.

"Oh, yes, he did," Cammie replied.

Austin smiled at the homemade lasagna and tiramisu sitting in the cooler. "He remembered, after all these years?"

"You know he never forgets your birthday. Remember, you're the one whose been gone, Uncle Austin. Daddy was so happy when you called. He talks about you all the time."

"Excuse me," Langston interrupted, clearing his throat for effect. "Austin, who is our guest? Is this my contact?"

"I guess so boss. I wasn't expecting Ms. Cammie, but she is the best, just like her father, from what I understand."

"I got it," Cammie interrupted. "I'm here on behalf of the Lawfton firm, after hours. Shall we get to the paintings?" Cammie said, pulling documents from her briefcase. "The prints were painted by a Ghanaian artist. After our research confirmed it, we went a step further for extra confirmation. Daddy hates errors," Cammie smiled. "These are additional prints from the same artist," Cammie said, spreading several photographs across the top of the custom-made bar. "Notice how the signatures and the dates are all the same, even on the old black and white prints."

"So? How does this prove who painted the sketches from my basement? Surely you don't think my painting was around in the 1800s?" Langston smiled smugly, as he stood towering over Cammie.

"Oh, Jr., of course not," Cammie smiled in return, seemingly enjoying herself a bit too much as she pulled another picture from her briefcase. "This is Effia, born and raised in Ghana. That signature and those dates belong to these people, her ancestors," Cammie stated as she pulled out more photographs and documents confirming the origins. "Unfortunately, they all passed away many years ago, before your dad used these designs."

"Then, how would my father get something like this? Before using these designs, we were damn near piss poor, surviving only on the family estate."

"Sure, if you wanna call living in a multimillion-dollar estate piss poor," Cammie mumbled.

"There was no money for trips to Ghana, Ms. Lawfton," Langston said. "Where did he get the prints?

"Kisi," Cammie replied as she produced another photo.

Hearing the name made Langston pause. "The nanny? You think Kisi painted these?"

Pulling more photos from her case, Cammie replied, "This is Kisi, in Ghana, standing next to her grandfather as he painted that print," Cammie said, pointing to the restored, framed-cylinder piece Langston was gifting to his mother for her anniversary.

"That can't be true. We checked the ingredients. That's my mother's recipe for her Signature line."

"Right and wrong, Mr. Sidreaux."

"Ms. Cammie, why don't you let me take it from here," Austin said.

"No, let her finish," Langston sternly replied.

Knowing that look all too well, Austin took his drink to the sofa in the corner of the sitting room.

"I present to you the fragrance that changed the world," Cammie said as she pulled the next photograph from her case. "This is Kisi's grandmother and grandfather, the parents of Effia, selling those very wooden cylinders that are in that photo. What a great artist her grandfather, Arban, was. Look at the resemblance of the designs? And here, we have this photo of Kisi in the U.S, with the actual cylinders on her dresser. I'm sure you can guess what was actually in them. Notice the dresser in the background. Isn't that the planta-I mean, the Sidreaux Family estate?" Cammie said, purposely stopping short of saying the word plantation.

"So, my family has an old African print that may have belonged to our nanny. Surely this all means something, or you wouldn't be here. Speak! You said I'm right and wrong, Ms. Lawfton. How?" Langston asked as his voice roared throughout the room

"Langston, please, son, lets me and you sit down like family and talk," Austin pleaded.

"It's okay, Austin," Cammie said, meeting Langston's glare as he peered into her eyes. "As you suggested to Austin, your father is, in fact, a thief. Kudos to you for that suspicion. However, while your parents did indeed pay for the ingredients and packaging, the Signature Body Butter is not Naomi's creation. It was Kisi who introduced your father to her family's recipe, adding additional ingredients to it to make it her own, right there in your father's kitchen."

"And how do you know this?" Langston asked.

"You see when Naomi's mother got sick and she went to stay with her for a while, Kisi took that opportunity to prove to your father that she was more than just a nanny, housekeeper. She wanted to make a life for herself, for her family back in Ghana. She wanted your father to represent her brand. Unfortunately, while Naomi was away tending to her mother, your father allegedly raped young Kisi. He then formed a relationship with her, housing her in the lake house several miles away from civilization. I think he may have fallen for her," Cammie blushed, "but well, he was already married to Naomi. The products, and the lotions he sold for Kisi brought in a decent amount of money, so he stole them for himself. Kisi couldn't do anything about it because she didn't have the means to fight him."

"Stop! Ms. Lawfton, you may know the law, but I know my parents," Langston chuckled. "I knew it," he said, laughing heartily. "As a matter of fact, I told Austin that I suspected all of this, the theft, the lies. Austin, you really didn't need to hire a connection for this, but I appreciate you for being so thorough," Langston said. "I can always count on you, he said shaking Austin's hand and patting his back like an old friend. What do ya say we have the kitchen fire up the grill, old man? For old times' sake?" Langston said.

"Mr. Langston, I'm not done," Cammie said.

"But I am," Langston replied. "Ms. Lawfton, as interesting as my father's infidelity may be to you, I'm an only child, yet I have siblings that are my age. There's nothing you can say about my parents that would shock me. I know my father well enough."

"Agreed, but do you know your mother? My purpose is not to expose Sidreaux Sr.," said Cammie. "I'm here representing this woman, your real mother," Cammie said as she pulled out a recent picture of Kisi. "Once she had you, your father kept her around, even purchased a brand-new house for her, so no one would know. Like I said, I think in his own twisted way, he'd fallen in love. Surely, she was in love with him. But once Naomi found out about their sordid love affair, she threatened to divorce him, and well, you know the Sidreaux Family laws. Who cares about an affair, but an illegitimate son? His only son? Long story short, your father had your real mother Kisi deported, and you became the son Naomi never had. She spent over a year in seclusion with you to ensure no one ever questioned your birth. Now, hats off to Naomi because she loved you like her own child. That's a lot to take in for a woman who kept having one miscarriage after another, seven or eight tops, I believe. Why would a woman with nothing vested stay in a relationship with a stank-ass man like that? Well, when somebody offers you your own fragrance line and a whole company to boot, you stay for at least eight years." Cammie said.

"Oh, and just in case you ever wondered why you never saw any baby pictures or any pictures of your mother pregnant with you, here they are," Cammie said, pulling photos of Langston as a baby from her briefcase. There were pictures of Kisi pregnant, sitting on Sidreaux Sr.'s lap at the lake house, another photo showed the two of them frolicking in the lake, and one of baby

Langston napping next to his real mother, Kisi, and his father. "Kisi's aunt was a great photographer," Cammie said. "Your father had no idea she was taking pictures. She took Kisi's old job, working at the house your father purchased."

After Cammie stopped speaking, silence filled the air for what seemed like an eternity. "You both can leave now," Langston whispered.

"Understood. When you're ready, Mr. Langston, we need to discuss your inheritance to Sari Unique. According to the bylaws, the heirs must be produced from marriage. I'm gonna leave my card on this table, and you can call me," Cammie said as she made her way towards the door. "Oh, and one more thing. You can tell your daddy, I'm coming for him," Cammie said as she placed the documents back into her briefcase.

"Langston, I'm so sorry, son," Austin said, "I didn't know about all of this."

"It's okay," Langston replied, Turning his back away from Cammie while trying to hide the frog in his throat. "Cammie? You look familiar. Were you a guest at the launch for the Sari campaign for Dani?"

"Yes! I was there for Dani," Cammie interjected, glaring at Langston's back like a lion marking her prey, unaware that he could see her reflection from the mirror on the wall.

"Well done," he whispered. "Well done, indeed. Cecil, can you please see them out please?" Langston called to his butler as he quietly drifted up the winding staircase. Once he was out of earshot, he rammed his fist through the glass mirror in the hallway. Breathing a sigh of relief, he pulled his hand back and rammed it into the wall, wishing the blood dripping from his hand was from his father's face. Unable to express his emotions, he longed to feel something to release the anger in his heart. Staring at himself between the pieces of cracked glass, Langston recalled a conversation he had with his father the evening of his tenth birthday party after all his guests had gone home. His father told him to sit down so he could talk with him.

"Your mother and I have been separated for two years. We're getting a divorce. Tomorrow you're leaving to attend school away from home. You'll come back every few months. During this time, you will learn how to become the heir of a billion-dollar company. As you know, I am not like your mother. So, do not expect any hugs or affection or play of any kind. I will never come to your games or school events."

"I don't understand, father. You're getting a divorce?" Langston whimpered. "What about me? What about my games? What if the school needs to see you?"

"Mr. Austin will be there," Sidreaux said.

"What if I get scared? I'll just go with Mom! I don't wanna go," Langston cried. "Please father, I'll go with mom," he wailed."

"No! You are my heir, and you'll do as I say. Stop crying. Now! Sidreaux Sr's roar echoed through the mansion. "Look at me," he said, grabbing Langston's face and looking angrily into his eyes. "You must never let another man see you cry. Ever! You are a billionaire's, son," he said. Sidreaux Sr then got down on his knees and faced his son. "Come, he said, as he held out his arms and embraced Langston Jr in loving embrace, allowing him to cry on

his shoulder. "You will yearn for my hugs, but you will never feel them again. This will be difficult at first, but one day you will thank me. My father did the same to me, and I turned a failing company into what it is today. It's the Sidreaux way, son. Do you understand?"

"Yes," Langston said, pulling away from his father and quickly wiping his tears.

From that day on, Langston and his father never spent twenty-four hours under the same roof. When he came home on school breaks, the house staff was waiting, but his father was gone. Langston spent most of his time at his mother's new house or on the estate alone, with the staff. Once he was in high school, he attended summer retreats, only going home for the holidays, when he officially met his father's new family. Sidreaux Sr. never told him he loved him or showed him any kind of parental love or affection ever again. Everything was strictly business.

Later that night, in his soundproof workout room, Langston wept loud, bitter screams, pausing only to catch his breath as his heart raced through his chest from beating the heavy bag. Hoping his anger would subside with every bare-handed punch, he slammed his bloody fist against the cold heavy bag over and over again. He was numb to the pieces of glass digging deeper into his flesh. Unable to control his rage, he continued on and on until his bone was protruding from his hand, and he could no longer make a fist. As if nothing had ever happened, he nonchalantly wrapped his wrist in a towel, wiped his face, and pressed the wall intercom for assistance.

"Cecil, I'm feeling a little hungry, have the kitchen prepare crab omelets, please."

"Yes, sir. Will that be all?"

"No, I'd like a whiskey milkshake after dinner."

"Right away, sir. Will there be anything else?"

"No. Yes, have Dr. Barry meet me at the hospital. I'll have my dinner when I return."

"Are you okay, Mr. Langston? Should I call Ms. Ebony, sir?"

"I'm fine. In fact, I couldn't be better," Langston happily replied. "Just got a little carried away in the weight room. You know, with the holidays coming," Langston said. "I'm making room for Mrs. Cecil's sweet potato pie."

"Well, I certainly do understand that" Cecil said cheerfully. "It is the best in town, sir."

"I couldn't agree more," Langston said.

"I'll have the car ready when you come down sir."

"Thank you, Cecil."

Just as Langston suspected, his wrist was broken. After all the glass was removed and a splint was in place, Langston canceled his dinner at home and opted to go into town for a local burger and shake. Sidreaux Sr. called while the doctor was setting his bone back in place.

"Son, are you on vacation?"

"Just a sore wrist, Dad, nothing of concern."

"A sore wrist. If you were in Paris, then PERHAPS YOUR WRIST WOULDN'T BE AN ISSUE! Damn, mutt," he mumbled.

Mutt? Langston wondered to himself. His father had been calling him a mutt since he was a child. Up until the age of ten, he assumed it was his middle name until his mother demanded his father call him by his name.

"Son, I don't have to tell you how important it is to stay ahead of the competition. Someone is always waiting to take your place—to claim your seat! We have a legacy to protect, a bloodline."

"Of course, father. Don't worry, I'm taking care of the bloodline. I'll see you soon."

Fifteen

DIAMOND IN THE ROUGH

"Dani Breaux? My name is Lawrence, your driver. I'm here to escort you to the Winston gala this evening."

"I'll be out in just a minute," Dani replied on the intercom as she took one final glance at herself in the mirror. "You look like a princess," she mumbled to her reflection. "I can't believe Adrian would do this," she said, admiring her dress. On the delivery card, Adrian wrote: *Because when it's time for diamonds in the rough to shine, honey, we make 'em holla!*

Adrian's amazing gift was fully realized when Dani opened her door first thing in the morning. There stood a makeup artist along with a hairstylist.

"Hello! I'm your hairstylist, Trey Mitchell," the gentleman beamed.

Dani stared at him, waiting for Trey to realize the irony of the situation.

With a smile, he simply said, "Oh, honey, you don't need hair. Watch me work!"

A few hours later, here she was, still staring at the finished product. She had to admit her bald head had never felt so supple and smooth. Her scalp was baby soft, even toned, and conditioned without the appearance of tan lines or makeup. Just as hair complemented a woman's style, Dani's bald head was doing the exact same thing, except it was effortlessly perfect.

"Shout out to the hairstylist who doesn't need hair to make it happen," Dani said, excited about her follow-up appointment with Trey.

The dress Adrian sent was a heavy floor-length silver corset ensemble covered in crystals with a thigh-high split on the side. She wore tiny teardrop earrings with a matching tennis bracelet and necklace. While the jewelry was simple, next to her melanin skin it, was enough to light up a room.

"I can't believe I look like this," Dani stared at her image in the mirror while blinking her eyes repeatedly to stop the tears from accumulating. "It's all me! Nothing but lashes to remove at the end of the night. Just a short time ago, she would have never gone to a ritzy event like this without a gorgeous custom lace front wig professionally installed. "Look at how far you've come," Dani whispered to her reflection as a tear escaped down her face. "Oh no, no, no," she said, quickly dabbing it away and touching up her face. "Well, here goes nothing. Jackson, wish me luck. Mama's got this in the bag," she said as she winked at her reflection and walked out the door.

READY, CAMERA, ACTION!

"Ladies and gentlemen, give it up for the entertainment tonight! Our celebrity guests have given us a concert right here in our own backyard," the emcee said to cheers and whistles from the crowd. "The Naomi Foundation donates millions to communities all over the world," he said as the stadium-size overhead screens featured videos of the foundation building homes for single mothers and funding various projects for children's shelters. The one that shocked Dani the most, was the surrogacy program for women unable to have children. Naomi uses her own money to pay full medical expenses and benefits to sponsor twenty surrogates every year.

"Wow, kudos to you," Dani mumbled.

"My dear, we love you, we salute you, and we honor you," the emcee said. "As for me, you are not just my boss. You are a self-made minority woman of power, something many of us who were raised in homeless shelters never had the opportunity to experience up close and personal. To your family, we thank you from the bottom of our hearts for sharing your queen with us," he said, as the audience cheered in response. "With that being said, uh, Ms. Naomi, come on up here and show these people how to walk, Ms. Thang," the emcee said, as Naomi rose to the occasion.

Naomi served a flawless runway walk down the red carpet and up to the stage like it was her job. She was an ageless beauty. Her dress was a simple emerald-green slip gown with the kind of thigh split that knew no bounds. She wore large diamond studs and a massive diamond ring. Her silvery hair was full, with thick loose curls flowing down her muscular back.

Dani had never seen Naomi smile this much. She wished Becca was here to see this, but she was happy that Lisa and Dr. Foster had flown in as her plus ones. When Dani arrived,

Cammie was the first person she noticed in the sea of people wearing a backless sequin white jumpsuit.

"I see you," Cammie mouthed to Dani, "but I need to take a call. Be right back," she said, turning to answer her phone.

In the meantime, Dani sipped a glass of wine while embracing the ambiance of the evening. The ballroom was stunning, everything and everyone in pearl white or silver, with the exception of Naomi. Always a woman of few words, after a couple of one-liners, she thanked her fans and proceeded to make her way toward the media. As the crowd began drifting outside to enjoy the dancers and fireworks, Dani locked eyes with a familiar face she hadn't seen in quite some time, Langston Jr. His gaze left her nervous as usual, but there was something different in his eyes. *Why does he look so sad,* Dani wondered? Forcing a slight smile in his direction, he nodded in response and tipped his glass towards her.

"Excuse me," she heard a familiar voice from behind.

"Ebony. How was Paris?" Dani said.

"At first, I had nothing but respect for you," Ebony said. "When everybody made fun of you, I always came to your defense. I was your biggest fan. But now, you disgust me! You should be ashamed of yourself," Ebony scowled, then tried to discreetly rub the back of her neck while two of her friends surrounded Dani on both sides.

Awww, poor Ebony, Dani thought as she watched Ebony rub the back of her neck several times. *Perhaps, she didn't use the right razor. I remember them days.*

"Would you look at that? Standing here looking like a blast from the past with that mini, baby-doll dress on and that choker around your neck," Cammie said. "Dani, remember them little plastic baby dolls you used to get for Christmas, with the white plastic shoes and the little pink bottle?"

"What?" Amused by their similarities, Dani said, "I can't believe we had the same baby dolls growing up."

"Well, apparently, Ms. Ebony had one too. Look at this travesty," Cammie said, glaring at Ebony's hot pink mini dress with an empire waist.

"Honey, all she need is some white baby doll lace to go around the trim," Becca said laughing as she approached the ladies. "What's this, a family reunion or a street fight? Either way, I ain't been to one in a minute, so I'm looking forward to it."

"Becca! I thought you were out of town with Javi," Dani said, reaching for a hug as if Ebony's girls weren't standing there.

"Are you kidding? I wouldn't miss this for the world honey," Becca said, directing a wide cheesy smile towards Ebony and her friends.

"This family is not what you think. You should watch your back," Ebony said as she walked past Dani with her friends in tow.

"And you should not have used a razor on the back of that neck," Cammie said. "Who shaved you like that?" Cammie asked the three of them as she inspected their bald heads. "I've seen better on my dog."

"It's true," said Dani, "Y'all gon be covered in razor bumps by next week. I can already see red blotches forming on the back of your neck."

"Can you see it on mines too? I'm sorry, Ebony, but my neck is on fire," said one of Ebony's girls.

"Mines, too," her other friend said, aggressively scratching her head. "Wait, I know you. Are you the same Dani that snuck in hot toddies and cold medicine when we was all sick last year?" her friend, Monique, asked.

"The one and only," Dani replied.

"Ebony, I told you Sidnae was lying. Something ain't right about that woman," Monique said.

"It's okay," Dani said. "Call Marcus and Trey on Ninth. Tell him Dani sent you. He'll clean that neck up and give you a good blend."

"Thank you so much, Dani," the ladies said, hugging her while searching their cell phone directory for Trey's number.

"You still should be careful," Ebony said as she walked away, assuming her rightful place next to Langston Jr.

Suddenly, Dani looked up and noticed Cammie's face on the football stadium-sized screens overhead, smiling her infamous Cheshire grin. Surprised to see herself on-screen with Cammie, Dani tried her best to move away from the camera, but Cammie's hand was attached to her arm.

"I know that look, Cammie. Please don't embarrass me. Stop thinking what you're thinking," Dani spoke through her teeth.

"Just relax and enjoy the show," Cammie said, looking towards the overhead screen where the reporters were competing for Naomi's attention.

"Naomi, over here, over here," a celebrity correspondent yelled. Two additional stadium screens were playing outside for those without tickets to view the event from the sidewalk. As a gift to the public, Naomi had the best chefs in town serving up hot food for anyone who wanted to partake.

Cammie loosened her grip around Dani's arm as she pulled a small bag of candy from her purse.

"Cammie-Liana, what are you doing?" Dani said between her teeth. "Shhh, we gon miss the show," Cammie replied, like they were watching a movie.

"Naomi, you look amazing," the famous celebrity media correspondent, Max Hayfield, said. "Every year, you always manage to outdo yourself. I am so honored to be on the red carpet interviewing the queen of the fashion industry again this year, but I almost missed it! At the last minute, the date was changed. What happened?"

"Ah, a little bit of this, a little bit of that, my love. We had to move some things around. As you know, this time of year is quite busy for us," she said.

"Hmmm, could it also be the massive surprise you have planned this evening," Max yelled as the crowd went mad. "Just last year, Naomi shocked everyone with the opening of two new warehouses, bringing jobs and competitive wages for thousands in the area."

"Patience, my love," Naomi responded with intrigue.

"Naomi", over here, another reporter called out. "Does the surprise have anything to do with the video challenge?"

A man whispered something into Naomi's ear, and apparently, that was her cue.

"Well," she said to Max, "since you pulled my arm, yes, it has everything to do with the challenge." As the crowd grew silent, Naomi continued, "That video really hit home for me and my family. Dani has become, well, Dani, where are you?" she said, looking over her shoulder?

"What? No, no, no, no," Dani said, "that's not the plan," she mumbled, as Cammie strong-gripped her arm, pulling her toward the camera.

"Dani," Cammie said through her teeth, "if you don't take this graceful walk up to that carpet, so help me, I will drag your ass up there and cuss each and everybody out who says anything TO me, and you know I will."

Knowing Cammie never gave idle threats, Dani walked the red carpet and locked arms with Naomi. She didn't notice the crowd cheering for her, but Cammie did as she quickly made a call.

"Cue it up; we're ready," Cammie said.

"Ladies and gentlemen, meet the writer behind the camera, my darling sweetheart," Naomi said, holding Dani around her waist.

"Wow, you are stunning," said Max.

"Exactly," Naomi replied, "and so are all the bald women and children out there. I, along with my ex-husband, Sidreaux Sr. from Sari Unique, immediately jumped on board and accepted this challenge. What we have in store is not just for bald women, but for anyone with skin sensitivities or autoimmune issues."

Sari Unique? What the heck was Naomi talking about? No one discussed Sari Unique being a part of anything, Dani thought while maintaining the perfect smile.

"I know you all didn't know this, but Ebony, my future daughter-in-law, is a bald woman. No one knew," Naomi said. "And it broke my heart that she felt like she had to hide herself from us," Naomi said, dabbing tears from eyes.

"Yes, Ebony Franks, the supermodel. I recently read her story," said Max. "I just have to say, that photo with the one eyebrow taking the mirror selfie, me and my wife were in tears watching her interview. Ebony, I know you're here, and I hope you're watching," Max said, turning towards the camera. "You are beautiful, inspiring, and amazing! We love you!" Max said, as the crowd went wild.

"Yes, that's my baby," Naomi gleamed like a proud parent. "I called Dani and I said, 'To hell with those other brands. Nobody out challenges me, not even the ex-husband,'" Naomi said as a large white curtain fell to the ground. "Ladies and gentlemen, this is a replica of our new office in New York completely dedicated to establishing the first-ever full line of Naomi's all-natural products. We want inclusivity for all people, regardless of their differences. And thanks to Sari Unique and my son Langston," Naomi said, pausing for fake tears, "we joined together behind the scenes. We completed an entire campaign featuring some really brave people in the industry who just said, to hell with it, and let it all hang out."

"Naomi, over here," a female reporter interrupted. "You mentioned collaborating with your ex-husband, Sidreaux Sr., isn't that Dani's boss?"

"Yes, dear. Listen, while old Sr. and I may not agree on everything," she said playfully scowling in his direction, to which he responded with his own pretend evil grin, "we both believe in doing what's right and will always advocate for our people," Naomi said to roaring applause.

"But isn't it true that Sari Unique fired Dani right after she made the video?" the female reporter asked. "According to our sources, didn't they steal her words and use her story to create a campaign of their own?"

"Naomi, over here," another reporter yelled. "Is it true that you had security escort Dani out of the office, and you fired her in front of everyone?"

"Mr. Sidreaux," another reporter shouted, "is it true that you shaved the heads of your own models and used the actual biographies from real women dealing with alopecia and cancer?"

"Wow, Naomi, is that true?" asked Max.

"Well, dear, there will always be rumors, upon rumors, upon rumors," Naomi waved her hand as she spoke as if brushing the rumors away. "I mean, come on. Sidreaux and I have been stars of rumors for year. This is nothing new," she laughed nonchalantly.

"Of course, and we love you, Naomi," said Max. "You've done so much for the people of this state. But I'm sorry, the viewers at home want to hear it from the horse's mouth. Dani, is it true? Were you fired from Sari Unique because of the social media challenge you released? Are the allegations surrounding your removal from Sari Unique true? Did they steal your words and use it for their own gain?" Max asked, shoving the microphone in Dani's face.

"Um, I…uh," Dani stuttered, struggling to find the right words as her heart raced within her chest. She could hear her voice, but her mouth wasn't moving. *Was she hearing things? Where the heck was Cammie?* Dani thought, as she could feel herself starting to panic. When she looked up at the monitor, she saw a video of herself being escorted from Sari with her box of belongings in tow. *Where the heck did that come from?* Dani thought. *That's not what we planned.* As if that wasn't enough, Dani suddenly heard her own voice, like a recording.

"Wait, I'm getting some recent footage here," said Max. "Listen up!"

> *"Dani, can you hear me? It's Sidnae here. Are you there?"*

> *"Yes, I'm still here."*

> *"Are you surprised? You know I told Talia that we have to pay homage to Dani in all of this. Without her life, her stories, and her journey, this whole campaign wouldn't*

be happening. I just wanted to personally let you know the press is all over the article. They loved it! It's real, it's raw, and emotional."

"Yeah, I know it's real because I lived it. But I didn't write that story, and I certainly didn't give you permission to use it. You can't just use my name and attach it to some photo shoot. I never gave anyone permission to use my life, especially in this context," said Dani.

"Come on, Dani. It's a story that you shared with Talia. Let's not get too emotional with the whole stealing thing. As a matter of fact, you asked us to give you a platform. Don't go into a hissy because things didn't go your way. Next time, sign an agreement before spilling the details of your life over a cheap lunch. Again, you should be thanking me instead of insulting my integrity. There are a lot of people waiting in line for jobs like yours. We can take the little temper tantrums here and there, but not too much, okay? I gotta go."

What in the heck was that? Dani thought. *That's not the exact words I recorded on the phone that day with Sidnae. And the plan was to send an ANONYMOUS tip to the media. Why the heck would I want them to play a recording of me backstabbing her, while I'm standing in bird's-eye view of Sidnae? Dammit Cammie!* Dani thought, trying her best to control her facial expressions as she briefly locked eyes with Sidnae, who had a death stare focused on Cammie. *What is she looking at Cammie like that for? How would she know?* Dani wondered. In the midst of the drama, Sidreaux Sr. was nowhere to be found. In the next clip,

Dani saw herself, her video. Except, this wasn't the first video Dani released from the comfort of her living room. This was the finished product that involved women from across the globe.

As the final copy played with Dani's voice narrating her original message, it featured clips from the spa retreat. The video featured excerpts of the Professional Bald Women's Network in Spain, having the time of their lives. And there in the middle of the floor, in a penthouse suite, the ladies tested product samples from Sari Unique and Naomi's most expensive line, followed by a newcomer brand, *Bells and Me*. The ladies submitted their vote. The bald women who submitted their video showing the world how they walked in their "normal" everyday received full jars of Naomi's Signature Body Butter and Catera's Bells and Me. They recorded themselves voting online for Bells and Me as their top choice. There was a special clip of Catera thanking the ladies for their support, promising that she would continue to dedicate her creative talents to the maintaining the health and wellness of others. As a treat, every woman in the video received individually wrapped gifts from Catera's line, courtesy of Cammie-Liana Lawfton.

When the video ended, different groups of bald women finished with a final message, "This is our normal!" a group of female bald doctors said from Texas. "This is our normal!" shouted a group of bald female soldiers from Virginia. "This is my normal!" a bald female flight airline pilot said from Tennessee. "This is our normal!" shouted a group of young, bald ballerinas from Maryland. "This is our normal!" a group of bald athletes shouted from a gym in Georgia. And the message went on and on with shout-outs from across the globe.

"Hey, it's live online!" someone yelled out.

"What?" Naomi said as she grabbed the strangers cell phone.

"Well, and there you have it, Max," Naomi said to the famous correspondent while pretending to clap like she was responsible for the unexpected turn of events. "I love my ex-husband, but I think everyone knows what he trashes, turns into my treasure, right? Without further ado, meet my new CEO and face of my new line, Dani Breaux, featuring my first line, Catera Bell Cosmetics."

"Wait, what?" Dani said, confused as the crowd went wild. Looking into the audience, she suddenly recognized all the ladies from the Professional Bald Women's Network applauding and cheering her on.

"Wow! Dani, it looks like your friends are representing tonight. I love this! Folks, you heard it here first. Did you see Dani's expression? Clearly, she had no idea of Naomi's surprise. I guess there's just one other question. Dani, do you accept the offer as the new face and CEO of Naomi Enterprise New York City?" Max asked, holding the microphone to Dani's mouth.

"I, uh...I," Dani stammered.

"We will discuss all the details later," Cammie said, suddenly appearing, handing a glass of wine to Dani and Naomi. Then gesturing to the waiter, she grabbed another glass, and handed one to Max. "For now, we celebrate this moment and the possibilities for the bald woman and children around the globe! Salud!" Cammie yelled to the stream of applause.

By the end of the night, Dani had hundreds of business cards shoved her way, which were all collected by her driver, Lawrence, who Cammie transitioned to be her security for the rest of the evening. Everything else was a blur. Dani watched as Ebony left alone in her own limo, and Naomi disappeared almost immediately following the fiasco, but not before whispering to Dani, "My office, seven am sharp."

"Eight will do just fine," Cammie interjected. "I'll be there bright-eyed, and bushy tailed."

"Good," Naomi replied. "You know, Cammie, you remind me of myself—this little stunt," she said waving her hand at the huge screens, implying the unauthorized takeover of her event. "This was so much like me back in my day. I can't wait to hear more of your ideas," she said as security cleared a path and the crowd parted for the queen's exit.

For the rest of the night, Dani met more powerful people and saw more famous faces than she ever had. And this was only the beginning. She was getting brand offers from various companies, in addition to writing opportunities. As she stood off to the side, texting her mother pictures of various celebrities, she felt someone intentionally brush up against her shoulder. She looked up to see Langston's back as he walked past and stepped into the back of his car. She held her breath to see if he would make eye contact.

"Ms. Breaux, Ms. Lawfton gave me orders to take you home now," Lawrence said. When Dani turned back towards Langston, the limo was pulling away from the curb.

"That's okay. I think I'll walk," Dani responded. Just then, her phone rang.

"I don't understand. If anything, this evening should have shown you is that I got eyes and ears on everything, and everybody, everywhcre. GET YO ASS IN THE CAR," Cammie yelled.

"Ok! Stop yelling," Dani laughed. "And Ms. Cammie? You and I need to talk about this newfound knowledge," Dani said. "Come on, Lawrence, let's go get a burger," Dani said.

"I could eat," Lawrence smiled as he ushered Dani into the back of the car and pulled into traffic, with Cammie's righthand man, Uncle Johnnie, following close behind.

After the anniversary party, Langston Jr. rushed to his mother's house. Somehow, he was convinced that his mother was also a victim in all of this, forced by his father into a life of lies and deceit. Sidreaux Sr. was controlling his mother, just like he did his Uncle Andrew.

"Ebony, I know you're avoiding my calls. I'm not sure what to say. I was an asshole tonight. I'm sorry," Langston said. I wish I could explain it all, but we will talk soon. For now, I need you to just trust me, steer clear of Sari and everyone there, please. I'll call you later."

Sidreaux Sr didn't tell him what he'd been up to the last few months. Langston agreed that Dani had to leave Sari, but he never signed off on security removing her from the building, nor did he know about using any of her personal experiences against her will.

While waiting for his mom, he decided to cook their favorite breakfast, vegan pancakes with fresh blueberry syrup. Langston felt there had to be some explanation for Kisi's part in this, but he had no doubt that Naomi Winston was his real mother.

"Ugh, mom never places pans where you need them." Langston stepped into the apartment-sized pantry to gather the pots and ingredients for the late-night breakfast. That's when he heard his mother's voice.

"Clearly, Sid. I mean, sometimes you do the most ridiculous things! I can't even imagine how we were ever married or how we ever managed to raise a son together!"

Langston smiled to himself, feeling more confident now more than ever that Naomi Winston was his mother. *How could I ever deny her?* Langston thought to himself while looking for cinnamon.

"Oh please, don't act like this wasn't your idea too."

"Dad," Langston whispered to himself as he listened to his father chastise his mother for not having his back.

"Now, people assume I'm a heartless man with no compassion for bald women or whatever the hell they are."

"Oh, shut up, you old fool! You and I both know that you care more about your image. That girl means nothing to you," Naomi said.

"Yeah, well, she clearly means something to Junior," recalling the look in his son's eyes when he talks about Dani or the way his face lights us when she walks into a room. "I've seen that look before," Sidreaux Sr. said. "That's the same way I feel when I look at you."

"Awww, poor Sidi," Naomi said as she gently caressed his face. "Once I finish with Dani and her lackies, Jr. will certainly lose interest. No need to worry, dear. Momma always takes care of her little men."

"Hmm, I love when you call me your little man," Sidreaux Sr. said.

"Well, clearly the shoe fits," Naomi laughed as he pushed her away in frustration.

"Make sure it's airtight, Naomi. If Jr. finds out we had anything to do with this, he'll start moping around the office and slacking again! I can't have him half-ass performing and ruining my name. You know how that boy gets all wrapped up in his feelings."

"Well, clearly, he didn't get that from me," Naomi said. "And nobody cares about that boy's feelings! Sidi, he has winter hair! You gave your heir to the son who views winter hair as a thing. I gave you sons with a much higher IQ and education. All you had to do was use them!" Naomi said.

"Those are not my sons."

"Neither are they mine, but what difference does it make?" said Naomi.

"Speaking of which, what time will your donor seed of a husband be home? Maybe we can spend a lil extra time together this evening," he smiled, pulling Naomi toward his chest.

"Sorry, Sidi, I haven't seen my love in weeks, and all of me will be here waiting for him when he walks through that door."

"Understood, as I'm sure that won't take long. When he passes out, you'll find me at the Embassy, in our favorite suite," he smiled confidently.

"Noted," Naomi replied. "When I need a LITTLE you time, I know where to find you. When I want the whole package, I'll wait for my man, but thank you for the occasional snack."

"You are so full of it," Sidreaux Sr. said as he walked toward the front door. "And get that bald-headed thing out of my company, and keep her away from my son, or so help me, I will throw your ass out on the street along with her."

"Don't test me, old man."

"Try me," Sidreaux Sr. said, slamming the front door behind him.

"Ugh, I can't stand that old fine-ass fool! I need a bath and a bottle. Steven!"

"Yes, madam, your bath is ready, and a bottle of white wine is waiting upstairs on ice."

"Oh, Steven, that's why I love you so much." Naomi blew air kisses to her butler as she sashayed up the winding staircase.

Once she was gone, Langston pressed stop on his cell phone recorder, slid to the floor and placed his head in his hands, and had another good cry. With a sudden clear direction of what to do next, he spent the next hour making calls. By the time he left his mother's pantry, there were no more doubts or tears.

"Cammie, this is Langston. We need to meet."

Sixteen

EVERYBODY HAS CHOICES

The long busy roads were lined with dream homes and a community of small businesses. Streetlights always shone bright, making the neighborhood feel like daytime at night. Dani didn't own a fancy luxury car or a summer house on the beach like her neighbors. She soon realized that it didn't matter. Mrs. Carson from across the street still invited her to random dinners and holiday parties. The Schmidts, on the corner, occasionally dropped off desserts and homemade doggie treats for Jackson. Halloween and seasonal barbeques were the best. And folding chairs lined the street for backyard bonfires and football games.

Dani spent hours at the neighborhood park playing with Jackson, rolling in the grass, and running up and down the stairs. The curb by the park had become her Zen spot for meditation and frequent talks with God. She wondered if chasing her dreams to New York involved giving up her blessings.

"Good job, Jacks! Good, boy," Dani said, catching her breath and collapsing on the curb under the streetlight where Lawrence could watch her from a short distance. After waiting in traffic for over an hour, Dani decided to forego the burger for an evening run. In keeping his promise to Cammie, Lawrence followed behind in his car like her own personal presidential detail. By the third mile, Dani managed to sweat out the three glasses of red wine she drank at Naomi's anniversary party. She was so high on the adrenaline rush from the evening that she didn't realize she was well on her way to a buzz beyond her control.

"This doesn't feel real," Dani said, flashing back to the sequence of events. "Jackson, mommy got a new bag. What you think about that, huh? Well, technically, mamma may have a few new bags. This is crazy. On one hand, I'm so excited," she said out of breath. "On the other hand, I don't want to mess this up. What we have, God, this relationship," she said, sitting on the sidewalk, as she found herself talking to God, "I don't wanna mess up the guidance that I prayed for. I can't believe I'm actually chasing my dreams, and it's not about just getting paid. I can't wait to tell people's stories so they can feel what I feel. There's so much more to life than just words and pain. Restoration is real, but God, I'm so scared. It seems like every time I take a risk or follow a dream, life happens, and it knocks the wind out of me. I don't think I can take another gut punch right now, God," Dani cried.

"I've been at this crossroads before. I chose the husband and the white picket fence," Dani sobbed in frustration. "I thought I made the right choices back then, but clearly, life said otherwise. So, this time, I won't budge until I hear from you. I don't care how many offers come or how much money is on the line. I need to know I'm making the right choice. I need reassurance, and not just any old kind. I need that Moses from the Bible type of assurance. When he was unsure of himself, you reassured him, and I think I need that."

"I know things happen in life, and sometimes it's beyond our control. I just need a break from running headfirst into the eye of a storm. If it's gonna rain, and I'm gonna have to start over, please let it be where I have some stability. You say to fast, pray, and believe. I did that, and I nearly died."

"Perhaps, the fasting and praying wasn't about what you lost. Maybe it was about where you are now," a voice said quietly. "Could it be that the other stuff was just a part of the journey? I'm sorry. I didn't mean to sneak up on you. I wasn't trying to eavesdrop. I was running the block, and I thought it was you, but I wasn't sure. I've never seen you out here this late by yourself before."

As Dani looked up from the sidewalk, he asked, "May I sit?"

Across town, Langston slowly paced the floor as he dictated his requests to Diane.

"Langston, perhaps we should slow down and think about this for a minute," Diane said.

"I'm not sure I understand what you mean," said Langston.

"Hmm, in the last seventy-two hours, you turned over evidence to The Lawfton Law Firm implicating Naomi Winston for *allegedly* breaking surrogacy laws and your father for, well, it would be easier to find laws that he didn't break. Honestly, I don't know what prompted you to call Cammie-Liana Lawfton. As your attorney, I would have given you a reference. Now you want to set up a lucrative trust for a former employee?"

"Allegedly? The board resigned both their positions to me and my stepbrothers. Why are we still discussing it?"

"Langston, even though your parents agreed to step down, the charges being brought against them are very serious," Diane said as Langston quietly stared back at her. Recognizing the familiar Sidreaux glare, Diane quickly moved on. "On top of the heavy settlement you added to the severance package, you're also maintaining her yearly salary to be put into a trust indefinitely, AND you're making her your beneficiary? Removing the planned inheritance for your children?"

"Perhaps, it's because I don't have any children, nor do I intend to have them," Langston said.

"What about your fiancée? You've had savings accounts set up for your future wife since you were twelve years old. Are you closing those as well? Have you discussed this with Ms. Ebony? If you close those accounts and anything happens to you, she won't get a dime."

"Diana, you're the family lawyer, not my counselor or my personal advisor," Langston said quietly. "I have handled my finances since I was twelve years old. Please try not to insult me any further," he grinned.

"Of course," Diana replied. "How would you like to proceed?"

"For generations, my family has lived and died for the love of money. Void of any type of love, kindness, or compassion towards anyone. Removing my father and changing the Sidreaux bylaws gives my successor the freedom to make their own choices with this company."

"So, they can choose their own heaven or hell. How noble of you," said Diane.

"Just because I don't believe in either, doesn't mean I want to decide for someone else. And if I *decide* to have children, allowing them to have choices would be my greatest gift to them. Besides, I'm a billionaire Diane. If they fail to profit from that, then that's their choice. As for Ebony, she has her own money. She doesn't need me to survive. I've made sure of that."

"As crazy as it sounds, if you're serious, I think it's one of the most noble things I've ever known a Sidreaux man to do."

"It's Langston from now on."

"Very well, Mr. Langston. Do you have any special instructions?"

"Technically, everything has already been handled. However, just for my benefit, I personally want to ensure Dani's signature is on the trust account and the beneficiary documents. Again, she must never know the source, just that it's a part of the benefit package promised upon her departure from the company. The settlement funds from the severance package will be directly transferred into her account by 9:00 am. Once the documents are signed, in the event that anything happens to me, nothing and no one will ever be able to change my wishes. Please forward me a copy of your documents as soon as it's done. I don't expect any errors. And Diane, thank you. For everything."

"My pleasure, Langston. Although I do have one last question," she said. "Why don't you just tell her that you love her?"

"Love? I'm not quite sure what that word even means or if I'm capable of it," Langston replied.

"Well, I would say what you've done for her up to this point is a great start."

"I'm not so sure it is," Langston said. "If that's the case, I love her just about as much as I love you."

"Oh, I don't know about that Mr. Langston. "I'm not the one sitting here with millions of dollars in my account."

"Are you sure about that? Maybe check it again. I'll leave you to it," Langston said, as he barely made it to the elevator before hearing Diana scream.

"Whew, maybe that is love," Langston smiled.

BECCA & JAVI

"So, you live in New York City? You have a building…and a rental in New York?" Javi repeated in disbelief as Becca stood outside his front door.

"I love you. I am in love with you, and I'm sorry I didn't share my plans, but it was so instant. I had to do this my way Javi. I wanna be everything you desire in a woman, but I have to be me, I have to keep my independence," she sobbed. "I know you prefer a woman who doesn't work. A beautiful, devoted little wife who always buys the perfect cut of meat. She exercises in the morning, cooks, and cleans in the afternoon. I can't stay home and fix your meals. I have to go out and make the bacon too. Heck we can hire someone to cook it. It tastes better that way," she mumbled.

"Becca, please come in and shut the door, honey," Javi said.

"I'm not done yet," Becca said. "I don't want to grocery shop, but if I want to pick up the check for dinner, then that's what I'm gonna do," she continued. "If I want to buy you a Ferrari on Tuesday, just because I can, then so be it. I don't wanna be some idea of a traditional relationship. I held back because, well, the one thing I can never give you Javi is a legacy. You're a wonderful man, and you deserve to have children of your own. Say something, Javi!"

"Is that what you think I want?" Javi asked. "The way that I feel about you has nothing to do with your career or tradition. It's your spirit my love. Everything that comes from here, he said as he touched her heart. Your compassion for others, your love for family. When you came to my house, and we put up a Christmas tree and baked cookies, I thought, wow, I've never done this with anybody before. The night was so magical, and I didn't want it to end. I thought to myself, God, if you could just leave that woman under my tree. To my surprise, the next day, you came back with all this food, and we cooked again and watched movies together. When I opened my Christmas present," Javi said, as he held back tears, "you had restored my grandfather's pocket watch. On the other side of the watch was a picture of you, it was under my tree. God gave me exactly what I wanted our very first Christmas together. Because of you, I have traditions to look forward to that I never knew before."

"Javi, that was a long time ago. We spend every Christmas together now. What are you saying?"

"Rebecca Lynn Carrington, you are my legacy. The way that I love with you? That's a foundation that I'm not willing to trade in for anything in this world."

"What about the other women?"

"Don't! You don't get to do that, Becs. For years you've been refusing to take me seriously. I'd give up my life for you. Don't you know that? If I ever lost you, I'd tear this world apart, one place at a time, to get you back," Javi said.

"Same," Becca cried. "I wanna be the couple who plans a future together. I wanna get married before shacking up. I believe in God now, Javi. I didn't know so much about that before, but when you know better, you have to do better, right? This won't work if we're not equally yoked," she said, pacing back and forth.

"Equally yoked," Javi said, slightly confused.

"Yes, it means that we're connected, and we have the same beliefs for all of etern—"

"I know what it means," Javi said, cutting Becca off before she could finish her sentence. "I've always believed in God. What changed about you? Will you please come inside, honey?"

"Let me finish," said Becca. "I know that we love each other, we both love hard, and always have. No matter what happens, I don't care how many women or men, or sickness, or family or whatever crap that comes our way, divorce will never be the answer!"

"Rebecca, I would never cheat on you, and I would never leave you."

"Let me finish! Do you have any idea how many men say that shit? Listen to me! I would much rather wake up to occasional drama with a man who loves me, who knows me, and who accepts me with all my shit than to wake up one day dead, lying next to a heartless demon who could care less."

"What? How would you know if you're already…"

"Javi!"

"Okay, okay. Becs, I love you so much," he said, amused and shaking his head. Her descriptive details were one of the things he loved about her the most. "I get it," Javi said, reaching for her hand."

"I'm not done! We know everything about each other. I know you work out six days a week, running three, lifting three. You fancy the occasional cigar with friends, you hate raw meat but love wild salmon when it's cooked just right. You only like simple carbs on the holidays unless it's something homemade, you order your toothpaste from Mick's online, and you sleep on the…"

"Rebecca, please," Javi anxiously interrupted. "It will take days, weeks, months to list everything we know about each other.

"Javi, you have to understand, refusing you was never my intent," Becca sobbed.

"Becs, why are you still standing outside? Come home, baby," Javi said, reaching out to her, waiting for her to take his hand.

Becca screamed with excitement as she jumped into his arms. "I am not living here until we're married, Javi. And we are not gonna be having all kinds of sex and all that anymore because why buy the cow when you can get the milk for free, right?"

"Whatever you say, my love."

"Don't even start," she yelped with laughter as Javi nuzzled her neck, tickling her with one arm and hoisting her off her feet with the other. Becca was finally home. For the first time in a long time, she knew without a doubt that she was exactly where she belonged.

"Hey Ric, there's a Cammie Lawfton here to see you, says it's pretty urgent."

"Tell her I'll be right out. Shit," he whispered under his breath as he stepped out the back of the food truck. "Ms. Lawfton, what can I do for you?"

"Ponytail! Is that you? You're the guy who owns the high-end men's stores, right? Boy you make that apron look good, look at you." Cammie said, admiring him from head to toe.

"Thank you, but my friends call me Ric. What can I do for you? Would you like something to drink?"

"I know it's not necessarily my business, but considering the history and all, I have a few questions," Cammie said. "You're not just ponytail from retail now, are you? Michael R. Chase,"

Cammie repeated from his business card. "Are you the gift box mystery man? The poetic poet? The genius behind the creole cuisines in Dani's freezer?"

"Ms. Lawfton, I think you have me confused with someone else."

"That's why I'm asking. Ever since I met you the other day, I've been waiting for Dani to figure out that her little retail crush is also the owner of her favorite local food truck, Le'Ric's. Isn't that right, Ric?"

"So? It's not a crime for a man to have multiple streams of income," said Ric.

"Maybe not, but life is not a fairytale, Ric, and I don't believe in all this coincidence stuff. What do you want?"

"All I want is for her to be happy," Ric said, taking a seat on a barstool.

"Michael, I'm gonna level with you. I hear my dad say that statement to people all the time. I'm gonna level with you." Cammie laughed. "It's a bit of a different approach for me, so bear with me. I've had a very, very busy week."

"Yeah, I noticed. I keep up with the news."

"Wonderful, then you understand. The point is, in the midst of my very, very busy week, I managed to run across a few things about you. Imagine what I can find when I really focus in. You don't want that."

"Okay, okay," Ric said, holding up his hands for a truce. "I'm not breaking any laws here. Contrary to what you may know about me, I am not a threat to Dani. We hardly know each other. She's leaving tomorrow, and I wish her the best."

"So, you go through all that gift-giving, letter writing, secretive undercover romance, popping up here and there, and now you just let go?"

"I'm not gonna be the reason why she stays or goes."

"Well, isn't that very serendipitous of you," Cammie said. "Only issue here is that I don't think any of your interactions are by chance."

"She came into my store," said Ric.

"True, but you live forty-five minutes to an hour away from here, in a very nice area. Why do you drive all the way to this neighborhood Monday through Friday to run in *this* park? George manages the food truck, and your employees take care of the retail store. Why are you here?"

"Are you watching me, Ms. Lawfton?"

"When it comes to my family? Always. See I'm not much on folks who only look good on paper. I think they're a bunch of self-righteous, narcissistic, ego-driven title holders. And as soon as they don't get what they want or life doesn't fit their script, they make trouble. And before anybody can call them out on it, they run. Cowards. Hurting people and making excuses to justify their actions along the way. The only good thing about them is that piece of paper with their name scribbled on it. If I had my way, I would rip that shit and burn it up before anyone had a chance to see it."

"Well, thankfully, that's not me. My silence does not mean that I'm running. Besides, Dani made her choice. What else am I supposed to do?"

"Shit, or get off the pot, Ric!" Realizing that he was just a scared little man-boy still trying to find himself, Cammie softened up a bit. "The fact is that you think you're smart enough to fool everybody, yet, here I am, and I know more than what you're sharing. As well written and beautiful as you may be, I don't have to smell a shit stain to know its shit," Cammie said. "Clean yourself up, get it together or disappear."

"And if I don't?"

"Google me," Cammie smiled. "Until then, I'll take that new vegan burger you have on the menu. Is that meatless? No, don't tell me, I wanna enjoy it like it's meat."

"Sure thing," Ric said, unsure if he should smile and go along with it or jump in his truck and run to the nearest police station for protection. "I'll hook it up for you, and I promise, you won't know the difference," he said, hoping the food would lighten the mood."

"No, no! Don't do that. Messing up my food is like messing with my life."

"Then, I guess I'm putting my life on the line here. Nobody cooks like me, I guarantee it. While you wait, try my new bacon grilled dates," he said as he grabbed the freshly made burger prepared for the next customer in line.

"Hmph," Cammie said, stuffing a warm wrap into her mouth. "Mmm, maple sugared bacon is my weakness," Cammie said as she bit into another piece of crispy bacon and creamy date. "I'd like to add bacon to my burger, please."

"Absolutely! Too bad we don't have any bacon."

"Then use some of these," she said, pointing to the samples on the complimentary tray. "This is bacon! I know when I'm eating bacon."

"Nope, not a shred of meat is on this truck," Ric said, handing Cammie the juicy double plant meat burger with vegan cheese.

"Oh my gosh," she said, taking a huge bite of the hot juicy burger. "You would do wonders for my diet."

For the next hour, Cammie tried everything Ric gave her and took a bag for the road. As she headed to the airport, she had to stop herself from calling Dani and blowing Ric's mystery man, letter writing cover, but she needed to do more research.

After boarding the plane, Cammie took the window seat and was in deep thought as she stared across the tarmac. *There's something about Ric that I just can't put my finger on,"* Cammie thought. *He may know the way to a girl's stomach, but it takes a whole lot more than some good food to hide his family secrets.* "Excuse me, what are you looking at?" Cammie said to the woman sitting across from her in first class. The lady was frowning like Cammie was contagious, and she didn't want her in the same space. "Look away before I breathe on you and make all your hair fall out," Cammie threatened as the woman took a drink of water, trying her best to stare straight ahead.

ONE YEAR LATER

"I'm coming! I'm coming!" Dani said.

"Dani, Javi's on the line. He said you have to leave now," said Marie, her assistant.

"Yes, I'm leaving. Tell him I'm on my way," Dani yelled back while running out into the New York streets to hail a cab. With the phone up to her ear, Dani spoke anxiously into the phone, "Cammie-Liana Lawfton, where are you? I've been calling you for the past thirty minutes. Answer your phone."

Dani couldn't help but smile, thinking about how everyone's life had changed so much over the last year. Cammie was right; the opportunities here were endless. Within six months, Becca's New York business ignited like a massive volcano. As Dani crossed the street to the waiting cab, she snapped a quick cellphone pic of Becca's new billboard, a strong, gorgeous athletic woman with prosthetic blades posing in the latest line of sports bras and underwear. The New York business generated more revenue than all the other locations combined. Becca's dream of starting her own design school was becoming a reality. With a baby girl on the way and a fiancé, Rebecca was living her New York fantasy.

"Hello, you better have a good reason why you're not in New York," Dani said, knowing it was Cammie on the other end of the line. "Being the perfect girlfriend to your boo is probably not gonna get you through this one Cam."

Cammie was enjoying the fruits of her labor, dedicated to being a real girlfriend to Harris, one of the highest-paid NBA players in the league. She attended every basketball game along with the other spouses. She cooked, cleaned, hosted parties, and actually enjoyed decorating her house and the new yoga spa she invested in the year before. For a while, Dani and Becca assumed she had transformed into a different person, a much nicer person. Unfortunately, their excitement was short-lived. As soon as she stepped into a courtroom or someone ruffled her feathers, the real Cammie proudly showed up.

"Nice try, Dani. We've been waiting here for you for hours, or maybe three minutes. Hurry up, Becca's ten minutes away," Cammie said, disconnecting the line.

How the heck did she get here before me? Dani thought. "Let me out here! This is fine," Dani said, quickly paying the driver and racing down the long driveway.

"Becca, please don't be here yet, please, please, please," Dani whined as she lightly jogged towards the door, careful not to break a leg in her Louboutin heels.

"Surprise!" the ladies chimed as Dani entered the foyer.

"That was a good one, guys. Next time, try not to yell so loud. We don't wanna scare her into labor; just give her a little love jolt," said Javi.

"It's her. Her car is pulling up now," Cammie said. "I had someone put a tracker on it a few months ago."

"Okay, guys, we're ready. Shhh," Javi said, "and Cammie, we'll talk later about that tracker," he whispered.

"Jessica, make sure we have everything ready for the D.C event," Becca said as she slowly walked up the driveway. "By then, this little alien who's taking over my body should be out.

Oh, honey, mama's sorry," Becca said, gently rubbing her stomach. "I love you, but you really need to keep your feet off of mommy's whooha. Otherwise, that means old Dr. Martin is gonna have to turn you again. I swear I don't know how women go through this. Who the hell wants to be nine months pregnant for a man? What the hell for?" Becca fussed.

"Honey, I been telling my teenage granddaughter the same thing. Her mama caught her necking with one of the neighborhood boys," Jessica said.

"Necking? Who is still necking? Look, you can't even see my neck," Becca said, rotating her head. "Here, take out your cell phone and record this," Becca said. "I got a sex prevention message for her.

"Hey! You see this," Becca said, pointing to her stomach. "This is what happens when you neck."

"That's right. Tell her about the breech and Dr. Martin turning your stomach," Jessica said.

"He rotated the insides of my body. He literally stuck his hands inside of me, Becca said slapping the front of her thigh, rights under her baby belly. Do you know why he did that? Because my baby was trying to walk out of my va-jay-jay! It's a hole the size of a penny. You better make sure you really like this neighborhood boy because the next thing you know, you have something the size of a watermelon sitting in your stomach, and the doctor has to slice you from the cooter to the boot just to get this little sucker out. Meanwhile, your little necker gets to sit over in the corner texting his friends while your body morphs into a walking, pissing hormone. Quit necking!"

"Cut. Now that was really good, Bec. I think this just might work."

"Oh, that felt good. But you can't use that, Jess. You can show it to her, but sure it don't post online. We have a brand to protect, she said swinging open the front door."

"Surprise!"

"What the? Why are all these people here? Javi!"

"Becca Boo, look at you and your wittle tummy," Cammie said.

"Well, it's about damn time! I haven't seen you in months, Cammie. Looks like you been living in the gym," Becca said.

"Mmmhmm, she does look extra fit," said Jessica.

"Heifer, please, I helped you set up the New York office," said Cammie.

"Well, I forgot. I just need to be mad at somebody, and I love Javi too much for that. But I also missed you, Cammie. You couldn't even come and eat a sandwich with me because you're too busy doing squats," Becca said as she started to cry. "Daniiiiii," she cried.

"Hey honey, come on, let's get you comfortable, get your feet up," Dani said. "Look at all that food."

"Dani, I'm two days past my due date," Becca whispered. "What if she never comes out? Why are all these people here? Why did you guys agree to this? You know I don't like people. I have gas so bad if anybody hugs me, they might get a surprise."

"Whatever you want. I'll ask them to leave," Dani said, wiping Becca's tears.

"Nooo, I love this! I love you guys," Becca said, allowing Javi to put her feet up on the couch. "Javi, you are amazing. Thank you for loving me so much, but why are the men here?"

"Hey! Men, get out," Dani said.

Agreeing with his future wife, Javi joined Dani in her request, "Guys, if my baby wants the men to leave, then leave we shall. Gentlemen, may I direct your attention to the insensitive man cave in the backyard. There, we will have classic men's food that includes four flavors of messy hot wings, barbeque sliders, and something to wash it all down with. We got pool tables, ping pong tables, classic drinks, and cigars."

"Hell yeah," the husbands grunted. "Welcome to the men's baby shower," Javi said, leading the pack out the back door.

As the ladies enjoyed a healthy spread of chicken salad, cucumber sandwiches, and fruit, Dani sat in the corner taking pictures, thinking about the captions she would write under each shot. Her next article would be exclusive on her best friend, Becca. Dani's life had become a whirlwind of adventure and repurposed dreams. Twenty-four hours after spilling her guts on ponytail's shoulder, a messenger showed up at her house with sealed documents requesting her presence at the bank. Dani would never forget the moment the branch manager, Molly, showed her the amount of money in her savings account.

"Congratulations, Ms. Breaux," the banker said, giving Dani a copy of the signed documents, keeping one on record and placing one to the side for the messenger.

"Okay, but it's just a severance. Is it normal for you to request my presence by messenger for a severance package?" Dani questioned as she read over the document, her eyes resting on the zeroes. "What does this mean?" Focusing on the legal line of numbers, Dani read them out loud, much louder than she intended, "Ten million dollars! They're suing me?"

"No, ma'am, that's the settlement for your severance. This is a copy of your trust. Here are all the details with your attorney's information at the bottom for any additional questions.

"Wait, so this says five thousand dollars a month into a trust, for how long? Is this in addition to the settlement? Where is it coming from?"

"Yes, this is in addition to the settlement."

"For how long?"

Molly replied, "There is no ending date. I encourage you to speak with your attorney about the specifics. We don't have any additional information."

As Dani walked home from the bank, she kept pinching herself, thinking she was dreaming and that at any moment she would wake up, and Molly would call her and say it was all a misunderstanding. Just last night, she was crying, wondering what she would do for long-term financial stability. A few freelance jobs here and there would not cover any surprise medical expenses. On her way home, her mother's words rang in her ear, "Stop expecting the enemy to show up in your life more than you expect God to." Halfway home her phone started to ring.

"It's okay, I know. It's Sari playing some type of game, trying to get back at me. Don't worry, I didn't touch the money. Well, I did sign the documents, but I didn't spend anything." Taking Cammie's silence on the other end of the line as a sign that she was right, Dani quickly said, "Cammie, I have to go."

"Don't you hang up this phone," Cammie said. "You're emotional. I hear you, and I get it. Just let me say this, and if you need a minute to get yourself together, I understand. No matter what anybody says or does, Becca and I, we got you. For life, we will always have each other. As long as I have, you have. Understand?" Hearing Dani crying through the phone broke Cammie's heart as she knew it was coming from a place that was tired of dealing with disappointment.

"I hear you," Dani said, feeling somewhat better.

"Good, I love you. Girl, New York, here we come! Okay? Tomorrow when you land, my driver will pick you up and drop you off at my penthouse. Make yourself at home, that's your place for as long as you need it."

"I appreciate that, but I just, okay," Dani said, feeling like there was no need to argue with Cammie. She understood Cammie's wish for her, and she agreed, but she was not letting her house in D.C go until she had another one with a secured job.

"Good, I'll see you later. Oh, wait, one more thing. Girl, I almost forgot, you won't need to stay in my penthouse long because you a damn millionaire now. So, I suggest you start looking at properties in the area, well, maybe not my area, that's big, but I may have a few suggestions."

"Wait, what? What did you say? Stop playing! Cammie, are you for real? Cammie, you still on the line? Hello? Cammie? Cammie? Cammmie? I think I lost my signal, shit!"

"Girl, you ain't lost no signal. I was just adding Becca to the call," Cammie said as she and Becca laughed, listening to Dani talking to herself.

"That first time seeing all of them zeroes in your bank account really jacks up your spirit," Becca said as Cammie screamed in laughter.

Dani laughed and cried until the ladies couldn't make out any of her words.

"Okay, okay, we gonna call you later," Cammie said. "Go pray, cry, and get it out. Just please get it out before you get here. We love you," she said as they disconnected.

Thinking back on that moment, Dani smiled, "Who would've thought?"

"I want some food. Dani, can you get me something from the men's cave. I want a slider sandwich from Javi," Becca pleaded.

"Slider burger coming right up," Dani said as she stepped into the backyard, inhaling the familiar scent of charcoal and meat. "Mmmm, it smells so yummy out here."

"Thank you. Vegan chicken sandwich, right?"

"Ric? What are you doing here?"

"Javi called me, said something about a men's shower and to bring my chef's hat, so here I am."

"Oh, I didn't know you were coming," Dani said, feeling disappointed. After that day in the park, she discovered ponytail was the actual owner of Le'Rics in addition to his chain of retail stores. She admittedly had a crush on him, but he never responded to her invitation to have dinner before her flight left the following day. She wanted to celebrate her night with him, but it was obvious he didn't feel the same. When he came to New York to help set up her new office, she had hopes, but again, they were short-lived. Every now and again, he called to check on her, almost like he was keeping tabs on her progress, asking how she was doing, how the business was coming, and was she happy. She remembered telling Becca it was like he was keeping a progress report. Although recently, he had been calling more often, especially since she told him about publishing her new book and using the proceeds for opening a retreat for cancer survivors.

While Dani was the face of Becca's brand, and she enjoyed the freedom of modeling for other designers, her joy and passion came from writing, inspired by the many different journeys of people who overcame obstacles to reach their goals. She'd created a space where their normal was different because their differences created their norm.

"I'm also here for a few business meetings, but I must admit, I'm so excited about the dinner party for your new venture. I booked my flight as soon as I heard."

Unable to control her smile, Dani said, "That's three weeks away."

"Well, I guess we have some catching up to do. I would like to take you to dinner tomorrow night, if you're not too busy."

"Me? You wanna take me out?"

Ric smiled his uncontrollable smile, "Yes, I would love to take you out."

"Then, I would love to go out with you," Dani smiled.

"What you smiling so much about?" Cammie said. "Ric? We got Chef Ric in the house! Hey boo, what you cooking? I want one."

"No! It's my baby shower, and he is here for me. Javi, I want a burger. Please get me a burger," Becca whined.

"Oh, girl, you gotta hurry up and have this baby," Dani said.

"Yes, please, the whining voice alone is triggering," Cammie said.

"Okay, sweetie daddies got you," Javi said. "Ladies, come on, it's for the baby. Please, Cammie, work with me."

"Thank you, honey," Becca replied. "Ric, I will have mine with the works. I want two meats, grilled onions, tomatoes, spicy mayo, slaw…"

"He knows what the works is. He made the menu," Cammie said.

"Hurry Ric! She's starving over here," Becca whined, rubbing her perfect little belly.

"I got you, mama, the works coming right up," he said, handing the plate to Becca.

Unfortunately, Becca didn't move fast enough, and Cammie swept in from the side and grabbed the paper plate, taking a huge bite while running in the opposite direction.

"Cammie, no! Javi! Dani!" Becca whined as she jumped up from her seat and tried her best to chase after Cammie.

Cammie walked slightly faster than Becca around the backyard, savoring the burger while fussing at Becca, "Stop whining!"

"Becca, he's got another one for you right here," Dani called out.

"I don't want another one. I want that one. The one he made with love," she whined.

"Becs, I think they're all the same. He's making them all with love, right Ric?" Dani asked?

"Not really, just one," he said, looking down at Dani.

Unsure of what he meant, and sensing that Cammie was coming in for a second round, Dani snatched the plate with the hot burger and ran towards Becca.

"Go Dani go, she's gaining on you," Javi said, waving his hands towards her as the other husbands cheered.

With Cammie coming in for a second helping, Dani passed the plate to Javi while she tackled Cammie to the ground, and the ladies laughed like a bunch of school kids.

"Cammie, your phone," Jessica said. "Someone is really trying to reach you sugar. It's ringing constantly."

"Thanks! Hello this is Cammie. Sam, what's up? What?"

"Hey Cammie, have you seen the news?" said one of the men from the party.

Reaching for their phones, Dani and Becca checked the newsfeed and on the first page was breaking news, *Double Whammy: NBA star Harris Mason's mother and father were found gagged and beaten, apparently held for ransom. While investigations are ongoing, our sources are telling us that this was a business deal gone bad, alleging that they owed money to some pretty dangerous people. According to their taped confession, Harris's parents had some financial issues with the family business several years ago before their son's mega NBA contract, and I quote, "We never paid it back," they said while constantly apologizing on camera to their children. Here's the double whammy, folks, after discovering the news from a text message sent to his phone, seemingly intoxicated, Harris Mason tripped on the stairs at his penthouse and was rushed to the hospital by his female companion. According to medical reports, he fractured his knee, dislocated his shoulder, and has several other bumps and bruises. This has got to be devastating for him right now. We're here for you, buddy. Get well soon.*

Fearing the worst, Dani and Becca sprang into action, attempting to talk to Cammie, but it was too late. Without saying a word, Cammie gave Becca and Dani a hug, slipped on her heels, and disappeared. It was no use talking to Cammie when she went to that faraway place in her head.

Thankfully, she didn't have that blank expression, Dani thought. *She looked shocked, and maybe scared. When she was ready to talk, she would talk.* Looking across the room, Dani made eye contact with Becca, and like sisters who spoke without words, they agreed.

As the sun went down, the ladies relaxed on the outdoor furniture surrounding Becca. They shared baby stories and sipped iced tea while the men about football. Dani lay quietly on the deck watching Jackson playing with the kids and glanced over at Ric, talking and laughing with the guys. She thought about what he said about making her burger with love, and it was a very good burger indeed, but she'd had better.

"Could it be him, somebody else, something else? Who knows?" Dani mumbled, smiling to herself.

"Are you talking to me?" Ric mouthed back from across the yard.

As she shook her head no, Dani looked around at her current setting, who she was now compared to who she used to be, and just the presence of knowing it was all God, made her smile.

"Wow! God is amazing," Dani said, smiling from ear to ear. "This feels good. Nothing and no one will come between what you have for me. That's what you told me, that's what you've shown me, and that's what I believe," she said, basking in the sunshine.

This time, instead of trying to control the narrative, and figure out this thing with Ric, and what it meant. Dani decided to just let it be, live her life, and trust God. If it was one thing that she learned throughout the years, it was that worrying would not change a thing, nor would it affect the hairs on her head, or the lack thereof. So, what was the point of being anxious about a love life, Ric, Becca or Cammie? She wasn't living for them. After years of stress, and punishing herself over everything and everybody, she found that most times, it was so much easier to just trust God and have faith. After all, it was impossible to please God, without it. And at the end of the day, that's all that really mattered.

Seventeen

ALL IS WELL

"Mr. Lawfton, your niece is here," Richard's assistant Shelly announced.

"Sweetheart come in. Take a seat," said Richard. "These next few weeks are gonna be pretty tough for Sari Unique. I'm sure you've heard about Sidreaux Sr. They found him this morning, hanging in his basement. I was afraid ole Sidi boy would do something like this."

"Yes, I'm aware," Talia said. "I guess the idea of possibly going to prison didn't fair too well. Apparently, Langston Jr was married this past weekend. He's off the grid, out of the country. We haven't been able to reach him just yet."

"Good for him. Keep an eye on boy wonder; make sure he sticks to his word. Let's close this chapter out Talia, so we can move on. Give him some time to grieve, maybe a month or two, then submit your two weeks' notice. Our work here is done," said Richard.

"Well, I have something to share with you as well," Talia said. "Over a year ago, Langston Jr. appointed Dani as his beneficiary, leaving her his majority stake and every penny he owns."

"So?"

"So, I'm not sure how the other board members will respond to that," said Talia.

"Hmph, sounds like a smart man to me."

"How so?"

"If anything were to ever happen to Langston, Dani would probably sell the shares, take the money, and move on with her life," said Richard. "She has no interest in Sari, or maybe she'll keep it and try to make something out of it. Giving that hellhole to someone with a heart may birth a fresh form of life into it, something honest and truthful, like it was intended."

"And if she doesn't have good intentions?"

"Well, we'll just have to make sure she's influenced in the right direction. In the meantime, we need to move on. Oh, and Talia? It's time you take a vacation. You've been working on this case for years. Go and spend some of the hard-earned money I'm paying you. Plan your wedding, for goodness sake," said Richard. "Langston Jr. will find himself another righthand to run the company."

"Of course, Uncle Richard. I'm going to quickly leave your office before you change your mind."

"Talia?" Richard said.

"I know, I know," she said. "Don't say *Uncle Richard* in the office," she said as she closed the door behind her.

Finally free, Richard Lawfton could officially retire, leaving the firm to his daughter, knowing that every ghost from his past was now officially buried. His family was safe, and no one from his past relationships would come after them. Maybe now Marie, the only woman he ever truly loved, would officially give him another chance.

"Marie, Richard here. What do you say about a nice long extended getaway with a debonair, handsome, young man who adores you, longing to cater to your every need, your every whim?"

"I'd say give him my number."

"Hmm, I love it when you play hard to get," said Richard. "Pick you up in half an hour?"

"I'll be waiting."

Thank you for taking this journey with me…..

TIPS FOR SELF-CARE DURING CANCER TREATMENTS

I am not a medical professional. These are things that worked for me. Every journey is different. Before trying any suggestions, I encourage you to do your research and speak with your physician about what works best for you.

Nutrition Tips:

Bone Broth- This was my go-to remedy, especially after chemotherapy treatments. While accredited to balancing gut health and a strong immune system, it was a good aid for my digestion and nausea. Also, it was very soothing to my mind and body.

Vegetable Broth- Sipping on this broth helped calm my stomach and quenched my thirst. However, by the end of the second week, I was experiencing thickened saliva, so I switched to solid foods like baked chicken or fish. I also kept plenty of ginger beer and ginger lollipops.

Vegetable Soups- I ate vegetable soups filled with mustard greens or pureed soups.

Oral Care:

During treatment, I experienced dry mouth and thickened saliva. When my mouth was dry, I used mouth rinse very often. It was difficult to drink a lot of water at times.

Exercise:

My chemotherapy came in two parts, with four treatments during each part. During the first phase of chemotherapy, I jogged a little and lifted more weights the week following the treatment. I moved as much as my body allowed me to move.

A CLOSEUP LOOK AT CHEMOTHERAPY

Chemotherapy Part 1: My first chemotherapy treatment took place in the month of October. I read so many articles about people passing out due to experiencing extreme nausea during treatment. Needless to say, I was terrified. Once the nurse flushed my port and administered the treatment, I felt fine. While the look, taste, and feel of the thick red stuff, Adriamycin, was something to behold, I still felt like my usual self. As a matter of fact, immediately following treatment, we went to the store to pick out Halloween costumes—yes, grown folks wear Halloween costumes and hand out candy, even if they don't have children. I remember saying over and over again that I must be incredibly strong because I don't feel anything, like a superhero.

The moment I got home; I immediately threw up everything I had ever eaten in life. At least that's how it felt. My head weighed a ton. It was all I could do to get out of bed to go to the bathroom for the next forty-eight hours. I had to learn quickly to take it easy on myself. If I was feeling better during that week, I took a nice walk or stretched my body. The superhero in me was definitely on pause.

Chemotherapy Part 2: I was less nauseous but in pain. I experienced soreness and tightness in my joints and muscles, many times to the point of tears. Daily walks, jogs, and strength training helped me to cope with the pain. I also followed Dr. Mark Hyman, where I learned to add baking soda and essential oils to my routine Epsom salt baths.

Maintaining a Daily Regimen- Keeping a schedule gave me the focus to continue moving forward. As crazy as it may sound to some, cleaning my house, exercising, and food prepping for the week kept me moving. On some days, I took extra care of my home environment to make it seem like a get away from all the things that were happening during the doctors' visits and scheduled treatments. I took baths by candlelight to pamper myself or enjoyed movie and popcorn nights at home with friends. This was very therapeutic for me. Things like candles surrounding the bathtub, pampering myself, or movie and popcorn nights at home with friends was very therapeutic for me.

REFERENCES AND RESOURCES

Dr. Mark Hyman:

https://drhyman.com/blog/2010/08/24/the-ultrasimple-diet-a-more-detailed-look-at-how-to-kick-start-your-metabolism/

Dr. Josh Axe:

https://draxe.com/nutrition/bone-broth-benefits/

https://draxe.com/

Rebecca Katz:

https://www.rebeccakatz.com/the-cancer-fighting-kitchen

The Susan G. Komen Breast Cancer Foundation:

https://www.komen.org/

National Alopecia Areata Foundation:

https://www.naaf.org/

The Bald Boss Network:

https://www.instagram.com/baldbossmovement/?hl=en

American Cancer Society:

https://www.cancer.org/treatment/treatments-and-side-effects/physical-side-effects/mouth-problems/dry-mouth.html

Greenbriar Fitness:

https://greenbrierfitness.com/

SPIRITUAL REFERENCES AND RESOURCES

Throughout this process, I learned that my daily thoughts, what's in my heart, and the words that flow from my mouth, could be manifested in my life. It was depressing to speak fear, pain, and negativity over my life, but in contrast, it was empowering to speak the Living Word. I sincerely hope that you can find something here that will inspire and encourage you.

NIV The Woman's Study Bible:

https://www.christianbook.com/niv-womans-imitation-leather-brown-color/9780785215110/pd/215114

Healed of Cancer. Author: Dottie Osteen.-

https://www.lakewoodchurch.com/store/product/DPB0001E

My sister's mother-in-law gifted me with this book. It is filled with healing scriptures and her own personal journey with cancer. I still read this book as a part of my time studying God's word.

Steven Furtick.

https://stevenfurtick.com/

Every teaching I listen to speaks directly to my experience in my walk with Jesus. I look forward to tuning in to his message every week.

T. D. Jakes.

https://www.tdjakes.org/

This is a daily spiritual feeding that not only gives me direction but also correction.

I Declare: 31 Promises to Speak Over Your Life. Joel Osteen.

https://www.barnesandnoble.com/w/i-declare-joel-osteen/1110913426

I thank God that his grace and mercy are new every day. Some days, as soon as I open my eyes, I am reminded of my struggles. My health issues, bills, work, appointments, and divorce. I'm learning to intentionally declare and speak God's word over my life first thing every day.

Youtube Music:

https://www.youtube.com/

Go to YouTube to listen to inspirational gospel music.

SNEAK PEEK
THE SEQUEL TO NORMAL IS DIFFERENT

BECCA AND JAVI

"Yes, hello? Hold on a sec. Jess, bring the cold teething ring, please. I feel a lil fever coming on. Mama's baby is just teething, aren't you," Becca said, holding baby Levi against her chest, calming his tears. Feeling like it was too early for teething, they took him to pediatricians, Dr. Jim and Ivy Thomas, their best friend couple. After getting pregnant less than a year after Isabella was born, Becca and Javi decided to confess the truth. They were already married. The day after Becca told Javi how she felt about him, Javi pulled some strings and surprised Becca with a secret ceremony the following week with the Thomas's as their witness.

"Oh shoot. The phone, I was on the phone. Hello, Jim? I'm so sorry, hon. Levi's been upset all morning. You know Javi's out of town with work. Did you try his cell?"

"Yeah, that's okay. How is Levi?"

"He's fine. I think he may be running a fever. Amazingly Bella is just as calm as a little princess, just like her father, I suppose. Hey Doc, what do you mean how is Levi?"

"One sec," Becca said, clicking the mute button. "Jess, call Javi. I have Dr. Thomas on the phone, he's asking about Levi. I think the test results are back."

"Oh, well, his wife, Dr. Thomas, is downstairs," Jess replied.

"You're kidding me? Okay, okay, okay. Something's wrong with Levi. She's just popping up and it's Sunday, and the other Dr. Thomas is on the line."

"Why would you think it has something to do with Levi? Oh shoot, the blood test," said Jess.

"Okay. Let's not panic just yet. Gimme your phone; I'm gonna call Javi. You go downstairs and see what the heck the other Dr. Thomas wants, and I'll see why this one is calling. Baby doctors don't just randomly pop up at your house and call you out of nowhere on Sundays, even if they're your best friends."

"Wait, I thought Javi took Levi to Dr. Smith for the follow-up? I think you were out of town, but I could have sworn Dr. Smith said Levi was fine," said Jess.

"No, Javi would have told me that. We never got the results back from the Thomas's. Why would he take Levi in for a follow-up? Mama's got you, baby. Oh gosh, he has a fever now. I can't do this, Jess. This is too much," Becca whispered, sitting in the rocking chair nervously, trying to calm Levi.

"Here, I'll take him," said Jess. "You call Javi, and me and Levi will go talk to the doctor downstairs."

"Jess, whatever she has to say, she can tell it to you. I'd much rather hear bad news coming from somebody I know. Where the hell are husbands at times like this?"

"Shhh, now don't get yourself all worked up in a hissy," Jess said, calming Becca with one hand and holding baby Levi against her chest with the other. "Let's just focus on one thing at a time, calling Javi. Okay?"

"Okay," Becca calmly replied. "Jess, do you think he has a fever? What if he's, I mean, what if something's wrong?"

"This is not the same situation," Jess said, recalling Becca's senior year in college when she lost her mom and got engaged in the same year. Baby Logan died of sudden infant death syndrome, and Becca's fiancé left her at the altar. She made Jess promise to never speak of that time in her life, not even to her closest friends.

"Yes, he is a little warm, but, honey, you have a whole pediatrician couple waiting in the wings. Let's get our boy some help. We don't wanna assume anything."

"You're right. You go. I'm gonna talk to Dr. Thomas up here, and you talk to the other Dr. Thomas down there," Becca said. The doctors had told Becca that having another child would be complicated but not impossible. Becca got pregnant almost instantly following her secret wedding to Javi. She lost the baby three months later and never told a soul. Somehow, she thought things would be different being married to Javi. This time she loved being pregnant, at least eighty percent of the time. She adored Javi and loved being a wife. She had never felt so secure and loved by anyone, not even her parents. She took care of herself one hundred percent of the time. No stress, no long nights, healthy eating, she did everything right.

"Hello, Jim? I'm so sorry for the long hold. Levi's just not feeling well, but I know you know this. So just spit it out. What's wrong with my baby? Please stop asking if Javi's here. I squeezed both these suckers out by myself. Ripped my ass to shreds. I think I can handle whatever it is. Hello? Jim? Dammit! This is my house, and my child," Becca mumbled. "I don't need a freaking man by my side to get test results. Besides, Javi could never handle pain like me. He cries when he can't breathe through his nose. I'll end up nursing him and the baby. Okay, I need to get this woman out of my house," she said, checking her reflection in the hallway mirror. "Jess, I'm on my way down," Becca called out as she made her way downstairs.

"Dr. Thomas, I'm so sorry to keep you waiting. Levi's been having these fevers and fits all night."

"Yes, Jess was just filling me in. He does have a slight temperature."

As Becca looked at Dr. Thomas's face, she was sure now more than ever that something was wrong with Levi. "Ivy, what's wrong with my boy? Before you ask where Javi is, he is out of the country. Shoot," Becca said, sitting at the bottom of the stairs. "I tried to tell Javi that I couldn't have children. My history with babies is not good. If you came here to tell me something's wrong with my son, please have a solution ready. Whatever it is, we're willing to try."

"Rebecca, I gave Javi medication for Levi when he stopped by the office on his way out of town. Maybe he forgot to drop it off, but I will get you more as soon as possible. I assure you, both Isabella and Levi are fine and healthy babies."

"Oh, thank you," Becca exhaled. "Thank you, thank you, thank you! See Jess, all that stress for nothing," Becca said. "You look like you've seen a ghost. You heard her, everything's fine. So, Ivy, what brings you my way? Are you fighting with Jim? You know he's been ringing the phone off the hook, calling for Javi all morning."

"Rebecca, when you and Javi were married, it was one of the greatest days. I mean, we always knew it was coming, but we were so excited when the day finally came. When you asked us to witness your wedding, Jim and I were ecstatic! We immediately cleared our schedules," Ivy cried.

"Oh, honey, it's alright," Becca sighed. "Oh shoot, Jess, get the wine. Come into the kitchen, ladies. Men, we can't live with 'em or without 'em, right?" Becca said, pouring Ivy a glass of wine. So, what did he do? Is it another woman?"

Taking a long sip of wine, Ivy continued, "When you guys were married, everything changed. I was no longer cooking for Jim and Javi, and no longer sending someone to check on Javi's place when he was out of town because of you and the babies, of course. You're his family now. I've never seen two people love each other so much," she cried."

"Ivy, just what are you trying to say? Well, honey, spit it out. You're a doctor, it can't be that difficult," Becca laughed.

"During all the hustle and bustle of everything, the emergency contact information was never changed. As you know, Javi doesn't have any other family, with his parents passing on some time ago. Rebecca, Jim and I, we received a visit from the police this morning. Javi's plane, it…he…I'm so sorry,

Rebecca. Javi's plane went down. The police said it would be impossible for anyone to survive."

Becca stared at Dr. Thomas, as if in shock. Suddenly, she lunged from her seat and slapped Dr. Thomas as hard as she could.

"Ow! Damn it, Rebecca," Dr. Thomas moaned, holding her hands over her mouth where Becca slapped her.

"Oh, no! I'm so sorry, Dr. Thomas," Jess said, clutching the baby to her chest while running to the kitchen for ice.

"I asked you not to let her give me bad news," Becca said, looking wild-eyed at Jess. "Didn't I say that? I said, 'Jess, don't let her give me bad news about anything.'"

"It's okay, Jess," Dr. Thomas said, holding her hand up to imply that she was alright. "She's just in shock, it's fine."

"Oh, she's just in shock. It's fine," Becca repeated, mocking Dr. Thomas in her English accent. "Don't you dare mistake my emotions for sadness. I'm hormonal, dammit! Let me ask you something Ivy, did you see my husband? Is he at the hospital?"

"Rebecca, his plane went down over the ocean. Jim made some calls, but we were unable to get any additional information."

"NO! I SAID did… *you…see…him?*"

"I can't say that I have," Dr. Thomas responded. "I don't think they…I'm not sure if they've located…him."

"You see, Dr. Thomas, to you, I may look like a bougie little princess with blond hair and blue eyes, but the truth of the matter is, I'm a Texas-born chick."

"Damn right, you tell her, Bec," said Jess.

"Did they pull his …did they pull him …" Becca tried to get the words out.

"It's alright, Bec, I got it, honey," Jess said, grabbing her hand. "I think what Ms. Becca means is that if Mr. Javi is not at that little hospital of yours, then you better hustle your ass on outta here while you still got time."

"Yeah. That's it," Becca said, pacing behind Jess like she was waiting to be tagged into a wrestling match. "And don't you bring your ass back here without my husband!"

"Now, sugar, you just can't come in here with these wild stories about planes crashing and whatnot," said Jess. "I been knowing Bec and Mr. Javi for years. Been knowing Becca since she was a little girl. That man is like a son to me," Jess said, holding Levi while trying her best to swallow her tears. "You best come back with something a whole lot more concrete than that, or don't come back here at all. I suggest you leave before I put this baby down."

"Of course," Dr. Thomas said calmly. "Rebecca, when you're ready to talk, you can call me anytime."

"GET OUT!" Becca shouted!

After Dr. Thomas left, Becca fixed herself a glass of wine and sat quietly at the table for over an hour, not moving, not talking, and never taking a sip. Finally, she looked at Jess with dazed eyes and said, "Jess, I uh…I have to uh…," her voice trailed off in a whisper.

"Don't worry, go. I got the babies," Jess said, with silent tears flowing like a fountain. "You go find our boy and bring him home."

"Yep. I'm gonna go bring him home," Becca said, now confident, as she ran upstairs and packed her bags. Becca took her time getting dressed, ensuring she was beautiful for when Javi saw her. "Come in here telling me about my husband. Who the hell she think she's talking to? I didn't feel that," she fussed. "God, I felt it when you called mama and daddy home, and grandma and grandpa," Becca said. I even felt it when you called my baby Logan. Remember when I kept having that same bad dream for two weeks straight? Right after he died, that dream went away. This is different, and you know it! Me and you, it's different now! You made promises to me. I believed you when you led me to Javi. I didn't have sex with him, I took my time getting to know him. I took my time getting to know you! Now we have babies. We have a beautiful family," she cried softly. Suddenly her tears were replaced with anger, "You mean to tell me that you gon call my husband home, and I didn't feel nothing? THIS IS NOT THE NATURE OF OUR RELATIONSHIP! Okay, okay, calm down," she said to herself. "I'm sorry, God. I know you wouldn't do that."

An hour later, a car was downstairs waiting to take her to the airport. Becca thought about turning one last time to look at her babies, but she couldn't do it, not without Javi. "Mama's going to get Daddy," Becca said, quickly closing the door behind her, knowing that if she hugged her babies, she would fall apart. She needed to put that emotion to the side and focus on the task at hand. She had her assignment and was determined to see it through. Again and again, she called Javi's phone, but it went straight to voicemail.

When she arrived at her destination, she reached out to her connections. As she sat in the back of the car, she thought about Javi's promise, *If I ever lost you, I would tear this world up, one place at a time, until I find you.* "Same," she whispered. "That's our promise. That's our vow. I'm coming, Javi, you hold tight. Please, God, please! Don't take my husband. Don't let my children grow up without a father."

DANI AND RIC

Well? What do you think?"

"It's some type of stew, right? A soup, maybe?"

"What?"

"Mmm, delicious," Ric said, discreetly scraping his teeth against his tongue to remove the taste. "It's spicy, meaty, flavorful, perfect for the holidays," he lied. "You know I love meat, but I was thinking maybe we could keep it light tonight. Maybe fry some cauli buffalo wings and some vegan nachos?"

"Okay, but I've been in the kitchen for quite some time, slaving away at this recipe. You know, preparing this gumbo and all," Dani said, feeling confused from Ric's reaction. "I'm a little tired, but the kitchen is all yours, knock yourself out."

"Cool, I'm good with it. I'm a little jet-lagged, but I love cooking for you too," Ric said sarcastically. "I'll order the ingredients, and you, my gorgeous queen, can put your feet up and relax. Oh, and before I forget, I bought you a surprise. Your friends are not the only ones who can bring a smile to that gorgeous face of yours. Drumroll, please," Ric said as he beat the countertops. "All the way from D.C., baby, your favorite dessert in its own little cooler. Can you guess what it is?"

"Oh, my gosh, lemon meringue pie, lemon meringue pie! You made me pie?" Dani said, suddenly feeling excited and jumping from one foot to the other.

"No, maybe your second favorite," Ric said, continuing to beat the counter like a drum. "Try again and get it right this time."

"Lemon pound cake with the crusty top? Seven-up pound cake with the crusty top? German chocolate cake? Mango ice cream?"

"What? Dani, none of any of that," Ric chuckled, slightly disappointed. "Fig tarts with cream cheese. You love my fig tarts."

"I do love your fig tarts. They are scrumptious."

"That's right, and you love them. Talking about lemon meringue pie," Ric said, playfully pinching Dani on her backside. "I did bring ice cream, though," he said, holding up a quart of his famous homemade ice cream.

"Mango ice cream," Dani cheered.

"Vanilla bean ice cream! What's gotten into you? You can't have mango ice cream with caramel fig tarts and cream cheese."

"Right," Dani said. "Thank you for thinking of me," she said, ensuring she had antacids for later. "I'm gonna shower before Cammie gets here with her surprise. I feel so loved today," Dani said as she playfully danced across the floor like a ballerina. "What is it? Did I say something wrong?" Dani asked as she saw the expression on Ric's face change.

"I was just hoping that we could spend the holidays together, just the two of us."

"The holidays? Who said anything about the holidays?"

"I'm just not in the mood for everyone tonight. I wanted to relax, just the two of us."

"Okay, but you know we planned this evening months ago," Dani said. "All of us have crazy schedules right now, and I'm pretty sure Cammie and Becca will be with their family for the holidays, and so will I."

"Wow, really, Dani! Way to ask me about my plans," Ric said sarcastically while fixing himself a drink.

"Alright. What's happening here? We never discussed getting together for the holidays, Ric. In fact, I haven't seen very much of you in the last six months. We barely even talk." *Clearly, the letters I've been receiving are not from him,* Dani thought to herself. *But Cammie said it was him, she said he confessed to it. Why won't he confess it to me? This is so weird. I feel like I should just say something, but that would betray her trust.*

"Dani, what's it been, like two years? I've been patient, giving you time and all, but I want more. I want to belong in this thing we have. I want intimacy. I want you."

"Intimacy," Dani repeated, slightly confused.

"Yes, intimacy. And I know for you that means a relationship, maybe even marriage. I just think that with everything you've been through, wouldn't it be nice to just live a little, uninhibited, unattached? Do whatever you feel? We don't have to be married or in some type of committed relationship to express our feelings toward each other. You know I'm crazy about you, but I can't commit to a woman I've never been intimate with before. I mean, don't get me wrong, if the sex is not earth-shattering, it won't be a deal-breaker."

"So, if it's not a deal-breaker, then why not commit?"

"I honestly don't feel like we've spent enough time together for that type of commitment, Dani. You've been traveling with work, and when you're not traveling for work, you're focused on trying to open a gym or running the magazine, or your modeling, or your friends. I guess we need to add your family to that list now."

"Oh, come on, Ric. Most of my travels are done in one or two days; then, I'm back in New York. You've been overseas for months. This is the first time I'm hearing about this. I'm sorry, but it's very confusing."

"What about us for the holidays, Dani?"

"I'm going to my mama's house for the holidays. Listen, for the first time as an adult, I get to spend time with my family without having to rush back home to help run somebody else's company. I'm going to Louisiana. Besides, I booked my flight in advance. It's too late to cancel. I didn't even think that you would be in the states."

"Exactly, Dani. You didn't think. You didn't think about me. You never think of me, of us," Ric said, gently placing the knife next to the cutting board, wiping his hands, and zipping up his jacket. "I think it was a mistake coming here today."

"HA! You're good. You're so good," Dani said in disbelief while shaking her head. "I know what this is, I know what you're doing, and you don't have to do this. Trust me," Dani said, pouring herself a glass of apple cider.

"What am I doing, Dani?"

"You're trying to intentionally start an issue to justify whatever it is that you want to do or that you have been doing. You don't have to do that. We are not a couple. You can do whatever you want. Let's just start over and enjoy the evening."

"Is that what you think this is? Wow, bravo, Dani. Way to make this all about you and your consistent life of drama. Enjoy whatever this…crap is. I'll be at my hotel for the rest of the night. Call me when you really want to talk."

"Hey, Ric, you can stay at your hotel until you go home," she calmly replied. "You're right, you may be full of it about most of the things you said tonight, but you are right on about one thing; I've had too much drama in my life. No more games for me."

"You're being serious right now? You're breaking off our friendship, just like that?"

"I'm sorry, I can't handle any drama right now," Dani said.

"You can walk away from me just like that? Good for you, Dani. I guess I should be thanking you for giving me a way out of this emotional bullshit you call a life."

"Please, shut the door on your way out," Dani said calmly as she walked across the room to place another log in the fireplace. Assuming he closed the door behind him, Dani checked her purse to grab her phone to call Cammie. "It's not here. Where is my ph–" She heard a noise and looked up to see Ric hadn't left. "Hey, you need to leave, now!" Dani sneered.

"Stupid bitch!" Ric said as he quickly backhanded Dani across her face. "Owww," he groaned, grabbing his hand and removing the bulky ring from his finger.

Dani's ears were ringing as she grabbed the side of her face. She tasted the blood gathering in her mouth. There were no voices in her head telling her what to do, no Daniesha. She couldn't believe Ric had the nerve to put his hands on her. She glared at him, shocked by this sudden change in his behavior.

"Shit, Dani, I'm sorry," he said, instantly regretting his actions. "Oh no, no, no," he said, grabbing his head, realizing that his temper was getting the best of him again. He hadn't hit a woman in over twenty years. The thought of having to start counseling again frustrated him. Cutting back on work would be their first suggestion. That's why he started the food truck as a way to relieve stress. Fashion was his true love. *Now is not the time to cut back,* he thought to himself. *I have expansion deals for California, Florida, and overseas.* "Dammit, Dani. Hey, is it too much to take care of your man sometimes? I flew all the way here from Italy to see you," he said, standing over Dani as she held on to the back of the couch. "I could have any woman I want," Ric calmly said.

Before counseling, beating his girlfriends was something he learned from watching his father. As far as he was concerned, if beating women was a sport, his father was the G.O.A.T. The man was a wealthy business owner. He was highly respected and admired for his millions in charitable contributions and the jobs he brought to the community. If the devil had an image, it was his father in his Rolls Royce and Armani suits driving through neighborhoods searching for his next young victim. Ric promised himself that he would never be that man.

"You can't speak to a man that way and expect him not to react," he said calmly as he went to the kitchen to grab ice for her face. "I'm really sorry I hit you. I lost my temper, been under a lot of stress," he said, as tears ran down his face. Here, let's put some ice on that before it swells," he said with remorse as he walked over to Dani.

When Dani heard his footsteps approaching, she opened her eyes and instantly felt rage and fear. *Oh, my God, he's headed this way,* she thought. Without second-guessing herself, she grabbed the large hot vanilla candle on the coffee table that had been burning for hours and threw it in his face.

"AHHH!" Ric moaned as the hot wax dripped down his face, sticking to his long thick curly hair. "Bitch," Ric screamed, lunging his body in her direction.

Without words, Dani picked up the clean piece of firewood next to her foot and slammed it across his shoulder. When he bent over, she hit him again across his back. Once he fell to the ground, she struck him again, and again, and again, until the heaviness of her head and the ringing in her ears forced her to stop. *You think you can come into my house and put your hands on me,* Dani thought as she slammed the thick wood against his shins.

"AHHH!"

Still silent, Dani walked over to the kitchen and reached under the sink where she kept one of many weapons. After a crazy date several years ago, she had guns hidden in different areas of her house. Jackson came running and barking into the living room and the kitchen. He barked over and over again as he ran back and forth through the house.

"Jackson, go away. GO BACK IN THE ROOM," Dani yelled, but he persisted, barking in her direction. Realizing that his bowl was empty, she poured him some water and held her face under the faucet until her heart stopped racing. She watched Jackson quickly lapping the water with his tongue. Unable to stop her hands from shaking, she poured herself a glass of water and drank it as fast as she could.

"Hey, hey, mama's okay. Come on, boy, here's a snack," Dani said, sticking some food into his mouth. She felt her heart calm down as her breathing became less intense, and her ears stopped ringing. Everything was fine until she glanced to the left and saw Ric on all fours struggling to get back on his feet. Dani quickly picked up Jackson and locked him in her bedroom. Realizing that Ric may be fully standing now, she cocked her gun as she stepped back into the living room. Still trying to regain his balance, Ric was on his hands and knees. Spotting her cell phone, she thought to call 911, but the idea brought tears of rage to her eyes. Without thinking, she slipped into her pointy-toe heels, walked over, and kicked him in the face and again on the side of his stomach. *That wax is falling right off his hair, it ain't even sticking,* Dani thought.

"Oh, heck, no," Dani said as she grabbed another burning candle and emptied the contents on his head.

Screaming, Ric yelled, "You win, you win! Come on, Dani, I only hit you once," he said, struggling to stop the blood gushing from his nose.

"That blood better not touch my floor," Dani whispered.

Unable to control it, Ric tried to catch the droplets with his shirt, but the fit was too tight. "Come on, Dani, I can't. I need a little help here."

"Tight ass shirt," she mumbled. "The letters. Did you write them?"

"What? Dani, come on. I'm hurting here," Ric pleaded.

"The boxes, the surprise gifts over the years…it wasn't you?" Dani asked while disconnecting the thick leather shoulder strap from her briefcase.

"Yes, I did. It was me," Ric said. "You already know that."

"You lied to Cammie and told her it was you."

"Dani, it's not that I don't wanna talk about that, because I really do wanna have this conversation with you. I just have to go, but I promise we can talk about this later. I think we both need to calm down."

"Oh, now you wanna leave," Dani said as she doused him with a pitcher of water. "Stew? How the heck did you cook a whole meal, ship it over here, and now you don't even know if it's stew or soup? You wanna talk about my drama when all you really wanted was some ass," she said as she swung the leather belt at his face.

"STOP!" Ric said, shielding his face with his arms.

"You learned all that cooking, but nobody… taught… you… to keep your… hands… off… women," she said, whipping his legs and his butt with the black, leather strap as he scrambled across the floor.

Ric grabbed the strap from her and threw it across the room. "Let me talk, please. I didn't just want sex from you. NO, NO, NO!" he yelled as Dani reached for the firewood, "Let me finish. I needed an interview. You have a lot of followers, and you worked for one of the biggest fashion companies in the world. I knew that if I could just get you to write something about me, give me a good review on a pair of heels or something, I could increase my retail traffic. I desperately needed the money. I don't have a relationship with my father, and I didn't know of any other way. The store and the food truck were bringing in revenue but not enough to cover the lease increase, especially with all the new restaurants in the neighborhood. When you expressed interest in Katera's lotions and candles, that brought in a lot of new business. Women would come in to purchase her products, and they would buy something for their man or some heels for themselves."

"So, you used me? Why not just ask? Why come to New York? Why would you come to my best friend's baby shower?"

"Because Katera left when Cammie introduced her to Becca and all these other companies. They started handling her manufacturing and distribution. Within a year, she moved to her own location. When Cammie mentioned the letters and mystery box stuff, I initially said no when she asked if it was me. I had no idea what she was talking about. Later on, I just went along with it. I assumed whoever this guy was, that he would back off since you were in New York, and I would be there, at least until, you know."

"Until I wrote a story on you, an interview," Dani said. "I still don't understand. When you came to New York, I wrote a whole piece on you. Becca even used your designs in her photoshoots, and she still does. Oh, wait, I see now. After you got what you needed, you left to go overseas. That's why you've been gone for the past six months. Damn, I'm so stupid."

"No, yes, kind of something like that. You're right, I got what I wanted, and I left. I came back because I didn't expect to still have feelings for you, but I do. It was something about when I saw you that night in the park, and you cried on my shoulder. I knew then that I wanted more, but it just wasn't a good time for me. Once I got what I needed, business was great for both if us. You were settled in New York, and I figured we could spend some time together and get to know each other. Start fresh. Then I saw the flowers in your office and— dammit, Dani, what the hell did you put in my hair?" Ric said, struggling to tie his hair in a bun?

Dani listened intently, taking it all in, not saying a word as she stared at him.

Realizing Dani was weirdly quiet, Ric talked faster. "I saw the fancy cheese, the flowers, and the expensive wine delivered to your office. I pretended like I wasn't surprised, like it was from me, but I wondered how did dude know exactly where to find you in New York? How did he have your office address when it was still in construction?"

Dani wondered the same thing, and she reported it to the local police, even allowing Cammie to put her driver, Sam, on it. After Cammie's confession that her secret admirer was Ric, Dani called off the investigation with the police. She assumed the gifts and the letters were Ric's way of getting to know her, and she was fine with taking things very slow. She actually was so busy that she stopped thinking about the letters altogether until she received the delivery this morning.

"I thought that if I spent some time with you that you would forget about this weird letter nonsense. I never had a woman choose a piece of paper over me before. No matter how much I tried, I could never compete with those stupid-ass letters and overpriced gifts. And dude bought cheese—you don't even eat cheese like that. The sad part was when you thought I was that guy, you looked at me differently, like you were falling for me too. I may have had a motive, but I really started feeling you. You just weren't feeling me."

"So, you used me and got what you wanted. When you couldn't get laid, you decided to put your hands on me and blame me for it," Dani said nonchalantly, picking up a Christmas globe from the bar and throwing it at him.

"Stop it," Ric said, catching the glass ball before it slammed into his chest. "You trying to kill me or something? You don't wanna do that. I'm not a woman beater, anymore. I haven't hit a woman in over twenty years. Needless to say, women have gotten a lot stronger since my old college days," Ric said, chuckling while wiping the blood from his nose. "I'm just a good-looking man with a lot of machismos, and who is sometimes under a lot of stress. I never meant to hurt you. But this mystery guy? This man could be dangerous, Dani. I didn't know this guy was delivering to your house. That means he has your home address. Look, I'm not mad at you," Ric said. "I actually like you more now than I did before. I'm pretty turned on, to be honest, but I'm willing to wait," Ric said quickly, raising his hands in surrender. "We can start over fresh."

Before he could say another word, Dani raced toward him, and wrapped the leather strap around his neck, kneeling behind him, strangling him. *Time and time again! Pray, Dani, pray! Read, Dani, read! Breathe, Dani, breathe,* the thoughts raced through her head. *Ignore it, be the bigger person, she said, pulling the belt tighter.* "Every time… I get something going good…. here comes another one of you…weak ass men…again, and again, and again! Why can't you just leave…me…alone?" Dani asked through clenched teeth. "Nah, then you wanna claim I gave up on you? I stopped believing in you? Nigga, I never stopped fighting! I never stop believing! If it wasn't for me fighting and believing, your punk ass would have fell flat a long time ago."

"Hey, hey, hey. Stop! What are you talking about?" Ric asked, struggling to pull the belt away from his throat.

"All you cared about was money!"

"Not true," Ric said as he used his body strength to press her against the wall and pull the belt from his neck. "Who the hell are you talking about? What the hell did he do to you?" asked Ric, catching his breath. You trying to kill me?"

"You got a sew-in," Dani said, releasing the leather strap as she noticed the hair stitching on his scalp. With the belt still wrapped around her fist, she held her hands to her mouth in shock as Ric stood up. The look of embarrassment on his face alone was more than the ass-whipping he endured. Unable to control herself, *Don't do it...don't you laugh at somebody else's hair loss,* she thought. Unfortunately, it was like a sneeze that could not be stopped. Dani laughed until tears fell from her eyes. Every time she looked at him, she laughed. She couldn't finish a sentence without laughing. "You said...you said you been growing it since you was a child," Dani laughed, now noticing where his real hair separated from the extensions. Thanks to the candle wax, his real hair was spiking like darts. "You said it takes hours to press it, takes a whole day to wash it," Dani laughed hysterically. "Dude, you ain't nothing but a coward."

"Dani, come on, don't do that. Enough! Don't laugh at what you don't understand. We both lost our tempers, and we should move on."

Dani cocked her gun and attempted to dialed 911. Before she pressed the last digit, Cammie appeared in the doorway.

"Well, hello. Seems like I missed the main event," Cammie said. "Ric left the door slightly ajar when he pretended to leave. As far as I'm concerned, it's self-defense," Cammie said, eyeing the gun in Dani's hand and the bloody bruise on her face. "I got here just in time, but not soon enough; at least that's what I'll say when the cops get here. Dani, feel free to do whatever you feel."

Slowly, Ric picked up his bag from the floor and limped towards the door, carefully walking past Cammie.

"Hey, Ric," Cammie whispered, "I'll see you later."

Looking down at her gun, Dani realized she had grabbed the one that was full of blanks. She fired a blank shot into the air, and Ric's slow limp turned into the fastest skip she'd ever seen.

"Run, Rapunzel, run," Cammie said. "Looks like Ponytail gon need a lace front."

"It's a sew-in," Dani said.

"Girl, shut up! Punzel got a sew-in? Daaang! He got a heck of a beautician, though," Cammie said as they laughed hysterically.

Dani sat at the bathroom vanity in silence as Cammie cleaned her lip and gave her an ice pack for her face. She listened to Cammie downstairs cleaning the mess she made with her scuffle with Ric. The old Dani would probably feel bad about hitting him like that, but the new Dani felt justified and wished she would have done a little bit more. "Hmph, Calling me a bitch. I should've scalped what little hair he had left."

"I told you to do whatever you wanted," Cammie said. "Although I must say, grasshopper, from where I was standing, you did a pretty bang-up job. First thing in the morning, I'll send him a real nice lace front."

"Add a butt pad. He gon need a butt pad," Dani said, giggling. She stopped short when she saw her reflection in the mirror and began to cry. The right side of her jaw and lip were so swollen that she didn't recognize herself.

"Yeah, looks like he used the hand where he wears his ring. As women, we don't always walk away without a cut or a bruise.

Sometimes it's on the inside, and sometimes it's on the outside. Either way, it sucks, and it should never happen, but it does. Some people see life, dating, and marriage as a game. They spend a lifetime competing with whatever perception of reality lives in their head. Most times, the other person doesn't even know when they're about to be tackled, ran over, or pimp slapped. The good thing is that you got up, and you fought back. You ever seen a man after a football game or a boxing match? Sometimes, even as women, we have to roll up our sleeves and fight back. Don't you ever feel bad about victory scars. Do you understand? You won this round. Or maybe I should say, weapons may form, but they don't prosper?"

"I get it," Dani said. "You don't always have to use scriptures for me to understand things," Dani said, frustrated.

"I don't do that for you. I do it for me, so I can understand. Anyway, I have to run, but I drew you a hot bath in the master bathroom. Clean yourself up. I put some wine on ice, ordered you some dinner. Oh, by the way, my surprise for you is waiting downstairs next to the Christmas tree. I'll call you later."

"Thanks, Cammie, for always being here." As Cammie saw herself out, Dani sent a text to her therapist: *I need an appointment, tomorrow.* As much as she respected Cammie's fighting spirit, she never wanted to feel that kind of rage again. If Cammie wouldn't have shown up, she wasn't sure what would have happened.

After a long hot bath, Dani slipped on her old sports t-shirt and went downstairs to check the locks. "I'm exhausted. I guess kicking ass can take a whole lot out of you. Come on, Jackson," Dani said as they went downstairs to check the doors and make a snack. Suddenly, Dani stopped halfway down the staircase, quickly scooped up Jackson and quietly ran back upstairs. Once in the bedroom, she locked Jackson in the shoe closet praying he would stick to his favorite toy and leave her shoes alone.

"No time to think about that now," Dani said, while grabbing her gun from the top shelf linen closet. Ensuring it was fully loaded, she slowly walked downstairs. Maybe it was a shadow of the tree outside, Dani thought. It was so quiet downstairs. Just when she was about to step off the last stair, a tall shadow moved through her living room. It was dark and the candles were lit so she couldn't see who it was. Ric? No, this fool did not come back to my house, she thought.

"I see I didn't make my message crystal clear. No worries, this time I won't miss," she said, cocking the gun and stepping into the living room. "Hello 911, I have an intruder whose been shot," she said as the man turned to face her. "Langston?"

Unfazed at the presence of a gun pointed in his direction, Langston sat calmly and nonchalantly sipped his cognac.

"How did you get in here? Before he could answer, Dani said, "Cammie!" Remembering that she was on an emergency call, she said, "Hello, I'm sorry 911, it's a false alarm. I'm sorry, yes, I know him and I'm fine," Dani said, trying to slip the phone into her pocket. "You're here, Dani said, searching for words, again trying to stick her cell phone into her pocket. She then realized that she didn't have any pockets because she wasn't wearing pants, just a t-shirt and underwear. "Oh my gosh! Dani said, struggling to stretch her shirt while embarrassingly walking backwards towards the staircase. I'll, I'll be right back," Dani nervously said as her phone started to ring. "I'm just gonna answer that and, I'll,-

"You'll be right back," Langston said.

"Right. Hello," Dani said, quickly running back upstairs to change clothes. "Cammie! I am going to kill you," she laughed. "What?" Dani said. For the third time tonight, she suddenly stopped in her tracks. Lowering herself to the edge of the bed, she sat, with the phone to her ear, staring into space.

CAMMIE AND HARRIS

"That's bullshit, Cammie, and you know it! For the past three years, I've asked you to marry me, and you said no every time. What the hell else was I supposed to do?" Harris said.

"Oh, I said no the last time you asked? Then I guess this ring on my finger is just for decoration," Cammie said.

"The same reason why you wore the last one, because it's pretty. Don't play me, Cammie! We been knowing each other since high school. You never said yes. It's been over a year, and you cringe whenever I mention the word, *wedding,* said Harris. "You treat that engagement ring like it's a promise ring to be my girlfriend. I'm a man, Cammie. I don't want a girl I want a woman, you! I want you to be my wife, the mother of my kids, adopted or not—I don't care. I wanna spend my life with you!"

"Whatever Harris! All that preaching, yet you found yourself spending your time with another woman."

"Here we go with this again," Harris said, sinking back into the bed, gently moving his body so as not to apply pressure to his bandaged elevated leg.

"Harris, look around. Look at your mom and your dad. I am not a good fit for you and your family. Your mother hates me. I want to spend my life with you too, but I can't. I just…I'm not the person you think I am."

"I know. I know all about you," Harris said. "Your brother Bennet filled me in on some things back in college. You a lil nutcase. I thought about walking away back then, but once I got to know you, we fit like a glove. We both bougie hood, with a little bit of crazy mixed in between. I don't have anything to hide from you Cammie. I accept you just as you are. You're the only person in my life that makes me feel like I can do anything. I've been playing ball since I could walk. Everybody in my circle would be just fine with me playing until I drop dead, except for you. When I talk to you about doing other business ventures, you don't laugh or tell me to just focus on the playoffs and that should be enough. You encourage me to go after my dreams, with no judgment. Even back in high school and during our college years, you knew about my past, but you never judged me. You just kept pushing me to focus on my game. To this day, my old man loves you for that."

"At least somebody in your family does," Cammie said.

"Babe, I'm a momma's boy, and my mother is a snob. That's not your issue, that's mine.

"Yeah, but it's not okay for me to ask you to choose between me and your mother."

"You damn right, it's not okay because you're my woman. I will always choose you first," Harris said as Cammie looked at him in disbelief. "At one time, it was always my mom first and everybody else second. I spent the first half of my life trying to find self-validation in her feelings for me, giving her everything she could ever imagine. I wasted years trying to get my dad to see that I also have a business mind, I'm not just another black man dribbling a basketball. I've done my part as their son. They don't want for nothing. It's my time now."

"Yep, you and what's her name?" Cammie said.

"So, I messed up, hanging out with an old friend. When you refused to marry me after the third time, that shit hurt. A couple months later, I heard she was pregnant, and I had to know if it was mine."

"You've already explained that," Cammie said.

"Then why you keep going back to it?"

"What I don't understand is why you couldn't tell me that you thought she was pregnant. Accepting me is being honest with me, too, Harris. Accepting me is knowing that I don't argue with folks unless I'm getting paid.

"True, but I know you enough not to put you in a situation that would initiate a *Cammie* reaction without cause."

"Without cause? Really? You sticking your man-man in somebody else is without cause? I thought you understood that what you do in the dark, I will always bring to light," said Cammie.

"Yeah, but you don't have to orchestrate evil acts to prove a point," Harris said, rubbing his bruised thigh and scratching at his bandage. Have a little faith Cammie. Isn't that what you always say to me? If it's something I need to know about you, I believe it will come out at some point."

"Well, I only have a certain amount of faith. That stuff seems to work wonders for others, but not so much for me," Cammie said. "I guess because of my dad's absence in my life, I see most people as what they are, ornaments on a Christmas tree. Something to keep around when needed, no commitment necessary. Then I met my dad and my sisters. I never thought I would ever meet him, let alone have a relationship. I have sisters that I've watched over the years, fighting all kinds of things from sickness to infertility to heartbreak, and some kind of way, they always end up okay, better even," Cammie said. "Sometimes I imagine myself fighting like them, believing in a power that's bigger than me, reading a scripture or two every day, treasuring those things about myself that are precious to me, hoping that it will mean something to me one day."

"Cammie, I got you. I just need for you to understand that we can't take from each other. This little stunt you pulled by paying off my parents' debt and sending that crazy-ass dude over there to get money like that, that shit was a bit drastic, Cammie. Seeing my mom tied to chairs and gagged…"

"Ahhh, Harris please! No one was going to kill your mother. I just wanted to remind her where she came from."

"Falling down those stairs could have ended my career Cammie. How would you live with yourself if I couldn't play ball again? Knowing that you took that away from me, from us."

"Yeah, well, you took my virginity from me," Cammie said. "Something that I've held on to my entire life until I met you, and you gave yourself to somebody else. A simpleton! A one-night stand because you didn't get the answer you wanted for marriage. So, if you can't play, you can't play. You won't find any sympathy here. However, I am sorry for hurting your mother. I needed you to see that she is not as flawless as she pretends to be, and she needs to stop randomly putting her mouth on me and spreading nasty rumors. You and I both know I've done some pretty scary things. She doesn't have to make anything up."

"True, but what's done is done. I'm sure you won't have to worry about my mom going forward. We good?"

"I don't know, Harris. I'm not sure."

"Whether you decide to be my wife or not, I'm not going nowhere."

"Seriously? I have to get out of here," Cammie said, turning toward the door. I hurt your parents, literally. Why would you want someone like that in your life? Not to mention, I may have ruined your career. You can't possibly be willing to overlook all of that."

"What if I am? This ain't the first time my momma been smacked around," Harris said. "She used to gossip really bad about folks in the neighborhood. Let's just say it got to a point where she couldn't sit outside in the yard for too long. She stopped for a while, but she so spoiled now, she just says whatever she wants. I'm sorry, I let it get that far. You don't ever have to worry about her mistreating you again. If she doesn't respect my wife, then she don't respect me. And I won't be pushed around in my own house. Give us a chance babe. We still learning each other, right?"

"Next time, it may be more than just your legs," Cammie replied, with tear-filled eyes, knowing she would end him if she felt like he was trying to destroy her.

"Well, I guess a leg for a life will have to do for now, huh? I think you love me too much to kill me. Besides, you ain't going nowhere. You gon be right here with me, pushing me in my wheelchair, helping me with rehab. You gon be my real-life ride-or-die wife. I don't want no other chick when I got a smart, beautiful woman by my side."

"Don't forget about sexy," Cammie said, walking back toward the hospital bed and laying down next to him.

"Forget? That's all I think about," he said, pulling her close as she lay her head on his chest.

"We gon have some real-life horror stories to tell our children. Kids, yo mama tried to kill your daddy."

"You better not!" Feeling her cell phone vibrate, Cammie glanced down at the caller ID.

"Nah, turn that ringer off. Baby, we could have some fun with these stirrups."

"Boy, hush, you can hardly move," Cammie chuckled putting the phone to her ear. "Hello, this is Cammie? What?"

ABOUT THE AUTHOR

Latilda Conyers holds a Bachelor's Degree in Health and Science. She is currently working on her Masters in Corporate Communications and Organizational Development.

She was born and raised in the Bayou State of Louisiana, a place known for its genuine Creole and Cajun culture, and a vast array of some of the best foods in the South. She grew up surrounded by a strong family unit, cultivated in love, faith, and relationships. Latilda believes that with God at the center of her life, all things are possible. When she's not working, you can nd her enjoying the outdoors with friends, relaxing with loved ones, or running around the park with the newest addition to the family, her brown eyed Goldendoodle, Fancy.

To connect with her visit www.latiempowers.com